Praise for Gordon Kent

'A lot of thrillers these days, you come away feeling like you've been in a simulator. Gordon Kent straps you into the real thing. Enjoy the ride!'   IAN RANKIN

'*Night Trap* is the real straight Navy stuff. Better strap yourself to the chair. I loved it.'   STEPHEN COONTS

'Told with all the authority of inside knowledge . . . an absorbing tale of international skulduggery.'
Irish News

'Consistently excellent . . . loaded with gunfights, snappy dialogue and the aerial hijinks of supersonic jet fighters. The high testosterone doses satisfy, but best is the complex and clever web of motive Kent weaves for the mole.'   *Publishers Weekly*

Visit www.AuthorTracker.co.uk for exclusive updates on Gordon Kent

D0995534

Also by Gordon Kent

GORDON KENT

DAMAGE CONTROL

HARPER

Harper
An imprint of HarperCollins*Publishers*
77–85 Fulham Palace Road,
Hammersmith, London W6 8JB

www.harpercollins.co.uk

This paperback edition 2006

1

First published in Great Britain by
HarperCollins 2006

A catalogue record for this book is
available from the British Library

ISBN-13: 978 0 00 717877 3
ISBN-10: 0 00 717877 8

Set in Meridien by Palimpsest Book Productions,
Polmont, Stirlingshire

Printed and bound in Great Britain by
Clays Ltd, St Ives plc

*To the men and women, Japanese and American
who stopped Aum Shinrikyo*

Author's Note

The notion of a terrorist group, no matter how motivated or extremist, that is dedicated to the immediate overthrow of a major world power and the extinction of all human life may seem far-fetched. Shoko Asahara and the Aum Shinrikyo had billions of dollars, dozens of top Japanese scientists as members, and the will to carry out an aggressive and deadly WMD campaign. As of this writing, Shoko Asahara has recently been sentenced to death, but his cult is still richer than many corporations, remains powerful in Japanese politics, and continues to carry his message.

Prologue

In a porcelain bowl floats a single lotus flower, waiting.

Meditation appears to the untrained as a passive activity. To the observer, the practitioner's body seems poised but relaxed, the breathing even, the face calm. Westerners speak dismissively of men "studying their belly buttons."

Mohenjo Daro sits easily on a low leather divan, his long legs crossed under him and his arms relaxed, hands resting easily on his knees. Aside from his pose, little about him suggests meditation. He wears a simple silk sweater from Italy and jeans. His face is that of a warrior from ancient Indian art, with rugged features and a pale walnut color. He was, and is, handsome, in a military way, the iron gray in his hair accenting the strong wrinkles in his skin. Nothing about him speaks of the ascetic except that his feet are bare.

His eyes are open. The pupils are huge, black, and blank, the irises almost as dark under heavy brows. And between them, exactly where a Brahmin's caste mark would be, there is a birthmark, a third eye placed by nature.

The lotus flower. Daro sees it, regards it as a composite of organic material, as a symbol, an object of power. He seeks to know it without effort, to comprehend both the flower before him and the totality of the lotus. And having accomplished this to his satisfaction, he watches this blossom curl and close and then open, the water undisturbed beneath it, the petals of the flower uncurling like stop-action photography. The petals reach their full, erotic opening, and then he watches them wilt and decay, the first touch of orange brown on the edges to the last black organic mold resting on the surface of the unmoving water. And then he begins to restore the flower, working the mold back to the ravaged blossom and then seeking the full bloom of perfect health. When the petals have risen from their watery grave and stand, shriveled but extant, once again attached to the stamen, Daro gives a sudden gasp as intense pain floods his abdomen, snapping his focus from the life of the flower to the dying of his own body.

In a porcelain bowl floats a single lotus flower, unchanged, but the man is writhing on his divan. The spasm passes, and he is angry, although the mood passes as quickly as the unfolding of the flower. He rises and zips on a pair of Spanish leather boots and crosses to the door, the flower abandoned. One hand remains on his abdomen.

He reentered his household when he left his meditation chamber. Outside waited the cares of the world as represented by his aide, Vashni, who bowed. He smiled at her. "Give me a lemon drop, Vash."

She produced one, her head tilted to one side. She could read that his meditation was not satisfactory. "I have all the reports, sir. Our military situation is good. I have reports from each of our member units with their status and preparedness. Only the *Nehru* has not reported in, which was to be expected."

"Excellent."

"Some of the financial information is late from Delhi because the government closed the exchange early."

"Really? Whatever for?"

"There was the threat of a terrorist act. Or so the television claims."

2

"Any effect on us?"

"None." She was confident, arrogant.

He was walking now, leaving meditation for business and chewing his lemon drop. She followed him, reading figures on the output of factories and the price quotes of stocks that he assimilated without need of a pen and paper in much the way he could know the fullness of the lotus. Details of military units loyal to him and prepared to act. As he expected. He was making enormous sums of money, also as expected. He went to his office, nodded gravely to his private secretary in greeting as he passed through the outer office and continued to his desk, his attention on Vash unwavering. She had already prepared his laptop with input from her own files and he clicked idly through PowerPoint slides that illustrated the points she was making.

"What a pity that we cannot simply buy the world and fix her," he said with a smile, looking at the vast sums of money they were compiling.

Vash smiled in return.

Daro touched a button on his desk and ordered tea. Then he reached under his shirt and withdrew a small golden plastic shell and plugged it into his laptop. The screen cleared and another image took its place, then passed away in a swirl of graphics, to be replaced by a word-processing screen.

His private secretary, once a devout Muslim, came in with a tray of tea and set it on his desk. He paused expectantly, and Daro motioned him to sit and join them. "Really, Ali, you might as well drink tea with us. A few more people might help create a sense of drama."

Both of them laughed. "Drama" was usually a word of opprobrium to the believers. In this case, the absence of drama was clear, and almost comic given the gravity of the moment.

"I could not sleep last night, sir," Ali murmured. He was an old man; the admission seemed boyish.

"Goodness, Ali. You don't have reservations? If you do, please tell me."

"Not reservations, sir." A certain gleam came into Ali's eyes, almost rakish. "Eagerness."

Vash nodded as well. "So long in the planning," she murmured. "So quick in the execution."

Daro smiled, opened his mouth, and was hit by another spasm. He put his head down and held his abdomen with both hands, and when he raised his head, much of the color had left his face. "It won't be so quick, my friends, because something will go wrong."

They looked startled.

He nodded and took a lemon drop from the bowl on his desk. "No plan survives contact with the enemy. We will act, and someone will react, and we will react to their reacting, and there will be conflict and uncertainty and death. Something will surprise us, and our true test will not be in the years we prepared but in the moments where we must react to something we have not expected. That is the way."

Vash, the consummate businesswoman, shook her head. "After all this preparation, I expect better. I expect victory." She sounded as if she demanded it.

"Have I taught you nothing?" The color was back in his face, and his left hand had moved from his abdomen. He sat straighter. He looked at Vash. "There will be no victory, Vash. Or if there is a victory, it will be so impersonal that we will not recognize it, and few of us will see it, or even enjoy it. That is what it means to be a servant rather than a master. We serve the earth. The earth will never thank us except by surviving and thriving when we are gone."

She nodded with her eyes cast down. "I spoke rashly."

"Excellent! If everyone remembered every lesson and had no thoughts of his own, we would be working for the opposite of entropy, I think. Are we ready?"

4

"I would have liked this naval exercise with the Americans to have finished."

"Like all elements in strategy, the naval exercise will pose us both problems and solutions. I admit that your part would be easier if there were no exercise, but the greater plan would be harder." He looked at Ali. "Are we ready?"

"Your household is ready to move to the secure location." He nodded sharply, as if, unlike Vash, he had no doubts and that scored him a point.

Daro turned his attention back to the laptop and typed "Chaos" into the screen.

He moved the mouse arrow to the send button and caught their eyes with his, deep pools of black that gave away little light.

"Here we go," he said, and clicked the mouse.

Day One

1

West Fleet HQ, Indian Navy, Mahe, India

For Commander Alan Craik, Fleet Exercise Lord of Light was the culmination of six months of work, and, with six minutes to startex, he was angry because he, as umpire, could see that one side was already cheating—the US side. He looked around the large room that housed exercise planning and control—banks of computers, a central console that blocked his view of part of the room, ratings and a couple of officers in Indian naval khakis, and his own two US personnel.

"Sir?" Benvenuto was a skinny kid from the boonies of northern New York, a long way from home in this Indian naval headquarters. "Admiral Rafehausen's on the net for you, sir."

Craik walked around the big console. In front of him was a bank of encrypted radios that kept him linked to the US forces at sea, four hundred miles to the west. He grabbed a head mike with earphones. "Good morning, sir."

"You're late." He knew Admiral Rafehausen's voice—an old friend, pilot of the first aircraft he ever flew on. "You sleep in, Al? Leaving Rose for a nautch dancer?"

"I don't think they even have nautch dancers anymore."

"You should get out more often, Commander. What you got for me?"

"I have startex minus six, and you have an S-3 way out of exercise start parameters, sir." He trailed the mike cord so

9

he could lean over the JOTS terminal—the Joint Operational Tactical System, which showed the entire exercise and could, if asked, show US and other forces all over the world—watching a lone S-3 Viking move at low altitude along the eastern edge of the Lakshadweep Islands. *Paul Stevens*, Alan thought to himself. *Hotdogging*. "I see him, Al. I guess he didn't get the message."

"I have to hold exercise start until that aircraft is within start parameters, sir."

"Hey, Al, lighten up. I got my beach recon teams in the water now. I've got my decks full of guys waiting to launch and I can't exactly call them off. My Combat Air Patrol is up and already needs fuel from the tankers on the deck. You know the drill, Al. Let's just say I'll ignore AG 702 for a while, okay? Can we get this thing underway?"

Alan ran the trackball over the American and Indian battle groups. The JOTS on Rafehausen's carrier would show only the Fifth Fleet units, and the Indian admiral on board the Indian light carrier *Vishnapatingham* would see only his. It had taken weeks of computer work by the two nerds in Alan's exercise detachment to make this mutual blindness happen, and now one pilot was screwing it all up. He wanted to argue, even to use his supposed power as umpire to stop the exercise, but the big point was to cooperate with India and make diplomatic points. Canceling would be *really* bad diplomacy.

Alan sighed. "Okay, we'll go for startex. But you're on your honor about reports from that S-3." In fact, Rafe probably wouldn't be forced to his honor; the S-3 was a long way south of the Indian battle group, and if Stevens turned on his radar before startex, he'd be admitting he was cheating.

The hell with it. Get it over with and go home. He *was* touchy because the umpire's job had been wished on him only forty-eight hours ago. He had been supposed to honcho the intel side for the US and then go home, where right now he could be enjoying his wife's birthday. *For once.*

"Four minutes to exercise start, then," he said into his mike. Then Rafe, knowing Alan was angry, maybe feeling guilty, made small talk for forty seconds, and they ended the conversation as friends.

Alan turned to Benvenuto. "Three minutes to exercise. Start the message traffic feed."

"Aye, aye, sir."

Across the room, Indian ratings were feeding the scenario setup into the two comm nets.

Everything was going to be fine.

Aboard Indian Submarine *Nehru*, Arabian Sea

The communications officer coughed into his fist for the second time and read the message again. He couldn't control his thoughts, which twisted and turned through his convictions and his fears faster than he could clutch at them.

The day.

Around him, the enlisted men on the comms station reacted to his all too visible nerves. Ram Vatek, his most senior technician, raised an eyebrow.

He knew Vatek as one of the faithful. He leaned back and coughed into his fist again, focusing on Vatek's loyalty, using the man's face as an anchor to reality. He took a deep breath and exhaled slowly.

"It's a new day," he murmured and watched Vatek's usually confident expression turn to apprehension.

The comms shack became still. Every man on duty knew what the words meant. Many of them knew parts of the overall plan. Knowing the plan and facing the grim reality of the message were different beasts.

No one in the comm shack flinched, however. They opened an arms locker that should not have been there behind the

11

central computer processor and took out pistols, Tokarevs loaded with special low-power ammunition.

He pressed the push-to-talk button on the main comms console and spoke to the whole ship.

"Today is a new day," he said, his voice unsteady as he spoke.

On the bridge, the navigator reached under his chart table and drew a Makarov pistol from its holster, turned, and shot the captain in the face. Under the pressure of the moment, he shot him repeatedly, pulling the trigger until the slide clicked open and the noise and smoke filled the bridge.

In the engine room, the second engineer drove a screwdriver into the abdomen of the engineer and stood appalled at the amount of blood that pooled on the smooth gray deck as his superior writhed. A rating shot the dying man in the head and seemed to enjoy the act. The engineer had not been a popular officer.

The second engineer looked at the blood on his hands and uniform and wanted to scream. And he looked at the wild eyes of the rating with the smoking gun and wondered what they had unleashed.

In the weapons space forward, two of the faithful shot their way through with smuggled Uzi Combat Commanders, killing every crewman in the space and inadvertently wrecking one of the operational weapons stations. A lot of the weapons techs were Sikhs and other unrecruitable sectarians, so they had to be killed.

In ninety seconds, the mutineers had control of the ship. Every man they believed might not be loyal to their cause, including a few who had received the indoctrination, was herded into the mess deck and locked down. Many others were killed because the mutineers, once blooded, were vicious. On the bridge, the navigator settled into the newly cleaned command chair and tried to ignore the smell of blood and feces.

"Make revolutions for five knots. Dive to one hundred fifty meters. Helmsman, make the course zero eight nine."

"Aye, aye, sir."

The Kilo-class submarine turned to port and headed away from the exercise area and back toward the west coast of India.

In the comms shack, the communications officer sent a coded message using the small golden egg he wore around his neck. The message went out through the VLF antenna and was received at West Fleet Headquarters, Mahe, where it was routed with other exercise traffic to its addressee at a small naval test facility in southern India—and to the Indian exercise-control officer at exercise headquarters, where Alan Craik waited.

West Fleet HQ, Mahe, India

Intel officers wait, Alan thought as he watched a digital clock tick down toward the beginning of the fleet exercise. Two minutes twenty to startex. *And worry*. He was standing by the JOTS repeater, staring at it as if memorizing the position of every ship in both fleets, but he was thinking about his wife, Rose, wanting to be with her. He tried to focus on the exercise. He called across to a female US rating, the only other American there besides him and Benvenuto. "Borgman, give me an update on my comms with the two fleet commands."

"Good to go, sir." Borgman was a heavy-bodied woman with an almost childishly pretty face, a plodder who got things done with tenacity rather than brilliance.

He nodded and went back to the JOTS terminal and the glowing blobs that represented the American and Indian ships. Nothing had changed. He looked up and let his eyes swing over the room. An Indian rating named Mehta looked up and let their glances meet as if to say, *We're doing the best we can here.*

A little more than a minute to go. Alan raised his eyebrows at Benvenuto.

"Good to go, sir," Benvenuto said. He was looking at something over Alan's shoulder as he said, "Data's streaming—"

Aware then of somebody behind him, Alan turned, saw an Indian officer standing there, registered the single star on the collar, produced a name without having to look at the man's tag—Commodore Chanda, the Indian exercise-control officer. Alan smiled, guessed that the answering scowl was prestart nervousness.

"Sir," Alan said.

The commodore was watching the clock, must have been watching it when Alan turned around. Across the room, a nervous Indian lieutenant was also staring at the orange numerals.

The commodore was standing too close. Alan wanted to elbow him out of the way, of course couldn't. He bent over the terminal, pretending to study the location of the American flagship. The commodore was right behind him. *Well, he's a commodore; he can stand where he—*

The crease in the commodore's trousers brushed the back of Alan's right thigh; Alan shifted left to make room for the more senior man, shifted his eyes for a fraction of a second off the terminal, catching a whiff of some scent the Indian officer used, then flashed back to the terminal as it—inexplicably, surprisingly—darkened and lost its picture, like an eye blinking. He caught movement below him—

—and saw a hand emerging from a uniform sleeve with a commodore's broad stripe on it, holding something glittering and brassy to the input port of the JOTS repeater.

"Hey—!" Alan started to say, grabbing, without thinking, at the hand. Then, too late, he said, "Sir—!" but the commodore's enraged eyes had already locked into his.

14

AG 702, 20 NM WSW of the Lakshadweep Islands

In AG 702, the cheating S-3 that Alan Craik had seen on the JOTS and complained about to Rafehausen, Commander Paul Stevens was enjoying his nugget TACCO's nerves. "Hey, Collins, you got that back end sweet yet?" Stevens tried not to lose an opportunity to give the kid the gears. In fact, as far as Stevens could tell, the "back end"—the big bank of antiquated computers that drove the airplane's sonar-receiving and tactical displays—was functioning as well as it ever did, but the new LTjg didn't know that.

"It's, uh, it's up, sir. I mean—"

"Jeez, Collins, either it's up or it ain't. I'm the pilot, not the TACCO. Which way do you want it?"

"It's up." Collins's voice rose so that the response sounded more like a question than an answer.

Stevens hit his intercom so that only his copilot could hear him. "Kids ought to be out of diapers before they leave the RAG."

"Give him a rest," she muttered. Lisa "Goldy" Goldstein had fought her way out of the girl jobs in naval aviation and she had plenty of spine to stand up to Stevens, who was a great pilot and an okay squadron CO, but sometimes a total asshole as a human being. "Skipper, you blow that kid's confidence, we still have to live with him the whole cruise."

Stevens smiled. He liked Goldstein, and he liked that she stood up to him. "I can hear the snot in his nose every time he talks."

"Yeah, skipper, and I can see the dust when you fart. Can we get this show on the road?"

Stevens grinned. "Roger that." He cycled the intercom to the back end. "Collins, if you've got us a working computer, you and Whitehorse better start thinking of your sonobuoy pattern."

Bobby Whitehorse, the enlisted SENSO Officer, or SENSO,

was a shy, silent Indian kid from a reserve in the Dakotas. He listened, said nothing, and started to enter his projected pattern into the computer in front of him. As his facial expression rarely changed, it was difficult for the other troops in the squadron to figure out whether he was sullen-silent or shy-silent.

Stevens saw the little symbols on his pilot's display. "Way over there?" he said. "You guys in back trying to run us out of fuel?"

"That's where the ASW module told us to go, skipper," Goldy said.

"Yeah, yeah. I came out this way to keep that big island between us and their radar." Stevens was holding the plane about ninety feet off the waves beneath them, flying with one hand and turning his head to Goldy when he talked. One bad twitch and they'd have a wing in the water, but Stevens always flew this way and his crews got used to it. And they *had* to be under the opposing force's radar horizon, because they were cheating—flying to a target before startex.

Stevens pushed the throttle forward and banked to the left, heading for the entry point to the pattern the SENSO had marked twenty nautical miles to the west.

"I have an ESM cut just beyond the island. Russian air-sweep radar, second generation." Collins sounded less nervous. He was better with the radar detection than with the sonar. "I'm putting it on screen. Second cut. Got a triangulation. See it, skipper?"

Stevens flicked his eyes from his instrument scan to the little screen on his console and winced. The Indians had at least a radar picket, maybe more, *much* closer to him than he had expected. This is where he and Rafe and the crotchety bastards in the anti-submarine warfare module had guessed they'd find the Indian sub early in the exercise. Rafe wanted it found and tagged from the get-go. And here the Indians were, with a radar picket right at the edge of the start area, looking out for someone like—

"Looks like we're all cheating together," Goldy said.

"Jeez, Craik might have warned us the Indians were this far south."

Out of the corner of his eye, Stevens saw the flash off her visor as Goldy turned her head and looked at him. Clearly she didn't agree with his views on cheating, either.

"Got another cut, skipper. Another air-search radar."

"They shouldn't be seeing us yet," Stevens said, banking sharply to keep the bulk of the forty-mile-long island between his plane and the radar pickets on the other coast.

"Startex in one minute," Goldy said. "I think we may be the first casualties in this thing."

"Not if I can help it. Whitehorse, put a long pattern down here."

Collins cut in. "We're still seven miles from the drop—"

"Let's put the first line in here and we'll sneak up the coast low, drop a few more, and see what we get."

Collins mumbled something about how far the Indian sub would have to be from her start position to be caught this far west.

"You got something to say, Mister Collins?"

"No, sir."

Clunk. Each sonobuoy had the passive systems to listen for an enemy sub within a thousand yards or so, and a tiny radio transceiver to broadcast the digital data back to the plane. When the sonobuoy survived the drop to the water and the transceivers worked, it was a great system.

"Number one in the water and I have a signal." Whitehorse had a flat, nasal voice.

Stevens thought it might have been the longest sentence he'd heard out of the boy.

Clunk.

"Number two in the water and—live. She's good."

Collins came in again. "Look at the salinity, Whitehorse. Where's the layer?"

Stevens cut the nerd babble from the rear seats. He didn't expect they'd find the sub, but it was an exercise and he didn't want to be remembered as the first casualty.

Clunk.

"Startex," Goldy said. The game was live; if anyone had seen them, they'd be called with an imaginary missile shot over the radio. Stevens looked at the digital readout on the encrypted comms without thinking, fearing the worst. Nothing came, and he smiled. He looked down where the live buoys from Whitehorse's drops were matched up with the projected pattern and prepared to turn west toward the island after the next drop. At this altitude, even at low speed, every turn was exciting.

Clunk.

"I—uh, skipper? We—shit, there it is again. Maybe a sub?" Collins, from the back seat, with nerves making him sound like a girl.

Stevens made the turn to put the next buoy in the pattern.

"Whitehorse? You concur?"

"It's a sub," Whitehorse said. Flat and confident. "Diesel running about five knots."

"Well, it's a pleasure to know they're cheating harder than we are," Goldy said. "He's at least a few miles off his start line."

"I got him on two buoys. I got a fix." Collins's voice rose an octave. "Hey! There he is!"

Goldy tapped her helmet and cut out the back seats. "Want me to call him in to the boat?"

"No. Let's drop an active on him so he's dead and *then* call him in. Those pickets are right over there; we may be under their radar horizon but they'll be on a broadcast like white on rice."

"Roger that."

"Whitehorse, you ready with an active drop?"

"Roger." Whitehorse sounded interested.

"Collins, you ready? You going to fuck this up?"

"No—ah, yes. Sir. No."

Goldy reached over and slapped Stevens on the helmet. Stevens gave her a smile that said, *Yeah, I'm an asshole.* Then he got the plane right down on the wave tops at the lowest speed he could manage and aimed for the datum, the little mark on his computer screen that told him where the sub was, one hundred and fifty meters down.

"Ready to drop," Whitehorse said.

The high-bypass turbofans screamed like asthmatic banshees as he aimed for the datum.

Clunk.

"In the water. Ready for active."

"Go," said Collins.

Breeeet!

Every man on the submarine's bridge heard the screech as the buoy went active. The former navigator froze, his mind blank.

"There is *not* another sub out here." The second engineer sounded less positive than his words implied.

"Whoever that is knows where we are and that we're leaving the exercise area. Battle stations!" the navigator said.

"It must be Americans from the exercise."

"What are they doing over here?"

"Cheating. They're famous for it." The second engineer got down on the chart table.

Breeeet!

"It has to be an aircraft."

Around them, sailors tumbled into their action stations, many of them looking sick and gray. The navigator still couldn't focus his mind on the problem. No one had planned for detection this early.

"We have to shoot it down," the second engineer said.

"What?"

"We have to shoot the American down."

"What if he's already passed on our location?"

"What if he has? It will be an hour before they can have another plane here. We'll be long gone."

The navigator hesitated and saw something he didn't like in the second engineer.

"This is my decision."

"Not if you endanger the mission."

The navigator saw the gulf yawning at his feet. They were no longer part of a service with a hundred years of tradition. His whole view of himself and his place in the ordered universe shredded. He was alone, the captain of a ship of mutineers. And the second engineer was prepared to walk over his corpse if he didn't act immediately.

"Surface!" he shouted. "Khuri, man the launcher. I want to hit him the moment the tower clears the water."

"Aye, aye, sir." Petty Officer Khuri was one of the few men qualified to fire the rotary missile launcher in the conning tower, and it could be fired only when they were surfaced.

"Satisfied?" he snarled to the second engineer.

The younger man nodded and shrugged, as if to say that events were his masters, not his servants. It was a popular saying among the faithful.

The navigator wondered how they would maintain discipline.

He felt the bow incline sharply.

"They're coming up!" Collins said.

"Jeez! Well, that's sporting. Goldy, snap a photo for the cruise book. Hey, Collins, you don't suck as much as I thought. Whitehorse, that was sweet."

"Can I call the boat?"

"Get the photo first."

Stevens took his time, banked the plane and climbed a little to get Goldy a better camera angle and pointed the nose back at the datum, just a mile ahead. He could see the disturbance in the water where her tower was cutting the surface. *Mighty fast for an exercise*, he thought. Then the tower was clear, a black square against the sun-dazzled sea.

A little click in the brain, as a neuron fired on some half remembered—

"What the fu—" *Not sun dazzle. Missile launch.* "FLARES!" Stevens bellowed.

Collins, busy enjoying his first operational success with a cup of coffee, took a precious second to toss it aside before reaching over his head for the flare toggle which, being a careful young man, he had set to a three-second burst pattern when he entered the plane.

Stevens had no altitude and very little airspeed, but he did what he could. He rammed the throttle past max to military and put the belly of the plane toward the launches. He thought they were real. It made no sense, but he believed it and acted. His response was almost enough.

The flare pods fired continuously as he turned. The first missile chased a flare that burned as hot as the sun and its warhead fired, taking a precious piece out of the vertical stabilizer because the flares hadn't had time or speed to deploy far from the aircraft. Stevens felt the change in handling and compensated. He was that good.

The second missile followed an earlier flare and detonated just off the port wing, its steel-cable warhead just missing the port engine and slicing through the aft cockpit, beheading Whitehorse in his seat and taking the top off the aft canopy. Wind and sun filled the airplane.

Stevens felt the change and reached down to pull the master eject as two more missiles slammed into his port wing, which separated from the plane as shrapnel shredded

Stevens's body and tipped his ejection seat as it fired to incinerate LT Goldstein before her seat could compensate.

A piece of the port engine struck Collins a glancing blow that broke most of his ribs. Because the first missile had ripped the canopy off the back seat, and Stevens's last piloting had oriented the plane at right angles to the water, his own ejection was clean, and his seat shot him sideways, parallel to the sea, unconscious and mutilated. His luck lay in his angle.

The fourth missile hit the tons of fuel in AG 702's belly and she exploded, but her death hid Collins's ejection from the shooter on the conning tower of the *Nehru*. By the time his chute deployed, the tower of the sub was clear for diving, and Collins's limp and bleeding body settled into the warm water more than a mile beyond the quickly sinking wreckage of his plane. His life vest inflated as it felt the salt, and a transceiver in the shoulder began to radiate his distress.

2

Mahe Naval Base, India
"Sir—!"

The Indian commodore's eyes, widened with anger, stared at Alan. "Take your hands off me!"

But Alan didn't let go. The other man's rank meant less to him right then than his touching the JOTS, which had worldwide connections and was as sacrosanct as any piece of classified hardware the Navy owned—the reason that Benvenuto was posted to ride herd on it. For this exercise, Indian monitoring personnel were allowed to look at it but most definitely not to insert data or play with the controls; when they wanted data or a change of view—there had been a briefing specifically about this—they were supposed to ask Benvenuto or Alan. They did *not* work the JOTS themselves.

"Sir!" Alan still had a grip on the brown hand, his own good hand closed over it just behind the knuckles so that whatever the commodore had inserted into the port was still locked into Alan's fingers "I'm very sorry, sir, but—"

"Let me go! This is an order! I will protest—"

"Sir, our orders are clear—nobody—"

The hand squirmed within his grip and the arm tried to pull away. "This is an outrage—!" Heads turned toward them. The Indian lieutenant who had been staring at the clock looked shocked now, an expression that Alan caught in a fraction of a second's glance and registered as fear. The commodore was pulling harder, putting his considerable weight behind his effort, and his hand backed four inches away from the JOTS and then jerked, and Alan's fingers, gripping harder still, slid down the long brown fingers and caught on something hard and smooth, and a gold chain attached to the glittering thing snapped and the commodore's hand pulled free.

And Alan found himself holding a shell-like, golden object with a protrusion made to fit a USB port.

The commodore made a grab for it. Alan pulled away. "Benvenuto—!" The JOTS tender, frozen at the sound-powered phone, launched himself at the terminal. At the same time, the commodore, face flushed a muddy red, was bellowing across the space at the Indian lieutenant, the Hindi words lost to Alan. He closed the golden shell inside his hand and rapped out, "Benvenuto, do not let this officer approach the JOTS terminal! That's an order!"

The hand came down and hovered near a sidearm. Alan took it in—the distorted face, the weapon, the rage—and wheeled to shout across the space to his communications specialist, "Borgman! Get Fifth Fleet HQ on Priority *now*! We have a situation here." He whirled back to confront the Indian commodore. "Sir—please back off! You're violating the terms of the agreement that set up this exercise. At once, sir!"

The commodore was shorter than Alan, trim, late forties. He hesitated long enough to meet Alan's eyes and make some inner calculation, and he shouted again at the lieutenant.

And the lieutenant unsnapped his own holster with his left hand and drew an automatic pistol with his right and put it almost against Petty Officer Borgman's head as she tried to raise Bahrain on the radio, and he pulled the trigger.

"No-o-o—!" Alan screamed. He would have gone after the lieutenant then, but he heard Benvenuto shout, and he turned and saw that the commodore had drawn his own weapon and was aiming it at him. Benvenuto caught the

24

man's arm and the gun roared, and Alan crossed the space between them in a stride and kicked the commodore in the groin, and then all hell broke loose.

The lieutenant took two shots at Alan and Benvenuto, and Alan hit the deck, pulling Benvenuto down with him. Somebody was screaming from the other side of the room. The commodore was on his knees, bent forward almost over Benvenuto's legs; as Alan looked, he vomited.

"Holy shit—!" Benvenuto groaned. Alan leaned across the sailor to punch the side of the commodore's head; the man lurched to Alan's right, revealing the gun he still held in his right hand. Alan hit him again and grabbed the gun.

The lieutenant's pistol barked and was met by a scream of pain from the doorway and a rattle of automatic-weapons fire; when Alan rolled back, he saw an Indian Marine sagging down the side of the entrance door, his hands closed over the front of a uniform blouse that was oozing blood. Another Marine, seen only as the forward half of an assault rifle and a pair of hands, was firing into the room, and another arm appeared and the hand grabbed the wounded man and pulled him out the door. Alan could look along the floor and see people lying flat around the room's periphery, except for the lieutenant, who showed as a pair of legs protected from the doorway by the central console. Then another pistol started to fire, the source hidden from Alan by the console—one of the other Indian ratings, the only people over there. *Jesus, they brought weapons and were waiting for their moment. But what the hell was all that with the golden thing and the JOTS?* And then, belatedly, *You don't kill people so you can win an exercise—*

He still had the golden device in his left hand, the bad one, the one with only three fingers because two had been blown off in a firefight years before. He wriggled the hand down into the leftside pocket of his khakis and leveled the commodore's pistol in front of him along the floor and took aim at the lieutenant's right foot.

"Sir!"

Benvenuto's strangled shout brought him around in time to see the commodore climb over the sailor's body, his left hand on Benvenuto's throat, and then the commodore was gone behind the JOTS terminal and Benvenuto was trying to suck air into lungs that had been flattened by the weight of the commodore's knees. He was a whiz-bang electronics tech but not much of a street fighter.

Then the automatic firing stopped, and there was a burst of pistol fire and a lot of shouting and the bang of a closing door, and then a sudden babble of voices that was like a kind of silence because there was no shooting under it.

"Sir, sir!" a voice shouted from the other side of the room. "Do not shoot us, sir! We know nothing about it, sir!"

Alan looked along the floor and saw Mehta's face at his level. It was strained but sane, the more remarkable because he was lying in Borgman's blood. "Sir—they went crazy—they are imposters or something—"

From habit, Alan glanced at the clock: the exercise had begun thirty-three seconds before.

Two new voices bellowed from the door, then a third. Alan rolled up and saw three Indian Marines with weapons pointed. He had a microsecond to make a decision, because one of the Marines was already looking at him and swinging his rifle. If they were with the commodore and the lieutenant, he was about to die and he should at least use the pistol in his hand; but if they were not with them—and they had returned the lieutenant's fire, after all—then the worst thing he could do was fire on them, for they would surely kill him.

Alan slid the pistol over the floor toward the Marines. "Alan Craik, Commander, United States Navy," he said. Saying it from a sitting position was not very dignified. Still, it seemed to work. The Marine's eyes met his, took in his collar and his oak leaves, and the rifle swung away.

Then there was a lot of shouting in other languages, and Alan crawled on all fours to Benvenuto and made sure he was okay, and then he stood, using the JOTS terminal as cover, and looked around the space. The steel door to the planning room was shut; an Indian enlisted man was collapsed in a far corner, one pant leg soaked with blood. Mehta and another rating were tearing at the pant leg and trying to fashion a tourniquet. On the side near the clock, a rattled Indian EM was trying to explain to the Marines what had happened, while another was bent over a cell phone. The first one pointed at Alan and made a gesture, acting out the shooting of Borgman. The lead Marine, a sergeant, shouted back and at once everybody shut up. As if cued to that silence, an explosion from overhead rocked the building, and trouble lights flashed all over the communications consoles. The rating who had been talking to the sergeant flung himself at a console and began to flip switches.

The sergeant stood, half-crouched, his head tilted. He turned to look at Alan. Dust filtered from the ceiling. A fluorescent fixture swung down and held on by its wires. In the new silence, a rattle of gunshots sounded somewhere else in the building, and Mehta, his hands bloody, groped his way to a wall box with a red symbol on it and began to pull out first-aid supplies.

The sergeant duckwalked to Alan, gave a cursory salute, and said, "Sergeant Swaminathan, sir." His voice had a pronounced lilt, the Indian accent that turns w to v.

"Is it a mutiny?"

The sergeant shook his head. "Very bad, sir. I think I have to take my men to barracks."

"But the three who were here—they murdered one of my people!—they went through that door—"

"All very bad, sir. Best return to barracks."

Alan wanted to storm the door to the next room to get at the commodore and the lieutenant. A steel door, no explosives, three Indian Marines. He looked them over—they were shiny-bright, spic and span, with knife-edged creases in their khakis and spit-shines on their shoes, dressed for display more than action. The sergeant was right; his best course was to find other Marines and make sense of what was going on. Plus there were four unarmed Indian enlisted personnel to worry about, one of them wounded, and Alan and Benvenuto and three more US personnel downstairs.

The commodore and the fleet exercise were the least of their worries.

An Indian communications man was shouting from the console. "All communications lost, sir—everything! I think it is the antenna array on the roof up there, blown all to flinders!"

"Can you telephone?"

The sergeant shouted at the Indian EM, who tried a telephone, shook his head, tried another and then another. The man with the cell phone was waving it. "No good—no good—no cell connection—!" He looked wide-eyed at Alan. "I cannot get through!" Whatever was happening was choking the cell-phone net.

"Very bad here, sir," the sergeant said. "I take you and these personnel to some safe place, then report to my barracks." He shook his head. "Very bad mess, sir."

Alan hesitated. "I can't just leave one of my people," he said.

"She is dead, sir."

Alan walked across to Borgman's body. Somewhere outside, another explosion erupted and was answered by more small-arms fire. He knelt. Borgman's face was partly gone, blood and tissue sprayed over the communications panels. Alan put his fingers where a pulse would have been in her throat, waited while twenty seconds ticked away on his Breitling.

Bahrain

They were all waiting for something, but nobody would say what it was, even though all four knew—Rose Siciliano Craik, assistant naval attaché, Bahrain; Harry O'Neill, big-bucks American convert to Islam; Mike Dukas, head of Naval Criminal Investigative Service, Bahrain; Leslie Kultzke, live-in interloper on Dukas's life after following him all the way from Washington. What they were waiting for was Alan Craik, but he wouldn't be home for more than three days.

When they had planned this gathering, he was supposed to be home, and then he had been made fleet-exercise umpire, and there went the notion that they would all be together for Rose's birthday. Alan was the glue that held them, and, without him, there was this strange sense of waiting for somebody who wouldn't show up.

The three old friends sat with their knees almost touching, laughing and mopping at spilled drops of coffee and licking fingers that had become coated with powdered sugar from Rose's biscotti. Leslie sat a little apart, like a good child allowed to sit with the grown-ups. She smiled when they laughed, otherwise sat with a pretty good imitation of interest on her round face. She was twenty-two. They were nearing forty, in Dukas's case more like forty-five.

Then the conversation ran down, and Harry said, "Shall we play a round of whatever-happened-to-old-so-and-so now?"

"We're going to play let's-help-Michael-lose-weight." Leslie smiled at him as she said it, pulling the plate of biscotti away from Dukas's hand. Quite opposite expressions flitted across their faces, his chastened, then irritated, hers mature and maternal. The change made Harry raise his eyebrows at Rose, who drew her own dark, thick brows together and gave him what her husband called "the look that kills." Then she turned away and said in that voice that announces clearly that the speaker is trying to change the subject, "What do you think Alan's doing right now? Mike—Harry—? What does the umpire *do* at the start of an exercise?"

Harry, who had been a junior intel officer ten years before, smiled and shrugged. "Stand around and try not to look bored, I suppose."

Northern India

A closed car speeds along a highway. Vashni, Mohenjo Daro's right hand, misses the comfort of their corporate headquarters, but she never questions Daro's impulse to leave it and become anonymous. The lack of an office does not separate her from her networks: she has her headset on, watching the markets and her e-mails on VR glasses while Daro chats with the driver, a Tamil who joined the movement years ago.

As they make the turn from the main highway to the permanent traffic jam around the airport, she sees a flood of e-mails hitting her server. She reads. She touches Daro's arm, her face averted, less because she continues to watch the screens in the VR goggles than because she doesn't want to see his face and know again that she sees a dying man. "The *Nehru* has shot down an American plane." She flips up her glasses. "Those idiots." She looks at him.

One of the virtues that Mohenjo Daro possessed as a leader was that he never wasted time on recrimination, although he would certainly have been justified now. He had spent three years putting his own crew on the submarine and getting it into a situation where it could disappear. The *Nehru* should have been invisible to the joint exercise. It should have had the additional invisibility of their carefully laid misdirection of the American JOTS system. And now it had shot down an American aircraft!

"So much for stealth," he said. He had rather liked stealth, she knew. He had hoped to avoid the messiness that came with open conflict. He smiled now as he saw the irony of it,

30

close to religious revelation. Of course, the path to anarchy and healing lay through conflict, as he often told her. It was more ironic that he had tried to avoid it. She knew that his mind would now start wandering down corridors of paradox; she put her hand on his arm to remind him that she was waiting for his order.

"Implement Shiva's Spear," he said. "Better look at the next two layers and have those brought up to readiness." He thought. "Assemble an operator team at one of our office locations."

"Which one?"

"Choose one at random."

Ahead, his gleaming helicopter waited on its pad. Mohenjo Daro sat back and contemplated the end of the world of men.

Mahe Naval Base, India

Running feet sounded outside in the corridor, then shouts and shots.

Alan had made his decision. "We have a vehicle in the fleet-exercise car park. I have to get to it."

"I will try, sir."

"Plus I got three more people downstairs." And he wasn't leaving without them, for sure.

The sergeant licked his lips, chewed on the upper one as if trying to bite the small moustache there. "Okay, we try."

"Benvenuto, you okay?"

The young man was rubbing his throat. "Little hoarse, sir."

"We have to disable the JOTS." Alan jerked his head. The terminal was critical hardware, its innards as highly classified as anything the Navy had. "Out the window. It's two floors down to asphalt."

Benvenuto's mouth opened. He was being asked to go from being the JOTS' mother hen to its terminator in one breath. "Ok-a-a-a-y, sir—"

They got two of the Indian EMs to help while one of the

Marines broke the unopenable window, and without ceremony they toppled the device over the sill. Alan leaned at
the corner of the window and watched it smash on the pavement below. There was more shooting out there now, and
when he raised his head he could see smoke billowing above
a row of trees.

The sergeant was instructing the other Marines and the
Indian personnel. Alan looked for the pistol he had tossed
away but didn't see it; he supposed that one of the Marines
had kicked it out of the way. The sergeant was already by
the door, bouncing up and down on his toes from tension.
Alan got down low, spotted the pistol under a computer table,
grabbed it, then looked around the ruined room, pausing for
a bitter moment at Borgman.

"All right, let's go."

3

"Admiral on the bridge!" The sailor braced.

"Stand easy." Rafe came off the starboard ladder and waved at the bridge crew. "You guys have coffee for an old man?" He turned to Rick Madje, his flag lieutenant, who was holding a phone out to him. Rafe raised his eyebrows.

"Captain Fraser on the *Picton*." HMCS *Picton* was a Canadian frigate attached to his battle group, the ship Alan had complained about because Rafe had put it way down south as a radar picket with orders to stay in Emissions Control, or EMCON—the regulation of outgoing EM transmissions across the spectrum—until she had a chance to shoot.

"Captain Fraser?"

"Sorry to break EMCON, Admiral, and I'm on satcom to make us harder to track."

"Sure, Alex, sure."

"Sir, I'm calling to protest two inbound 'missiles.' I've called Exercise Control four times to note them as intercepted and they don't respond." The "missiles" would really be aircraft imitating missiles as part of the exercise.

"Roger, Alex. I hear you. We haven't been able to raise ExCon since a few seconds after startex ourselves. Something's gone down at their end."

Rafe could hear the relief in the Canadian's voice. "That's

okay, then. But be aware that two Indian Air Force Jaguars went over my position about six minutes back and went into a missile profile."

"Got it, Alex. I'll pass that to Air Ops."

"Out here, sir."

"Stay alive, Alex. Keep up the good work."

Rafe turned to Madje. "You get all that?"

"Yes, sir."

"Get it through to Air Ops and Supplot." Supplementary Plot was where electronic-warfare-intelligence information and various other sources were cross-indexed to update the carrier's picture of the ocean around her. Rafe turned to the boat's captain, a former F-18 pilot. His leather flight jacket's patch said "Hank Rogers." Only a score of old buddies like Rafe knew his name was really Reginald.

"Hank? Launch the alert five, okay? I have to put some teeth down there to cover the Canucks."

"On the way," Hank murmured, already on the phone to the air boss.

AG 703, in the Stack 2NM NNE of the USS *Thomas Jefferson*

Lieutenant Evan Soleck's had been the fourth plane to launch after the local Combat Air Patrol and he got it into the air without a hitch. He had no back end to worry about, because he was a mission tanker for a sea-strike package that would launch later in the event—twenty thousand pounds of fuel to give while airborne—but intellectual curiosity made him get the back end up from his pilot console so that he could run his passive electronic-surveillance antennas and follow the action.

His copilot, a nugget from Iowa called "Guppy" because of the facial expressions he generated while concentrating on his instruments, had his hands full merely following the checklists and couldn't believe his pilot was wasting time on backseater crap. "If the skipper wanted us doing that stuff, he'd have sent us up with guys in the back," Guppy said in a put-upon tone.

Soleck watched him flail through the checklist. *That was me, last cruise*, he thought. And continued the ritualistic pattern of bringing the computers on line. *Oh, for the MARI we had at the det.* New computers, enhanced antennas, the works. Soleck had flown in a special det under Al Craik and it had spoiled him for these old planes and their antique systems.

USS *Thomas Jefferson*

In the windowed bubble below the *Jefferson's* bridge, the air boss was trying to launch forty aircraft for the opening reconnaissance of the exercise. Every F-18, every S-3, all the EA-6B Prowlers—it was a major launch, and it took his full concentration to keep the overcrowded flight deck from becoming a disaster. A sailor pushed a yellow sticky into his line of sight. *Launch the alert five AAW.*

The air boss looked at the line waiting to get off cats three and four. The event had started, and he had planes five deep in the queue already.

"Tell the tower to hold three and four until the alert is launched." The alert—an aircraft held on the shortest tether, ready to launch in five minutes—was sitting on cat two, with the second plane somewhere toward the stern. He held the note out to a spotter and motioned that they needed to get that second plane through the traffic jam and on the cat.

"Now launch the alert five AAW," the air boss said into the ship's 1MC. He cycled his comms from the Guard frequency that he monitored in his headset to the AAW net while trying to read the spidery writing on the launch board behind him. *Donitz. AG 203.*

"Alpha Gulf 203, you ready?" he said.

"Green and green."

Lieutenant-Commander Chris Donitz was already in the shuttle. The air boss watched the twin vertical stabilizers tremble in the heat distortion as Donitz moved the plane to full power, and then he was off, rotating just off the cat to clear the hull of the ship.

Alpha Whiskey, the air warfare commander off to starboard on the missile cruiser *Fort Klock*, came up before the air boss had toggled back to Guard, giving orders to Donitz as he roared away from the ship in his F-18. "Alpha Gulf 203, intercept two goblins inbound on the 090 radial at 9000."

Somewhere above him, Donitz said, "Roger," before the air boss had switched freqs and noted from his comm card that "goblins" were Indian Air Force Jaguars. He didn't question why Indian Jaguars had to be intercepted; his job was down here. He watched a sailor put a check next to AG 203 on the launch board, then looked down at the deck and saw that AG 114 was next to launch for the alert five.

"Spot, you got 114 moving yet?"

"Trying to get the S-3 off cat three so I can move the E-2 and get him space."

The air boss looked down at the deck again and saw the S-3 on cat three as the jet-blast deflector rose out of the deck to protect the planes waiting behind her from the backwash of her engines. "What's that S-3 doing?" he said into his mike.

"Something about their shuttle."

The air boss stifled his desire to say something savage. Out on the deck, a sweating kid was struggling with some bent piece of metal under the nose wheel of a plane older than he was, surrounded by fumes and jet blast and God knew what else. No amount of attitude from the air boss would make it happen any faster.

"Got it," Soleck said, looking at a first harvest of ESM cuts from his S-3's back end.

"You said we were in EMCON, Ev."

"We *are* in EMCON. I'm not radiating anything; I'm looking at what other folks are radiating."

Against his own inclination, Guppy leaned forward to look at the screen on his armrest.

"See? That's the air-search radar on one of the Indian picket ships." Soleck put his cursor over one of the signals so that Guppy could see it.

"You don't *know* that."

Soleck exhaled in frustration. "Yeah, Gup, I do. So would you if you learned your radar parameters. That's not one of ours, and it's too much in the air-search freq to be anything but one of theirs. Civilian ships don't mount antennas like that, right? See the sweep? And anyway, that's Owl Screech, a Russian targeting radar on one of their Russian-built ships."

"And you just know all that."

"Yeah. I also know that we're off our altitude by a long shot and starting a long turn to the right because the copilot isn't really paying attention."

Guppy swung his eyes to the instruments and the plane snapped to attention. "You—"

Soleck thought *Yeah, I'm being unfair. Whatever.* He ran the cursor over the battle group and looked. He could read some low-power emissions from the flight deck, guys talking to the tower for launch at radio freqs. In full EMCON, they wouldn't do even that. Otherwise, the battle group was pretty invisible. Looked tight. He kept widening his search ring, keeping one eye on his nugget's flying and one ear on the launch of their strike package. He could hear the air boss berating 706, the other S-3, which had some kind of mechanical failure while in tension.

He got distracted by air-search radar off to the south,

followed almost immediately by a targeting radar. His stomach fluttered. He understood as soon as he got a second cut. That would be *Fort Klock*, probably engaging the first Indian strikes. *Cool.* Soleck liked to see what was going on, and he liked to figure things out. He intended to be an admiral himself, one day.

"706 is ready to launch," Guppy said.

Soleck decided not to tell Guppy that he could listen to the radio, too. He got another cut way to the north, up near the Lakshadweep Islands, very weak. He played with it a little, got a second cut. The parameters were way up in the comms range and looked naggingly familiar.

Alpha Whiskey came up on the air command freq and passed a vector to an F-18 just launching. Soleck smiled when he heard Chris Donitz responding in his Minnesota voice. Donitz—"Donuts" to everybody who flew—had just made lieutenant-commander. Donitz was being told to intercept a couple of Indian Jaguars. *Old aircraft, no match for the F-18,* Soleck thought, *probably simulating missiles. Get 'em, Donuts!*

USS *Thomas Jefferson*

"Where the hell is Al Craik?" Rafe barked at his flag lieutenant.

"Nothing on any of our freqs. Nothing on satcom. It's like the whole of Mahe has gone off the air."

"Fuck me." Rafe realized that he had uttered the words and regretted them. Admirals were encouraged to avoid the foul language so normal at every other level. Hank flashed him a smile, as if he was glad that Rafe was still one of the boys.

"Skipper?" a sailor behind the captain said. "CAG on two. He has a plane missing."

Rafe looked at Hank while he took the call. "Yeah," was all he said, and a few seconds later "yeah" again. Then, to Rafe, "AG 702 hasn't been up on link or radar for ten minutes and CAG is worried." AG 702 was the S-3 that Rafe had allowed to go out early.

"Stevens is lying low out there." Rafe was staring at the mess around cat three. "He's in EMCON, too."

"Yeah," said Hank.

"Tell CAG that once the E-2 is airborne, we'll get a squeak out of 702."

"Yeah." The captain murmured into his headset. "He says thanks."

Rafe thought that the CAG was a nervous ninny who had been promoted above his level of competence, but he kept that view strictly to himself. So far, the worst thing about being a battle group commander was finding that many of the people he liked as drinking buddies were not up to the challenges of big command. Right now, for example, he was ready to kill Alan Craik, whose silence was ruining his day.

"Alpha Whiskey for you, sir."

"Admiral, 203 is a minute from intercept with those goblins and they won't respond to radio calls. 203 wants to know how you want to play it."

This was the gray area where exercise and reality and pride and pilot envy could all get messed up. Rafe didn't want the Indians to even have an argument that their "missiles" had hit his ship. He worried, too, that the Indian "missiles" would turn back into airplanes when they spotted 203 and prompt an engagement that would waste fuel. He wanted them to admit that they were exercise-dead—and stay that way.

"Tell 203 to get them up on exercise guard and tell them they're dead from surface-to-air-missiles back before their launch point. If they ignore him, he's to engage."

Even while he spoke, the S-3 on catapult three rolled forward into the shuttle at long last, dipped her nose as she went under tension, and leaped like a fat old cat into the air. That S-3 had cost his ship five minutes of launch time, and he could imagine the mayhem it had wreaked down in

Air Ops, with pilots aloft clamoring for gas and pilots on the deck eager to launch. *He* was hot even in the air-conditioned comfort of the flag bridge. Rafe looked at the flag JOTS repeater and waved to one of his staff. "Can you raise Commander Craik on the JOTS?" Even if all of Mahe was down, Al's JOTS should still function. *Why isn't he thinking this shit?* Rafe thought irritably. He took a swallow of coffee. *Cold. Ugh.*

On the screen of the JOTS, Rafe saw 203 intercept the two Indian Jaguars. One of them turned away at once and headed back for the coast, changing his flight speed and course as prescribed in the exercise book to show that he was exercise-dead. *Score one for the good guys.*

But the other kept coming.

"Goblin Two will not respond to calls and is inbound toward the missile engagement zone," Alpha Whiskey said.

The ship's captain called from his big chair on the port side. "I want to turn to starboard to unmask my aft CIWS." The Close-In Weapons System was a cannon capable of incredible bursts of very accurate fire to hit missiles at close range.

Rafe wanted to ignore the "dead" Jaguar and continue the launch of aircraft, but he understood that exercises were to train *everybody* and that ship handling mattered, too. Faced with real missiles, the captain would try to get every defense system on target. *Broadside on, just like the age of Nelson.*

"Do it."

Hank leaned over his mike. "Execute," he said.

Instantly the noise of the ship changed and she rolled to starboard as her helm was put over. It was one of the fastest turns he'd experienced on a carrier.

Madje caught his eye and pointed at the JOTS, shaking his head. "Mahe master terminal is off the air," he said.

Rafe felt a little chill in his gut.

The ship leaned harder to starboard. The whole deck was

vibrating. Rafe saw Hank's grin, realized that Hank had planned this maneuver and was on the ball. It was well executed, too, and he saw the helmsman beaming.

Good for them, he thought. *Glad I let him.* Somewhere in the back of his mind where he kept score, Hank Rogers got a little plus sign on a future fitrep.

Down a level, the air boss was putting the whole deck on hold as they heeled sharply. He'd had less than a minute's warning about what the captain intended. The flight deck was still jammed, but the respite was giving the spotters time to get the second alert five up to cat two and the E-2 command plane up to cat three, despite the cant to the deck.

Almost there, he thought.

AG 703

"Turn us to 180, Gup," Soleck said, craning his neck. "Sounds to me like the Indians jumped the gun and we have a missile strike coming in." He looked out over the sunlit sea and up to the clouds, trying to find the two Indian Jaguars mentioned on the AAW frequency. They were clearly in radar silence, as he didn't have anything on the S-3's primitive ESM. *Now if they were in the water—*

In the water fired a synapse somewhere in his brain. That weak signal up north was a rescue transponder. That's why the freq looked familiar. *Man in the water!*

He was reaching for the radio when he saw the Jaguar, a high glinting in the sunlight, starting its steep descent to imitate a missile heading for its target—the carrier.

USS *Thomas Jefferson*

"Goblin's not responding to the tower."

"Fuck him." Rafe couldn't remember an exercise with such dicked-up comms. *Was the guy really an asshole, or had someone put out the wrong freqs? Who knew?*

"He's less than a minute out and starting his pop."

A pop-up was a typical terminal maneuver in most anti-ship missiles. The missile would climb sharply after it chose its target, then come down as nearly vertical into the deck of the target as possible. The Indian pilot was going for realism.

"He's too fucking close," from Air Ops.

The *Jefferson* was still turning, her aft anti-missile systems unmasked and "firing" for exercise purposes, but the rate of turn had slowed and Rafe felt the *thunk* of a plane launching, almost certainly the second F-18, headed south.

"Get him the fuck out of our airspace!" the same voice in Air Ops shouted.

Rafe glanced around, and something moved in his peripheral vision, and then the world exploded.

AG 703

Soleck was two miles to the north of the stack of the carrier and just turning inbound to establish his refueling track, more attention on his armrest data screen than on his instruments, when movement in his peripheral vision caused his eyes to flick into an instrument scan and out over sea—

"Holy mother of God," Soleck said.

There was a fireball rising from the deck of the carrier like a Hollywood special effect, orange and white and spreading from the bow to the stern, the violent red pulses punctuated by streaks of white rising from the flames. The fireball itself rose so high that the island, the command node of the carrier, vanished in an orange bloom.

His plane shook, and then a fist of air nearly struck them from the sky.

4

Mahe Naval Base, India

The commodore's pistol was a Czech CZ75 with a full fifteen-round clip but no extra ammo. Alan figured it would be about as good as a peashooter against the automatic weaponry he could hear, but it helped him fight a feeling of loss of control.

The Marines were herding them like school kids down a back stairway, two of them leading and one covering the rear. "I feel like I'm back at Adirondack High," Benvenuto muttered. "Fucking fire drill."

Crossing the third-floor foyer, the Marines had met two others; there had been a tense moment when both groups had got ready to shoot, and then they had identified themselves, and the two newcomers had said something to the sergeant and veered off down another corridor toward the office of the Commander, West Fleet—God knew what they'd find there. The building was chaos, three bodies and a wounded man scattered along the central corridor like sacks dropped off a truck, a trail of blood down the tile where the first wounded Marine had been dragged. Twice, they had seen other people at a distance; both times, everybody had flinched, crouched, and then the others had run away and they had moved on in their hurrying file. *Indian file*, he had thought grimly. *But different Indians.* They passed office after office with closed doors. Inside, he suspected, unarmed people were trying to wait out whatever was going on. Or were dead.

USS *Thomas Jefferson*
Fire. All around him, fire, and something on his legs.

Rafe flailed his arms, seeking to get them free. A tumble of images, separated by flashes of darkness.

"Sir! Stop fighting me! Sir!"

Rafe pushed against something and the vertebrae of his back impacted against a sharp corner, sending more pain through his body in a jolt. He curled up, and the weight settled all over him. Weight and pain. He lay still. More tumbles. No sense of time.

"That leg might be broken. Move him carefully."

"Sir, we got to get him clear of the bridge. The whole fucker could go!"

"Roger that. Down to the O-3 level."

"Anyone else alive up here?"

"Captain Rogers is dead. Helmsman is over there, I tried to wrap him, everyone forward of this bulkhead died when the fucker hit us. Admiral was coming back for coffee, that's why he's—"

Rafe moved his head under the fire blanket and tried to speak. "—hit us?" he tried to say, but it only came out as a croak. He *hurt*. But time was moving now.

He felt them putting him in a clamshell. His back and legs hurt so much he couldn't really think, felt himself going into shock, tried to breathe. The fire blanket fell back from his face.

"—what hit us?" he tried, but again, it was like a hiss of air.

Madje's face appeared in his arc of vision. It was red and there wasn't any hair on it.

"Sir? Can you hear me?"

"*Whahitus?*" Rafe got out.

44

Madje leaned closer. "That Indian plane hit the deck just forward, sir. The fires are pretty bad. We're moving you to the O-3 level, and we're fighting the fires."

"*Whuzinc'mand?*"

Madje shook his head. "Captain Rogers died a few feet from you. CAG Lushner may be alive but the flight deck is— no one can go out there."

Rafe scrabbled at Madje like a corpse rising from the grave. His hands were burned claws and the angry red flesh on his sides showed under the ruins of his flight suit, but he rose almost to a sitting position.

"*You—find senior now! Take command!*"

Madje nodded, almost saluted, but Rafehausen had fallen back into the stretcher. The admiral coughed in pain as a portion of his left index finger, complete with the nail, remained stuck to the clamshell where he had gripped it to sit up.

AG 703

From the moment Soleck saw the Indian fighter plow into the after deck of the *Jefferson*, his mind focused on what would have to be the prime interest of every airplane aloft. *Fuel*.

Soleck's AG 703, flying as a mission tanker, had twenty thousand pounds of JP-5 to give when the carrier ceased to be a haven. AG 706, the last plane to launch before the catastrophe, had as much again. Scattered across two hundred miles of ocean were eleven other planes, mostly F-18 Hornets, famous for their short legs and suddenly bereft of their home base. Some of them had been on Combat Air Patrol since the last launch event more than an hour before, and their fuel tanks were as close to dry as their flight parameters and safety allowed. Down to the south, Donitz had already gone to burner and made at least one turn against exercise opposition from another flight of Indian Air Force

Jaguars before the accident; he had less fuel than any of the others. Up to the north, two F-14 Tomcats from VF-171 were on picket with the northernmost fleet elements, and somewhere up there was supposed to be Stevens's S-3 with a buddy store holding more gas. The rest of the planes were close at hand, waiting in the stack for the launch of the rest of a sea-strike package that would never come.

"Where we gon' to land?" Guppy said. He was shaken, his voice a monotone, his face as gray as his flight helmet.

Soleck had the plane under control and the altitude even. Now he was trying to watch the whole sky for other planes. The tower had been off the air from the moment of the accident. He could see that the initial explosion and the resulting fire had stripped every antenna from the carrier, and that meant that the planes in the stack were on their own. Soleck feared that other pilots might leave their assigned altitudes and start flailing around, increasing the risk of collision.

"Gup, we could fly to China with this much gas. Shut up and get me Alpha Whiskey on radio two. And try and raise the skipper in 701."

Soleck could hear a babble of pilot exchanges on Alpha Whiskey, with every plane in the stack clamoring for fuel and information. Alpha Whiskey, the radio frequency reserved for air-warfare command and usually controlled from the Ticonderoga-class cruiser *Fort Klock*, was being clobbered. "Start writing that shit down, Gup. Get their fuel states. Hey, *Guppy*! Stay with me, man."

Soleck had completed his turn at the north end of their track, and they were now nose-on to the burning carrier, just a mile out. The plume of smoke rose more than a thousand feet, and the tower leaned out over the starboard side. Guppy couldn't take his eyes off it.

Soleck reached over and slapped the side of his helmet. "Gup!"

"Sorry." Guppy mumbled something but opened his knee-board pad and started following the voices on AW.

USS *Thomas Jefferson*

Madje had been lucky, protected by the heavy central bulkhead when the first explosion happened. Madje had dragged the admiral clear of the fire on adrenaline alone, put a fire blanket over him, and donned a breathing apparatus, then rescued the helmsman. He would never remember doing any of these things. His first conscious action had been getting the firefighting team to help him get the admiral out of the smoke.

But the thing he would never forget was the sheet of flame covering the whole deck as the fire spread, interspersed with fountains of fire as aircrews punched out of their stranded planes. He had seen it for only a moment, a second, before the forward part of the bridge started to warp and collapse. He must have been moving the admiral by then. Things were missing—time, space, fire, pain. It was as if the last hour was a movie, and all he had was the promos.

He put a hand to his head and hair came away, burned. His face felt as if he had a bad sunburn. He shook his head inside the respirator mask.

Who was next in command?

Figure the CAG as dead, burned in his cockpit, or ejecting into the water and thus unavailable. The boat's skipper was dead. That left the flag captain, the navigator, and the engineer, all captains. The flag captain ought to be down on the O-3 level in the flag spaces, where Madje had planned to move Admiral Rafehausen. Seemed like a good place to start. He shone a flashlight down the ladder well through the smoke. *Where had he got a flashlight?*

"Looks clear," he shouted through the hatch.

"Lead the way, sir. We'll bring the admiral."

A blast from outside the tower rocked it, moved it by

several inches and distorted the bulkhead to his left. He touched it cautiously and it burned him.

"Down! Now! Quick as you can! This wall is hot! Go, go!"

They ran and fell and fought down the steel ladder, around a platform and down again, with wrenching noises above them and a roaring like a jet engine. Madje knew that the flight deck was just the other side of *this* hatch, and he could see from the distortion all along the wall that the other side was exposed to extreme temperature. The heat came through the respirator, burned his face again and scorched his hands.

When this wall burned through, the tower would collapse. The structural beams visible on the vertical surface were spalding, huge flakes of hot metal shooting off them in response to impacts from elsewhere. For the first time, it occurred to Madje that the carrier might not recover.

Radio India

"We interrupt the regularly scheduled program for a special bulletin. Residents of the city of Mahe report the sound of explosions and what they describe as 'rapid gunfire' from the nearby Mahe Naval Base. Radio India is trying to establish contact with the local naval headquarters. Elsewhere in the nation, two incidents of what also appears to be fighting have occurred, one in Pondicherry, one in the far north of Uttar Pradesh state. A government spokesman denied that any such thing was occurring and pooh-poohed the idea of terrorism. A spokesman told this reporter that, quote, 'Military fire practice rounds here all the time.' Amal Gupta, Delhi."

USS *Thomas Jefferson*

Madje followed the stretcher-bearers down the ladder to the O-2 level, below the flight deck. It was full of smoke, it was hot as hell, and there was already water up to their ankles. His arms and back were hurting through the adrenaline from the effort of carrying the helmsman.

"Shit!" the lead man on the stretcher shouted. "We sinkin'?"

"Fire hoses!" Madje shouted. "Move! Move!"

Around another platform, through another hatch and down to O-3. Water was pouring through the ladder well, all run-off from the fire hoses fighting the fires in the corridor above. A sailor in a respirator was standing at the bottom of the ladder.

"Where you boys coming from?" he said harshly. Close up, Madje could see he was a Chief Petty Officer.

"That's Admiral Rafehausen, hurt bad. The guy over my shoulder's the helmsman from the bridge. I'm Lieutenant Madje."

The CPO looked as if he might let Madje off this time. "Get t'admiral forward. Doc has Ready Room Two for casualties. Then get your asses up to Chief White forward. Sir, I have to ask you to join a fire team."

"Chief, I have a last order from the admiral. Then I'll be back."

Even through the respirator, Madje could read the chief's contempt, as if officers could be expected to find excuses to avoid firefighting. Maybe they could. Madje followed the stretcher down the starboard passageway to Ready Room Two, passed the unmoving helmsman to a triage team, and got a spasm of pleasure when they gave him a thumbs-up. He watched two corpsmen hovering over the admiral, loitered for a moment, and realized that there was nothing, *nothing* he could do here. He sloshed back out into the passageway, got a look from the chief, and headed forward. He squeezed past a hose team preparing to go topside, climbed over the knee knockers at frame 133, and found himself squelching into the relatively clean flag area and its brilliantly polished blue tile floor. He looked in flag ops and flag intel and the living quarters. No flag captain.

It was quiet, and he was tired. He stood in the flag briefing room, alone, insulated from the fires three decks above, and thought how easy it would be to sit down. Then he did. His legs hurt and his back felt as if he had twisted it, and his face felt swollen. It probably was. He lifted the respirator off his chest—and got back up.

"Fuck," he said aloud. He put the respirator back on, felt it tug at the fatigue in his spine, and got a twinge of his own eventual middle age.

Bangalore, India

A Toyota panel truck backed up to the loading dock of Building Three of the New World Technological Center. Three figures wearing heavy coveralls, gloves, and hoods got out. While one pulled up the loading gate to the interior, the other two opened the rear doors of the truck and took out two large fans, which they carried into the building. Unreeling electrical cords while two of the building's workers watched and did nothing—the people in the coveralls, one of them a woman, smiled at them—they plugged the fans into a wall socket. The third figure unreeled a hose from the panel truck. All three people put on goggles and respirators, and one of them went to the truck's driver's seat. The others turned on the fans. Sarin gas began to flow through the hose.

USS *Thomas Jefferson*

Madje went back out into the passageway, headed aft. He passed another fire party checking a hose, and then he got to the big steel hatch labeled "Combat Information Center." It was dogged shut. He rapped at it with his knuckles. "Flag lieutenant!" he shouted. Heads turned in the passageway, he was so loud.

Inside, somebody undogged the hatch. He pushed through and they dogged it behind him.

"Flag captain here?"

He could see from the kid's patches he was from the S-3

50

squadron and probably attached to the ASW module just forward. The kid just shook his head. He looked numb.

He passed the ASuW station and walked into the domain of the tactical action officer. There was a little smoke here, but no smell of fire. The screens were lit and functioning.

"TAO?"

"Mister Madje?"

"Sir, the admiral sent me to find out who the senior officer is and place him in command. The skipper is dead. I think the CAG is gone, too."

The TAO nodded. "CAG died in the first hit. His Tomcat was on cat four."

"I'm trying to find the flag captain."

"I can't help you, Madje. I can tell you that I'm conning the ship from here and waiting for somebody senior to take command." The TAO was a mere lieutenant-commander.

The huge screen in front of the TAO was repeated from a JOTS terminal. It showed the *Fort Klock* alongside the wounded *Jefferson*, with other ships supporting her fire-fighting efforts.

"Tell the admiral we're going to get through this. We have four ships alongside putting water and chemicals on the fire, and we've cleared the O-2 level of fires and started to take back the flight deck. How is he?"

"Badly burned, I think. But he spoke to me a couple of times."

"That's good. As to command, eventually some son-of-a-bitch will realize that he's senior to me and come relieve me."

A sailor held a radiophone out to the TAO. "Captain Lash on the *Fort Klock*, sir."

"Give it here," the TAO said wearily. "TAO, *Jefferson*. Go ahead."

"*Jefferson*, what's the status on command? Air Ops says the CAG and Captain Rogers are out. Where's Admiral Rafehausen?"

51

"Sir, I have his flag lieutenant right here. The admiral is injured but should recover, over."

"Copy injured." Pause. "*Jefferson*, I'm taking command of the battle group effective twelve forty-nine GMT."

"Roger, copy. *Fort Klock* has taken command." The TAO looked around as if he was hoping someone senior would come in the scuttle.

"I'm taking the exercise; effective immediately. I want a status on your fires when you can pass it, and I want to know the fuel status of every plane up, TAO."

"Air Ops is working on that, sir. We have—" the TAO looked at a sheet of paper being held in front of him—"eleven planes up. Sorry, make that thirteen."

"Get me their fuel status."

"I'm on it."

"You have hull-integrity issues?"

"No, sir. We've cleared the fires off the O-2 level, we're working forward from the bow of the flight deck, and the stern is on fire. I have no working elevator and cat two may be savable. That's what I know now, sir."

"Keep me apprised. I'll get a smallboy on your stern. Does she steer?"

"She does."

"I have to put out a sitrep to Fifth Fleet ASAP. Any idea of your casualties?"

"No idea, sir. No idea at all."

Pause. The TAO was looking at the hatch to Air Ops, where an officer was trying to get his attention.

"Stay in touch, TAO."

"Aye, aye, sir."

Madje felt that he knew too much. He was sagging, done with his immediate duty and frightened of the prospect before them. He cleared his throat. "I'll—I'll go fight fires. Sir."

"That sounds like sense to me." The TAO turned away

from him to the officer who had just entered from Air Ops. "Those the fuel figures?"

"Yes, sir."

"Somebody's going for a swim."

"Yes, sir."

Madje took a deep breath, tried to ignore his back, and got the scared kid at the hatch to let him out. And then he went to fight fires.

5

AG 703

Soleck was keeping his eyes on the air traffic and his brain on the fuel. "Gup, as soon as you get their fuel states, start working out what they need to get to—" He looked down at his card of the day, registered the primary bingo field, the precleared field where planes could land in an emergency, as Mahe. This was certainly an emergency. "—Mahe, India. It's on your kneeboard." Guppy looked over at him, trying to say something about being in over his head. "Just *do it*, Gup. Fudge the numbers. *Guess.*"

"I'll try."

"Good." Soleck fed radio one into his helmet and dialed up AG 706 on the squadron frequency.

"AG 706, this is 703, over?"

Pause.

"703, go ahead." That was Scarlatti, known to the air wing as "Mozart," a nugget only a little more experienced than Guppy, and *damn* Stevens for taking Goldy. They were an inexperienced squadron and Soleck wasn't sure he was ready to do what had to be done.

"Mozart, this is Soleck. Listen up; we've got all the gas that's in the air and close to the stack. You and me. We're going to have to set up a fueling station headed inbound as soon as AW gives us a bingo field, and we tank the Hornets until they can go feet-dry. You copy all that, Mozart?"

Pause. Soleck could almost hear the gears grinding in Mozart's mind.

"Roger, 703, I copy. What do you want me to do *right now*?"

"Stay on your assigned track and altitude until I come up again. Stay on this freq and monitor guard and AW. I'll get back to you. Soleck, out."

"AW on one, sir." Soleck wondered if Guppy had ever called him "sir" before. "And nothing from Mister Stevens."

The AW said, "703, what is your status and give?"

Soleck was pretty sure that was Captain Lash—Alpha Whiskey—himself, not some designated junior officer. That alone told Soleck plenty.

"AW, this is 703. We have twenty-two thousand pounds to give on original mission parameters. AG 706 has the same. AW, I'm prepared to set a track to a designated bingo and tank en route. Request ID on senior officer in the air, and request location of bingo. My card of the day says Mahe Naval Air Station. Over?"

"Wait one, 703."

Soleck breathed out, relaxed his grip on the controls a fraction. Somebody was in charge down there; the world had not ended; and AW was on the air.

"703, this is AW. I have Air Ops on handheld; I have to transfer fuel data via another line because they have lost their antennas. Copy?"

"Roger, AW." Soleck tried to imagine the difficulty. Air Ops, if they were in business, would know the fuel needs of every plane—more important, unlike the bridge of a cruiser, Air Ops would be full of pilots who could work the numbers on fuel problems. And Air Ops was where bingo fields were set. But, according to AW, all that information had to flow across a handheld, probably a walkie-talkie.

The AW came back on. "I have Lieutenant-Commander Donitz as senior officer in the air. And 703, just so you know the whole deal, our best information is that Mahe is down or not responding. We have no response from Calicut, either. We're trying to find you a bingo field, but something is going down in India, over."

Soleck felt a cold ball form in his gut.

Mahe Naval Base, India

They had picked up the other three Americans from the HQ building's bottom storey—an ex-SEAL named Fidelio, whom everybody called Fidel; a female petty officer, Dee Clavers, who had been an almost-Women's NBA center; and a female jg named Ong, an *anime* princess so small she had barely managed to make the Navy minimum.

There were too many of them now, Alan thought—five Americans and four Indians and the three Indian Marines. Too few with weapons and too many who'd never been in a fight. He muttered to Fidel, whom he'd served with before, "This isn't any good, Chief."

Fidel grunted. "What's the plan?"

"I have to get to something I can communicate with Fifth Fleet on. Everything's out here, cell-phone system's swamped."

"Hotel."

"Yeah, exactly what I think." They were staying at a beach hotel ten miles away. The hotel was as close to a home as they had.

Fidel nodded. "Car park, the van, then hotel, gotcha. You any good with that gun?"

"Not bad."

"I'm a lot better than not bad." Fidel held out his hand for the gun. "You lead, I shoot, Commander."

AG 703

"Sri Lanka," Soleck said quietly. Every airfield he could find and plot, he had entered into a chart on his computer, complete with range rings.

"203 is inbound for gas, figures he has eight minutes of fuel remaining." Gup still spoke in a monotone, but tracking the fuel for eleven other planes was keeping his mind occupied.

Soleck had walled off the emergency, taken a bite out of his own responsibilities and was chewing hard. He cycled frequencies on the radio until he had AW. "AW, this is 703, over."

"Go ahead, 703." Different voice.

"Any luck on a bingo?"

"Negative, 703." The speaker's voice went up an octave. "We're trying to raise anyone in southern India and we're—"

Soleck cut him off. "Can you raise Trincomalee in Sri Lanka? They're a little over five hundred nautical miles from us. Different country. Maybe whatever's going down in India isn't there. We're going to splash a Hornet if we don't start tanking."

"Wait one."

Soleck watched his instruments for a few seconds, thinking of the decision process that would have to happen on the bridge of the *Fort Klock*—the country clearance, the levels of military bureaucracy. He made his decision and turned the plane east, pointing the nose toward the distant island of Sri Lanka. Then he dialed up strike common, which was being used by all the pilots airborne. "203, this is 703, over."

"703, this is 203, go ahead." Donitz sounded professional, unhurried, despite the fact that his plane was running on fumes.

"203, am I correct that you are strike lead?"

"703, no one has told me that, but yeah, I think I'm the only el kadar in the air."

"Sir, I'd like to get the stack moving towards Trincomalee, Sri Lanka. I'm assuming that their field is open and they'll let us in. The distance is five seven five nautical miles from my position and my best guess is that we can get all of you there with enough gas to land."

"Soleck, I don't even have Trincomalee on my bingo card."

"Me, either, sir. But Alpha Whiskey says southern India is down and it's the best I can come up with. Every minute we stay here wastes gas. Worst case, we'll be feet-dry in an hour and someone will give us a vector to an Indian field."

"Do it. I don't have the comms or computers to figure this out. You sure?"

"Sure as I can be. It'll be close. Break, break. All planes, this is 703. 706 will rendezvous on 703 at angels one-one course 110, speed two hundred knots. Planes will tank as called by 703 in fuel priority. Sound off."

Soleck was pleased to watch Gup making check marks next to the planes he had listed on his kneeboard as they called in.

The thing was doable.

Mahe Naval Base, India
They parted company with the Marines and the Indian sailors outside the headquarters building and then huddled in a window embrasure while shooting sounded in the street. A car had been blown up down the block, maybe by a rocket-propelled grenade, and the Marine sergeant said that a lot of the firing was coming from a security building down there.

"We'll have to go the back way," Alan said. He pointed. Down behind the buildings was a chain-link fence and then weeds—grass, scrub bushes, a few trees. "There's a creek down there somewhere. Wasteland." He knew what the base looked like on a map, knew that the creek divided it so completely that a bridge had been built over it. The wasteland might give them cover. He looked at Fidel. "Unless you want to hole up inside again."

Fidel held up the CZ. "With one handgun? Any kid with

58

a weapon could waste the lot of us." He shook his head. "Lead us to the wasteland, Commander."

AG 703

A voice in Soleck's headset said, "This is AG 101, two hundred miles north of your position, will rendezvous en route; I'm good for fuel and can probably make Trincomalee from here, over." 101 was a Tomcat up north, which rang a bell in Soleck's head. Two bells, in fact.

"Where's Stevens?" he said aloud. And he remembered the ESM cut on the rescue frequency. He pressed buttons on his armrest, minimizing the display of the Indian airfields and going back to his ESM screen, where the computer had taken enough cuts on the transmission to locate the original transmission to a point. He overlaid 101's position and grunted.

"101, this is 703, I have you in the link. Can you turn east to my mark in the link and investigate a transmission on search and rescue, over? We've got a plane missing."

"Roger, 703, I see your mark. I'll be there in two. Stand by."

Soleck switched freqs to Alpha Whiskey. "AW, this is 703, over."

"Go ahead."

"AW, I've conferred with Strike Lead in 203 and we're taking the stack east toward India with hopes of making Trincomalee, Sri Lanka. Hope you'll get us permission to land there or another field in the area."

"703, this is Captain Lash. Make it so, 703." Lash was decisive, which helped. It was going to be close. Worse than close, if Soleck's fears for his squadron commander were proven correct.

"Roger. Out."

"203's six minutes to empty, two minutes out from us." Guppy was trying to do three things at once and having some success.

"Get the drogue out, deploy the FLIR camera. We'll watch them come in, save time and gas."

"Roger." The sound of the fuel line deploying was audible even through his helmet.

"203, you're first at the basket. Drogue should be out and deployed."

"Copy. I see it. On the way."

"Roger."

Strike common was blinking. Soleck dialed it up. "Go ahead?"

"703, this is 101. I have eyeballs on a man in the water, no response on the radio, over."

"One of ours?" Soleck knew it was. It had to be somebody from Stevens's plane; there was no use pretending otherwise. Even strict emissions-control procedures wouldn't have kept Stevens from hearing what was going on on virtually every frequency.

"I'm turning again. Yeah. He's not waving. Not moving much—shit!"

The last was in a different tone of voice. Soleck listened for a moment and called, "101? This is 703, please respond, over."

Silence. Not static, but silence. Soleck switched to cockpit-only. "Sorry, Gup. Recalculate your fuel assuming no give from Commander Stevens. Get Air Ops to do it, too. Tell me how it comes out."

He already had a figure in his head, and it wasn't good. He looked down, flipped his screen image to FLIR and rotated the FLIR pod to look back and down at the refueling drogue. Almost immediately, he saw Donitz's plane climbing toward them.

"203, I see you."

"I'm coming in, 703."

Donitz's approach was smooth and even. His probe was out and he rode a spot of turbulence that threw his nose off-center and then put the probe in the drogue with a little flip that was so fast it was hard to follow in the glowing green image on the FLIR.

"How much are we giving 203?" Soleck asked.

Guppy looked up from pencil and paper calculations. "Uh, well. Three thousand pounds?"

"Donuts, will three thousand pounds get you into Trincomalee?"

"Not with any margin."

"We'll talk about margin in a minute. Wait one. Break, break. 207, you're next for Texaco on 706."

"Roger, 703."

"706, give 207 three thousand pounds."

"Roger, copy."

Not for the last time, Soleck wished for a break, for the control of an E-2, for the steadying voices from the tower and the air boss. He had no idea whether three thousand pounds would get an F-18 across 575 miles of ocean. He wanted to know what was happening in the north, and he took his screen off FLIR and back to the datalink. He had to cycle past the ESM screen and he saw that the display was now littered with cuts from radars, lines of bright green radiating from two points just north and west of the datum he had assigned to the man in the water, and an obvious radar cut from one of the Tomcats.

"101, this is 703, please respond, over."

"703! We are under fire, repeat, under fire; unknown vessel fired two SAMs."

Soleck stared at the screen, his mind numb. Then he focused and was able to say, "Roger, 101, copy your under fire from unknown vessel." His voice was shaky. "Can you provide any ID?"

"Mac says it's some kinda Russian destroyer."

"101, is that a Kashin-class destroyer?" Soleck forced himself to focus. He was watching his ESM screen, trying to fly the plane and dial up the AW frequency while maintaining a perfectly steady platform for Donitz's tanking. He still had time to think that Tomcat jocks never bothered to watch their recce slides and learn ship types, and this was going to prove the pudding. But he had cuts from a modified Godavari-class frigate and a modified Kashin up there where 101 was, about nine miles apart and both close enough to the datum to fire SAMs at the northernmost Tomcat. He fed the ships' locations from his ESM into the datalink, knowing that without an E-2 aloft to transfer the data and without the bandwidth provided by the antenna array on the carrier, it was unlikely that the information would ever appear on the bridge of the *Fort Klock*.

"Jeez, 703!"

Soleck took a deep breath. "101, please ID your attacker. You can see him. I can't." He left strike common up, called Alpha Whiskey. "AW, this is 703, do you copy 101?"

"Roger. 101 is on strike common."

I know that! "AW, this is 703. 101 is under fire from unknown enemy vessel. 703 has two possible unid Indian vessels in vicinity and placed them in the link. Do you have the link?"

"Negative link. Repeat that, 703?"

Guppy was waving for his attention. "203 has three thousand pounds and a little."

"Cut him loose, call the next one in."

"Who?"

"You decide, you did the math." No time to baby Gup now. He was swimming so far, and Soleck was gaining confidence in him. He leaned back. "Take the plane, Gup."

"I got her."

Soleck took his hands off the controls and flexed them, realizing he had been flying like a nugget with a clench. He looked at ESM, saw a targeting radar come up on the Kashin-class destroyer.

"101, prepare for another missile. Get out of there!"

"Roger, evading. Going to burner. Chaff and flares."

Soleck pulled up a factoid from his remarkable memory. "Missiles will be first-generation radar-homing."

"Thanks, 703."

"101, they should suck at look-down."

"Roger, copy, going on the deck."

Soleck waited. He was sure the old Russian missiles would be poor at finding targets below them. Almost sure. For a moment, he could *see* the missiles on ESM as their radar homing warheads flickered. Then they vanished.

Then 101's voice: "Two missiles past timeout overhead, I can see the exhaust at burnout. Owe you a beer."

Soleck made himself breathe. He activated his radio. "AW, this is 703. 101 is under fire from an Indian Navy vessel, Kashin class." *And if I had a Harpoon, I could whack him from here.*

"Copy, 703." Captain Lash, again. "Break, break, 101, what's your status?"

"Peachy, Alpha Whiskey."

Soleck thought that was just adrenaline talking. In fact, if that Tomcat had just turned low with his burners on, he'd used more fuel than he had to spare, and Soleck didn't have any extra. He unclipped his harness, leaned way out over Gup and plucked the kneeboard off his lap.

"We're going to need gas, Alpha Whiskey," 101 said.

Yeah. And without Stevens, he could see they were already short. Somebody wasn't going to make it. He did the math while 101 reported the incident to AW and repeated that there was a man in the water. Soleck walled off the idea that Stevens and Goldy might be gone. He was walling a lot off. He heard Alpha Whiskey scramble his own helo, already busy doing search and rescue on pilots who had punched off the *Jefferson*'s burning deck, to get the man in the water up north.

He went to the Alpha Whiskey freq and requested another line. He wasn't ready to go public yet. Then he got 203 on Donitz's squadron freq. "Donuts?"

"Yeah, Soleck?"

"I got a problem. The Tomcat had to burn gas—"

"I heard."

"And Stevens's plane is down. Somebody is screwed for Trincomalee. Or anywhere."

"Relax, Ev. We're not. I can make it—altitude's good. And if I can make it, all the Hornets—"

"Not the Hornets, Chris."

Four of the Hornets had already tanked. They couldn't give the gas back if they wanted. The Tomcats farther north had limited options and their options were getting smaller by the second.

"Gotcha." Donuts had thought it through without Soleck's having to spell it out: one of the Tomcats was going in the drink. Almost certainly the one that had just saved itself from that very fate. And Soleck was telling Donuts that he was going to have to make the call. *Welcome to command.*

Even while he listened for Donuts, Soleck was back on the ESM, watching the Godavari-class destroyer as she closed with the Kashin-class. She had a number of radars, French, German, and Russian, and while they baffled even Soleck's knowledge he could see their types. The Modified Godavari, a middle-aged Indian ship with a curious mix of British and Russian technology, was illuminating something with a high PRF radar that almost had to be for gun-control. She was *way* out of range of the Tomcats.

That meant she was about to shoot the Kashin.

The world was going to hell

Bahrain

Two thousand miles away in Bahrain, there was no thought of guns or of death from the sky. Harry O'Neill had taken

Mike Dukas off to show him his new Hummer. Harry ran a security company that had contracts all over the Middle East; an armored Humvee was just the thing for the CEO to drive. Leslie had stayed behind with Rose, ostensibly to help with dinner, really to talk. Or try to talk. Younger by fifteen years, she was shy—a once noisy, overweight, semi-literate young woman who had found her real self in the Naval Criminal Investigative Service's bureaucracy—and in Mike Dukas.

"So what do you do with your days?" Rose asked her as they were dipping lush tomatoes into boiling water and then peeling them.

"I take classes. Distance learning, you know. Plus Arabic at U. of Bahrain. Plus I do some temping."

"I'm impressed."

"Michael says I'm an over-achiever." She put a peeled tomato on the cutting board between them, and Rose cut a cross in the bottom and squeezed seeds and pulp into a blue plastic bowl. "I'm going to be an NCIS special agent, just like him."

"What does he say to that?"

Leslie made an unhappy face. "He says things like, 'Dream on.'"

"That's not fair."

"He doesn't mean it like that. He means—it's hard, and there aren't that many jobs for women. And he means it's *me*." She stopped peeling, looked down at the board, knife in one hand, tomato in the other. "Leslie, the trailer-park-trash queen."

"Honey." Rose wiped her hands on a paper towel. "Hey. You're smarter than he is, that's the trouble."

"No, I'm not."

"Leslie, I *know* Mike. You're smarter."

"He's in love with you." Leslie smiled. "It's okay. But I know he is." The smile became shaky. "He isn't in love with me, though."

"Honey, you two live together!"

"Michael likes sex, right?" Leslie passed the back of the tomato-holding hand under her nose and sniffed. "I chase him across the Atlantic Ocean, I show up at his door, he hasn't got a woman in Bahrain yet—dah-dah! How nice to see you, Leslie, why don't you lie down and spread your legs." Tears welled in her eyes. She sniffed again.

Rose put her arms around her. "Oh, honey, he isn't like that. He's, he's—"

Leslie let her hands hang at her sides, let herself be hugged. She said, "I'm pregnant."

"Oh, Les—!" Rose swayed back, her hands on Leslie's upper arms. "That's—" She studied Leslie's face, thought better of saying it was wonderful. "Does he know?"

Leslie shook her head. "He'll think I did it on purpose. You know, to—"

"You have to tell him!"

"I'm thinking, maybe—maybe if I, you know, didn't have it, then he wouldn't feel—" She shuddered. "Trapped. Whatever."

Rose held her arms. "I've been *praying* to get pregnant again. I was going to have our last one here, shore tour, it would be easy. Then I had a miscarriage. Les, it's hell when you want one and you can't."

"It's kind of hell when you got one and you figure he doesn't want it." She searched Rose's face. "I'm sorry I dumped my shit on you, and you're—you got more reason to—"

"No, no!" Rose laughed a little shakily. "I'm pregnant, too! If I can make it to three months, maybe this time it'll be okay! Ten more days."

"Does Alan know?"

"He's been away, so busy, it's just one more—" She shrugged. "Maybe it's unlucky to tell him until I'm sure, you know?"

The two women let their eyes meet, then put their arms around each other, laughing that partly mad laughter that is near tears.

In a pool of white sunlight, five red tomatoes gleamed beside the bright blue bowl.

6

Mahe Naval Base, India

They found chain-link fences behind the naval base's buildings. Fences that had to be climbed. And there were five of them. And one was a woman with the upper-body strength of a child.

Ong had to be helped from behind by Alan or Fidel and pulled to the top by Clavers, who made it in one graceful jump, grab, and swing. Fidel and Alan went over like monkeys. Benvenuto managed to get over by grabs and gasps, but it wasn't pretty.

"Whadya think?" Fidel said when the little group had made it over their third fence. They were huddling in a dumpster storage yard that smelled mostly of things that had been in the dumpsters too long.

"I think the lieutenant's about had it."

Ong was collapsed on a stack of wooden pallets, her head in her hands, saying "I can't" and weeping.

"We need some fucking guns." Fidel said it as if guns would get Ong over the fences faster. The words were not quite out when a man with a gun stepped around a dumpster fifty feet away. He was eighteen or nineteen, thin, in Indian naval working dress. He had an AK-47 and there was no way to tell what side of this strange conflict he was on.

Fidel raised his right arm and shot him. Just like that. Alan would have sworn Fidel hadn't had time to aim.

"Jesus, Fidel—"

"You wait to ask who he is, you die." Fidel was already over the body, the AK in one hand, the other ripping through pockets for extra clips. He found one, then another. "That shot'll bring shit down on us, Jesus—" Other gunshots were still popping out on the street, but nothing close by.

He tossed Alan the CZ and bent over the boy's body again, looking for more ammunition, but his head was up to watch the place where the boy had first appeared. Alan went to the corner of the dumpster and looked around it, finding nothing. Above them, the wall of the building was windowless for four storeys; above that, a single row of floor-to-ceiling windows ran the entire width. *VIP country*, he thought. He supposed the building had something to do with the dumpsters—maintenance, or facilities and grounds. Would those people be involved in a mutiny? Could the building be a safe haven for Americans?

Fidel backed himself against another dumpster twenty feet away. He pointed at Alan, then at the space that he could see and Alan couldn't. The finger pointed again at Alan: *You—go!*

Alan went around the corner of the iron dumpster, the CZ ready, took in at a glance that they were between two rows of dumpsters, five on each side, and he raced to the next one and sheltered there, looked back and nodded at Fidel, who ran forward. So they made their way up the rows, covering each other, until they reached the third pair. Alan was leaning against the sun-warmed metal, Fidel just signaled to come on, when a brown hand splayed itself against the edge of the dumpster opposite. Fidel was already running.

Black hair appeared by the hand, then a face, brown eyes like a deer's, young and feminine. The boy tried to swing a weapon into position; Alan had time to see that it was a bolt-action rifle, and then he fired the CZ, shooting on instinct as he had been taught—index finger along the side of the pistol, third finger on the trigger.

Point and shoot.

An astonished expression replaced the fear on the young face, and the kid screamed. He had been hit just below the collarbone on the right side. Then Fidel was there blocking Alan's view, and the AK was hammering, and it was over.

Alan found himself looking at two bodies. The smell of blood was sickening, lush, warm. Twitching, the two boys lay on the violated earth, dirt impregnated with broken glass and bolts and hard plastic knobs that stuck out like bones, blood on them now. "Jesus Christ, Fidel!" Alan said. "They're kids."

"You think I'm fucking proud of it?!"

"We don't have to kill everybody we see!"

Fidel's face was twisted. "You want to take the fucking gun—*sir*?" He held out the AK-47.

"You know you're better with it."

"Yeah, well just keep that in mind—*sir!*"

Alan suppressed the angry things that sprang to his tongue. They stared into each other's eyes, neither flinching. Finally, Alan said, "You're out of line with that tone, Chief," and turned away, exposing his back to the other man and his anger and his weapon. But Fidel was better than that.

They picked up the two rifles, old British .303s, beautifully maintained and oiled but half a century out of date. Each of the sailors had had a full box magazine and five more rounds.

"The poor bastards were like mall security guards," Alan said with disgust. He turned away because flies were already gathering. Thinking, *No safe haven here after we've killed three of their guys, no matter who they are.* He looked at the next chain-link fence and then at Ong and the others. "This sucks."

"No shit."

"We're going farther down toward the creek. It'll be crap, but there'll be no fences and no people." *And nobody we have to shoot,* he thought, looking at Fidel. "Well?"

Fidel looked toward the scrub jungle through which the maps said a creek flowed. "I think we're gonna wind up humping some people on our backs, but—" He shrugged. "O-ka-a-a-y!"

AG 703
Soleck cycled through the screens on his computer while warming the ISAR—Inverse Synthetic Aperture Radar— which used the doppler of a target's movement to create a two-dimensional digital image, a radar photograph. It was best against targets on the water; it could be cranky, was often attenuated by atmospherics, but when it worked, it could reach over the horizon through ducts and reflections to image a ship that lay hundreds of miles away.

"Gup, you did leave *us* enough gas to make Trincomalee?"

Guppy didn't rise to it. "Roger that," he said. "And a thousand pounds reserve for whoever needs it. Both planes."

Soleck wanted to check the figures but Guppy had a head for math and somebody in Air Ops must have done it, too. Gup was doing very well indeed. In fact, by the end of this flight, he might have shed nugget status forever.

Soleck had the radar in surface-search mode; he could see the Indian battle group to the north, now well spread out, with elements dispersed over ninety miles of ocean. He overlaid the position of the Tomcats and the man in the water and the ESM cuts, shading his small screen with a hand and trying to work with the minimal inputs available to the front seat.

There. Two bananas on the surface-search that corresponded to his ESM cuts. He pressed the image button on the Indian Kashin-class and had the satisfaction of seeing her come up immediately. The image wavered and rotated twice; she was almost bow on. As he watched, the shape of her superstructure developed two major radar returns that showed as bright spikes above her hull.

71

Has to be damage, he said to himself. He also thought he could see her forward turret rotating and something changing amidships. *More damage?*

The ESM told the story—launch parameters for a Styx IIc anti-ship missile. He watched it go to homing and then terminal and then vanish as the Indian Godavari-class's close-in weapons took it out. He got on the comm.

"Alpha Whiskey, this is 703. An Indian Navy Mod Kashin fired on 101. That ship is now taking fire from an Indian Navy Mod Godavari. The Kashin has suffered damage. 703 is monitoring via ISAR and ESM."

"Copy, 703."

Donuts spoke up. "Alpha Whiskey, the mission tankers don't have enough gas to get 101 to the beach." Soleck could see him flying a thousand feet above him and a mile away.

"Roger, 203. Concur. What do you recommend?"

"Strike Lead recommends Alpha Whiskey advise on sending an SAR helo into a hot zone."

"203, I'm hesitant to send an unescorted helo up there."

Soleck, his eyes on the computer screen, cut in. "Kashin's air-search radar went off the air during the last exchange, Alpha Whiskey. Hasn't come back up. Still taking hits from the Godavari and seems to be listing to port."

"Roger, 703, copy all. 203, I'll risk the helo. What's on your mind?"

The nasal quality of Donuts's voice came through clearly. "I want 102 to turn south and head for the tankers. I want 101 to hang with the man in the water until gas is an issue or better yet until the helo shows; make it look like we have teeth. Then punch out or ditch, pilot's choice, and the helo picks them all up."

Wow, thought Soleck, *Donuts can be a cold bastard*. But the more he thought it through, the better the plan seemed— except for the two guys who would have to punch out of a perfectly good plane.

72

"203, I see your plan. I was thinking of ordering them to try and bingo at Lakshadweep."

"Copy, Alpha Whiskey. I'm concerned with the Indian Navy." Probably one of Donuts's best understatements.

"Roger, 203. Concur. Helo is on the way."

Soleck listened to Donuts repeat it all to 101. The pilot in 101 showed his sangfroid. "203, this is 101, concur. Always enjoy spending the taxpayer's money."

On his computer screen, Soleck could see the Kashin-class listing more and more heavily. Flames and smoke didn't register on ISAR, but damage did, and her superstructure was a spike of radar reflections twice the height of the original image. None of her radars showed on ESM.

In the last light of the setting sun, he could just see the smudge of smoke to the north. Way out over the horizon there, the Kashin-class was burning, a plume of smoke rising thousands of feet into the air. Behind him in the quick dusk of the Arabian Sea, the black pall of the deck fires on the *Jefferson* rose to meet it.

Soleck watched the computer and the gas and prayed.

Donitz pulled on the stick and turned his nose south and east until his compass read 140 and his GPS arrow lined up with Soleck's pointer for Trincomalee. He checked his altitude, his profile, did the math on his fuel one more time, and shifted his butt in his seat. Long ride, and the fuel was too close to call all the way there.

"All planes, this is Strike Lead. See you in Trin."

Ten sets of *Roger*.

And 101 came up last. "Have a beer for me, Strike Lead. We're punching out in a minute."

Donitz listened to the pilot in 101 count the time down, his voice flat through the count. And then he said "Eject," and he was gone.

Bahrain, Fifth Fleet HQ

The flag lieutenant, resplendent in whites and chicken guts, cut straight to the head of the morning line in the hotel lobby. "Is Admiral Pilchard in the hotel, please?" he asked. A full commander in the line glared at him, and Spinner smiled back. *You may be some shit somewhere, pal*, Spinner's look said, *but not with me. Not right now.*

"He's in the pub, sir." The woman behind the desk smiled. Spinner was used to that smile, but right now he had other fish to fry. Ignoring the outraged stares of the line, Spinner marched across the lobby of the Gulf Hotel and into the pub.

Pilchard was planning to play a round of golf with the new ambassador and an old buddy; he was wearing an ancient navy sweatshirt and jeans and Spinner thought he looked old and undignified. He and his buddy were laughing, the only patrons in the bar; just two ill-dressed old men drinking coffee.

Pilchard's head came up as soon as he saw Spinner's uniform.

"Sorry to interrupt, sir." Spinner paused for dramatic effect. This was what he liked best, center stage. "There's been a serious accident on board the *Jefferson*."

"How serious?"

Spinner felt as if he were watching Pilchard age, as if it was some cheap horror movie. The laugh was gone; the face looked gray. *Time to retire, old-timer.* "We don't know for sure, sir, but the first look is that a plane, possibly Indian, hit the deck of the *Jefferson*. Her flight deck is on fire and she has fires on the O-2 level and above. Captain Rogers is dead and Admiral Rafehausen is badly injured. Captain Lash of the *Fort Klock* has taken command. He's ordered the fleet exercise canceled." Spinner was keeping his voice very low.

"Jesus," Pilchard's guest murmured.

"I have to go," Pilchard said, pulling a windbreaker from the back of his chair. "You drive?" he asked. Spinner winced.

"Yes, sir." *Kiss the afternoon goodbye.*

"Get me out to HQ." Pilchard waved to his friend and started out to the lobby, Spinner hurrying to keep pace.

Pilchard had his phone open and was dialing. He glanced up at Spinner, who pointed at the waiting car. "Shelley?" Spinner wished he could hear Captain Lurgwitz on the other end. She was Pilchard's flag captain and she didn't like Spinner, thus kept him out of a lot of good information. "Yeah, Spinner's here. I got it. Was it Indian? What do they say?" There was a pause. By now, Spinner was at the wheel and Pilchard was folding his height into the cockpit of Spinner's BMW. He nodded at something.

"How long have they been off the air?" A low buzz as Lurgwitz spoke. "You tried calling Al Craik at Mahe?"

Spinner's stomach growled at the mere mention of Craik, who had reprimanded him for some trivial message attachment once and didn't seem to play the game the way the other staff officers did. *Blow-hard glory hound.*

Pilchard glanced over at him, and Spinner wondered what showed on his face. The admiral was still gabbing on the phone. "I'll look at the rest when I'm in. No press till we know, right. Yeah, Shelley, I remember the *Forrestal*. If you can't get Mahe, get me HQ Delhi or even their attaché here, okay? And get me Al Craik."

Near Jodhpur, India
A cell-phone tower rose from a dusty plain like a damaged tree. A poorly paved road ran by it. A motorbike came down the road, two people on it, a man and a woman, the woman riding behind.

The motorbike stopped by the cell-phone tower, and the driver dropped it in the dry grass. He looked up and down the road—people walking, four cyclists, a distant truck—and removed two blocks of C-4 from the bike's saddle bags. The woman was already wrapping wire around two of the tower's supports.

75

They attached the C-4 and connected wires buried in it to a cellular phone by alligator clips. Then they got back on the bike and putt-putted along the road for half a mile, where they stopped and made a cell-phone call, and the tower collapsed. Joke: the tower handled the call that triggered the explosives.

Bahrain

Admiral Pilchard came up a corridor in Fifth Fleet headquarters with his flag captain beside him and his flag lieutenant running interference. All three looked grim: they had just come from a meeting about the *Jefferson*.

"Spinner!"

"Sir!"

"Get me the Public Information Officer—my office. Now!"

"Sir!"

That's what Spinner seemed to do best—do things to please people. He was almost running in his eagerness to get the PIO.

Pilchard turned into the flag deck, waved a hand at people who were perfunctorily rising, and banged right through into his private office, a whirlwind pulling Lurgwitz in his wake. She was a stocky, intense woman who would one day have stars on her collar like Pilchard's.

"What d'you think?" he demanded, throwing himself down in his chair.

"I don't see the pony yet."

Pilchard put his forehead on the heel of one hand. "What a mess! Jesus, Shelley—" He looked at her. "Sit down, for Christ's sake!" He blew out breath. "Okay. I want CAP for the carrier, even if we have to go to the goddam US Air Force for it. Two, I want liaison with the embassy about the Indians and whatever the hell is going on over there. A, there's the question of relations with their navy—get their attaché, what's his name? Roopack, Jesus, what a birdbrain,

76

but he's what they sent—calm him down if need be, make sure he gets the message and relays it home that we deeply regret, etcetera, not our doing. A full investigation—make that a full *joint* investigation—will follow. Don't mention the *Jefferson* unless he does; if he does, not word one that we think it's one of their birds that went into our deck or whose fault it was. Okay? B, put intel on finding out what the hell is going down in India itself. Find out why we haven't heard from Craik and get on his ass if you can find him. Then—"

He looked up at a knock, bellowed to come in. Spinner put his pleasant face around the door, waited to be signaled in, and then let the Public Information Officer go first. Then, even as the admiral started speaking, Spinner was arranging chairs, making sure there were notepads, and fetching coffee from the admiral's pot.

"We have a situation," Pilchard said to the PIO. "Your job is to put a wall around it."

The PIO, a commander with degrees in journalism and mass communications, nodded.

"The *Jefferson*, that's the BG flagship, has had an accident. It's bad. We don't know how bad, but the boat's crippled and people are dead. Right now, the deck's closed and she's got no air cover." Pilchard picked up a pen and tossed it back on the desk. "We can't let word about it get out until we know just what we've got and how we can cover. If the media pick up on it, we're going to have every hardhead in the Middle East trying to pick off the BG. Understand?"

"You want a soothing-syrup story or no story at all?"

"No story today. Maybe syrup tomorrow. *No* press briefing." He picked up the pen again. "Can we keep five thousand sailors on the *Jeff* from phoning home about it? So far, maybe—acting BG CO is 'taking steps.' If that holds, we'll be okay for a day." He cleared his throat. "*If* the story gets out—if you're asked, volunteer nothing—then you say that the ship is underway and doing its job. Got it? That's the bottom line—the ship is still the biggest piece of force projection in the world, on station and on duty."

"Uhh—" The PIO cleared his throat. "What's Washington's spin on it?" By *Washington*, he meant not the Navy, but the politicians in the executive branch.

"Washington doesn't know yet. I'm reporting to the CNO as soon as this meeting ends. From there, he can do what he wants with the civilian spin-doctors." He didn't add, *And if I had my way, they'd never find out.*

Radio Pakistan
"Alert Bulletin—Alert Bulletin—Alert Bulletin!

"Forward elements of the Pakistani Army have been put on alert along the border in India. Unconfirmed reports present a wave of violence sweeping across India. Gunfire, including heavy weapons, has been heard in many places. Monitors of Radio India report accounts of murder, arson, and vandalism. Attempts by this reporter to contact India have failed, suggesting massive damage to the telephone system. Our army and air force reserves have been alerted to stand ready. Bulletins will be issued as more is known. Fahd Firadawsi, Lahore."

7

Mahe Naval Base, India

They had mud-clotted shoes and calves by the time they had reached a clump of trees that promised shade, if not protection. Pant legs were black from mid-calf down, and the heat had ruined khakis put on for the air-conditioned spit and polish of the West Fleet Command building. Underarms were dark, hair lank. "This sucks," Benvenuto growled.

"No pain, no gain," Clavers said.

Ong moaned.

Benvenuto, perhaps out of sympathy for somebody even nerdier than he, reached back and grabbed her right hand and pulled her across a stretch of black mud.

They stopped under the trees, pushing wet hair off their foreheads and leaving mud stains. Fidel looked toward where the creek was supposed to be and shook his head. "Too easy," he said. "We won't be the only ones thought of coming this way." He looked at Alan.

Alan grinned. "If I'd had time, I'd have ordered in a chopper."

"We need flankers. Okay?"

"Okay by me."

"Gotta be you guys with the rifles. Still okay by you?"

Alan grinned again, nodded. He had one of the old .303s, Benvenuto the other; Clavers had the CZ, because she said she had done a private combat handgun course—she said.

Fidel sent Alan thirty feet to the left and twenty feet ahead and put Benvenuto on the other side, almost on the fence. Fidel took point. When they moved out, Alan lost Benvenuto at once, and then he could see Fidel only between clumps of grass.

And then he was in the mud.

He plodded forward, seeming to drag the creek bed with him. The heat was oppressive, even after Bahrain, worse because the air was saturated. The effort made him hyperventilate, and he drew up on a tussock of grass, gasping, knelt to catch a moment's rest. When he looked up, movement registered in the yellow-brown wasteland ahead of him.

He stared. Nothing. Then he saw it again—tan moving past darker brown, then into sun-blasted near-white. Tan pant legs, brown hands. Brown *gunstock*.

And other movement closer to the creek.

He looked for Fidel but didn't see him. Farther back, he saw a flicker of something dark. Benvenuto's hair or Ong's.

Then a sound to his left like a woman's wail, quickly muffled.

Oh, shit, shit, no—

A voice called, birdlike, nervous, from in front of him, was answered from ahead on his left, and he heard Fidel shout, "Hit the dirt—down, down!" and an automatic rifle opened up. Alan, still kneeling, put the .303 to his cheek and fired where he had seen the gun, then swiveled and started to fire toward the movement closer to the creek and thought better of it, remembering that female wail. Fidel shouted again and began to fire three-shot bursts. Alan dove into the mud, propped his elbows on the next grass clump and fired again where he thought the shooter was.

That was two of his ten cartridges.

Where ignorant armies clash by night. From a poem. High school. It had struck him even then, what clashing by night would be like. This was not so different, clashing in the tall grass with an enemy who may have been a friend.

"Americans!" he shouted. "We're Americans! American Navy!"

He heard single reports from his right: Benvenuto with the .303. Fidel must have shot a full clip, because there was a pause. How many clips had he found on that kid? Not many—

Somebody female was screaming ahead and to his left. He swept the sights that way, then back, hunting for the shooter on that side. The screamer was a woman. Was she hit? Would mutineers include women?

Fidel fired a burst.

"Fidel! Fidel, goddamit—stop firing—!" Then, in the silence, "Friends!" he shouted. "American Navy!"

A long silence, then the woman's sobs. Not one of his.

"US Navy!"

Another voice, calling in an incomprehensible language.

"US Navy over here! Friends!"

Then another voice. "Show yourself." The voice had authority, timbre.

"Jesus, don't!" Fidel.

"Who are you?" Alan shouted.

"Show yourself."

He waited. He was trying to pierce the grasses with his stare, willing them to part and show him who it was. But what difference would it make? His neck hurt from craning upward; he dropped his head forward, stared into the mud. It might, he thought, be almost the last thing he was ever to see. *Oh, Rose, what a mess—*

He pushed himself upright. His hands were caked with mud, his uniform shirt filthy, his face streaked. "Commander Alan Craik, United States Navy."

He heard the unmistakable sound of a foot being sucked out of the mud, then the swish of grass.

"Fidel, don't for Christ's sake shoot."

The man who emerged from the yellow grass had gray hair, a complexion more olive than brown, heavy circles under his eyes. He stood as straight as it was possible for a human being to stand, his look imperious—head a little back, eyebrows arched. "Commander Ramanpur Upadhyay, Indian Navy." He looked at least as disheveled as Alan.

Alan bent and picked up the .303, never taking his eyes from the Indian officer. He held the rifle well away from him to show he wasn't going to use it and, with slow, deliberate steps, crossed on his toes to him. Neither man was wearing a hat: no saluting. Instead, Alan smiled. "Commander."

"Commander." They shook hands.

"I hope you have no casualties, Commander."

"A credit to the depth of the mud here, I daresay." He had no Indian accent whatsoever, in fact sounded more British than a Brit—an Indian type Alan had learned to recognize. "Most of mine are civilians. Yours?"

"American naval personnel."

"I am trying to take mine to the hospital, where there is an attempt to gather loyal forces. I regret that we thought you were—an enemy."

"So it *is* a mutiny?"

"God only knows what it is." He spoke over his shoulder in another language. Alan, looking back, saw Fidel and the others struggling to their feet. *Like two tribes meeting in a jungle.*

"We're trying to get to our vehicle. In the fleet-exercise parking lot."

"I hardly know this part of the base. I am a lawyer, actually. We were trying a court-martial in the JAG building when this dustup started. There will be a good many more courts-martial soon, I daresay." He gave a hint of a smile. "Perhaps you would join us?" He gestured toward his path ahead. It sounded as if he was proposing a stroll with the family.

Alan thought of what it would mean to get through the mud to the bridge and then try to cross it. "I have to get my people off the base."

The Indian commander nodded. "Quite the best plan, I'm sure. However, we had a garbled order to move to the hospital."

His people, also filthy and disheveled, had arranged themselves behind him—an enlisted man with an old, wood-stocked AK, two astonished-looking younger officers who were, Alan guessed, also lawyers, and five civilian women, two in saris.

"Well—" Alan looked around, focusing on where the fence must be. "If we stand out here, we'll bring trouble."

"Quite. Best be moving on." Again, a hint of a smile. "Our separate ways—ships that pass, and so on." They shook hands again. "My profoundest apologies for the shooting."

"No harm done."

The two lines of people passed each other without words, individuals exchanging rueful smiles, especially the women on both sides. Fidel looked disgusted. Alan looked the others over—Benvenuto smiling nervously, Ong bedraggled but oddly calm, Clavers jerking down one side of her mouth in a nervous tic. *Never fun to get shot at.*

Fidelio muttered in Alan's ear, "I fucking didn't kill anybody this time, okay?"

"And you did right. Fidel, it's for the best—they're the good guys."

Fidel frowned, unconvinced. "They all look alike to me."

When the straggling line of Indians had vanished into the yellow grass, Alan gathered the others close, their faces strained, eyes wary. "I think the car's about a hundred yards along. We'll probably have to go over another fence to get to it. Everybody ready?"

He took silence for an answer.

"Let's go." It would hardly have made any difference if

83

they'd said they weren't ready. It was get to the car or die—
and then get to the hotel or die. And then—

Bahrain

In the parking lot of Fifth Fleet headquarters, Spinner could
hardly wait until he was out of the building before he was
on his cell phone to his father in Washington. The other
times he'd passed information along, he'd sent e-mails
because he'd heard they were more secure, but now time
was everything. If he could scoop the intel agencies with his
dad, he'd score points, and his father would score points with
the White House. Scoring points was very big medicine with
both of them—Spinner because he felt in his gut that he
never pleased his father, and the old man because he loved
power.

"Dad!"

"Hey, boyo. How's public service?"

"Listen, Dad, are you watching the news?"

"I'm in a meeting." The implied comment was that he was
doing something too important to be interrupted but could
make time for his son.

"Dad, turn on CNN. There's something going down in
India."

"Ray, I'm *in a meeting*—" Warning sign. Dad was not a
patient man, as Ray's mother had discovered.

"Dad, this is more important!" Spinner had the windows
of his car rolled up despite the heat, his cell phone clutched
to one ear. "Dad, now hear this: an Indian fighter jet just
crashed into the deck of a carrier called the *Jefferson*. The
doomsayers are telling the admiral it could have been deliberate. Pilchard is asking his staff for scenarios for *intervention* in India." Spinner grinned. "I thought you'd want to
know."

There was a pause at the other end of the line, and Spinner
could picture his father waving apologetically at somebody

powerful and walking out of the leather-upholstered meeting room in the Mass Avenue office and heading to the staff lounge down the hall where the TV was.

"The President doesn't want to waste resources on a country like India."

"Yeah, Dad, no kidding. Like, that's why I called."

TV sounds bled through the digital connection.

"Okay, India's in chaos. What's Pilchard up to?"

"He has people on the ground there because of a fleet exercise, and they're panicked that the carrier accident might have some connection. Plus just now we got a report that a destroyer may have been *fired at* by an Indian vessel."

"I think this goes right to my guy." His "guy" was a deputy to the National Security Advisor. "Call me the instant you know more."

"You bet! Out here."

He punched off and looked around the parking lot. Had anybody seen him? Would anybody be suspicious, seeing an officer with a cell phone at his ear, at this hour? No, everybody had his own problems to think about. And everybody used cell phones all the time. And a plane had hit a carrier, so who gave a damn about a phone call?

And he was *Ray Spinner*. Born to win. Born to make out. Born to rule.

Mahe Naval Base, India

The fleet-exercise parking lot was a trapezoid that held about eighty vehicles. They had reached the back of it—yellow grass and livid green weeds, black mud and the odd scrub tree. The mud ran almost to the fence, and the walking was worse. Clavers and Fidel plodded ahead, but Benvenuto and Ong were holding each other up, staggering, no longer caring about mud or grass or firm ground.

Alan knelt where there was bamboo and some kind of thorned cane. "I'm going to do a recon up the far side to see if I can check out our vehicle and if there's anybody at the gate. If the gate's down, we've got another problem."

"Go through it," Fidel muttered.

Alan shot him a look but said nothing. "Meanwhile, I want you guys to look for a way in without going over the fence."

Benvenuto, who was lying flat, said, "Don't raise the river, lower the bridge."

"Talk English," Fidel growled.

"Like, dig—dig?" Benvenuto giggled. "Go under, get it?"

Alan made himself sound confident, trying to pump them up. "Use whatever works. Only big enough for the biggest of us to squeeze through—I guess that's you, Fidel." He stood in a half-crouch. "I'll be back." He glanced at Ong, who was next senior to him and should have been told to take charge. Nothing.

Fidel got up. "I'm coming with you."

"Better alone."

"Unh-unh—*sir*. By the time you get that antique into firing position, you'd be in two pieces. You go; I cover you."

Alan grinned. "Okay, Mom, I'll take the pistol." He handed Clavers the .303; she looked hurt, but she turned over the CZ. Alan grinned at them. "Dig good."

He and Fidel went along the rear of the parking lot to the corner and turned up the long side. They hadn't gone ten yards when Alan stopped, hearing a sound he knew he shouldn't hear, an anomalous *clink*, then silence, then a soft sound of two things brushing together. He motioned Fidel back, knelt. Seconds later, an Indian noncom in fatigues appeared inside the fence thirty yards away, a new, black-plastic-stocked AK in his hands.

"Shit." He pushed Fidel down as a signal for him to stay there and hurried, crouching, back the way they had come. When he reached the others, Clavers and Benvenuto were scraping in the earth with their pocketknives, a pile of dirt between them.

"Bag it!" he whispered. "Guy coming inside the fence. No shooting!" He looked down at the pile of dirt. "Kick it out of the way, push grass over it—!"

He waited with them until the noncom had come into view, come down the fence in a crouch, and gone past. The man was edgy, worried more about what was ahead of and behind him than what might be outside the fence.

"He see them?" Fidel said when Alan rejoined him.

"You think I'd be standing here if he had?"

At the far end of the fence, they knelt and studied the gate. An officer and three EMs were there, all armed. The arm of the gate was down and two cars had been parked bumper to bumper across the road.

"Iffy."

Fidel grunted. "Maybe they're good guys." He was being sarcastic.

Alan watched. And waited. Nothing happened—and then the officer's cell phone must have rung, because he took a device from a pocket and put it against his ear. An alarm went off in Alan's head: these guys somehow had a cell-phone net that was still functioning. And then the officer reached inside his shirt and withdrew something, the gesture alone telling Alan that it was on a chain or lanyard. The thing gleamed in the sunlight. Then the officer took it in his fingers and connected it to the cell phone.

"Bingo," Alan said. Fidel pulled his brows together. Alan felt for the thing he had taken from the Indian commodore and put, yes, right there in his left-hand pants pocket. He had pretty much forgotten it in everything that had happened; now, he took it out. It lay, golden, shell-like, in his palm, the USB-port connection a small extrusion at one end.

"What the hell's that?"

"Something that tells me those aren't the good guys. Come on."

Bahrain

Admiral Pilchard banged his secure phone into its cradle and opened a desk drawer and then slammed it shut with all the force he could muster. He buzzed. "Get the flag captain in here!" he shouted.

He tried to do paperwork while he waited, but he couldn't, and she was there in thirty seconds, anyway. When she came in, he stood up and put his fists on the desk and said, "Washington knows! I just got my ass chewed by the President's personal political cocksucker because I didn't inform them *first* about the *Jefferson*!" He banged a fist on the desk and took two strides away. "Not a word about the danger to the fleet—not a word about the kids who may be dead or dying—!" He swung into a vicious parody of Southern smarm. "'Don't you ri-uh-lahze the po-li-ti-cal potenshee-al foah damage heah?' He's reading *me* out because I didn't call him personally so he can do political damage control!" He stared at her. "Well?"

"Well, sir—" She spread her hands. "I think we've got somebody who's leaking top secret information."

Mahe Naval Base, India

The hole under the fence was big enough for Fidel to wriggle through on his back. Clavers followed, then Ong, pulled through by the two inside. Benvenuto went in on his belly, jumped up and brushed himself off with a surprising burst of vigor.

"Save it; you'll need it," Alan said. He wriggled through, face up.

They crouched between two cars in the row nearest the fence. He looked at Ong. "Lieutenant? Can you make it to our vehicle?"

She nodded. Tears were running down her cheeks. She looked like a very dirty Oriental doll that would cry if you put it on its back.

"Okay." He motioned Clavers and Benvenuto in closer, put a hand on Fidel's back to get his attention. "There are four guys at the gate, plus the guy walking the perimeter. Maybe more, but we didn't see them. We're going to try to take them without shooting. Hear me, Fidel?"

He saw the back of Fidel's head move in a nod.

"We're going to get as close as we can—the front row of cars, with the cars as cover—I'll already have stood up and said something. Okay? The signal is 'friends.' You hear me say 'friends,' you're behind cover, weapon cocked and locked and ready to shoot."

"You don't want us to shoot, you said." Fidel's voice was like rocks rattling together.

"I don't, but I don't want us to get killed, either. If they shoot, then we shoot."

Fidel turned his head. "You gonna let them shoot first?"

"If they *try* to shoot, we shoot."

Fidel grunted. "You stand up, you say, 'Friends,' they shoot you, we shoot them. Okay, if that's the way you want it." He shrugged—quite an elaborate shrug.

"It's a matter of timing."

"Sure is."

If they'd been alone, he would have read Fidel out. He took a breath, exhaled, said, "You got a better plan?"

"Yeah—waste 'em."

Alan looked at Clavers and Benvenuto. "The goal is to take the gate with minimum damage on either side. Clear?"

Both nodded.

"Fidel?"

Fidel nodded as they had. "When I see your head blown apart, I can feel free to waste them."

Alan looked at him. Hard. "If you don't like my way of doing things, give me the gun and I'll do it alone."

"A-a-a-h—shit, I'm just mouthing off, Commander. I'll do it your way. But it's going to be a split-second thing. If our

89

guys were trained snipers, it would be one thing—" He turned on Benvenuto. "How good are you with that rifle?"

"If it shoots okay, I can hit a paper plate at a hunnerd and fifty yards." He swallowed. "I hunted a lot of deer. With my dad." He looked from one to the other. "*Honest!*"

Fidel looked back at Alan, raised his eyebrows, shrugged. "He'll be a lot closer than a hundred and fifty yards. Maybe a hundred and fifty *feet*. My idea is, Benvenuto aims at the officer. He makes any move when you pop up, he shoots him. The officer's down, the other guys may fold."

Alan cocked his lower jaw forward, thinking about it. "Can you do it, Benvenuto? Shoot a man, not a deer?" He tried to make it as brutal as he could, so the kid would get it. "A man's head is about the size of a paper plate."

Benvenuto swallowed again. "Yes, sir. If that's the plan, sir."

"Okay, that's the plan. But—" How to make it clear to a twenty-year-old who wasn't really a warrior? "You've got to watch him. If he doesn't make a hostile move, don't shoot. But Fidel's right—if he goes for a gun or orders the others to shoot me or—anything, then you shoot. Okay?"

"And don't *think*," Fidel said. "You think, you're too late. Just *do* it."

Alan thought it was a big order for a kid who had been told all his life to think.

8

Mahe Naval Base, India

Alan's mixed bag of troops—a former SEAL, a boy, a woman, an officer who didn't like shooting people—trickled down the parking lot between the cars, moving so that they couldn't be seen from the gate. They had left Ong hunkered down beside their van, halfway down the lot.

The gate was off-center toward the end of the lot, so that Alan was the only one to its right; the others were staggered up the line of cars on the other side. Alan lost them after they crossed the last roadway, and he pulled up in the lee of a Honda sedan and waited, using the front wheel to mask himself from the gate. He had said he would count to sixty to give them time to get into position. Now that he was there, he saw how difficult it was going to be for Benvenuto, who would have to aim—and shoot, if he made that judgment—in a split second. Maybe it would have been better if Fidel had taken Benvenuto's role, using the AK, but then they'd have no automatic fire ready if the others opened up. Well, Fidel was right—if you were going to do this in a combat situation, you'd give no warning and you'd want only to kill.

As if this wasn't a combat situation. No, the trouble here was that Alan was trying to apply an ethic that came from a place outside combat and that was, unless you were an idealist, irrelevant.

So he was an idealist.

He watched the last seconds tick down and checked the CZ. He put his index finger along the frame and hooked his third finger into the trigger guard. *Well, the second time today. If I've been stupid, Rose, forgive me—*

"Friends!"

He was standing. He had the CZ in his right hand, raised to shoulder height but not pointed at them, the barrel up and the side of the pistol toward them. The hood of the Honda protected his gut and legs, but he was exposed from his belt up. In his peripheral vision he saw Fidel rise on his right, a silhouette in the violent sunlight.

All five of the Indians were near the gate, three of them focused on the street. One of the others saw him even before he spoke; the man hesitated, then reacted, reaching for the weapon he had leaned against the gatehouse. Reacting to him, the officer turned to follow the man's eyes, then Alan's voice, and his eyes widened.

For a microsecond, Alan's and the officer's eyes met. And in the officer's face was unmistakable recognition. *Of him.*

The officer shouted and scrabbled at his side for his pistol, and a rifle shot banged and echoed and the officer whirled and went down and lay on the ground, legs flailing. At the same time, the man who had reached for his AK heard the shot and saw Fidel and again hesitated; the other three turned, and Fidel fired a burst just over their heads, and the first man dropped his weapon, and then it was too late for the others to respond, three of them looking at four armed men behind cover. One of them held his weapon in hip-firing position while the other two lowered theirs. He swung the weapon toward Alan, and Alan pointed his index finger and fired and the shot ricocheted off the gatehouse wall and Fidel hollered at the three, his voice hoarse, eyes bulging, bellowing like a bull because he wanted to gun them down and instead he was doing what his commanding officer had told him to do.

And the guns went down.

Benvenuto was pumping his fist in the air; Fidel was red-faced, breathing hard; Clavers was blowing out her cheeks and muttering, "Holy God, Holy God—"

Alan touched Fidel's shoulder. "Beautiful." Fidel shot him a look, went back to communicating to the four men with the barrel of his AK: lie down, don't move, shut up or I'll blow your fucking guts out. The international language.

"You okay?" Alan said to Benvenuto. "You were great." The boy hardly heard him, riding an adrenaline high. Alan made a mental note to keep an eye on him, because he was likely to crash. He sent Clavers to get Ong and the van, and then he and Fidel organized the captured four into a team to move the cars apart while Benvenuto held one of their own AKs on them.

The officer was still on the ground, blood vivid and hot around him on the yellow earth. Alan bent over him, saw that the man was still alive, looked away; he wanted the golden thing inside the man's shirt. He had to go through blood to get it, found it on a fine gold chain. Then the officer was dead.

Alan held the thing up. "See who else has one of these," he said to Fidel. "Maybe on a chain around their necks."

The cell phone was in the officer's pants pocket. It was a new Japanese model, expensive, with a small screen that could show pictures as well as text—the best and newest, perhaps unusual for an underpaid Indian officer.

Alan turned it on. The LCD lit up.

He was looking at a picture of himself. In full color. With text in English: "Kill on sight."

"What the —?" Fidel was looking over his shoulder. "Shit, man, that's you!"

"Yeah."

"Hey." Fidel pulled him partway around. "Hey, Commander, what the fuck? These guys had a cell phone that works; they got your picture—this isn't some fucking two-bit mutiny!"

The van pulled up. Clavers began picking up guns and throwing them inside. Fidel, after a look at Alan, went into the gatehouse and raised the barrier and then herded the captives inside. Benvenuto, still high and now shaking a little, stood next to Alan. "We're ready to go, Commander. Commander? Sir?"

Alan was frowning, thinking that Fidel was right: that it made no sense that this officer had had his picture and an order to kill; thinking that this cell phone could get a signal when the system had been jammed; thinking that this was more than a mutiny—

"Let's go."

USS *Thomas Jefferson*

Rafe came to with the notion that he had overslept. His dreams were colorful, even ornate, and he felt as if he had spent too much time in bed. The feeling of the wrappings and bandages came to him slowly, followed by the claxon of the pain.

He could get only one eye open, and even that required a struggle. The eye was gummy, and once it was open he could feel his eyelid as a pain separate from all the others, the worst in his left leg. He looked down, but his head wouldn't move much and the leg was too far away.

"He's awake!" someone called in the distance.

He opened his mouth. It was dry sandpaper, as if he'd gone on a bender and this was the hangover day. That thought crossed his feeling that he'd slept too long and took him down a corridor of waking dream about life in his first squadron, until something else pressed at his abbreviated senses.

"Sir? Admiral Rafehausen?"

He opened his eye again, saw a blur. Someone pushed a straw into his mouth, and the rush of water was a pure

94

joy like few things he'd ever felt. He drank greedily.

"That's a damn good sign," said a voice in the background. "Give him all he'll take. Dempsey, see if you can swab that eye. It looks like it still has some particulate matter in it."

"Sure thing, Doc."

Rafe felt something on his eye and he blinked. There was a burst of stinging pain more intense than the pain in his leg, but it didn't last. When he blinked a few more times, the figures around him grew more distinct.

"Dempsey, get the admiral's flag lieutenant. I think he's coming around. Let's back off that drip a little now that he's awake. You with us, Admiral?"

Rafe moved his head a fraction.

"Good. Lot of folks waiting to talk to you. You're pretty shot up and the boat ain't sinking, so don't waste your energy. Give him more water."

"*Wathitus?*" he croaked.

"What's that? Listen to me, Admiral. I'd like to do this differently, but I know you're waking up. I had to amputate your left leg a little below the knee, and I'm not sure I can save your left eye. You have some burns, none of them really bad, but the aggregate—well, you ought to be in a burn unit, but I have a lot of worse cases."

Amputated leg? "Leg hurts!" Rafe said, quite clearly.

The face by him wandered back and forth. Rafe realized he was shaking his head.

"That's just nerve memory. I'm sorry."

Rafe gathered himself. It was hard to concentrate, but he had things to do. "*What hit us?*" he hissed.

"I'll let your flag lieutenant fill you in. He'll be right up."

Time passed.

"Sir?" Madje's voice.

God, Rafe was able to think, *he sounds like hell.* His eye blinked open. "Report!" he croaked. Someone pushed the straw back into his mouth.

Madje made a short and brutal report and finished by saying, "We're still picking up aircrew who punched out from the deck."

Rafe took a deep breath, which tightened the bandages and hurt him more than he had expected. He coughed water and mucus and his eye blurred.

"Doc? He's coughing."

"Raise the level on the drip. Sorry, Lieutenant. He's in rough shape. I'd rather you didn't use him up."

"No!" Rafe tried to shout, coughed again. "Planes aloft? Bingo?"

Madje's head moved. "The TAO is trying to get them into Sri Lanka. The Indians aren't responding, sir."

"TAO?" Rafe's whole body moved. "Who's—in charge?"

"There's an O-5 in reactor who's the senior man we can find, sir, but he doesn't feel he can leave the engines." That was a short form for an argument that had dragged Madje away from a firefighting team and into a labyrinth of the fears and hesitancy of an officer who clearly couldn't accept the reality that he was in command.

Rafe snorted. It sounded like an abbreviated cough. "TAO," he said.

Madje nodded. "Yes, sir."

"Get—planes down. Cats working?"

"Cat two's down but shows green. The fire hasn't touched it."

"Madje—have to know!" Rafe was looking down an increasingly colorful tunnel. He hated it. *Drugs.* "Get planes down. Report."

Bahrain

The tomatoes were simmering in olive oil; their odor, supported by garlic, filled the kitchen. Rose had taken down an already-open bottle of white wine and was wrestling with the cork when the telephone rang.

"I'll get it," Leslie said.

"Oh, would you? This goddam thing—"

Leslie was good at answering phones. She had done it for a year for Mike Dukas when she was a ditz-brained newcomer and he was NCIS's hottest agent, and then she had done it for a year for Dukas's assistant when she was no longer a ditz-brain and Dukas went off to head NCIS, Bahrain. "Craik-Siciliano," she said. Her voice was crisp—gone were the thuggish accent of three years before, the tears of half an hour ago. She looked at Rose as she listened to the other end. She gestured, held out the phone. "Your office. Urgent."

"Oh, shit—" Rose banged the bottle on the countertop. Her voice switched to professional chill as she spoke into the phone. "Commander Siciliano here."

Leslie picked up the wine bottle and, holding the neck in her palms, pushed the recalcitrant cork out with her thumbs. She tried not to listen, but the room was small.

"My God, when? How bad is it? But it can't—" Rose caught Leslie's eye, shook her head. Then, seeing the open bottle, she pointed at the heavy skillet, made a pouring gesture before turning away. "What about the exercise? Is that firm? Do we know who's in command? I can be there in—" She listened. "Okay, I'll hang by the phone. Absolutely. Yes. Thanks for keeping me posted." She hung up, hesitated. Her eyes met Leslie's again. "There's a fire on the *Jefferson*, the BG flagship. All hell's breaking loose."

"How did it—?"

"Plane crash, that's all they're saying. But it's bad, because Fifth Fleet has tanked the fleet exercise." She hugged herself as if she was cold. "We've got a lot of friends on the *Jefferson*. Mike has, too."

Leslie had never been on an aircraft carrier, thought of one only as a huge and invulnerable ship. "How bad can it be?"

"If the flight deck's packed with aircraft, it can be the end of the world. If it was right at the beginning of the exercise, they'd all be full of fuel, packed together. A carrier called the *Forrestal* went up that way during Nam. More than eight hundred dead." She looked away. "God."

"But— They have sprinklers and firefighting stuff and, and—everything—"

Rose shook her head. "It could be hell with steel walls."

Then there was the sound of the front door opening, and Harry and Dukas came in, talking loud and laughing, and Dukas stopped dead in the kitchen doorway and looked at the two women and said, "What's happened?"

"A plane went into the *Jefferson*. It's bad."

The four shocked faces exchanged looks, searching for comfort, not finding it. "I've got to find Alan," Rose said and turned back to the telephone. Dukas looked at Leslie. "I better call the office."

"There's another line in the den," Leslie said, leading him out. She didn't explain how she knew that. Leslie was, as Rose had said, smart.

Harry patted Rose's shoulder as she tried to get through to West Fleet HQ, Mahe. Her face went through shades of hope, frustration, anger. Finally, she crashed the telephone back into its cradle. "'Out of service.' How can a goddam navy base be out of service? 'India is out of service.' It's fucking *India*, for Christ's sake, not some two-bit third-world shithole! How the fuck can they be out of service?"

"Keep trying."

"Keep trying what? I just fucking tried—!" Then she heard herself. She put a hand on her abdomen as if checking the fetus that she hoped still lived. Her jaws clenched; her eyes closed; she inhaled. "Sorry, sorry, sorry. I'm being a hysterical asshole."

Harry smiled at her and kissed her cheek. He had a way of looking at people just slightly sideways because he had only one eye; the other, lost to torture in Africa, had been replaced by a beautiful but useless plastic one. "You're being Rosie Siciliano, the terror of the Sisters of the Annunciation."

She pushed him away. "You know too much about my misspent youth." She started to dial again.

"What hotel's Al staying at?"

"The Mahe International—the number's on the pad in the den—" She turned away to concentrate on something going on in the telephone. Harry got the number from the den, nodding at Dukas while he was jabbering at somebody at NCIS, smiled at Leslie. Harry wandered into the big living room, tapping numbers into his cell phone. Waited. Waited. Then a British-accented female voice said, "Mahe International Hotel, may I be of service?"

The woman on the other end was good. She knew within half a minute that Commander Craik wasn't there. Had he tried the naval base? Then Dukas and Leslie came in, and Rose stood in the kitchen doorway with the telephone still in her hand, and the three-year-old, Bobby, woke from his nap and wandered in with the nanny from the bedroom wing. And then Mike—the other Mike, named after Mike Dukas—Alan's and Rose's nine-year-old son, came in from outside, looking at all the adults with the wisdom born of years among such people, and said, "What's wrong now?" Then, with the condescension that only a child can show to his mother, he said, "Mom, you're burning the tomato sauce again."

Northern India

A continent away from Rose's burned sauce, the sharp smell of rancid ghee carried over the industrial antiseptic and mold to burn in Daro's throat. He coughed, his hand automatically rubbing his abdomen. Despite the discomfort, he savored the anonymity of his new headquarters.

They now occupied a former telemarketing center over a

restaurant. The walls were gray-green, the carpet dull and moldy. There were no posters, no personal photographs, no cartoons, no graffiti. Three cheap digital clocks provided the only relief for the eye. On the floor, desks formed a long curve with a bank of small flat-screen displays against the far wall.

Mohenjo Daro paced the floor in front of the screens, often pausing opposite the desk of one of his operators to hear a report, curled into himself by pain despite his discipline.

Vashni, on the other hand, sat to one side with three laptops open in front of her, collating data. She raised her head from her screen. "The Americans have cancelled the exercise. We have a report that their carrier is on fire."

Daro nodded. He was leaning over another operator, reading her screen.

Vashni raised her voice, unsure whether her news had been heard. "Shiva's Spear was a success."

"Hundreds of men and women are dead, Vash. Try not to sound so pleased."

She swung her hair. "We can move to phase two. Americans are the greatest offenders against this planet—"

Daro was shaking his head even as she started to speak. "I wish we could have recruited there more effectively."

"In America? All they care about is money and primitive religion." Vash's facade of civility cracked and her voice grew shriller. "No one would have joined."

He ignored her, placed a hand on his stomach, shrugged. "So—let us move on to phase two, then."

Daro clapped his hands. The operators looked up.

"Phase two, my friends."

Conversation stilled. The gentle tapping of fingers on keyboards became the only sound, intense concentration the only expression. Phase two would turn India into chaos.

An hour passed. Two men in white lab coats served food, which was eaten automatically.

Daro moved around the room, scanning screens, making suggestions and responses, praising much and reproving little. Three times in the hour he stopped, hands at his waist, head down. After the hour's walking, he was visibly weaker.

Despite her own tasks, Vashni watched him from the cover of her computer screens. She was sure that the bouts were coming quicker and hitting him harder.

One of the men at the left of the room punched a fist in the air, and Daro walked over to look at his screen, where a data stream was made visible as a digital waterfall. "I'm in," the man said, indicating his screen. Then his fingers flew over the keyboard. As he typed, flat screens on the front wall lit up and provided images, all black and white. Nine of them showed corridors, one showed a desk with a guard; a few showed outside views of a low concrete building, and three showed the top of a dam. One showed a low concrete building with a heavy blast door marked "Bldg. 37." Altogether, there were twenty-seven screens, and, even as Daro watched, they changed to a new set of views: more landscapes, a helipad, more security stations. Distant mountains showed in some views, and a dam, and the lake behind it, and twelve huge turbines; factories, power storage, power transmission, a nuclear reactor. The whole of the Ambur Regional Electrical Power Facility, the most extensive in India, unfolded across the wall in the frames of the flat paneled screens.

Daro reached out a hand toward Ali, his assistant, and snapped his fingers, and Ali unwrapped a new cell phone from its plastic and handed it to Daro, who opened it and dialed a long number. The crackling of the discarded plastic was the loudest sound in the room.

"Ready?" he asked. Something about the reply amused him, and he smiled. "You should have the feed now. Three minutes? I think we can wait that long. Very good." He pressed a button to end the call, and handed the phone to

Ali while he watched the screens, leaning the weight of his torso on one arm on the back of a chair.

"Station Two will insert loops as soon as they have sufficient footage for each camera. Our views will continue to be live," he said.

"I have control of all their SCADA functions," the man said at the end of the table.

"Station Two will give you the cue to cut the lights."

The man nodded, his head back down on his screen.

The rest of the center remained quiet. Even Vashni had stopped working to watch the screens that flickered away, changing scenes every five seconds. There were hundreds of views, with guard stations, exteriors, interiors, machinery, more power turbines. The clocks counted down three minutes. Several of the computers gave low chimes, the sound of arriving e-mail.

"Our troops are going in." A small woman in the center took a deep breath.

"Lights out—now," said one of Daro's operators.

Daro caught a movement in one of the scenes because he had been watching for it. A man in black appeared by one of the security stations. Most of the screens went black. The external views of the power facility dimmed as the artificial lights in the compound went out.

Daro motioned for another cup of tea. "I think it is time to move again, Vash," he said, his face old now, pinched. He pointed at the operator on the end. "Stay online."

Vashni reached in her purse and brought out a hand bell, which she rang sharply. One of the two doors to the room opened and a group of men in white overalls marked "Dow Chem" walked in, pushing industrial carts. The operators began unplugging their laptops and loading them on the carts while the white overalls took down the display monitors and the digital clocks. Several of the monitors were showing bursts of automatic weapons fire as they were unplugged.

"Leave that one," Daro said, pointing to a monitor that showed a helipad. The operator nodded.

Daro exhaled sharply and bent over, his face moon pale.

Vashni surprised herself by placing a hand under his elbow. He turned his head, locked her eyes with his, gasped. Then he shook her off and tried to stand straight, rubbing his abdomen.

The room emptied. Daro's operators left.

On the screen, a helicopter landed on the pad.

Daro gave a weak wave and another cell phone was unwrapped and passed to him. He dialed. Listened. "Excellent," he whispered. Closed the phone and handed it to Ali, who extracted the guts and broke them between his hands.

"Lights," he said to the operator.

The operator pressed a key and squinted at the screen. "Back on," he said.

The views of the power plant were illuminated, one showing a body with a surprising pool of dark liquid around it, the others empty corridors, and then back to the helicopter, its blades still rotating.

Daro took a lemon drop and chewed it. Vashni was working on a tiny palmtop.

The operator continued to type ferociously. "I have control of the turbines, now. Shall I run them backward?"

"Not yet," Daro said. On the screen, dark figures were pushing a heavy metal cart toward the helicopter; another cart followed, then a third. The uncertain light shone on reflective tape outlining the edges of the carts, and the distorted image glowed. The glow framed matte black cradles in each cart.

It took six men to lift the payload from one cart into the helicopter. By the time they reached the third cart, Daro could sense their fatigue. He watched them lift the last black cradle off the cart and swing it up to reach the open door

103

of the helicopter. Their effort fell short. The cradle swung back and one of the men fell away, clutching his arm.

Daro looked at his watch. Another man appeared in the frame with a rifle slung over his back, and then another. They helped to lift the last cradle aboard the helicopter.

Daro watched them as he had watched the lotus, his attention tuned to their actions, his wretched abdomen churning in response to their struggles. Even Vashni watched them, her eyes flicking to her palmtop and then back to the men loading the helicopter.

Then the copter stirred on the pad. It began to lift, lights blinking. In seconds it vanished from the screen, tail high.

Daro sighed as if he had been holding his breath. "Let's go," he said.

He was now the possessor of three nuclear warheads

CIA HQ, Langley, Virginia

Mary Totten stood looking at a TV screen in the CIA's Center for Weapons of Mass Destruction and felt an adrenaline rush—the first good feeling since she'd been transferred out of Operations. A map of India was on the screen, and a talking head was telling them about the destruction of a power station at a place called Ambur. That was what had triggered the adrenaline—Ambur! She knew a lot about Ambur. *Ambur is more than an electrical power station, sweetie. Ambur is a secret nuclear-storage site.*

She ran for her desk, hungry to be the first. She grabbed her phone, checked on the fly that it was secure, and whammed the top button.

"This is Mary Totten at WMD," she said to the Deputy Director for Intelligence. "We have a situation."

9

Mahe, India

They got to their hotel by back roads and industrial streets; what was normally a ten-mile cruise from their hotel door to the Mahe naval base's main gate became a hurried, nervous search through a very different, very unfamiliar India. When, at last, they pulled up at the hotel's glass and marble front, Fidel said, "Amen," and Clavers, who was driving, screamed, "Hey, whoa—we made it!" Ong burst into tears. Benvenuto, whose high had crashed, looked as if he'd been sandbagged. Fidel told Clavers not to turn the engine off and waited for her to get out, then slid behind the wheel and said, "I'll park it around back." He glanced at Alan as if expecting an objection. Alan only nodded.

Clavers seemed to take it personally. "What the hell for?"

"Because I don't want it around front." He looked at Alan again, then back at Clavers. He put his right hand on the gearshift. "Always find the back way out—right?"

Alan herded the rest of them into the hotel. The air-conditioned lobby, not over-large but handsomely done up in shades of red and brown, seemed odd to him, different— and then it struck him: *Nobody's sitting or waiting or checking in. The place is* empty.

"Commander Craik!" The high female voice seemed to echo in the space. "Commander Craik!" A woman was calling, almost screaming, to him from the front desk.

Alan shouted back at his crew as he crossed the lobby, "Nobody go out! Everybody stay close to a phone!" The woman at the desk was holding up message slips, and he was thinking that there had been a dozen calls for him from Bahrain, angry people wondering why he wasn't at Mahe, why they couldn't reach him, what was going on— He turned back to his ragtag army. "And don't get in the shower!" Looks of shock. "If the phone rings, I want you to pick up!" They were already at the elevators, headed for their rooms.

"Commander Craik!" The tall young woman coming around the reception counter was Miss Chitrakar. In this hotel, where the reception clerks also functioned as concierges, she had been wonderful all week. Now, she looked terrified.

"Messages, messages—" She started back for the high marble and almost fell. "People calling and calling—especially—" She handed him a slip of paper.

The message said, *Stay where you are until I get you. Important! Harry.*

Harry? Harry wasn't Fifth Fleet. Still—

"The telly said the Pakistanis are preparing to attack!"

He looked at her, saw her frightened eyes, then realized that a small television set was on behind the counter, images of soldiers filling its screen.

Then the telephone rang and she flinched and answered and almost at once jerked, her head and looked at him, listened, nodded, tried to speak, listened, held out the phone. "Your friend."

Their fingers touched. She flinched as if shocked.

"Harry?"

"My God, you're a hard man to find. Al, what the hell is happening there—? I tried the navy base, the phones are down!"

"Harry—I can't talk—I've got to call Fifth Fleet—"

Miss Chitrakar moved away.

106

"Al, shut up! Listen—something's happened to the *Jefferson*. Some sort of accident. What do you know about it?"

Alan was watching the mini-TV. The picture was incomprehensible—a building on fire, a talking head, an air shot of the fire, a flasher in the corner that said "Calcutta".

"Harry, what're you calling *me* for?"

"Something's going down, Al. Rose got a call from her office; the word is that the exercise was canceled—"

"Yeah, but that's because—"

"—and the *Jeff*'s not answering any comm link—'

"Wait a minute, Harry, that can't be—*my* comm was down, not—"

"—plus there's some weird shit going on where you are. *Weird* shit—"

The picture on the mini-TV changed to show a shattered cell-phone tower, the flashing name "Delhi." The talking head returned.

"Harry, I've been out of touch for a couple of hours. Tell me about the *Jefferson*."

"They think it was a crash on the deck; that's all they'll say. Fifth Fleet don't know whether to shit or go blind. Al— are you guys okay?"

Alan saw Fidel come into the lobby from a rear door. He was carrying a long bundle wrapped in filthy newspaper.

"Harry, I can't talk. Physically, I'm fine. We're at the hotel and we're going to hunker down here. But—yeah, something's going on—I can't—"

He was watching a burning gas station on the mini-TV, the title "Mumbai." And abruptly, the set went black.

And the hotel lights went out.

Fidel stopped where he was, shifted his grip on the long bundle, and looked around.

And Miss Chitrakar screamed as the floor-to-ceiling front window by the hotel door exploded inward.

"Al—Al—what's going on—Al—?"

CIA HQ

Mary Totten hung up the phone after her call to the DDI, the wash of adrenaline fading, leaving her feeling cleansed. She had got the okay to head for India to find out what was going on at the secret nuclear-weapons site at Ambur. *I'm getting out of here!* she screamed inside her head.

She was a graying but still handsome woman, angular and tough and sometimes abrasive. Good at her job but not so good at politics. Made for the field, not a desk.

She burrowed in a drawer for her fly-away kit, which she rifled briefly, checking for the essential items—*flashlight, med kit, knife, toilet paper, birth-control pills, tampons, money, condoms, a good book. Need to draw a pistol from the station when I'm in-country.* The DDI had told her to assemble a team: she was to have the crisis-center plane, support from Special Operations Group, the works.

A team. Might as well start right here. The guy's a jerk, but he's brilliant.

She started around the cubicles.

"Bill?"

"Yeah, oh, Mary, hi—" Bill Caddis mumbled with his head down at his screen. He had a can of caffeine-free Diet Pepsi in one hand and a computer mouse in the other.

"Bill, I need you to go to India. Tonight."

"Sure. Yeah, sure, as soon as I have this thing fixed up. Sorry it's late, Mary. India? Whoa, as in *go to India*?"

"Go home, pack a bag. Get your passport with your cover name, if you ever got one. Expect to be gone a week. Maybe two. And take a shower, Bill."

"Oh, yeah. Hmmm. Sorry."

She went back to her desk, and threw herself into the chair so that the wheels screamed. She began to make a list. And the telephone rang. The security window said "DDI."

She had just talked to him. The DDI never called back with good news.

Oh, shit.
She picked up the phone.

Bahrain

Harry O'Neill was pushing the cell phone against his ear so hard the cartilage hurt. He was hunkered over, not wanting Rose or young Mike to hear him or the sounds coming from the device. In his ear, automatic gunfire popped like corn, and a woman screamed. A heavy clunk-crash meant that Alan had dropped the phone at his end. Or worse.

Harry made his way to the front door and stepped into the late-afternoon heat. "Al? Al, can you hear me?"

Mahe, India

Alan glimpsed at least four uniformed men shooting from the street before he dove behind the marble counter, taking Miss Chitrakar with him. She screamed even louder. He had time to realize, as he worked the CZ out of his belt, that the attackers could have recognized him through the big plate-glass windows, meaning that, whatever his picture and the message to kill on sight meant in the long run, right now it meant that their pursuit wasn't confined to the naval base.

Miss Chitrakar was in a fetal position, elegant, stockinged legs drawn up, screaming into the floor. He envied her; he wanted to curl up and scream, too.

He put his right cheek against the inside edge of the high counter and peered around, protected from the street by the depth of the counter itself—twelve inches of shelves, with an inch of marble on the outside. Chips of stone had spattered over the terrazzo floor immediately in front of him; beyond them and across fifteen feet of open space, Fidel, surrounded by torn newspaper, was crouched behind a pillar with an AK-47.

Good on you, Alan thought. He admitted to himself that he'd probably have told Fidel not to bring a weapon into the hotel if he'd known it was what he planned. Fidel fired a three-round burst, and somebody bellowed and then screamed. Behind Alan, Miss Chitrakar screamed in response. Fidel looked his way, saw the CZ, pointed toward the street.

Alan, using the gun left-handed, the butt held clumsily because of his missing fingers, eased the muzzle around the marble facing of the counter and tried to get enough of his left eye out there to see what was going on. As he did, Fidel fired again and full-auto fire responded, walking up the wall beside the reception counter and trying to swing over to Fidel's pillar. *Piss-poor shooting.* He looked out, one-eyed, saw a figure leaning over the hood of a car parked just beyond the sidewalk in front of the hotel. Alan steadied the big 9mm with his right hand and double-tapped, missing the mostly hidden shooter but sending him ducking behind the car as bullets thunked into the hood. *Deadeye Dick shoots again.*

"Just keep that shithead pinned down!" Fidel shouted at him. "There's two other guys—I got one—!" He disappeared around the far side of the pillar and reappeared as a slithering shape on the glass-littered floor. Alan raked his eyes over the windows, saw movement outside to his left, snapped off a shot, swung back to see his man on this side trying to look around the front bumper of the car he was using as cover. Alan fired at him, missed again but put the fear of God in him.

How many shots left? Nine? Eight?

Fidel was behind another pillar on the far side of the lobby now. When one of the shooters over there tried to back into the street so that he could throw something through the smashed-out window, Fidel took him with a burst, then ducked. It didn't register on Alan, then did, and he got his eye and hand behind the counter as the grenade exploded in the street; something pinged on the marble, and dust swirled where a ceiling tile had been ripped away near the door.

Fidel was already through the empty window, firing; Alan followed, the CZ pushed in front of him in his good hand now, the left hand supporting, third finger on the trigger. *Use it like a knife*, the instructor had said, *it's a knife—* He reached the window. Fidel was firing on full auto.

The shooter behind the nearest car popped up. He had blood on his shirt. Alan had time to take in the terrified eyes, the half-stagger as the man tried to swing the weapon first toward Fidel, then toward Alan.

He's trying not to run.

Alan double-tapped, double-tapped; the man exploded backward.

Oh, Christ, I hate this.

The street was silent. Far away, a siren wailed.

"Fucking amateurs." Fidel came in through the hole where the plate-glass doors had been. "Fucking *amateurs!*" He was in a rage. Alan guessed that he hated it, too. "Don't even know enough to try to shoot through fucking plate glass!"

"You okay, Fidel?"

"How do I look, dead? We gotta get outa here, Commander! Those weirdos were fucking *after* us—I saw one of them goddam *point* at you before they started shooting! What the hell goes on, here, anyway?"

"Is that all of them?" Alan wanted to sit down.

"Yeah, four. What kind of navy sends four fucking amateurs to get five people?" Fidel frowned even more deeply, a scary sight. "Hey, Commander, level with me—are we at war with India?"

"No. Absolutely not." He thought that over. "But part of India may be at war with us. With me." He shook his head. "Look, I'll tell you about it later, okay? For now, we have to get out of here." In truth he didn't want to move. Shock, fatigue, the self-disgust that came after killing swept over him. He wiped his face on his left sleeve. "We have to get out of here," he said again. He couldn't think.

111

CIA HQ

Mary Totten put the telephone to her ear.

"Sorry, Mary." His voice was weary. "It's off. You don't go. I've been ordered to take no action."

"Why the *fuck*?" Her voice rose to an unprofessional shriek on the last word. She reached up and tugged at one of her earrings, a bad habit left from adolescence.

"The President told the security advisor an hour ago that India is not a US interest."

"How the hell was the President making a decision about India an *hour* ago? It just happened!"

"Apparently the White House had another source on a, mmm, related matter."

She took a breath, tried not to sound like a child who'd just been told that Christmas was off. "*No* action?"

"NSC had an Indian story in front of the President before we did. Not Ambur—something else."

"Sir, do the President and the National Security Council know that the Indians probably build and store nuclear weapons at Ambur?"

"Mary, I tried. Maybe we can put something together tomorrow."

"Does the Navy know what's at stake here?" She cast her eyes desperately over the papers on her desk, a jumble of top-secret trash, before she found what she wanted; the Director, Naval Intelligence Daily Intelligence Summary. "The Navy's got a huge fucking exercise with the Indian Navy, Lord of Light, starting today!"

"Mary, this is a need-to-know issue, but I'll tell you this much—it was something to do with the Navy and the exercise that got to the President an hour ago. The exercise has been canceled—that's classified, not to be repeated; they're keeping it close to the vest so far. There's been an incident, okay? They're trying to keep it off the evening news until they can spin it. We're talking dead American military—

112

next to that, Ambur doesn't loom very large with this bunch."

"But if there are Indian nukes—!"

"Indian nukes don't vote; dead sailors' families do. They're focused on damage control."

"But—the Navy must have people on the ground there." She thought fast. "Look, cut me orders to go to Bahrain and support Fifth Fleet, sir. Screw the plane. Give me a country team for India and a couple of jocks from Special Operations Group and let me go to Bahrain to support the Navy. They'll love it, we'll look cooperative as hell, and the moment the NSC realizes what's really at stake, we'll be twelve hours ahead." She wanted to say *Please*. As in *I beg you. On my knees*.

"Well," he said, "I dunno—" But the tone was right, as if he was saying, Well, maybe, just this once, we could have Christmas—

10

Mahe, India

In the bullet-scarred hotel lobby, Alan became aware of a whimpering from behind the pocked marble counter, and he looked over and saw the lovely, still fetal Miss Chitrakar. He tried to mumble something comforting, and she moaned, and a round, brown, big-eyed young man with oiled hair staggered out of the office behind the reception counter and stared around the lobby. He put his hand over his mouth. He was the assistant manager, and he was going to be sick.

Having somebody else's problem to solve made Alan feel temporarily better. "Generator," Alan said.

The young man stared at him.

"Generator. For electricity!"

"Automatic."

Alan pointed at the dead TV. "I don't think the automatic part worked."

"Oh. Oh—oh—" He vanished.

Alan's attention was taken by the telephone, which still lay on the high counter, untouched and emitting rather high-pitched squawks that resolved into a voice calling, "Al—Al—" He leaned on the counter, glad for its support, unconsciously listening to a distant siren.

Harry was still on the line.

"Harry, hold for a sec—" He forced himself to focus, pulling himself back together. *Get people out.* He had to force himself

114

through it a step at a time. *Get them downstairs. Get them into the van.* He told Fidel to get on a house phone and get everybody downstairs and into the car. He tried to make himself sound brisk, confident. "We pull out in three minutes, no ifs, ands, or buts. No showers, no sacktime, no nothing! Go."

"No electricity, no elevators." Fidel grinned, again a scary sight. "Nine flights, Commander."

"Tell them to jump. We're getting out of here." *Before the cops arrive*, he was thinking. He didn't mind cops, in fact normally would have welcomed them—*Oh, boy, to just sink into the back of a cop car and let somebody else do all the organizing*—but what was happening was now so unpredictable that he wanted only to get them all to a safe place.

"Harry?"

"What the hell's goin' on, champ?"

"People with guns."

"You don't sound too good, bud."

"Look, the shit's hit the fan here. The base was chaos— like a mutiny. I don't know what's happening now; all I know is, people are shooting at us and for some reason they've put out a bulletin with my photo and 'shoot to kill' on it."

"Bulletin! What kind of bulletin?"

"Like a, like a Palm Pilot with a cell phone—little screen—" He was listening to the distant siren, now closer. Out in the street, a few civilians with shocked, silent faces were looking at the hotel, then at the bodies in the street.

"Who's shooting at you?"

"Harry, if I knew, things would be a hell of a lot better."

The siren seemed to be closer, and then there was an explosion, and then there was no siren.

CIA HQ
Mary Totten was holding the telephone as if she wanted to crush it in her fist. She could hear the DDI talking to

115

somebody on the other end, but she couldn't understand what they were saying. On and on. Discussing her future, her chance to get out of this fucking place! And he couldn't simply say "Go!", no, he had to mumble and mumble and— Bill Caddis passed her, watching her, and she waved him in, thinking momentarily that she would tell him that it was off, then deciding it was bad luck to say such a thing.

Then the DDI was on again. His voice was doubtful. "Well—okay." He sounded as if he didn't believe a word he was saying. "I'll cut you orders for Bahrain. But no team. No shooters, nothing like that—"

She looked at Bill. "One analyst? He's a specialist, sir, the best—"

"One, okay, one analyst. But I want you to notify Fifth Fleet yourself. Keep this as low-key as you can—really low-key. I'm out on a limb here, Mary."

"Yes, sir." She cleared her throat, trying to hide her excitement. "And, sir, uh—one more thing?" She bit her lip and tugged at the earring again, took the plunge. "I'd like to activate Persian Rug."

Persian Rug was a deep-cover asset in Bahrain with Indian contacts.

The DDI sounded shocked. "He's not a WMD asset!"

"Sure, sir. But he's submitted all the reports we have on Ambur and he clearly has contacts we can use. I can send you his last report—"

"Mary, now you're putting me out on *two* limbs. I'm sorry, I have to ask DDO. Give me another ten minutes."

"Thank you, sir." She reckoned it a done deal; the current DDI was actually close to the DDO, unlike past administrations. But she had also just placed herself in a must-win position; she'd have to produce something to justify the effort. *No problem!* She smiled and ended the connection, turning to beam the smile at Bill Caddis, who had slumped into a chair.

"Bill? Move your ass. We're going."

She made a couple of telephone calls and stared at the wall and thought about things like communications and guns, and she went through her classified Rolodex until she found the number she wanted at Fifth Fleet intelligence, Bahrain—a very attractive commander named Alan Craik.

Bahrain

Outside the Craiks' house in Bahrain, Harry O'Neill was sitting in a white plastic lounge chair beside the blue swimming pool, a laptop open on his long legs, and pressing the phone against his ear. He heard in it a distant siren and a muffled explosion, and then some sound as Alan lost the telephone and recovered it. Now, in the silence that followed, he could hear Alan's breathing.

What Alan had said about a mutiny didn't make much sense, but combat never made sense when you were in it. What worried Harry, however, was the feeling that Alan's entire environment, even India itself, might be going mad. The accident on the *Jefferson* triggered his security-officer response; it was unimaginable that what had happened to the carrier and what was happening to Alan could be only coincidence. Except that in an environment gone mad, coincidence became a kind of logic. He began to tap queries into his laptop as he spoke to Alan on the cell phone, his head slightly cocked so he could watch the screen with his good eye.

"Al, listen up. I'm going to put you on hold for no more than one minute, I swear to God. Then I'm going to get back to you, and hopefully by then I'll have some information. You'll hold?"

Alan sounded dubious. "I've got to get my people out of here, Harry."

"It's *for* you and your people, dumbfuck!"

"Okay, one minute, *one* minute—"

Harry cut the voice off and hit 11 on his phone and went direct to his office and his VP there, Dave Djalik, a former Navy SEAL.

"Yeah."

"Dave, Harry. Two things, most urgent: I want to know in the next fifty seconds what you're getting on India, southwestern India particularly. Get on that while you listen to me. Two, I want to know what flights there are out of Mahe, M-A-H-E, India and where they go—any flights to friendly countries, sooner the better. Get on it."

"Hold."

Harry looked around the oasis of the Craiks' garden. A desert garden, to be sure, but beautifully tended, beautiful to look at. As Harry sat admiring a desert rose, Mike Dukas came out of the house and stood next to him, his eyebrows raised in a question. Harry shook his head.

Djalik came back on the phone to say, "Weird things going down in India. CNN reporting terrorist attacks, but we're getting in-country client reports about mostly small stuff—a cell tower one place, fires another, somewhere somebody poured animal shit all over the floor of a resort hotel—just weird stuff. Got a report of spreading blackouts all over western India—looks like the electricity grid is doing a domino—Mumbai, Pondicherry, Mahe—yeah, that's the place you asked about— Hold on."

He was gone for nine seconds. Dukas started to ask a question, but Harry waved a hand, looked away. Then Djalik was back: "India's closed."

"The *whole country*?"

"Just declared. All major airports closed, no penetration of Indian airspace allowed. Forget the flights out of Mahe."

Harry pursed his lips, then made a popping sound. "Stay on this, Dave. Put out a company-wide alert, information-only, prep for possible complications in India and up all incoming intel to level three, my eyes personally."

"Got it."

Harry looked up and met Dukas's eyes. "Dave, give me ASAP a landing field near Mahe that will take the Lear jet. Can't be anything big—discreet, easy-on, easy-off—"

"I'm on it."

Harry brought up a mapping program on the laptop and switched back to Alan. "You there?"

CIA HQ

Two telephone calls convinced Mary Totten that Alan Craik wasn't in Bahrain, and there wasn't anybody else at Fifth Fleet intelligence senior enough to be worth talking to. Fair enough. She left messages to create a clear trail of having tried to do it the right way and then flipped slowly through her list of other Navy numbers in Bahrain until she came to a handwritten note that said *Mike Dukas new SAC NCIS Bahrain*. She hadn't met Dukas but she'd heard of him. *Tough, smart, dogged. Unmarried. Oh, goody.*

Mahe, India

Harry was back on the line to Alan.

"Fifty-seven seconds, not bad," Alan said. He was wincing because Fidel was standing halfway across the hotel lobby, making urgent *Let's get going* signs. All Alan wanted to do was lie down.

"India's closed," Harry said. "I'm coming to get you."

Closed? "What the hell?"

"We're getting intel of a general breakdown, Al—murmurs so far, I don't know what they mean, but the country's closed. I'm coming to get you. Hold on."

"Harry—!"

He watched his people straggle in a door on the far side of the lobby. They looked like walking ragbags, half-dressed, carrying the bundles and plastic shopping bags and anomalous luggage of refugees. Ong came out almost at a trot, trying to tuck a clean blouse into clean slacks, propelled from behind by a push from Clavers, who bustled through the door shouting, "She was taking a fucking bath! A *bath*!"

"Al!"

"Yo."

"An airfield thirty miles from you, bearing about 315 from— You're at the International, right? Yeah, 315 from the hotel. About five miles south of a town called Prenningerash. Got it? *Prenningerash!* The field is called the Bhulta Valley Agricultural Facility. General av, no commercial air, one tarmac strip. I'll pick you up there in the morning. Hey, how many people you got?"

"Five. Including me. But Jesus, Harry—"

"No prob. Early a.m. tomorrow, friend—be there."

"Harry—if the country's closed—"

"Get a grip Al, this is *me*. I'll pick you up in the morning. You guys just be there. We on the same page?"

Alan saw things complicating, spiraling up, heading toward utter incoherence. He glanced at his group, saw their tension, their weariness, their confusion, then felt again his own after-shooting depression. He forced himself out of it. "You're the best, Harry. Tell Rose I'm okay, and pass the word to Fifth Fleet, okay?" He raced through the details—Borgman's death and the need to get somebody responsible in India to recover the body; his current status; the mutiny. The hell with security—it was all over the TV, what did he care about an open phone?

Fidel was pushing the others toward the back of the hotel. Ong was hopping on one foot, trying to get a shoe on; Benvenuto was carrying her makeup case and a matching suit-bag and a big red plastic shopping bag with "Lala Land" on it in orange. Clavers was humping a duffel bag and a fishing-rod case.

Alan trotted after them. He and Fidel hadn't even got to their rooms. *Traveling light.*

"This is a bitched-up can of worms," Fidel growled when Alan caught up.

"You don't know the half of it."

Fidel glanced aside at him. "You call Fifth Fleet?"

Alan laughed and wondered if he was cracking up.

Bahrain

When Dukas saw Harry close the little phone, he said, "You're flying to India to get Al?"

"Country's closed. Al's a little rattled, but he said something about a mutiny."

"Oh, Jesus." Dukas sat on a plastic chair next to Harry's. "I hate to tell Rose."

"Rose is tough. Look, she has to be told. And Fifth Fleet has to be called to tell them about Al. Which do you want?"

Dukas stood. "I want to go home." He headed into the house.

Leslie met him at the door. "Where were you?"

"Out." He pulled her aside. "Look, there's some sort of massive problem in India, and the country's—"

"Closed, I know. I called downtown."

Dukas stared at her, a slow grin changing his face. "You tell Rose?"

Leslie made a face. "Yeah. She's bummed."

"Okay, go tell her Harry was just on the phone with Al. He's okay, but the environment is unstable. Harry's going to fly in and get him tomorrow a.m. Make it sound like a good idea."

"It *is* a good idea." She kissed him. The kiss made him smile, then blush, then look around to see who was looking. Dukas wasn't accustomed to being loved by somebody young enough to be his daughter. "Go tell Rose," he said. He patted her ass as she turned, and she chuckled; then a look of pain shadowed her face, and he knew she didn't believe it, didn't believe him, thought he was indulging her. Dukas turned away.

In the den, he called his office again. He got the special

agent, a man he hardly knew, somebody who'd come out from the States only the week before. "NCIS, Special Agent Greenbaum."

"It's Dukas. Give me Rattner," he growled.

"Rattner's in transit."

"In transit where?"

"He said he had business."

"I bet." Dukas reflected that this was what he got for sending all his good agents off on jobs. "Okay. I want you to try to get in touch with the agents on the *Jefferson*." Every carrier had two NCIS special agents on board; those on the *Jefferson* weren't under Dukas's command, but they could give him immediate and reliable information.

"I tried."

"Try again. And keep trying. I want to be ready to start an investigation the moment we can get aboard the *Jeff*."

"Investigation of what?"

Dukas thought there was the possibility that he would be going in to investigate the crash on the *Jefferson* as a terrorist act. He wasn't, however, going to say that over the phone to a newbie agent whose previous experience of investigations had been confined to six years on the Racine, Wisconsin, police department.

When he turned from the telephone, Leslie was in the doorway. "I gotta go to the office," he said. "I'll tell Rose."

"Rose is talking to an Indian admiral." She giggled. "He's the Indian naval attaché. I think he's coming on to her. I think he's trying to pump her about the exercise being cancelled. He knows about it, anyway."

"Rose is a big girl." He turned to go.

"Can I come?" She looked determined to be cheerful. "I'm a pretty good office assistant—remember?"

He thought of the danger of bringing a woman he was living with into the office, and then he thought of Special Agent Greenbaum. "Come on," he said.

CIA HQ, Virginia

While she waited to get a call back from the man named Mike Dukas, who was "out of the office" in Bahrain—and Mary Totten disapproved of people who were out of the office when all hell was breaking loose—she made lists and drafted a message for the agent code-named Persian Rug:

> To: CEO, Ethos Security, Bahrain
> From: Coven-Tope Venture Investments, DpiU
> We would like to get together with you to enumerate details of the security contract already discussed (see e-mails copied below) and activate it at your earliest convenience. We want to move quickly on this and we believe that our entry into the Gulf market can be enhanced by your participation.
> (signed) C. L. Brevard

The message would go out as an encrypted e-mail. Nonetheless, because no encryption was entirely secure, only three terms in it were in fact significant: "DPiU," (lower-case is essential), which authenticated the sender; "activate," which meant that the covert operator who was the recipient should activate at once; and the not-quite-correctly used "enumerate," which referred to a communications plan for a meeting twenty-four hours later at the Benetton shop on the second level of the Manama Mall.

C.L. Brevard was Cindy Lee Brevard—one of her cover names.

As she got ready to send the message, a new summary came up on her main screen. India was now having an epidemic of small-scale terrorist acts.

Fiddle-dee-dee, I'll worry about that tomorrow out in Bahrain.

11

Bahrain

When the message came in on Harry O'Neill's cell phone, he was in the Craiks' kitchen, helping Rose to put away the half-prepared, now-cancelled dinner. Rose was in office clothes now; she, too, had been called in and was on her way to the embassy because of a diplomatic wrangle over aircraft from the *Jefferson* needing to land in Sri Lanka. She was rushing, telling the nanny what to do for the kids' breakfasts if she didn't get home, banging things into cupboards as she talked. The nanny, an un-pretty, cheerful Bosnian girl, kept nodding.

Harry ignored the cell phone's tone, but it nagged on, and, thinking it was Djalik from his office, he leaned against the kitchen counter and put the device to his ear.

"O'Neill."

He heard the sounds of electronic space, then a comput-erized female voice. "Please call Jan at home. She is waiting for your call."

He shut the cell phone and gave Rose a smile, just as if he hadn't just received a coded message that told him to check his encrypted e-mail.

"Bad news for me, too, Rose. Crisis at the office." He kissed her and went out.

In his Hummer, he opened his laptop, brought up the message. *C.L. Brevard. Where the fuck do they get these code names?* He pictured Brevard, some self-styled tough guy with a balding head and a cover-your-ass approach to everything. He looked over the text, noted the authenticator, saw the "activate" and winced, saw the code word that meant a meeting, but he couldn't remember the comm plan and so didn't know where or when. As he drove away, he was planning how he would cover the moves he knew he would have to make to maintain his real self as a Muslim, black, foreign entrepreneur in an Arab country.

He also went over again the years-old adjustment to being known by the ridiculous code name "Persian Rug."

North of Mahe, India

The countryside was black, with only the flares of a distant refinery visible where the coast must have been. The beach-resort area had been madness as darkness fell—electricity gone, people frightened, cars blaring their horns and flashing their lights in their rush to get home and off the streets. Now, as the houses thinned on the dark road, the soft glow of kerosene lamps marked windows. Once, they saw the redness of an outdoor cooking fire.

Fidel was driving, trying to find his way down the strange road in what had become a blackout. Everybody in the van had offered advice, none of it useful; finally, Alan had had to shut them all up and move to the front seat to try to puzzle it out for him. Then Benvenuto had said from the back, "Excuse me—Commander—can I talk?"

"What?" The tone meant "No!"

"Yes, sir, only, I'm not trying to interfere, only—can you give me the name where we're headed, sir?"

Alan gritted his teeth. "Prenningerash."

"Can you spell that, sir?"

"Benvenuto, not now!"

He was surprised to hear Ong's small, liquid voice. "He's only trying to help, Alan. We have a GPS program going back here."

Alan turned hard around in the seat. The interior was dark; Clavers was half-asleep in the second seat. Behind her, Benvenuto and Ong were silhouettes against the dimness of the rear window, their faces visible in the glow of their laptops. Alan looked at where he thought Ong's eyes must be. He spelled Prenningerash—or tried to anyway.

Fingers tapped lightly on computer keys.

"Northeast of Mahe—that one, sir?"

"Benvenuto, you mean you have a *map* of this place?"

"Oh, it's Lieutenant Ong's map, sir—"

Ong overlapped. "We're using my laptop for the GPS plug-in. Benny's looking for the destination." Her voice was a reprimand. "I picked up my personal laptop at the hotel, although I hardly had time."

Benny?

Alan wanted to laugh. Or perhaps scream. "Yeah, the Prenningerash northeast of our hotel about thirty miles— bearing 315. That look about right?"

"Oh, yes," Ong said. She seemed to have made a wonderful recovery. Could one interrupted bath do that? He saw her head move from Benvenuto's laptop to her own; a hand was silhouetted against the back window as she pointed something out to Benvenuto. "We're on the same page now, except Benny doesn't have GPS. Yeah, we're on the coast highway there—see—?"

"Yeah, right—" Benvenuto sounded half delirious. What was better, after combat, than sitting in the dark with an older woman and working on your computers together?

"Can you see an airfield?"

"Oh, yes." Ong was twirling her trackball. Keys clacked. "Bhulta Field."

"Well, my source said the Bhulta Valley Agricultural Facility."

"I have Bhulta Field. Runway sixteen hundred and forty-one meters. Radio frequency—we don't care about that—

manned one hour before sunrise to one hour after sundown, no radar, landing lights on runway only, hangar space for light aircraft. Sound right?"

"Get us there!"

Ong murmured something to Benvenuto, who sniggered, moaned, giggled. Ong said in a louder voice, "Master Chief Fidelio, we're coming up on an intersection. Take an unpaved road on your right."

Fidel looked aside at Alan, his eyes reflections of the dash lights. Alan settled back in the seat. "Do what they say. We're in the hands of the nerds."

NCIS Bahrain

Dukas had been in his office an hour, disgusted and tense at the same time because he'd taken a day of leave and now he was using it to work, and because the message traffic about India was grim, and because something horrendous had happened to the *Jefferson*. He had put Greenbaum to sorting incoming traffic and trying to find the missing agent, Rattner, who so far had been tracked to the Jockey Club, where he had managed to disappear.

"Secure phone call," Leslie said. She was so much better in the office than anybody else he had that he was tempted to hire her—until he remembered what everybody would say. "Woman. Secure line."

Dukas grunted and punched buttons and scribbled a message for Leslie: *Ambur—find what we know about Ambur— electrical complex attacked earlier—*

"Yeah, Dukas here."

"Mister Dukas, I'm Mary Totten at the WMD Center." Dukas didn't get it immediately, then remembered a call slip that Greenbaum had given him, some female at the CIA Weapons of Mass Destruction center. Just what he needed now. She had a good voice, though, maybe a little too self-confident, one of those voices that said that anything it uttered was worth listening to, so pay attention. "Mister Dukas, I realize this isn't, strictly speaking, your purview, but I've tried Fifth Fleet intel and everyone seems to be out. I'd like to come out to Bahrain with a team and provide support to the Navy for the ongoing crisis in India."

Purview, Dukas thought, *Jesus Christ*. The word brought the woman into focus. "Oh, yeah?" he said. He didn't comment on "ongoing crisis," which was a term he wasn't ready to use yet.

"Are you following what's on the news?" she asked—impatiently, he thought.

"Yeah, we get television here."

The voice changed. She was quick. "Look, sorry, I'm rushing. Mister Dukas, the electric power facility that the terrorists hit? At Ambur?"

"Yeah?" He was wondering if a CIA team wasn't the next best thing to a case of shingles.

"Mister Dukas, we have reason to believe that Ambur is a nuclear weapons fabrication facility. They build and store warheads there, we think."

Dukas thought about that. Maybe he did want a CIA team. "Can I pass that information to Fifth Fleet?" He was temporizing.

"Absolutely. Look, I know that's where I should have started—I called everyplace there, tried to get a guy I know named Craik—the intel? But I couldn't, and time is of the essence, and I *want* to come out there and provide a WMD cell for support."

"I don't have the authority to authorize that," Dukas said, speaking with perfect truth but knowing that if he told her it was okay, it would be okay. "What kind of support you got in mind?"

She was ready for that one—boy, was she ready! Probably she even had notes. She went through the spiel in less than a minute—team size (some team, one guy), security levels, special knowledge, direct links to the WMD Center, skills. "We bring very special and very particular capabilities, Mister Dukas. I don't know a lot about the Naval Criminal Investigative Service, but I don't think you have those capabilities ready to hit the ground the way we do—do you?"

Dukas, thinking of the special capabilities of Greenbaum and Rattner, made a noncommittal sound. What he was in fact hearing from her, he thought, was that she didn't have shit for support from the Agency, but she wanted a trip to India. "Give me some time to contact Admiral Pilchard and I'll get back to you."

"I'll be *sitting* on the phone. Thanks, Mister—is it Mike?"

Everybody in the Navy called him Mike, but this woman sounded to him like an A-number-one CIA horse's ass, and it never paid to give them an inch. Still— "Yeah, Mike, of course. Absolutely."

But he didn't call Fifth Fleet HQ immediately. In fact, a minor invasion by the CIA was not to him a top-priority problem—Dukas was a political infighter, but so far he didn't see that a temporary in-country team could do much more than irritate the shit out of him—and so he checked on Greenbaum, found that Rattner was still invisible; checked with Leslie, found she was on the Internet. She had pulled up stock photos of Ambur when it was brand-new, and had data on something called SCADA, which was complex techno-speak but made him laugh.

"It's funny?" Leslie said.

"SCADA. 'Skata' is Greek for shit."

"Oh, as in scatology, oh, yeah!" She laughed, too. Dukas didn't ask her how she had learned a word like "scatology". Anyway SCADA wasn't shit but a technology for controlling things like electrical flow with computers.

Back at his desk, he eyeballed what they had on terrorist groups in India, at the same time dialling a number from his dog-eared private address book. Somebody else picked up, but on one hop he got through to the man he wanted—Carl Menzes, a guy in CIA Internal Affairs who knew everybody in the Agency. He asked for the creds on a woman named Totten.

Menzes was good at his job because he was cautious. "Mary Totten?"

"That's the one. WMD Center."

"I know nothing about her."

"Hey, Carl—come on! You know everything about everybody!"

"You're fishing, Dukas. I'm not biting."

Dukas sighed. "Look, Carl, she's offered help to the Navy, and that's so unlike anybody there in the crystal palace that I think she's either a flake or a fake. Help me out here, okay?"

Menzes hesitated. Then, "We're not investigating her or anything of that sort. Otherwise—I'm not in the business of repeating gossip."

"Well, I am. Give me the gossip. I gotta go to an admiral with something so he can make a decision, for Christ's sake."

Again, Menzes was silent. Dukas remembered how hard it was to drag information out of him—the reason he was so good at his job, in fact. Finally, Menzes said, "She's got this nickname. Not to her face, but, you know, somebody talking about her. 'Hottin' Totten.'"

"What's that mean?"

"It means either that she's a gunner or that her pants are on fire, what d'you think it means? And I heard a woman say it, not a man, otherwise I'd think it was just sexist bull-shit. She's okay, good officer, hard worker, just she's been in and out of a lot of beds, they say—that's not to be repeated to your admiral."

"But she's legit? I mean, she wants to come out here, she says 'support' us, which would be an Agency first, so I'm a little wary. Wha'd'you think?"

"If she wants to come out there, I'd say, what I've heard

130

about her, it's because of what's going down has got her interested. She's a gunner. She likes action."

"Your seal of approval?"

Menzes was a cynic—he knew it and Dukas knew it. He didn't give seals of approval. "I'd say she'll do a job if she says she will."

"Okay, good enough. I owe you one."

Menzes laughed. "I've heard that before. Every time you owe me, Dukas, I find my ass in a meat-grinder. Consider this a freebie."

Only then did Dukas call Fifth Fleet, and it was clear at once that he wasn't getting through to Admiral Pilchard without clout, so he used Al Craik's name and the words *urgent* and *classified information* and finally got through to the flag captain, and he had pretty much to tell her the whole story before she'd break in on whatever Pilchard was doing.

"Pilchard," the admiral said by way of greeting. "I can give you two minutes."

"Dukas, NCIS, sir. I've got a CIA agent who says the Indian electrical-production facility that got attacked a couple of hours ago is a nuclear-weapons site, and she wants to come out here with a team and quote 'support' us."

Pause. "How sound is that information about nukes?"

"Pretty sound, I think—she's a honcho at CIA's WMD center."

"Jesus Christ. You're Dukas, right?"

"Yessir."

"You up to speed on what Al Craik's doing?" Pilchard didn't miss much. He knew that Dukas and Craik were good friends.

"I was up to an hour ago, sir. He'd left the base at Mahe and—"

"I got all that from another friend of his."

"O'Neill."

"Yeah. He still under contract to us? He's trustworthy, anyway, right?"

"Very."

"Jesus, nukes. CIA got any handle on what the hell's going on over there? We're up to our ass in alligators over the accident on the *Jefferson*; we don't know what's going on with Craik, this talk of mutiny. Your office getting anything?"

"Sir, are you sure what happened on the *Jefferson* was an accident? Officially, I have to suspect it might be—*might* be— terrorism. A cop's way of thinking, sir."

"You have any evidence of that?"

"No, sir, but—"

"Keep it to yourself, then. But it's a—" Pilchard hesitated. His voice was tired, no longer brisk. "You better get over here and see what we've got. That's a good idea, anyway— look, come to the flag deck when you get here—I want to see you on another matter. I won't go into it now, but I've got a leaker over here. It's got to be stopped. We'll talk." Dukas heard him sigh. "As for the CIA people, you have my permission to say it's okay for them to come as far as Bahrain. What happens next depends on what we learn. And Dukas— make it very clear to them that when they get off the plane in Manama, they're mine to command. We've got a military situation here, and I'm the theater commander. Just make that clear to them, or home they go."

"Yes, sir." Dukas had a half-grin on his face. What Pilchard had said would take care of any ambitions the Agency might have with this one, no matter how much of a gunner Mary Totten was.

Trincomalee, Sri Lanka

"203 is on the tarmac," Donitz said. "All the Hornets are in the nest."

Soleck was grimy and sweaty and the taste in his mouth said he'd been in an ejection seat for way too long. He hit his "push to talk" key. "Mozart, you good to go?"

"Roger, sir." Scarlatti sounded scared.

The two S-3s had probably given too much gas to get the hornets down, and now 706 had less than a thousand pounds and a nugget pilot to get her down. Soleck tried not to think about his own plane; he figured they had less than six hundred pounds. The gauge had stopped reading while 203 was on final. "Don't get fancy, Scarlatti. Just put all three wheels on the ground."

"Roger that, sir."

Soleck started a slow turn to starboard, keeping the field's lights in sight all the way through his turn, losing altitude slowly to save fuel. He touched the throttle again, taking it down further, his speed the absolute minimum to keep his plane in the air. But he was determined to be the last plane down.

The last light of the equatorial day was passing quickly, but the field was still rose-colored from its rammed-earth berms to the old concrete aprons, studded with tropical trees and brilliant flowers that were like splashes of paint in the last light. The danger of the landings seemed less real with safety so close.

Off to starboard and well beneath him, Scarlatti's navigation lights flashed as he turned on final. His wings were steady, and then his nose gave a little shake and he was down.

"706 on the tarmac."

Next to Soleck, Guppy passed their landing information to the tower. Soleck cut right across the stack and made a tight turn, trading altitude for speed. He wasn't sure he had the fuel to go around the field again, and since Trincomalee had been kind to them and cleared the pattern, he didn't have to worry about accidents.

It was a dead easy landing, the kind of landing through which a veteran pilot would continue to make small talk. Soleck was a veteran, but he was silent. The last four hours made even the simplest decisions seem immense.

His attention slipped for a few seconds as he listened to the tower confirm their status as the last US plane to land. They were the last refugees from the *Jefferson*. He glanced once more at the fuel gauge. It continued to read "zero." He concentrated on his landing and found that during his moment of inattention, his hands had put the plane on speed and altitude, the nose lined up with the runway. *Good to go.*

The starboard turbine coughed.

The plane shook.

"Fuck," said Soleck. They were a half-mile shy of the runway and six hundred feet high.

The starboard engine coughed again, and then the port engine joined in. The nose came down. Soleck pushed it further down to gain a little more speed. He could *see the runway*, for God's sake, a wide pink ribbon stretching away to a distant huddle of white hangars. Four hundred feet of altitude, still too far from the runway.

"Ejection positions," he said, and flipped his ejection lever from all seats to front. He took a deep breath, reviewed everything he could remember about fuel flow in the S-3 and put his hand on the throttle. The engines coughed together, and he rammed the throttle forward.

The response was immediate; a burst of power. He raised the nose and got back a hundred feet of altitude in a second before the two engines went silent. Then he let the nose sink again. Twelve hundred feet to go.

He lost the altitude he'd picked up with the last fuel in the line. His airspeed was good.

"We're going to ride her down. Stay ready. This could be rough."

Guppy was silent. *He's okay*, Soleck thought.

The ground rose to meet him, the tarmac almost filling his viewscreen it was so close. Soleck raised the nose a fraction, touched his flaps. At some point, it became clear to him that he had the altitude to get the wheels on to pavement.

His gear touched, all together, a three-point landing from a glide.

He breathed again, and then he was using the sixty knots he'd landed with to try and roll them out to the other end of the field. They were only moving about ten knots when they rolled abreast of the other planes and turned to fill the last spot in the line. Soleck's parking wasn't great. They stopped. He and Guppy looked at each other.

"Least you don't have to shut anything down," Guppy said, the quaver almost gone from his voice.

Donitz was waiting out on the apron. The small man shocked him by giving him a bear hug. The other pilots were standing in a loose huddle, and then they all picked up their helmet bags and started to walk down the apron, past the last eleven planes from the air wing of the USS *Thomas Jefferson*.

At the far end of the line, Guppy looked back at the planes and slapped Soleck on the back. "We made it!" he said, as if it had just occurred to him that he was going to live.

CIA HQ

After a phone call from Mike Dukas gave Mary Totten the bad news that if she wanted to play, she was going to have play by the Navy's rules—meaning that she was under operational command of some admiral—and after she'd got mad and got over it, and when she was ready to go home and find somebody to take care of her cat while she was gone, the duty officer told her she had an encrypted e-mail.

She had been half out the door, but back she went, because it was from the deep-cover asset, Persian Rug. And it made her furious because it was one more goddam thing she couldn't control:

> We regret that we cannot accept the contract at this point because of prior commitments. Please keep in touch, as we value your business.

Shit!

In India, it was already night. Alan Craik was asleep under the van, a gentle rain falling only inches from his right hand. A hundred yards away, a leopard coughed, but he didn't wake.

Five hundred miles south in Sri Lanka, Evan Soleck looked at the starry sky and wondered how the hell they were going to get out of Trincomalee now they were there. The Sri Lankans were unhappy and the airfield was miserly with gas. At least everybody had got there.

It was night now in Bahrain, too. Rose Siciliano Craik was at her office in the American embassy, trying to cope with the problem of having armed Navy aircraft on the ground in a country that had no US naval attaché and no liking for armed intrusion. Mike Dukas was only a few hundred yards away, sitting in a conference room trying to keep his head down while angry, confused naval officers tried to predict what an attack on a nuclear-weapons site might mean for their next twelve hours.

Leslie Kultzke lay awake in the bed she shared most nights with Dukas. She was thinking about love and pregnancy and the risks of betting everything on one throw of the dice. She was thinking about what it would mean to lose.

Harry O'Neill was on his way to Manama Airport with Dave Djalik, two crates of bootlegged MREs ("Meals Ready to Eat," the twenty-first century's K-rations) bought in the Bahrain souk, and an assortment of weapons that wouldn't have disgraced a SWAT team.

The moon rose. It was brilliant in the desert air, a huge, illuminated pearl in the black sky. In the Craiks' shadowy garden, it lighted a white-painted piece of one-by-two that stood up from the soil. On it, Alan Craik had printed with a Magic Marker "Bloofer." At the top, a hand that could be recognized as Rose Craik's had written with a ball-point pen,

"Bye, Bloofer," and, near the bottom, a child's printing said, "Come back I miss you." Bloofer had lived in Florida, Texas, Virginia, Maryland, and Bahrain, and now his ashes settled into the sand under this bright Arabian moon. Such it is to be a Navy family's dog.

Day Two

12

Bhulta Airfield, India

The sun came up green, then a blazing gold that burned into amber on the undersides of the scattered clouds. Alan saw it all, waking at the first paling of the starry sky. He needed sleep, wanted sleep, but his brain wanted daylight and activity and distraction from chewing over the violence of the day before. His brain wanted to get on with the burden of getting his people out.

Green. It was a green land, in a place of some of the heaviest rainfall in the world. Lush grass grew around the van and lay like a carpet between them and the scattered buildings of the airfield, the single runway a dark stripe on it, half a dozen light aircraft tied down where the grass ended and two rusty metal hangars leaned. Surrounding the airfield were green trees, then green fields, then the bluer green of hills behind them to the east. Silhouetted now against the brightness, distant mountains.

They had found the place in darkness, their lights rousing a guard in a dhoti and a low-collared old shirt who had waved a cudgel at them as he stood in the headlight glare behind a gate that was nothing but a sagging metal pole between two posts. He was an old man, red-eyed; later they decided he was drunk. Alan had got out and kept saying "American Navy" and waving a piece of paper, which was actually a letter from a Navy reserve association but it did

141

have an embossed letterhead with a gold eagle. Still talking, he had pulled the metal pole aside and got back in and they had driven through, the old man shouting at them, and he had run after them as they drove to the only taxiway and across the runway and over the grass, and back there somewhere he had given up. It was just as well that the telephone system was down, or he might have called somebody.

Standing now, Alan looked south, the way they had come, and could see the curving glitter of a small river. Beyond, drainage ditches shimmered, full of water, and egrets dotted the green between the silver lines. The air smelled like flowers.

He wished he had a toothbrush. And coffee. They had stopped at a duka out in the country and found a couple of cans of vegetarian curry and a plastic pack of Jamun's Best Chappatis and some bottled water. That had been dinner, eaten sitting in the dark by the van, using their fingers and the spoon on Benvenuto's knife.

He heard Fidel growl, "Shit—", and saw his legs and feet disappear under the far side of the van. When the rain had started, the three men had rolled under the vehicle; the two women had slept inside.

"Morning," Alan said. Fidel may have grunted, maybe not; anyway, he kept on going away from the van, and Alan saw that he wasn't the only one who had a hangover from the firefights. Fidel was looking out over the flat, green landscape, and Alan saw that he was watching a white cow that was eating somebody's bean crop. "Sacred animal," he muttered.

Fidel grunted again. "Kind of nice, having a sacred animal."

"You're full of surprises."

Fidel looked at him. "I'm not just a guy who kills people, Commander." He wandered away toward some low bush.

Dee Clavers slid the van door open on Alan's side and crawled out, butt first, and then closed the door as if she was running away from home and whispered, "I'm getting too old for this. What d'you see, Commander?"

"I see a bunch of people without toothbrushes."

"That's life in the nav." Clavers ran her tongue over her front teeth. "You got a point, though. I'd kill for some coffee."

A female voice murmured behind them. "If you have a way to heat water, I have coffee." It was Lieutenant jg Ong. She had opened a sliding window and was looking out at the morning. She smiled at them. "You two look terrible." She looked, well, cute, a little puffy-eyed, her lips swollen as if she had been necking.

"What coffee?" Clavers demanded.

"Packets—you know? French roast. We need hot water." It was hard to believe—Ong the Unprepared, with coffee! That she was offering to other people! And then she said, "I guess after what we've all been through, you can share my toothbrush, too."

Alan ticked off on his fingers the other things they didn't have. "Pot, cups, fire—"

"I have a French press and one cup." Ong's small face frowned. "But I don't have fire."

"Let's ask the guard guy," Clavers said. "Worst he can do is beat us to death with his stick."

"We'll breathe on him and kill him first."

The knee-high grass swished against their legs and left their dirty khakis drenched after twenty steps. At the runway, they stamped their feet to shake the water off, then plunged into the grass on the other side and were drenched again. At the house by the hangar, the guard woke up and grabbed his cudgel, his turban unclean and half-unwound. He shouted at them in Malayalam, and when Alan held up money he shouted louder. Clavers made drinking motions; finally, she got through, and the frightened old man pointed at a bucket by the foundation of the house. He smelled of beer.

The bottom was covered with an organic mat that could have been rotting leaves or could have been animal, even human, shit. Alan smelled it. "We boil it a *long* time," he said. He pulled the loose matter out and swabbed the inside with grass and then filled the bucket from a tap, and they took turns carrying it across the airfield as the old man capered behind them, waving his stick and shouting, until his dhoti got wet and his bare feet seemed to hurt, and then he gave up for the second time and went back to his plastic lawn chair.

"Benny is gathering wood for a fire," Ong said. Her smile dazzled. "Fidelio is gathering paper and a lighter."

Alan grinned at her. "You have organizational skills I never guessed at, Miss Ong."

"Oh, I always get what I want." She said it without any suggestion of boasting, more as if she were giving the facts of geology. "I've also pulled together our food supply." She pointed at the front passenger seat, on which were laid out two Snickers bars, a half-eaten Toblerone, and three Indian sweets. "Anything to add?"

Alan had nothing. Fidel, to his surprise, had a granola bar.

USS *Thomas Jefferson*

"Sir?"

Madje tried to cling to sleep, so far down that his hand's pushing the voice away was unconscious.

"Sir?" from a hesitant voice and a hand on his shoulder, shaking him. Again. In the background, another voice insisted that he be waked. His conscious mind got the name *Admiral Rafehausen* out of the conversations around him.

He stirred, his legs kicking, and his eyes opened to light, movement all around him. He wasn't in his rack in a state-room, and this disoriented him so that he couldn't place where he was or how he had come here. Something about *Admiral Rafehausen*.

"Sir! The admiral wants you." A petty officer in a rumpled flight suit was kneeling next to him.

Madje's eyes caught the chalkboard a few feet away on the wall, the colorful linoleum tiles laid into the floor under him representing the squadron crest of VFA-139, and he was awake, aware that he was lying curled up on the floor of one of the forward ready rooms, his breathing apparatus still strapped to his chest and a poncho liner wrapped around his legs. He felt like hell.

"You're the flag lieutenant, right, sir?" the petty officer asked.

"Yeah," Madje groaned, rubbing his eyes. He caught sight of his hands, streaks of black over bright red skin, filthy nails. "How's the admiral?"

"Doc says he's better. He's awake again and he wants you. You been out for hours. Skipper said to let you sleep, but—" The man trailed off. He was young, maybe twenty-one, but dark circles under puffy eyes made him look older. "I got to get back to the desk."

Madje got to his feet and steadied himself on the rail of the chalkboard and a wave of vertigo hit him. He felt as if he could go back to sleep standing up. He stretched, pulled the poncho liner off his legs and threw it on top of a pile in a corner of the ready room and pushed out into the passageway, headed aft.

Trincomalee, Sri Lanka
Donitz found that his ear was stuck to the receiver of the phone. He'd been sitting on his bed, a bed that wouldn't have passed muster in a highway motel in the States, trying to use a rotary phone from colonial times.

"Fuck," he said. And then, "Jesus fuck."

Too loud. Soleck rolled over in his bed, the mattress sounding tinny.

"What's the problem, Donuts?"

"I can't get this fucking thing to—go to sleep, Soleck."

Soleck sat up and stretched. He'd got two hours of sleep after bedding down the birds and the scramble to find lodging, talk to the airfield, talk to Sri Lankan customs. The struggle that Donitz was still in.

"Sir, with all due respect—"

"Say it." Donuts was looking for something to lash out at. And mature enough to keep himself in check, but Soleck had some irritating habits at the best of times.

"You don't delegate well, sir. You're the det commander. Why don't you get some sleep and I'll sort out the phones?"

"Yeah?" Donuts balanced between anger and admission. "Yeah?" He shrugged, felt the tension in his shoulders and the emptiness behind his eyes. When he shut them, he could see his instrument panel and the heads-up display in his cockpit. "Okay, Mister Soleck. Have a ball. We need to get a clearance, we need to inform Fifth Fleet of our status, and we need gas. Here's my list. And I don't have a fucking phone number for any of them." He waited for Soleck to do the junior officer shuffle and dump it all back on him, which would give him the excuse to launch a salvo. "And we need a way to talk to the boat."

"Got it." Soleck smiled at him, a reassuring smile that robbed Donitz of his anger. "Get some sleep. I'll do this from the desk." He looked at his watch. "You got to fly in two hours."

"No shit. Wake me if—" Donitz began, but the room door closed with a bang, and Soleck was gone.

Bhulta Airfield, India

Alan took over the organizing of the coffee. He got a fire built, sent for more water. They boiled the water for twelve minutes and let the coffee steep for five in the French press. By then, Alan had told them about the photograph and the "Kill on sight" message, and he had passed around the palm device he had taken from the officer in the parking lot. He felt efficient, up, able to do several things at once and really get stuff done. He was surprised, therefore, when Fidel tapped his arm and said, "Could you slow down a little, Commander? You're making people nervous." Perhaps because Alan looked astonished, Fidel said, "It hits some people like that—like popcorn in a hot pan. Me, I get real quiet." And, to prove it, he turned away and got real quiet again.

Then the coffee was done and they passed the cup around, a sip for each, until the press was empty, and then they made another. And another. Ong's stock, until then somewhere below zero, went way up.

And Alan, having made himself neither say nor do anything for at least three minutes, handed Ong the golden object he had wrestled from the commodore in the first moments of disaster. It seemed a hundred years ago.

"Why, it's a USB key," Ong said. Benvenuto nodded.

"What does it do?"

"Oh, it *can* do lots of things. You plug it into your USB port and— Benny, reach down your laptop." She held the thing up. "It's wicked cute."

"The officer in the parking lot had one, too"

"So did the guys with him," Fidel said. "I put them under my seat inside." The words came out as if he had had to pay a lot for each of them.

"On chains around their necks," Alan said, "like—medal-lions?" He had almost said "amulets," but he didn't like the implication of magic.

"Like a club key," Benvenuto said. "Maybe they belong to the Calcutta Playboy Club."

Clavers groaned and rolled her eyes.

Benvenuto handed Ong his laptop, and she plugged the key into its USB port. The screen, which had been showing Benvenuto's hard-rock screen-saver, went black.

"Oh," she said. "Oh, dear."

147

"Shi-i-i-t!" Benvenuto roared. "It ate my screen-saver."

The blank screen was replaced by bright colors and some sort of logo that moved around the screen like a fly in a room, never settling. There was music, neither quite Indian nor quite Western. The logo danced across words: *Servants of the Earth*. Then that screen vanished and was replaced by animated figures and more music and voices.

"Oh, cute!" Ong said.

"What the hell's that?" Clavers said.

The figures were engaged in a balletic fight with a three-headed dragon.

"Kiddie cartoons," Fidel growled.

"That's *anime*!" Ong howled. "It's cutting-edge animation!"

"Like I said, kiddie cartoons."

The figures looked like Ong, big-eyed and black-haired and slender. Their fight turned into a conversation into a flirtation into a journey, all in about forty seconds.

"Commercial," Alan said. "It's a commercial for Servants of the Earth, whatever that is."

"It's so *cute*," Ong purred.

The screen turned golden, and letters in bright blue wrote themselves across it: *Do a random act of service for the earth each day.*

"Sounds like a bunch of tree-huggers," Clavers said. "Who's for more coffee? Everybody? Benvenuto—more firewood."

Benvenuto wanted to stay, because it was his laptop that was being used, but he was the lowest rank, so off he went. By the time he had come back, they had tried all six of the golden keys, and they all had the same logo and message and animated story. And they all urged random acts of service. Then Ong tapped on her own computer and plugged the commodore's key in and said, "There's *lots* more on it. It's huge for storage, that little thing."

"Any idea what it is?"

She tapped the keys, shook her head. "I'm afraid to let it

in until I like know what it is. You saw Benny's computer—it just seized the whole thing so it could get its message in." Benvenuto's computer was on the grass. It still showed the Servants of the Earth message. Benvenuto looked at it sadly. "It's okay, Benny," she said. "We'll de-bug it later, right? Trust me."

Alan squatted, looking over her shoulder. "Can you get it off your own computer?"

She turned her head. Her hair brushed his chin. She smelled good. "Watch." She hit a key and the Servants of the Earth vanished. She swung around, the computer still on her crossed legs. He was aware that they were too close together and he sat back on his heels. "It's basically a worm, which my axe is prepped to deal with. I tried to get into it, but it's pretty resistant, but like I *know* there's a *lot* of data in there."

"The guy plugged it into the JOTS. The JOTS sort of blinked, but that was all—no message, no animation. What's that mean?"

"I don't know until I get into it. But it probably means it's preprogrammed for the JOTS—like if it was going to do the worm thing, it didn't want to be seen on the screen."

"So it left the JOTS image up there?"

"Well—" She sniffed. She was really pretty in the morning, he was thinking. "Well, you know, like if I was going to do that, I mean plant a worm, the worm would probably have to do with what came up on the JOTS screen, wouldn't it? I mean, wouldn't that be the point?" Her eyes held his. He wasn't sure that either of them was concentrating on computers.

"And?"

"Well— Maybe it was going to plant data in the JOTS. To screw up the exercise? Or maybe it was going to suck data *out* of the JOTS? I mean, there had to be a reason he put it into the JOTS, okay?"

Alan remembered thinking at the time that the commodore was somehow going to help the Indian side cheat. Could you do that by somehow screwing up the data in the JOTS? By, let's say, changing the screen so that—

"Aircraft," Fidel said.

Alan looked where Fidel was pointing. Silver flashed in the sky. Alan stood, working the stiffness out of his knees, found he was glad to have an excuse to get away from Miss Ong, whose effect on him close up was a lot stronger than he would have guessed. He had more sympathy for Benvenuto.

Fidel was getting weapons from the van; he handed an AK to Alan, held another out to Benvenuto. He began to dole out clips. Overhead, the flash of silver became a distant aircraft dropping down toward the green fields.

"Did you see it first or hear it first?" Alan said. He couldn't hear it yet.

"Both."

The plane leveled and came toward them, and then he could hear it, the thin roar of the jets and the scream of air over the flaps and spoilers. It passed over the field at several hundred feet and turned north and dwindled to a speck. Alan looked along the valley and saw smoke rising from a house—straight up. No wind. The pilot would have seen that, too.

By the time the Lear jet was identifiable again it was on its final for the runway. The old man was running out to the taxiway, waving his cudgel at it and shouting. The plane dropped and skimmed the green fields that ran right up to the runway and touched down not more than twenty feet from the end. The engines screamed as the pilot fought to hold his rollout to the small field, and then he was speeding past them, the plane dazzling in the early morning sunlight. When it had passed, Alan saw the old man sitting in the long grass like a bundle of sticks, staring after it.

"Our ride," Alan said to Fidel.

"Hey, I'm not complaining."

The plane spun a slow half-circle at the runway's end and taxied back. Alan and Fidel trotted toward the hangars, the others straggling along. When they caught up with the plane on the taxiway, it had stopped and the pilot was laughing and jabbering out his window with the old man and tossing money down in little bundles. Harry O'Neill got out a couple of minutes later, elegant in a blue silk polo shirt and jeans and a white jacket. Dave Djalik, whom Alan knew, stood in the doorway behind him, scanning everything. O'Neill stretched, looked at the morning, came down the steps toward Alan's filthy crew as if he was about to give an interview. "Nice place you have here," he said.

"We're kind of glad to see you," Alan answered.

"Can't imagine why." Harry introduced himself, went around shaking hands. A black man stepping from a silver jet seemed to surprise them. Ong looked bowled over. Alan figured she'd just met the man of her dreams.

"When do we leave?" Fidel demanded.

Harry smiled. "No hurry, no hurry. You people had breakfast? We brought a great selection of MREs. Anybody for the Four Fingers of Death? Follow the chuck-wagon to a parking spot." He led them away from the plane; they all fell in behind as if he was the Pied Piper, until Alan sent Clavers back for the van. When they were all clear, the steps went up and the engine sound rose an octave and the plane taxied off toward the hangars, the old man trotting ahead and trying to fasten up his turban as he went.

"When *do* we leave?" Alan muttered to Harry.

"Some new developments." Harry put on aviator sunglasses, beneath which his smile was toothy and deliberately false. "Uncle Sam wants *you*, kid."

Alan sighed. Nothing was ever easy.

They straggled along behind the plane.

"Madje, you look worse than me." Admiral Rafehausen was propped on pillows, his head only a little higher than his chest. A metal crane elevated his left knee, and his left arm was clamped into a mechanical device that had a sheen of condensation over it. His eyes were dull, his face as pale as the gray bulkhead behind him.

Madje looked around for the doctor. He'd been sent in to see the admiral as soon as he'd reported at the entrance to the sick bay; this time, there were no orderlies waiting to put the admiral back under. Madje tried to hide his reaction to Rafehausen's appearance. "Good to see you, sir."

"You get—orders to—TAO?"

"Yes, sir. Skipper on the *Fort Klock* has the battle group."

"Yeah? Lash?" Rafehausen moved his head and glared, and then his eyes grew duller, and there was a long silence.

Madje tried not to read too much into the tone with which the admiral said, "Lash." After a while he thought the admiral was drifting off to sleep. He got up quietly.

"I'm not—done with you, mister. Go—get a shower, clean up." Rafe gave an approximation of a smile. "You look like shit." Long pause. "Need—eyes—ears."

"Yes, sir."

"Good." The admiral's eyes flicked away to the blank wall by his bed, lost focus for a few seconds, and wandered back to Madje. "Where we—headed?"

His abrupt change left Madje confused. *Headed?* "Sir?"

"Where—is—battle group *going*?" The admiral almost raised his head, his eagerness communicated in fractional movements.

"Sorry, sir. I was fighting fires—"

"Yeah." The energy drained out of his face. "Yeah. Good—you. Get cleaned up, and—" The admiral's eyes closed. He muttered, "Lash," and shook his head.

Madje bent over him and was reassured by a snore. He

got the picture. *Get cleaned up and find out for me what's going on.* He rose from the folding chair as quietly as he could and headed toward a shower.

Bhulta Airfield, India

Fidel and Djalik had identified each other immediately, Djalik picking up on Fidel's SEAL patch. They tossed SEAL references back and forth—groups, names, places—and laughed, getting comfortable with each other.

Djalik said, "How you getting along with Tom Terrific?" He jerked his head at Alan, who was walking twenty feet ahead.

"Hey, you know him?"

Djalik held up his left hand, which was a mass of scars and was missing two fingers.

"He do that?"

"He was in command."

"Shit, man. He's got a hand like that, himself." Fidel put his head closer to Djalik's. "You got a problem with him?"

"Oh—he's okay. He just wouldn't know he was dead until they nailed the lid down on him, he's such a gunner." Djalik was wearing sunglasses; when he grinned, his face went from threatening to gleeful. "You know the old nav story about John Paul Jones? He's on the *Bonhomme Richard*; the fucking rigging's shot away, the masts are shot away, they got a hole below the waterline, and Jones waves his sword and shouts, 'I have just begun to fight!' And down on the gun deck, this old salt, who's up to his ass in blood and body parts, says, 'There's always some sonofabitch doesn't get the word!'" Djalik tittered, then pointed at Alan. "Him and John Paul, they'd be a pair!"

Fidel rubbed his unshaven chin. "So far, I'd rather have him on my side than the other side."

Djalik stared at Alan's back. "Well—yeah."

13

In the Air, London–Bahrain

Mary Totten had slept on the flight from London, after a fashion, or at least rested—after a fashion. Now, three hours from Bahrain, she came to, pushed up the blind on the window next to her, saw endless cloud and a lightening sky.

"Jeez, you can really sleep on these things! That's amazing!" Bill Caddis was pushing his face, eyeglasses first, toward hers. She pulled back. He still didn't smell too good.

"I didn't really sleep."

"You were snoring! Sure coulda fooled me." He laughed a stupid, hurtful laugh because he didn't know that he was being hurtful.

He had a laptop in front of him, the screen bright with a report on the electrical facility at Ambur, and she said, "Isn't that classified?"

"The Tamurlane place."

"Ambur?"

"Ambur, Tamur, whatever. Yeah. Multiple-feed electrical production. Hydro, coal-fired, and a nuclear breeder. All built by ABB, according to this guy." ABB was a multinational construction firm with a US headquarters.

She winced. "Which guy is that, Bill?"

"Closed source. Must be from a NOC. Good writer." She winced again. A NOC was a Non Official Cover, a covert operator who was off the books—and the only NOC who

154

wrote reports about Ambur was the same Persian Rug who couldn't meet her in Bahrain. Bill was rattling on. "Anyway, it says that he got all this stuff on the plant from the ABB office in Bahrain. All the SCADA stuff, protocols, programs. I could turn the lights out all over India from here."

"Bill, the lights *are* out all over India. What's SCADA?"

"Oh, well, you know."

"Pretend I don't know." She was watching a flight attendant who might have access to a coffee pot.

He wrinkled his nose up so far that his glasses moved up. He pushed them into place with a grubby finger. "SCADA stands for—wow, long time since I actually looked that up— there it is: Supervisory Control And Data Acquisition. That's a long way of saying it's an automated system that allows the operator to control electrical power grids or sewage or water pressure or any systems over distance."

"Like the Indian power company?"

"Like any power company. They got SCADA systems, you bet. Probably hundreds, all wired to even more complex supervisory systems. At the other end of the whole mess are RTUs." She looked blank. "Remote terminal units. Things like valves and switches that get turned on and off by the SCADA system."

Mary was willing the flight attendant to look her way. "Why did you say you could turn the lights out from here?"

"Oh. Yeah, well, the problem with really sophisticated SCADA systems is that the more sophisticated and digital you build them, the more vulnerable they are. So if I know all the passwords and stuff for a SCADA system, I can hack in and run the thing—literally turn off the lights."

"With a computer somewhere else."

"Well, yeah."

"But you have to make contact with the other computer."

He tittered. *Anybody can do that*, his tittering said. Hurtful again. Irritated, she said, "Bill, an airplane is a public place, and we don't put classified stuff on our laptops. Wipe it."

He turned his eyeglasses on her. He shrugged. He hit a key. "Satisfied?"

"I want *everything* classified on that computer wiped. Now."

He shrugged again and hit keys. He wiped his nose on his sleeve. "I was through with it anyhow."

Trincomalee, Sri Lanka

Chris Donitz could see Soleck waiting for him by the van before his plane rolled out, and he knew the news wouldn't be good. The Trincomalee tower had been frosty all the way down, asking him his weapons status and advising him that no more flights would be authorized. He taxied to the line of waiting F-18s and S-3s, with one Tomcat at the end of line, and started his post-flight, shutting his engines down after a look at their status, and finding that they were about to go overdue for maintenance. Then he popped the canopy.

"They won't let us get any more gas," Soleck shouted.

Donitz was still doing his post-flight notes on a kneeboard, his engines still giving off visible waves, even in the steaming heat. He had bags under his eyes and an angry red mark across the bridge of his nose from too many hours in an oxygen mask.

"What the fuck?" he called down to Soleck.

"I got on to Fifth Fleet; we're good there. I cleared us with their customs guys. I got a radio from an expat that can raise the *Fort Klock*. But the Sri Lankan fuels guy here at the field says we can't have any more gas unless we pay for it, and the tower says it won't clear any more planes for flights without orders from Colombo."

Donitz shrugged. "Colombo?"

"The capital of Sri Lanka?" Soleck waved an arm toward the east. "Where these guys get their orders?"

Donitz shook his head hard, as if to clear it. "Yeah," he grunted, feeling ignorant. Then he levered himself out of his

156

seat and climbed down from the cockpit to the wing and jumped heavily to the ground. Among the hundreds of things they didn't have were crew ladders to make getting in and out of their planes less acrobatic. Donitz was short, too short to take the drop from the wing lightly.

"Tell me some good news."

"I got a bunch of stuff from Fifth Fleet. They're sending a plane out with more pilots and a maintenance section and a bunch of stuff to keep us flying. Rose Craik's going to talk to the Sri Lankans and get us permission to fly."

Donitz brightened for a moment, then frowned. "She coming out?"

"Yeah." Soleck sounded happy.

"She's an O-5. She'll take command." Donitz started for the van they used as an office, a rental that Soleck had arranged on his own credit card. Donitz couldn't decide whether someone else taking command was a good thing or a bad thing.

"What do you want to do about the fuel? We've got enough in the air to keep 105 and 203 on CAP until Commander Craik gets here, but those guys—"

Donitz could see them, trapped in their seats for an extra three hours, nowhere to piss. The only other option was to leave the carrier naked. "Tell them to stay on CAP. I'll try and talk to the guy in charge here." His next crew rest was getting farther and farther away. So much for getting sleep. He grunted. "Hey, Soleck."

"Sir?"

"Good job."

Bahrain

Mike Dukas had had three hours' sleep and was in his office early. The night at Fifth Fleet HQ had been gritty insanity, everybody going nuts between lack of information and the urge to action, between go-slow messages from Washington on the one hand and testosterone on the other. The staff had been left to do nothing and go nuts.

He had called Special Agent Rattner at home at six-thirty and then, leaving Leslie still asleep, he had driven to the office, stopping to pick up a box of a dozen at the Bahrain Dunkin' Donuts, with two extra-large black coffees. If Rattner didn't want one, Dukas would drink both. He got to the office first, looked at the night's message traffic—everything was about India, and the duty officer, Greenbaum, had flagged it all urgent and important. He'd have to have another talk with Greenbaum.

Rattner was in his late fifties, big, a little paunchy, experienced but therefore sometimes careless. His head was a little down now when he came in, bullish, but he started by trying to be so cheerful that Dukas wanted to hit him. Dukas didn't like cheerful at best, least of all in the morning.

Dukas did the amenities with the donuts and the coffee— Rattner took the coffee, as it turned out—and said without introduction, "I couldn't find you yesterday. All hell broke loose, and I couldn't find you. No good."

"I was on a case."

"This case take you to the Jockey Club?"

"No, as a matter of fact, lunch took me to the Jockey Club. I'm not allowed to eat lunch?"

Dukas pointed a piece of jelly donut at him. "Don't be a smartass. I'm new here; you're a very experienced agent; but you were out of line yesterday. Don't give me shit."

Rattner started to say something, shrugged.

"Say it. Come on, let's get it on the table."

"I've got five weeks to go. I don't give a shit what you think of me."

"I'm your boss; it matters what I think of you as a matter of principle. You don't believe in principle, you shouldn't be in NCIS. Look, Rattner, the shit hit the fan yesterday; I needed an experienced man here, you're not here! Greenbaum can't run this office alone. Five weeks, five days, five minutes, you work for me, I expect you to be here."

"Forget it."

Dukas grunted. "We'll get along better if you never say to me, 'Forget it.' I don't forget. Will you for Christ's sake admit that you were out of line not to tell us where you were going yesterday?"

"How could I know the fleet exercise was going to go to hell?"

Dukas stared at him. It was a cop look, but Rattner was also a cop, therefore probably immune to the look. Still, he shrugged. Dukas said, "Will you please for Christ's sake admit you were out of line?"

"Okay, I was out of line. Now what?"

"Now let's have another donut. Don't do it again, okay? I need you. You may not need me, but I need you." He looked into the donut box. "What I need you for right now is this new task the admiral just gave me." There was one donut left. "Somebody took more than his half."

"It was you. I counted."

Dukas shoved the box over. "Pilchard's got a leaker who spilled his guts to somebody in Washington about the *Jefferson*. The White House is on his ass because he didn't inform them so they could spin it—this in the face of very clear rules about how he's supposed to report and who to. So he wants the leaker. Big time."

"They had a leaker, they thought, a few months ago. Nothing came of it."

"This time, something's going to come of it. *You're* going to make something come of it. Pilchard's flag captain has a list of people who knew early on about the *Jefferson*. It's a pretty long list. You get over there and pick it up—no fax, no e-mail on this one. And on your way back pick up some more donuts." Dukas wiggled his eyebrows up and down. "See why I need you in the office?"

Bhulta Airfield, India

The sun was early-morning high and the day was already hot. They sprawled in the shade of the aircraft and ate MREs and made jokes about going home, leaving dear old India, how they'd miss it all! Harry signaled Alan with his eyes and walked him off into the shade of one of the private aircraft, a high-wing monoplane that had come out of the old Soviet Union in the seventies. They sat under it, shading their eyes against the glare. Harry told Alan what he knew about the *Jefferson*.

Alan couldn't bring himself to ask about Rafe. Instead, he said, "Who's in command?" he said.

"Last I heard, some captain was commanding the BG from the missile cruiser."

That was bad; it meant that Rafe was at least badly injured, maybe dead.

Harry looked at him, understanding everything. "Your friend Rafehausen's pretty smashed up, but alive the last I heard. But everything's fluid—they got no comms; they can't launch or receive; they're sitting out in the ocean without the one weapon that makes them worth a shit, aircraft. Pilchard's shitting bricks trying to figure out whether India's planning to attack the carrier. Fifth Fleet ASW is going nuts thinking that one sub could take out maybe the CV and the cruiser both. The last I heard, the President was on the phone trying to find somebody in India who'd tell him he could go to bed because India was really a peaceful nation that flew a plane into one of his toys by mistake."

"You know a lot, Harry."

"Of course I know a lot. This is big-time fuckup time, Charlie. This is the day that the diplomats earn their stripes. People are talking about war. Late news I got in the air had some of the cavemen in the Congress talking about nukes. US Secretary of Defense was waving his dick around and telling everybody to see how big it is. White House was saying just the opposite—make peace, not war. Pilchard just keeps shaking his head and telling people to deal with what they got, not what dicked-up people in Washington are afraid of."

"You were *with* Pilchard?"

"Oh, yeah. So was Dukas. Just before I left, so was Rose— she's in the middle of the diplomatic side of it. The *Jeff* left eleven aircraft airborne and no place to go, and a smart young kid named Soleck got them all to Trincomalee by doling out gas by the teaspoon. Now they're on the ground, and the Sri Lankans want them out, out, out, and it looks like your wife is going to have to go down there and make some sense out of it."

Alan was frowning. "Back up a sec—you were *with* Pilchard?"

"Yeah, yeah."

"Harry—you're a civilian. What the hell were you doing with the CO of Fifth Fleet?"

Harry took off his sunglasses and looked at Alan and puffed his cheeks and blew out the air in little puffing pops. "I knew we'd get to this point. This is the hard part." He put the sunglasses back on and tipped his head back. "I have to make a confession, Father. You do absolutions?"

"Friendship means never having to say 'You're absolved.' Confess, already."

Harry, the coolest man Alan knew, was actually embarrassed. "I'm an Agency NOC," he said. He waited. "You know what a NOC is, don't you?"

"*You?*"

Harry shrugged. "Deep cover the last eight years."

"Jesus Christ, Harry, I knew you had contacts at the Agency, but— Kind of risky, living in Bahrain and being in your business, isn't it?" What he meant was, *You never told me, your best friend, and I'm in the business,* and Harry knew of course that that was what he meant.

Harry shrugged again. "Somebody tried to blow me up

161

once. Djalik had to shoot a guy another time. No, my cover works, Al—I confuse them, big entrepreneur, honcho of a heavy security operation, but I'm a Muslim and I'm to them an African. Plus I pass on some decent stuff to a guy in Saudi and a guy in Pakistan, which the Agency has already vetted for me, so the word in some circles is that O'Neill is a spy for Islam, and the word generally is that he isn't one of them and he isn't one of us, he's just O'Neill—big, money-grubbing Muslim nigger." He plucked a stem of grass, bit it. "Okay, am I absolved?"

"You're telling me this for a reason, right?"

Harry nodded. "I've been given an assignment in India. A big layout at a place called Ambur. It got hit by part of whatever's going on here, and it's a secret nuke storage site. That's why I was with Pilchard."

Alan looked at him. "You mean you're not flying back to Bahrain."

Harry nodded.

"So none of us is flying back to Bahrain."

"You're to call Admiral Pilchard when we're through talking."

Alan stared at him. He frowned. "You mean, you've been given an assignment by the Agency, and I'm going to be given an assignment by Pilchard."

"I don't know what you're going to be given."

Neither of them was smiling now.

Alan said, "You should have told me."

"Is that the way you'd want your assets to behave—they out themselves to their friends?" Harry's voice rose. "Is that the code now, you only blow your cover to your best friends and family members and the people you sleep with?"

Alan slumped down beside him. "I'm sorry, man. Shit, of course." Alan laughed. "'I thought an exception would be made in my case.' You know that joke? Jesus, I'm sorry."

"Hurt your feelings, huh?"

"Yes, if you have to ask." Both men laughed. Alan clapped his hand on Harry's shoulder. "Okay, your secret's safe with me, Sidney. How do I call Pilchard?"

Harry pointed at his plane. "He'll want everything you know. I don't think he's made a decision about what you do next."

They stood up, pulling their grass-wetted clothes away from their skin. Harry said, "Sidney?"

"Riley." He laughed and put his arm over Harry's shoulders, and they walked toward the jet.

14

Bhulta Airfield, India

Harry's airplane was equipped as a traveling office and communications center—secure sat phone, radio, computer connections. Alan put Lieutenant jg Ong in a forward seat to send the contents of the six gold USB devices to Fifth Fleet while he and Harry sat in the rear.

"Once you're on, I'll move up and do some work," Harry said. "You want privacy, and I don't want your jg up there knowing too much about my connections."

"Look out, or she'll have you working for her. She has a way with men."

"I have a way with women."

"You're married."

"Yeah?" Harry grinned and showed him how to work the equipment, until he was through to Fifth Fleet and the screen said secure, and then Harry moved away. He was put through straight to Admiral Pilchard.

"Al!'

"Yes, sir."

"My God, it's good to hear that voice. We were worried about you. Listen, I'm having people paged, and I'm going to put this on a speaker-phone as soon as they're here. In the meantime, tell me what happened yesterday." The voice was weary.

Alan ran through it as succinctly as he could; he'd spent

part of the night getting it straight. Pilchard didn't interrupt, but when Alan was done, he said, "This device the Indian commodore put into the JOTS—it had computer graphics on it?"

"Animation, sir. Really a little commercial—maybe a recruiting message. I've got somebody checking into the Servants of the Earth right now."

"They wanted to do something to the JOTS, that fails because you catch him at it, they go right to violence?"

"He shot Borgman because I'd told her to get in touch with you, urgent."

Pilchard was silent. Alan could picture him, knowing his office—the thin, balding man sitting in short-sleeved khakis behind the big desk, phone caught between his head and his shoulder, playing with a paper clip, as he did when he was troubled. "You think there's a connection with the *Jefferson*?" the admiral said.

"I don't know enough about the *Jefferson* to say anything, sir."

"You hear that we also lost an S-3?" Pilchard told him about Stevens's plane, said it could have been an act of war.

"Where I was, it looked more like a mutiny, sir—Indians fighting Indians—"

"Yeah, well, we had a report of one Indian destroyer taking out another. Mass confusion." Pilchard said that they knew now that the Indian Jaguar had been on a missile profile as if it was flying an exercise missile strike and should have pulled up, but eyewitnesses from the *Fort Klock* and in the air said there had been no attempt to pull up: the plane had gone into the deck exactly as if aiming at it.

"How's Admiral Rafehausen, sir?"

"Lost a leg. Burns. He'll probably recover."

Not his career. Inwardly, Alan winced.

Pilchard gave him the *Jefferson*'s stats: two hundred and

twenty-seven dead, almost four hundred injured, most with burns; sixty percent of the air wing destroyed on the deck, the rest trapped on the hangar deck with no functioning elevator. Eleven planes had been in the air and had bingoed to Trincomalee. "Now—as for you and your friend O'Neill. He tell you?"

"Yes, sir."

"I've had confirmation from the Agency. Remind him that this is a Navy operation, and he and his folks work for me, not the other way around, okay?"

"Yes, sir, and, uh—'operation?'"

"Yeah, that's what I was coming to." Pilchard's volume changed. "Hey, Jack, how you doing—" Pilchard talked to somebody and then came back. "Al, you still there?"

"Here, sir."

"Okay." He told Alan what Harry had already told him about Ambur and possible nukes. "I have to know what the hell that attack means, Al. If it was just—what the hell, just what? Just another piece of terrorism—by some people who didn't know there were nukes there and wouldn't know a nuke if they fell over one, that's one thing. But if that attack was connected with the nukes—if, worst-case, the attack was to *get* the nukes, we're in deep shit. I mean, you understand the implications if somebody's running around India with a couple of nuclear warheads."

"Especially with an unprotected carrier group sitting only a few hundred miles away."

"O'Neill is there to get you and your guys out. But his people have told him to find out what the straight story is on Ambur and the nukes. And I want you to support him."

"Yes, sir." Alan kept his disappointment out of his voice. "How about my people, sir?"

"Use them. Doesn't matter for what, Al. That aircraft isn't coming back to Bahrain until you guys are done. So your people are there, unless India clears and we get something in sooner."

And they're mine to get home. "Yes, sir."

"I'm sending you into the shit, Al, but I got no other choice."

"Yes, sir." *And thank you for giving me the chance to volunteer, sir.* "Who's in charge, sir? Between me and O'Neill, I mean."

"You operationally. You all the way, in fact. But O'Neill's got the contacts there."

"And the aircraft, sir." And the MREs and the weapons and the money and the clothes. "Related matter, sir. I want to send the contents of these USB keys for decryption; we can't decrypt them here. I'd like to use O'Neill's secure link with his Bahrain office. There's an ex-Navy man there named Valdez who's the best computer guy I know. Better than anybody you have. He was my wife's petty officer before he left the Navy, top secret clearance back then. Can I use him?"

Pilchard said nothing for several seconds. Alan could picture him, rubbing the bridge of his nose and closing his eyes. Then he said, "I have a list that clears a Valdez, a Djalik, and a Moad as already approved by the Agency." That was news to Alan. In other words, Harry had staffed key posts in his security firm with ex-Navy people who also had become Agency NOCs. *What your best friend won't tell you.*

"Okay, you have permission to use O'Neill's contacts and his computer guy. Get on it. Now—last item, Al: you're walking into a diplomatic minefield. The White House is not exactly behind us on this. There's mixed signals, but what I'm getting from the President and the NSC sounds like they're satisfied if it turns into a regional war that leaves us out of it. Even though we all know that it wouldn't stay a regional war. I mean, I had one of those assistant-to-the-president phone calls last night kind of probing the edges of 'What if we brought the *Jefferson* into a friendly port and just got out of the Indian Ocean until things blow over?' I hit the ceiling. They won't quit, though. It'll get worse."

Then somebody put the speaker-phone on and Alan went over much of it again. There were questions, many of them unfocused. The disaster on the *Jefferson* had knocked the legs from under all of them, and they sounded stunned, some of them snappish and some dumbfounded. He wondered if he'd sound any better if he was there, starved of information, being badgered for answers.

Still, it would be better than being in a country that was tearing itself apart.

Maybe.

USS *Thomas Jefferson*

Madje felt better in a clean flight suit, despite a tepid shower and a cheek gouged by his hurried cold-water shave. He went all the way forward to the dirty-shirt wardroom and found the overhead buckled and twisted, the space empty except for a work party cutting at the buckled metal with torches. Then he worked his way aft on the port side, past repair parties cutting away damage and fire parties standing idle or sleeping up against the bulkhead. Twice he crossed knee knockers to find the section beyond the hatch flooded a foot deep with water and foam runoff from operations on the flight deck. He waded through both until he passed the deserted flag spaces and squelched up to the hatch for CIC. It was open, a reassuring change from the night before. He stepped over the knee knocker that kept the hatch well above the level of water runoff and craned his head around a smaller hatch to look into the ASW space to the right. He could *smell* the coffee. Chief Warrant Officer O'Leary was a stickler for coffee, and he was presiding over the ASW watch in person, a parallel ruler in one hand and a grease pencil in the other. Madje caught his eye and O'Leary, a short man with a broad face and a moustache to match, waved him in. "Looking for coffee, Lieutenant?"

"Dirty shirt's closed," Madje muttered as he took a clean cup from the rack by the chart table.

"You're welcome, boyo," O'Leary said as Madje took a swig. "How's the admiral?"

"He's—uh—better than you'd expect." Madje took another gulp of coffee, refilled the cup. "He wants to know what's going on."

O'Leary pointed to the chart table, where a broad blue stripe showed the carrier's track. "We're headed for Sri Lanka. We can only make about five knots."

"What are you tracking?" Madje asked.

O'Leary shook his head. "I'm dicking around. There's a sub out there, right? An Indian Kilo-class. I'm keeping a far-on circle updated to show where it might be." The forward edge of the circle was still fifty miles north of the carrier.

Madje looked at the penciled lines radiating from a note in the upper right margin of the chart. The note said *position at startex?* Madje was an A-6 guy; he didn't know anything about subs, but he wanted another cup of coffee, so he looked interested. "So he *could* be heading to intercept us. Got anything to look for him?"

"Nothin'. All the helos are still doing search and rescue or moving casualties. Cat two shows green but the TAO's not ready to send any planes off until he's fired a test load; rumour is it has steam problems. They're replating the deck aft of 133 as soon as they can; then they'll rig new arresting gear. I'm trying to get the TAO to move a frigate up north with a tail deployed. I think he'll go for that now the fires are out."

"The TAO? Not Captain Lash?"

O'Leary blinked, swallowed his coffee and looked away. "Not Lash," he said carefully.

"Any reason to expect the sub's hostile?"

"Nope. But I got nothin' better to do, and frankly I gotta assume he's hostile until the Indian Navy gets its shit together."

Madje nodded, finished his second cup of coffee and squeezed around the chart table. "Thanks for the coffee." He wondered if the sub problem was worth repeating to the admiral. Talking to O'Leary brought home to him how difficult it would be to sort information and pass it without either taxing a wounded man or oversimplifying the tactical situation.

Bhulta Airfield, India

After his telephone call with the admiral, Alan talked to his assistant at Fifth Fleet intel, a lanky lieutenant-commander named Lapierre, whom everybody called "Dickie." Alan went in detail over everything that had happened, said again that he wanted somebody to recover Borgman's body.

Finally, he called home, got the nanny, then Mikey. Rose was dressing, he was told, but suddenly she was there, gasping for breath. "I heard the kids," she said. She sounded raspy. She yawned—she had got in at four, she said. They talked parent talk, then lovers' talk, then business—the *Jefferson*, the bingoed planes at Trincomalee. She was going there soonest, she said; somebody had to negotiate with the Sri Lankans, and she was it. "De facto, I'll be taking command of the *Jeff's* bingoed planes." She hesitated. "I'm F-18 qualified."

"Jesus, Rose—you're not combat qualified!"

"Well, no—but they need everybody they can get. It's a mess." She made her voice cheerful. "Chris Donitz is senior officer; he an okay guy?"

"Donuts is great." Although, he thought, he'd never seen Donuts in a command situation. "I hear Ev Soleck's down there, too."

"Yeah, from the sound of it, he should be getting an air medal, at the least. How're you?"

He gave her a sanitized version of the day before, skating quickly over "Kill on sight," getting to the gold devices and the Servants of the Earth.

"Hey, that rings a bell," she said. "Remember Admiral Roopack? From the Indian embassy, he pissed you off at the Indonesians' party because he—"

"Held your hand for half an hour and kept looking down your dress, yeah."

"It wasn't half an hour." She giggled. "He did sort of have his nose between my boobs, though. Anyway, *he* mentioned Servants of the Earth. He called me last night to tell me that his country was 'undergoing a small upset,' blah-blah-blah, and I tried to pick his brains about it, and he said it was under control, blah-blah-blah, and he rattled off a dozen or so groups that might be causing what he called 'these localized troubles.' You can maybe talk to him when you get here."

"Well—uh—Pilchard's given me another assignment. That's for your ears only."

Her voice turned hollow. "How long?"

"Not long." As in *It won't be long before we either knock this or get killed.*

"I've heard that before."

"We obey orders, babe."

"Yeah." Long pause. "Trouble is, I love you."

"Yeah." Pause. "What a cheerful couple."

"Yeah." A sigh. "Talk to Mikey while I cry."

Mikey wanted to talk about hitting a triple in a pickup softball game. A welcome change.

USS *Thomas Jefferson*

Madje, trying to be Rafehausen's eyes and ears, made his way to the Tactical Action Officer's spaces and found a new TAO in charge—the ship's intel officer, an aristocratic O-6 from Massachusetts named Hawkins.

"Morning, Mister Madje."

"Morning, sir. The admiral sent me around to see what was happening. He wants a report."

"That's the best news I've heard this morning." He swiveled his chair to look down his nose at Madje. "You qualified as a TAO?"

"I've done the quals, stood a few watches as flag TAO."

"I thought you could hack it. We've only got four on the watch bill right now. Can you do it?"

Madje couldn't think of a reason not to do it; he had no duties when the admiral was asleep. "I can help out, sir. But the admiral—"

"Good. When you don't have other duties, report down here. Want a dump for the admiral?"

"Yessir."

"Marley, print a screen from the JOTS and give it to Mister Madje." Captain Hawkins swiveled to face the glowing blue screen that filled the after bulkhead. The screen was filled with symbols denoting ships as hostile, neutral, and friendly; symbols that also indicated whether the unit they represented was a ship, a submarine, or an aircraft. Madje knew enough about the JOTS system to know that the white numbers next to each symbol represented the age of the information that fixed its location. Up to the north, the ages of most of the Indian symbols went back hours, in some cases back to the start of the exercise.

Captain Hawkins was a New Englander and sounded it. "We're nearly blind," he said quietly. "I've got Supplot working flat out and I'm using every ELINT tool in the book, but the Indians have pretty good transmission discipline." He rubbed his eyes, passed a hand over his face as if washing it. "Can you get the admiral to override Captain Lash and get one of the S-3's in Trincomalee to go up on a recce flight?"

Madje was used to staff politics, but this was a new level—operational politics. Politics in the face of the

172

enemy—whoever the enemy was. *Why am I surprised?* He asked himself. All he said was "Sorry, sir?" with a look of incomprehension.

"Captain Lash has decided not to fly any planes where they could quote provoke end quote the mutineers." Hawkins swiveled to face Madje, held up his hands as if to prevent argument. "Hear me out. I think this boat is under threat, first, from a possible submarine attack, second, from mainland air strikes, third, from surface action. I don't even know which of the exercise ships is friendly and which is enemy. There were some attempts to communicate, early on; we know their carrier was friendly and is now heavily damaged. If they targeted us and fired a missile salvo, we wouldn't even be able to strike back over the horizon. Captain Lash is aware of all this but sees it as his duty to make the best speed for Sri Lanka and avoid further contact."

"You think he's wrong." *And O'Leary didn't like Lash, either.*

Madje felt as if he were sinking in mud. He'd experienced this sort of thing before, bad enough when the admiral was an active player and he had a flag captain and a chief of staff to fall back on to filter the politics for him. Now, he alone had the access to the admiral. And Hawkins knew it. Madje admired Hawkins, a former surface-warfare officer with real decorations and an admirable record, but he was known to be *very* political. "You think we need to know what's over the horizon."

"Damn straight."

The trouble was, it made too much sense. Hawkins was *right*, as far as Madje could see. One of the S-3s out of Sri Lanka could stay fifty miles to the south of them, giving gas, and still get them some kind of radar picture of the forces to the north. Madje knew how it could be done. He couldn't see any risk. "I'll see what I can do, sir," he said cautiously. "The admiral isn't in really good shape." *Understatement of the year.*

"Rafehausen would *never* let this happen if he were aware," Hawkins said with conviction. He raised an eyebrow.

Madje got the clear impression that Hawkins was asking him to lie—to call Lash and claim the admiral had given him an order.

"I'll put it to him, sir," he said. "That's the best I can do."

Hawkins swiveled back to his screen, wiped his face again, and ran his hand through his hair. "Good. Then get your ass back here and take a watch."

Bhulta Airfield, India

After his phone calls, Alan gathered his troops in the shade of Harry's jet. They had put on clean clothes, those who had them, and Alan was in some of Harry's. All the men but Alan had shaved. They had a new energy and a new eagerness because they thought they were getting out.

"There's been a change," Alan said. The faces closed, and Fidel started nodding. "We've had new orders." And he told them.

Fidel looked at him with disgust. "I knew it."

Alan pulled him aside while the others cleaned out the van. "Fidel, you're a great man to have around when there's real trouble, but I sure don't need you making wiseass comments when I'm trying to talk to the troops."

Fidel's face got red, less with embarrassment than anger, Alan thought. "I apologize," Fidel said.

"That isn't good enough. *Don't do it again.* You understand me?"

"Yes, sir."

"You know what morale means, Fidel?"

"Yes, sir."

"You know what one bad mouth can do to morale?"

"Yes, sir."

"Well, help me out, can't you?" Alan grabbed his arm. "It's no secret, I need you. Without you yesterday, we'd be dead.

I want to go home, too. But I have orders and I'm going to do what I've been told to do, without any remarks and without any bitching. I'm only asking you to do the same."

Fidel grinned. "You've just begun to fight, right?"

"What the hell's that mean?"

"John Paul Jones."

Alan didn't get it, gave up trying to figure it out. "We on the same page now?"

"Yes, sir. Sorry I mouthed off."

"Okay. What I want you to do is make sure all the weapons are out of the van and in the aircraft. Police it for cartridges, casings, anything. When all this is over, the Indians will start accounting for some of their deaths. I don't want them finding a rifle that killed one of their people in a car that we rented—*capisce*?"

"What about the van?"

It was on Alan's credit card. He'd already decided he had to take the hit. "Lock it and leave it. I told Bahrain to tell the company to pick it up."

Fidel laughed. "By the time they get here, we'll be lucky if it's got doors on it."

15

In the Air, Bhulta–Ambur

"The Servants of the Earth are a philanthropic environmental society. That's what their website says, anyway."

Ong was briefing Alan and Harry as the plane flew across southern India. Ong had gone to Google and got more than twenty good hits before they began to scatter off into irrelevance.

"Their aims are to bring the earth back from environmental catastrophe. They don't say right out how they're going to do this, but 'random acts of service' is a phrase that crops up a lot." She looked at her notes. "They have a surprising amount of money. That's not on their website, except by implication, but they have several 'projects' that have to cost a bundle.

"They also have some interesting people. The website is a recruiting tool—by the way, the same animation is on the website as on the USB keys, but it's tied specifically to recruiting. In fact there are several animated sections, really cute, very professional— speaks to technical know-how.

"They're very up-front about recruiting. They say they want 'India's best'—by the way, this is a specifically Indian thing; you can access the website in English and eleven Indian languages but no others, which says to me they don't want Europeans or Chinese or whatever. Anyway—" She looked at her notes again. "Oh, yeah, 'India's best.' They give the specs for the ideal member: twenty-two to fifty-two, at least a college degree, makes eighteen thousand US or more a year, and in India, that's pretty good, is in the sciences, technology, the military, or local or national government."

Ong scratched in her black hair with the end of a pencil. She frowned. "They make themselves sound squeaky-clean, but some other websites say they're real bad news. I dunno—not enough sources and no criteria to judge, you know? I do think they're connected with Hindu nationalism, maybe pretty far right. The leader is somebody named Mohenjo Daro, who's a businessman, but there's one source that says he was connected with the destruction of a Sikh thing called the Golden Temple. Before my time." She smirked. "Couple of newspaper pieces about them that really sensationalize them. Called a cult. But another calls them 'the cutting-edge business conglomerate.' I have yet to research that part, the businesses, I mean. What I could deduce, they seem to own stuff—a dairy company, big deal, but a petrochemical plant, an outfit that's into genetic engineering, a smalltime pharmaceuticals company—I don't know, I don't have details and these things don't hang together very well."

Alan said, "Sounds like real money. How'd they get it?"

Alan and Harry were sitting in the seats farthest back toward the tail; Harry had showed her how to reverse the seatback of the next row, so she was facing them with a pull-down table and her laptop between them.

"We-e-e-ll—" Ong had learned a lot of her gestures and expressions from TV. "Most of the stuff on the net is positive, I mean, it's PR stuff. Maybe put out by members? But the negative stuff is some of it really rough. One website, this is a fringe thing, I admit, is named 'Servants of the Worst' and is a kind of riff on the Servants' own site—animations, that logo that buzzes around like a bee, a parody of their tone. What it says is that these folks are bad, they're violent, they've got big plans and they're out to destroy India. It's pretty melodramatic."

"Whose site?"

"One of the SOE sites says it was put together by a patient in a mental institution. The site itself says he or she was a novice member and got fed up—'nauseated' is the word—and tried to leave and was threatened, then got beat up, finally changed his or her name and left the country. Which brings me to the kicker, because I'm almost done."

"And—?"

"This person who says he/she was a novice member says that when there are 'in-gatherings,' which are like weekly meetings, every member carries a key, which he plugs into 'the yoni of the earth' as they enter the meeting. I had to look up 'yoni.'" She smiled and may have tried to blush. "It means 'vagina.' Call it what you will, it's a computer port, because 'on the screen,' the novice says, quote, 'we were told that every day we should look around us and choose for destruction the greatest insult we could find to earth and nature.' Then you were supposed to keep a list and prioritize it so that, quote, 'you as servant of the earth can focus the forces of Shiva when the moment comes.'"

"The forces of Shiva," Harry said. He looked at Alan. "Shiva's a destroyer; that's all we know and all we need to know. Make a list of local-level targets and go after them when the day comes."

"Like cell-phone towers, high-rises, strip malls—"

"Power plants, untreated sewage, chicken factories—in fact, most of exactly what's been hit all over India."

Alan looked at Ong. "How many people in this outfit?"

"Nobody knows. Estimates run from ten thousand to a hundred thousand."

Harry shook his head. "Not important; question is, what people? If they really have technocrats, scientists, government

178

workers, the military—and we know they've got some of the military—that's news."

"But they'd have to be fanatics."

"Oh, really? What kind of guy you think power-dives a jet into an aircraft carrier?"

Bahrain

Mike Dukas was at Manama's airport only ten minutes before Mary Totten's flight was scheduled to land. The way he was running behind, he figured he should be grateful he wasn't half an hour late. He had meant to send Greenbaum, but it had made more sense to leave Greenbaum in the office with Leslie, who was giving him a crash course in Not Pissing Off Mike Dukas.

He went straight to the VIP office and pulled into his wake the greeter and the two security men who were waiting for him. They made it to the top of the ramp in the arrival lounge with two minutes to spare, which Dukas spent on a cell phone checking out Rattner's progress on the terrorist-attack prep. Then the aircraft whined up to the gate and the door opened and they walked down, and the VIP greeter was in the door as soon as it opened, contacting the CIA woman by seat number—to him, she was Ms Brevard—and bringing her out before anybody else could embark.

Dukas introduced himself, looked over her shoulder, saw a sad-sack guy who looked like something from a Dilbert cartoon.

"My special assistant," Mary Totten said.

Nerd city.

In Customs and Immigration, the nerd caused a small flurry because he didn't respond to the name on his passport and had to be reminded that he was using the name Bill Grayling. Smiles all around.

"Early in the day," Dukas said, although it was noon. When they were getting into his car, he said to the nerd, "You new at this?"

"No. Yes. Well, no—I'm really an analyst—"

"I could have guessed." Dukas put him in the back and had Mary Totten sit in front next to him. "Well, if you never leave Bahrain, you'll be okay."

"Never leave Bahrain, my ass! I'm outa here on the first plane I can get."

"If you mean India, there are no planes. India's closed."

"The Navy can lay on a clandestine flight for us."

Dukas grinned. This woman was going to be fun. "Miz Totten—Mary—Miz Brevard—there's something you need to understand." He risked a look away from the traffic and grinned at her. "The Navy isn't laying on anything for anybody."

She was a very good-looking woman, he decided, even after a night and part of a day on an airplane. A few lines to give her face character, a few gray hairs, a good body— heavy-boned, fit, tall—and eyes that didn't take any shit from anybody. *Hottin' Totten.*

"I can either take you straight to your hotel, or we can stop at my office, you can look at some recent message traffic"

"What I want to do, Mike, is get the hell out of Bahrain."

"Gee, Mary," Bill said from the back, "we lost a lot of sleep. Let's go to the—"

"Let's go to your office," she said. "Then I want to see Admiral Pilchard."

Dukas laughed. "I think if you're real lucky, the assistant intel officer might have time for you." She wasn't amused.

16

In the Air Near Ambur, India

Harry O'Neill was sitting in the righthand seat of the Lear jet with earphones on his head and one hand on a radio dial. His pilot, Luis Moad, was beside him. "Keep trying," Moad said. He was Goan-American, a former Navy pilot with a multi-engine qualification.

"Zip," Harry said. "Ambur's off the air, or I don't know what the hell I'm doing."

"My guess is you know what you're doing." Moad grinned. "You *better* know what you're doing, Harry—this heap has enough fuel to get to Ambur, and then it's white-knuckles time."

Harry changed frequencies, checking against a kneeboard card. Navy habits still ruled—kneeboard cards, comm cards, briefings, however cursory. Harry hadn't been a flying officer in his tour with the Navy, so sitting up here hadn't come easily to him at first; now, he was at home with the jargon and the drill.

"Intelligent life!" he muttered as their earphones filled with talk. He clicked his mike to intercom, said, "Chittoor," aside to Moad. "Fifty K from Ambur."

Moad glanced at his fuel gauges, nodded.

"Chittoor, this is BN756 registered to Ethos Security of Manama, inbound on heading 040, estimate 150 kilometers. What's your status, over?"

181

"756, this is air-traffic control Chittoor, repeat, please."

"Chittoor, what is the status of your field? Are you receiving aircraft, over?"

"756, Chittoor is open to limited traffic only. Are you an emergency?"

Harry looked at Moad; he nodded.

"Chittoor, this is 756, we filed a flight plan for Ambur but can't raise them; we have fuel for only—"

Moad held up five fingers, pumped them. Harry made an "I don't get you" gesture—five minutes? Five hundred kilometers? Miles? Moad switched on his own mike. "Chittoor, this is 756, we have one thousand pounds, estimate Chittoor in two minutes, request clear for immediate landing."

"756, Ambur is closed because of military activity. Avoid Ambur air space because of known antiaircraft incidents there. Do you have fuel to detour around Ambur and make Chittoor?"

"Can do. Are we cleared?"

There was some garble and then the voice, accented but intelligible, told them they were cleared for immediate landing on 235, and then there was some chat about where they were coming from and did they have papers and did they realize that Chittoor was not an international point of entry.

"Chittoor, this is 756, we filed a flight plan at Bhulta, repeat Bhulta, no immigration necessary." Harry didn't say that their flight plan had been left on the plastic lawn chair belonging to the old security guard, or that he and his people were carrying false passports with false immigration stamps. Why make waves?

Bahrain
Dukas sat on the edge of Rattner's desk, half-smiling at Mary Totten. "Maybe you got lucky. Navy may have a flight

heading for Sri Lanka late today—depends on whether a couple of pilots get here from Naples in time. You want to be on it?"

"I've zero interest in going to Sri Lanka."

Dukas shrugged. "It's that or Bahrain."

"What's in Sri Lanka?"

"Bunch of aircraft from the *Jefferson*." He'd told her about the accident.

"*They* could fly me into India. How far can it be?"

"That would be up to the senior officer on the ground, subject to approval from Fifth Fleet."

"Who's the senior officer?"

"Right now, I guess it's Commander Siciliano."

"What's he like?"

Dukas grinned. "Not your type, would be my guess." He waited for her reaction, which was guarded. "He's a she."

"Oh, shit." She made a face. "I really do relate better to men. Well—can you get me on this plane?"

"I can ask for space for you and your analyst. If you don't get bumped, and the flight goes, you'll be okay."

"Dukas, what I'm doing here is important! A lot more important than anything else that can be going on a goddam airplane!"

Dukas shook his head. "Believe it or not, the Navy believes that protecting its aircraft carrier is more important than providing transport for the CIA. You'd be higher on the list if you were a jet engine mechanic or a hydraulics specialist or an F-18 pilot. Right now, you can get bumped by an E-3 just out of weapons school."

"You don't think it's important to your carrier that there may be nukes floating around loose in India?"

"Yeah, well, 'may be' doesn't cut much ice next to the certainty that the carrier's got no working deck. If I can get you on the flight, I'll get you on the flight; if not—you've got a room at a good hotel."

She stood. "What're you doing this evening, if I don't get on the flight?"

Dukas glanced at Leslie, who was bending over Greenbaum on the far side of the office. "I'm working. There's one more thing."

"Oh, shit." She sat. "I hate 'one more thing.'"

"Yeah, don't we all. Listen, you said you got the okay to come here with a big team and a brass band, and then you got negatived down to just you and your nerd because the White House interfered." She had told him the story of her calls to and from the DDI. "Why?"

"They don't want India on their screen, I guess."

"Fast work, considering everything has to go through about six layers there."

"They knew what was going on even before I did. I thought I was the first horse out of the gate, you know? I saw it on CNN, I *ran* to the phone and got the DDO, and he said yes. Minutes, I mean *minutes* later, it was no. NSC knew more than I did, he said, knew more than he did, and the word was No."

"They mention the accident on the *Jefferson*?"

"No, just—" She slitted her eyes, looked at him with real interest. "As a matter of fact, the DDI did say something about the Navy. Something about need to know, and I didn't need to know."

Dukas was frowning. "What time did you have this conversation?"

"Oh, shit— What difference does it make?"

"Just a thought. Write it out for me while I drive you to your hotel, okay?" He lowered his voice. "And get your analyst to take a bath, will you? Between you and me, he makes the office smell like the zoo."

Trincomalee

Rose had spent the flight from Bahrain making lists. She had wanted to start making them back in Bahrain, but the process

184

of getting to Sri Lanka had itself proven a major undertaking, and the moment that Fifth Fleet admin was notified by Fifth Fleet ops that she would be the senior officer at Trincomalee, she had become, de facto, the person responsible for anything that could be signed for—aircrew transfers and TDYs, maintenance personnel, spare parts inventories.

Fuel.

Two queries to Chris Donitz had not brought her any information; a junior officer named Soleck had called twice but no one had thought to transfer his calls to her, and that left her too ignorant and too late. So she had signed everything, okayed everything, found a senior chief aviation bosun's mate to honcho the spare parts, and got herself to the plane.

The first list had to do with her immediate crisis—a diplomatic/military liaison mission to the Sri Lankan government to wrest permission for her planes to fly armed so that they could provide combat air patrol for the *Jefferson*. She continued to hope that the situation would be resolved by the time her flight landed, but the list had to be made. If she had to go, the transport would take her straight on to Colombo.

Contact embassy

Contact Sri L. DoD

Get status agreement

It was a short list, but the difficulties at each stage could be— "Don't borrow trouble," she said aloud. And thought about the baby in her belly. *The fetus*. Three months along and worried that she'd miscarry again. She'd *volunteered* for this. What was she thinking of?

"Sorry, ma'am?" The man in the seat next to her was a veteran F-18 pilot whom she knew only as Hawk. He'd come off the command ship at Bahrain, where he had been on the Fifth Fleet staff as the targets officer. He was typical of the pilots she was bringing with her; all well trained, all a year or more out of the cockpit. She shook her head. "Talking to myself."

He gave her a quick smile, put his cap over his eyes, and went instantly back to sleep.

She started to tackle the longer second list. She had run a chopper squadron and could do this in her sleep.

Fuel!

Space/habitation

Maintenance inventory

Comms

Planes

Personnel/rotation/flight sched/duty roster

By the time they turned on final for Trincomalee, she had twenty-four pages of written orders and sixteen checklists, and most of them had names already assigned. She looked at Hawk, who had become her maintenance officer because his short dossier said he had been assistant MO in his last squadron and he was unlucky enough to be asleep next to her. *Sleep while you can, buddy*, she thought.

Chris Donitz met her on the tarmac, his flight suit rumpled and stained and suggesting that he hadn't been out of it in more than a day. He saluted her crisply, his face tired, closed.

"Is this NAS Trincomalee?" she asked, keeping her tone light and willing him to respond in the same vein. All the new people were coming off the plane behind her and she didn't need a scene on the runway, and it was obvious to her from Donitz's body language that he wasn't entirely happy to see her.

He watched the line of people coming down the boarding ramp and gave a half smile. "Looks like it will be, soon enough. Ma'am."

"Tell me what's going on."

"We've got four birds over the *Jeff* right now and two more on alert. None of them are armed beyond rounds for the 30mm because the authorities here won't let us take off with missiles. I already have one plane down for maintenance with a landing-gear fluid leak and another coming up on a major engine-maintenance number. We don't have a hangar and the aircrews are sleeping at a sleezebag hotel in town." He took a breath. "You're Al Craik's wife."

"Call me Rose. They call you 'Donuts,' right?" She turned back to the line. "Hawk!"

He was taller standing up than he had looked on the plane. He had short-cropped blond hair and a flat-top, and his glasses sparkled. When he joined them, he looked about five feet taller than Donitz and twice as clean.

"Ma'am?"

"As of now, you're the detachment maintenance officer. Get with Donuts here, and find out who needs what. Here's a list of things I need you to do ASAP. Get Chief Sardo on the inventory. Any news on getting fuel?"

Donitz crossed his arms. He looked defensive, if not downright resentful. "You're taking command, ma'am?"

No way to sweet-talk around it. Naval tradition required Donitz to accept his loss of status, but long experience had taught Rose that no officer worth a crap ever liked losing a command, however temporary.

"You'll be my XO. This is, as of now, Det 161, or Det Trincomalee. One of those, whenever Fifth Fleet makes up its mind. Here are my orders."

Donitz sagged a little, uncrossed his arms. "Shit, ma'am, I didn't mean you had to give me the paperwork."

She nodded. "We have a space?" Space was Navy jargon for a hangar, offices, and maintenance area—everything that went with having planes and their impediments.

"Nada. We own the tarmac our planes are on."

"Okay." Privately, she thought that Donitz could have got something from the Sri Lankans; she could see an empty hangar, big, white, and British-built, down at the end of the runway. "Who owns that thing?"

Donitz's arms were crossed again, and he backed up a step. "Don't know." The question seemed to accuse him. "Never thought to ask."

She could see why Al liked him. He didn't bother to make an excuse. She gave him her best smile. "You had other shit to do. When did you last sleep?"

"I got a few hours this morning. I'm good to go."

"Okay. I need you to hold the fort for a while. My first duty here is to get the Sri Lankans off our backs so we can put our birds up armed. I brought an admin guy who can pay for civilian gas—for a while. That's going to take time. I brought a bunch of people, some good stuff, and some clout. Here's a list of my priorities for today. If you want to change the order, go ahead; you're the XO. But getting space is the top, and that hangar looks good to me. And get me a flight sched. Everyone qualed flies. That includes me—put me on the sked for tonight. I gotta go to Colombo first and play diplomat. Figure me back in six hours."

Before she could decide whether he needed to be handled, he was deep in her stack of lists with Hawk, and the transport pilot was telling her that he was cleared for Colombo if she was ready to ride.

Chittoor, India

The Lear jet was parked at the end of a row of grounded commercial aircraft, so it was a long walk from the terminal. Alan let Harry and Moad make the walk while he kept his people discreetly near the plane. Shaven and dressed in some of Harry's clothes, he felt better, if a little unfashionable—Harry was two sizes bigger.

He gathered them inside the plane, handed out assignments: Ong and Benvenuto were to concentrate on the Servants of the Earth, gleaning everything they could from the Internet. Clavers, housekeeping and security—"That means you keep these two safe, fed, and watered while they work."

"This is a long way from my designator, sir."

"Yeah, there's a lot of that going around."

Alan gestured to Fidel. "Let's talk." He led the way to the front of the aircraft and sat them both down. Keeping his voice low, he told him what he knew about the Ambur electrical facility, the attack on it, and the likelihood that it was a nuclear storage site. "Harry's on our side. I don't want to say any more than that."

"I kind of figured he was."

"Air traffic control said there's military activity around Ambur, including maybe SAMs—antiaircraft, anyway. I've been ordered to find out if there were nukes in there and, if so, what happened to them. Mister O'Neill has a source who maybe can tell him, so we're going there. You've already done your part, Fidel—you took a lot of risks, you saved our buns, you got us out of Mahe. You can stay here and run security."

"Or?"

"Or you can come with us and go through it all again—risk, the whole nine yards. Ambur's a war zone."

"You asking me to volunteer?"

"No. I mean it—you can stay here and run security on the plane and I'll think to my dying day you did your duty and then some."

Fidel looked at him, leaning forward in the airplane seat and turning, then looked out the small window and turned back. "You and I have some differences of viewpoint, Commander. I guess that came out yesterday."

"I was wrong yesterday. You did what you had to do."

"I want you to understand that I don't get my kicks from it. I've seen a couple guys did—got so they killed for fun. They were nuts; I knew they were nuts, and they finally got put away for being nuts. I'm not like that. But yesterday, that's what I *do*. And it's what you do, too, if you're honest about it."

"Not without a lot of guilt."

Fidel stared at him. "Well, if you didn't feel something, you'd be nuts, you see what I'm saying?"

"You feel it, too."

"I don't let it bend me out of shape, though. I don't make a big thing out of it."

Alan half-smiled. "You're not the one in command."

Fidel absorbed that, grunted. "Djalik says you're okay, but a gunner. I'll go."

"You don't have to—"

"I'll *go*! Jesus, sir, I volunteer, okay?" He got up and made his way to the aisle. "You and me are never going to be asshole buddies, but I think we're more alike than you maybe want to admit."

He went down the aisle. Alan sat there. At that moment, if the plane had taken itself off and flown toward Bahrain, he would have cheered. But it wouldn't, and he wouldn't, so he hauled himself up and called down the plane, "Lieutenant Ong, could I see you for a minute, please?"

He moved so she wouldn't have to climb over him. He wasn't sure that close contact with Ong was a great idea. She sat next to him and said "Hi," in a bright voice.

"Ah—Lieutenant, I want you to, mmm, back off a little from Petty Officer Benvenuto, okay?"

Her smile vanished. "What are you saying to me?"

"Benvenuto is twenty years old. He's never been out of East Jesus, New York. He doesn't understand people's signals yet."

"Why are you telling me this?" Her voice rose.

"Lieutenant, you've got him running around in circles. You were holding *hands* with him. That's improper behavior; you're an officer in the United States Navy!"

"I—was scared. I—needed to, um, depend—he's strong."

"Benvenuto is not a strong man. He's a kid. You, on the other hand, are an officer. I'm sorry, you were out of line."

She turned the big, teary lamps of her eyes on him. "Why don't you like me?" she said.

Oh, shit. "I like you well enough, Lieutenant. But military relationships—"

"I told you, I need a strong man! You won't do it; I need somebody! My father is strong, *very* strong; I was raised to depend on him."

"What does your father do?"

"He owns a chain of Chinese-language newspapers. He thought I was insane to go into the Navy, such little jobs, and now I think he was right!" She began to sob. Quietly.

Alan let her get through it. He didn't have even a Kleenex to offer, so he simply sat there. When she was calm, he said, "You did join the Navy, is the trouble. You *are* an officer. There are things you do and things you don't do. Please don't touch Benvenuto anymore; please stop calling him 'Benny'— he's Petty Officer Benvenuto—and please stop using him as a personal flunkey." He changed his position in the seat and lightened his voice. "Now, you'll be in command while I'm gone."

"I don't want to command!"

"You're the officer."

"It's an accident I'm an officer; I'm really a computer specialist!"

"Yeah, well, now we're here, and you're an officer, and I'm going away and you're in command. If I don't come back in three days, you take the aircraft and return to Bahrain; the pilot will know that's the plan. If Mister O'Neill comes back and I don't, you support him within the parameters of your own good judgment; consult with Fifth Fleet as you see fit. And remember that you have a responsibility to the people under you—most of all to get them home in one piece."

"I don't know anything about that stuff!" she cried.

"Yeah, well—" He exhaled loudly. "You do your best and take your lumps." He put his hands on the seatback in front of him as a signal that he was going. "Remember what I said about Benvenuto." She swung her knees out of the way, seeming to cringe into the seat so that she wouldn't touch him. Tears made her eyes glisten.

Alan walked down to Clavers. "Lieutenant Ong will be in command while I'm gone. Any questions?"

Clavers blew out her lips. "You know any good prayers?"

The sun made heat mirages along the runway like pools of moving oil. Nothing else was moving out in the heat except Moad, his pilot, headed for the plane after making his peace with the tower.

Harry opened the antenna on his satellite phone and waited for a signal, sweat forming on his forehead and running down his sides. He was tired of this kind of work. He didn't really believe in the causes anymore. Living in the Middle East made American policy difficult to accept.

Time to go.

Despite which, he dialed the number on the slip of paper in his left hand. The number rang twice and was answered automatically. There was no message, and a short beep. Harry pushed in a string of numbers. A simple code: date, meeting time, fallback, urgency.

His agent, Lottery Ticket, would know to meet today, and where, and that in the litany of urgency codes, this one rated the highest.

Harry stood in the sun, facing Mecca, and waited, praying. In time, the phone vibrated once and a string of digits appeared on the screen, accepting the meeting.

BBC World News
"The unrest that has gripped India increased overnight and

has spread to cyberspace and the financial sector. Although it's increasingly hard to confirm reports here as mobiles go dead and the long-line telephone system breaks down, it appears that at least one virulent computer worm has been launched, and three major attacks have been made on computerized systems. The worm, called 'Shakuntala' after a word in its subject line, removes part of all Windows XP and 2000 operating systems. My sources say that it is spreading exponentially in India because of language links.

"In addition, both the computerized rail system and the air-traffic control system have been the targets of what one official has called 'cyberterrorism.' Both seem to have been launched about two a.m. New Delhi time; by the beginning of the working day, major airports in Delhi, Mumbai, and Calcutta were closed and international flights were reported to have been diverted out of country. Radio bulletins say that the rail system is operating at less than half capacity and very low speeds because of the loss of computerized signals control, with one wreck reported on the main Calcutta–Lucknow line.

"In the centers of India's computer industry—New Delhi, Bangalore, Mumbai, and Hyderabad—high-tech companies that handle huge quantities of American and European outsourcing have gone down with computer failures. I heard an industry spokesperson promise a quick fix, but, in a country now teetering on the brink of chaos, with a government that is itself giving wildly conflicting statements about the situation, and the benchmark Mumbai stock index down twenty-one percent in the first hour of trading, many people here are hoarding food and petrol and preparing for what they fear will be a long ordeal. Nick LaHaye, Mumbai."

17

"We need to get to Ambur." Harry said it baldly, just like that. Alan could tell that he was already in a hurry. More quietly, he said, "I want to get this over with."

Djalik grunted.

Harry gave Fidel a long look. "I don't really like adding to the people on my need-to-know list. Just so you know, this is my last show for these folks." He jerked his thumb out the window at America, Washington DC, Langley.

Alan shrugged. "We're in this together. I want Fidel to know what's going on."

Harry was silent for a few seconds, his chin in his hand, looking out the window at the tarmac and the white stucco of the passenger building in the sun. Then he turned back to face Alan, opened his laptop and looked at the screen.

"I have two goals. I need to meet a source, an agent. And I want to look at the site, in particular, Buildings Thirty-seven and One-eighteen. That's a lower priority, especially if I can meet this guy."

Alan leaned over the table and looked at the map. "The facility is almost a mile square, Harry."

"Yeah. They packed everything into one basket; hydro from the dam, a coal-fired plant here on the north side of the river, and a nuke plant here." Harry pointed to a set of buildings on a photograph, laid the photograph on the map so that it was oriented correctly. "WMD office at CIA says that Building Thirty-seven, that's this low building here, is a quote possible nuclear weapons storage facility end quote."

Djalik nodded, and Fidel said "whoa" quietly.

Harry nodded back. "I'd like the four of us, armed. My source says the roads are clear, or at least they were last night when he left me a message."

"Where exactly are we going?" Fidel asked.

Harry pulled out a map and put it on the table. He had a big orange marking pen and he drew a circle around a point on a ridge just south of the power facility. "There's a gas station with a restaurant and a market right here. It services the trucks going down to Ambur. It's high enough that we'll be able to see the whole layout. If that doesn't work, I need to go to Mohir. That's over here." Harry pointed at another spot on the ridge, closer, but farther west.

Fidel and Djalik put their heads down over the map and the photo so that Alan couldn't see it. Djalik said, "It's just about twenty klicks. If the roads are clear, we can be back before this evening." The way he said it suggested that he didn't really believe the roads were clear, but Harry nodded.

"Good. Let's go."

Fidel and Djalik exchanged a look. "Need more of a plan than that, Mister O'Neill. Ingress, egress, evasion. A rally point if we get split up. Stuff like that."

Harry sighed. "If this was a commando raid, I'd do all that. We're supposed to drive over there, you guys take some photos, I meet my guy. That's it. And we need to move. My first meeting window is in an hour and thirty minutes."

"Meeting window?" Fidel asked.

Djalik raised his eyebrows. "You ever do clandestine? The guy who's waiting, he'll only wait a set time, usually just a couple of minutes. That's the window. If nobody shows in the window that looks right, he takes off, goes to a fallback meeting site."

"Okay," Fidel said. "And the fallback's Mohir?"

Harry began to drum his fingers on the table. He was impatient to start, that much Alan could see. And he clearly hated this open discussion.

Fidel caught Harry's mood too, but he wasn't going to let up. "So if we get there late, we miss the guy, and then we have to hustle to the next place. Right?"

"Yes."

"That's another fifteen klicks." Fidel turned to Alan as if appealing to him. "That's a lot of driving around the countryside on a tight schedule. Mister O'Neill says the roads are clear. What if they ain't? Do we shoot our way through?"

Alan thought about the day before, the fight just to get off the Indian navy base. "He's got a point, Harry."

Harry's fingers drummed faster. "Yeah. Yeah, I can see all that, but every minute we sit here, we're not driving. Anything could happen on the road. We take it one step at a time. I expect there will be troops, Indian Army troops, moving in this morning to retake the facility from the terrorists. Probably roadblocks. The longer we wait, the harder it will be to get there. All we can do is take things as they come."

"Weapons?" Djalik asked.

Harry nodded, and Djalik led the way to the arms locker in the tail. Fidel followed him like a kid heading for a toy store. Alan waited until Fidel was through the cabin with Djalik and then grabbed Harry's arm.

"You're meeting your source at the gas station, right?"

Harry looked and gave him a very slight nod.

"How are we going to handle that?" Alan asked brusquely.

"I'll wander off."

Alan digested this. He might be nominally in charge, but Harry wasn't going to tell him much. "Wander off?"

"You want your own copy of the comm plan?" Harry asked.

Alan was tempted for a moment to say, *Yes, I'm in charge,*

I have the need to know. "Fidel may be a little short on social graces, Harry, but his point is valid. We can't support you if we don't know what you're doing."

"Look, Alan, I have a comm plan. I activated by a signal to the guy's computer about twenty minutes ago. I can't take the signal back now, and I can't change the meeting places. Right? You know how this stuff works. We go, we get to the truck stop, and I hope he's sitting in the tea shop. If we can't get to the truck stop, or he can't, then four hours later in another tea shop in the village to the west." Harry didn't look at Alan while he spoke, as if he regretted passing even that much information. Then he pushed past. "If we're going to do this, we have to move."

Alan wished that he knew Harry's whole plan. He wished Harry's shorts fit him. As he passed through the main cabin, he snatched up his cold coffee and drained it and then went back aft to get a weapon.

Fidel had a semiautomatic shotgun and a pistol. Djalik, whose missing fingers mirrored Alan's, was limited to things he could handle with one hand. He took an Uzi machine pistol. Whatever Harry had chosen was already stuffed in a long zipped bag with a big Canadian flag. Alan looked over the limited selection and pointed to an M-16-clone carbine with a short barrel and a folding stock.

"Is that thing accurate?" he asked.

"Not bad," Fidel said.

"Pretty sharp," Djalik said at the same time. They both laughed.

"Can I manage it?" Alan asked Fidel, holding up his maimed left hand.

"Sure, sir. Doesn't weigh anything."

Harry leaned over him and picked up a green holster. "Rose sent this." Alan's Belgian Browning. He smiled, more at the thought of Rose than the sight of the gun.

Under the gun was a grubby green nylon helmet bag and

a backpack. Alan grabbed them—no clothes, but his spare toilet kit and some underwear and his flight gear.

Moad leaned in from the front. "I have a car."

Harry hoisted the Canadian bag. "Let's go."

Fifth Fleet HQ, Bahrain

"Admiral Rafehausen's requesting permission to put a recce flight up near the Indians." Captain Lurgwitz waved a message sheet as she came into Pilchard's office.

Pilchard grabbed it, pulled it close to his eyes and then looked up at her. "Rafehausen? Sent a message? He's doped to his eyeballs and strapped to a rack, according to Captain Lash."

Lurgwitz shrugged. "That's why I brought it in person, sir. Something's going on out there."

Pilchard read the message again. He started writing on the bottom of the sheet, his printing nearly illegible. "Doesn't matter. That recce needs to go down anyway; Lash is being too goddam cautious and he's blind. But get somebody on the *Jefferson* and find out who the—blazes put out a message over Rafehausen's name." He kept writing. He showed her his note. "Okay? One plane out of Trin, okay? That's all we have, and it can't look like a strike. Try for some distance work first. No closer than five-zero miles to any hostile. Got it?"

"Aye, aye, sir." Captain Lurgwitz took the proffered sheet. "Washington could call that a provocation." She waved a hand. "My job to point this shit out, sir."

The admiral shrugged, as if accepting the weight of the decision on his bony shoulders. "Yeah. Thanks. But losing the *Jefferson*'s more of a worry than provoking the mutineers." His eyes were already down on another message. "Get that out."

"Yessir."

North of Ambur Electrical Power Facility

"This is insane," Alan said almost to himself. His words were drowned by the noise of the Land Rover as Djalik shifted gears rounding a sharp bend and slowing for a mass of people on the road.

"Refugees," Djalik said. He shifted into reverse, but they were all around the car, a few young men beating on the hood with their fists, more standing still or shuffling along under heavy loads of plastic bowls, furniture, and bags of rice.

"Look sharp," Fidel said. "I see guns."

"Fuck," Djalik said. In the front seat, both suddenly had guns; Fidel had the automatic shotgun across his legs, and Djalik had the machine pistol in his lap. He kept both hands on the wheel.

Alan and Harry were in the back. Harry frowned. "My guy said the roads were clear."

A burst of firing came clear over the engine noise, loud whams all together from a big automatic rifle followed by a scream from the crowd. The crowd vanished as fast as it had appeared, leaving two old women trampled next to the wreck of a plywood tea shop and two twitching bodies that Alan took to be recent gunshot victims on his side of the car.

Djalik didn't wait for orders. He clashed the gears and the Land Rover shot forward, going over something with a soft bump and swaying as he shifted again and took a curve at high speed. According to the map, they should have been in open country, but this was India, and the road out of the town was lined with small shacks, tea shops, cabins; only behind them could the rows of sugar fields be glimpsed, interspersed with dense clumps of bamboo and lush trees.

Another burst of fire and simultaneously a single neat perforation appeared in the left rear side panel, just a few inches beyond Alan's shoulder. The bullet vanished into his seatback.

Alan leaned against the side as the vehicle swung around a pothole and accelerated. Over the seatback, he could see another bend in the road, the middle distance screened by a big stand of bamboo.

"I've got a crossroads coming up, no vehicles, and more refugees beyond. Could be a checkpoint." Djalik put on the brakes, and Alan raised his head. Around the bend, a glint of metal showed for a moment. Alan could see a heavy log across the road.

Harry leaned forward over the seats for a look. "That a regular army checkpoint?"

"Kinda too late to decide now."

Two soldiers in dirty uniforms stepped out from the bamboo in front of them and took aim at the windshield.

Alan saw their turbans. "Sikhs. Probably loyalists," he said quietly, although there was no way the men on the road could hear him.

Djalik and Fidel had their weapons out of sight. The Land Rover came to a stop. The first soldier yelled and motioned with the barrel of his rifle. The second kept his on target.

"How you want to play this, Harry?" Djalik asked quietly. He kept both hands on the wheel.

"Me first. You guys stay in until I talk, or tell you."

He opened the door slowly and put his feet on the road, keeping the door between him and the rifles as long as he could. The two soldiers didn't move. Harry closed the door and raised his hands.

"Speak English?" he asked as he climbed out.

The man who had shouted raised his rifle and motioned Harry forward. The nearer man shouted again. The other soldier yelled at Harry.

"We're American. American!" Harry shouted.

"Hemiriken?" said the soldier nearest to Alan's door. His head rose from behind the sights of his rifle. He turned his head and shouted behind him at the roadblock. Alan thought they were speaking Hindi.

The other soldier shouted at Harry and he tried to respond in different languages—first French, and then another that had to be Arabic, and then a third. The word "American" came up in each. Neither of the soldiers seemed to understand. The one outside Alan's window waved his rifle at the men in the car and spoke again, apparently to his partner.

A third soldier approached them at a run, his rifle held in both hands, his eyes moving to the landscape to their right. He had three broad stripes on his left shoulder. He came up to the soldiers and they had a rapid exchange, the soldiers both speaking at once, their eyes never leaving the vehicle and Harry.

Harry waited and then cleared his throat. "Sergeant?" he asked.

"Yez. I speak English, thank you. Please state your business?" His uniform was covered in dust and his armpits were black with sweat. He'd been in it a while. He sounded calm and professional, even courteous, except that his men had their assault rifles aimed and ready.

"We're trying to get to Mohir, near Ambur. Can you tell me what's going on, Sergeant?"

"Past this post is war," the sergeant said.

Well ahead of them to the south, where the ground started to rise toward the mountains, a big gun fired. Alan saw the flash first, then heard a dull crump as the sound carried over the five or six miles. Before he could remark on it, a missile rose from a position to his right and crossed the intervening miles in seconds, detonating in roughly the position of the original firer. There was a sudden burst of fire beyond the bamboo, big guns like howitzers that made speech impossible and threw a line of dust eruptions from exploding shells up the ridge. All three soldiers were off the road and in the ditch to Alan's left before the last explosion sounded.

Answering fire from beyond the ridge struck somewhere in front of them, again screened by the bamboo, raising geysers of earth over the tops of the highest plants.

More shooting off to the right. The sergeant said something and crawled out on the road. His men stayed in the ditch, but their rifles were back on the car.

Harry climbed to his feet, no longer a picture of groomed safari wear. "How long have you been fighting here?" Harry asked. He sat back against the fender of the Land Rover. A pack of cigarettes, only slightly banged about, appeared in his hand. He looked more relaxed than anyone there.

In the front seat, both of the men moved restlessly.

The sergeant squatted, took a cigarette, nodded his thanks and lit it with a butane lighter from his breast pocket. He took a long drag on the cigarette and waved it to the north. "My regiment attacked Ambur ridge last night. We were not completely successful." He smoked again, looking at the ridge. Suddenly, his flow became more rapid, as if he wanted to talk about it.

Post-combat stress disorder, Alan thought, listening from the back seat. He had his door open in case the shells came again.

"Nor did we completely fail. Now we are slowly pushing them off the rest of the ridge with artillery. Ours came up a few hours ago, yes?" He asked the last as if he expected they had seen it. But he didn't wait for an answer. "Off east, they attack us this morning. We were not entirely surprised, yes? But we took some losses, and now they hold the road over there." He pointed across the sugarcane fields, past rising ground covered in deep green scrub, to a trio of low buildings several miles to the east. Alan realized that this was the ground that the soldiers had been looking at every time they glanced away from his group, as if they anticipated an attack.

"We are supposed to go to Ambur," Harry said.

The howitzer battery fired again up the road and more

guns answered it. Again rounds fell long and detonated near enough to make them all take cover. Alan rolled out of the car and over until he was lying alongside Harry.

"Time to go for the fallback at Mohir."

"Yeah." Harry's voice was flat.

Alan smelled the sweet tobacco smoke from one of the cigarettes and felt a flutter in his stomach; he was an old smoker, a frequent backslider, and stress always increased his longing.

"Got the map?" Alan asked Harry. Harry rolled on his side and pulled it out of a cargo pocket. Alan squirmed to face him across the map. The sandy soil was working between his shorts and his skin, and something was crawling on his leg. Just like Africa. He looked at the map.

"Where are we? Here?" he asked, pointing at a crossroads at the base of the ridge. The facility was south and west along over the ridge, three or four kilometers away.

"Or here," Harry said, pointing to the next junction south. "I didn't count the crossroads."

Alan pulled the map around. He traced the line of the ridge to the east, looking at the low ground where the enemy—how quickly these things crystallize—had his tanks.

The sergeant was calling orders in his own language. His men began to move back toward the dug-in weapon.

"How far is Mohir?" Harry asked, pointing toward where he hoped the village was located to the west.

The sergeant finished his cigarette with professional intensity. "Their infantry is moving this way."

"Do you know this village? Mohir?" Harry asked again.

The sergeant looked at the map, ran his fingers unerringly over the area where the attack was staging, then glanced west, at the village.

"Yes," he said. "Workers' housing for the power plants. Right there. Maybe four kilometers." He looked at his men, back at the ridge. "You need to go."

Harry brightened, and Djalik and Fidel exchanged glances, rolled their eyes, swore inwardly.

"Will you let us go that way?"

"Go. Just go. Yes, go that way—back along the road is cut now. Go!"

Alan was back in, noting that his seatback was cut up and his window broken; he dusted the glass off the seat and settled himself. Harry was hanging out his own door, still talking to the sergeant.

Djalik was rolling. The Land Rover moved up to the downed log, two crouched soldiers moved it just enough for Djalik to squeeze by, and they were out of the bamboo. Then Djalik gunned the engine, shot around the curve and took the corner at the intersection, headed west. The high center of gravity caused them to sway once, almost out of control, and then they steadied with a thump.

"Those guys were pretty good, for grunts," Fidel said. He had the shotgun again.

Harry leaned up between the seats as they hit a hole— pothole, shell hole, something in the narrow track that Djalik couldn't get around. Harry's head hit the roof with a crack and he cursed. "Bit my tongue," he said, shaking his head.

Alan laughed, and Harry took a swing at him, a mock swing that Alan avoided by sitting back heavily. Harry leaned back over the seat, keeping his head down.

"Another intersection here, then we turn right on to a paved road that doubles back and up the ridge here. See it?"

"Got it," Djalik said. "Where's it go?"

"Small valley, there. Then Mohir."

Fidel let out a grunt of frustration. "How do we know somebody's not fighting over that, too?"

"We don't." Harry looked at Alan. "Let's go."

18

Bahrain

It was late in the day, and Dukas felt as if he'd been cleaning the floor with his tongue. Deep fatigue can be like a bad hangover, he decided. He knew bad hangovers pretty well, had had quite a few of them until Leslie had moved in.

He had a draft plan for a counterterrorist investigation of the *Jefferson* on his desk, plus a case of probable domestic abuse in a Marine family at the embassy, plus three thefts, a racial incident, and a homosexual allegation on Navy ships in his area. The homosexual allegation made him groan aloud. "We're wasting our resources on bullshit!" he growled.

Leslie was cleaning up the files she'd been working on with Greenbaum, who had already gone. She smiled at him. "A wise old man named Mike Dukas once told me that nothing NCIS did was unimportant."

"He was an idiot." He looked at her. "I was trying to teach you an ethic."

"Well, you did."

"Where the hell's Greenbaum, that you're doing his work?"

"He said he was interviewing somebody's wife."

"Oh, Christ." Dukas was annoyed all over again, now because Greenbaum had escaped him. "I'm going to bounce that sonofabitch right out of this office."

"He's all you got."

Dukas opened his mouth and looked at her, eyes big. He closed his mouth. "Go home," he said.

"You coming?"

"Later."

"You going to be home for dinner? I thought I'd make pizza." When she said this, she didn't mean she'd hump in a pizza from Domino's; she meant she had the dough already made and in the fridge, ready for a final rise, and she'd make sauce and put on fresh mushrooms from India and fresh tomatoes from Palestine and fresh cheese from Italy and a lot of other good stuff, exactly as he had taught her.

"I can't make any promises, babe."

"Well, I'll put it all together; I can throw it in the oven when I hear you. Okay?"

"Yeah, yeah." He was already reading the report.

"I got Ripley on the Trincomalee flight."

"Ripley?" He was trying to read.

"*Alien?* God, Michael, haven't you seen *anything*?"

"You talking about Totten—Brevard, to you?"

"And her house nerd. Twenty-hundred takeoff."

"You didn't like her." His head went down over the page again, then came up. "She's a type you see in the Agency— maybe you don't like her, but my guess is she's great in the field. Here in the office, not so good." He bent his head over his reading again.

Minutes later, she said, "Goodnight, Michael."

"Yeah."

Dukas read on, editing as he went—it was his own writing, not too bad but always full of typos. He heard a noise and looked up and was surprised to see Rattner, not Leslie, and only then did he realize that of course Leslie had left.

"Hey, Rattner."

Rattner put his hand on his heart, said, "The Great Rattner has arrived."

"What're you doing here, anyway?"

"Wanted to throw some crap into a file." Rattner crossed his arms. "What's new on the *Jeff*?"

"Only able to make five knots. How you doing with the leaker?"

Rattner shrugged. "I'm checking the list from Fifth Fleet, but shit—"

"A woman arrived here today from a certain agency we both know and love; she told me that the White House and NSC knew something about the Navy before the official word ever left Fifth Fleet. Before *her* place knew about it. That grab you?"

"No shit! Where is she?"

"Headed for Trincomalee."

"Aw, fuck—if I knew the times—"

"I got the times." Dukas took a slip of paper from the bottom of the pile and pushed it across the desk. "I made her write it down before she left. Don't tell me I never did anything for you."

"I could use another guy. How about Greenbaum?" Before Dukas could object, he said, "Give him a chance, Mike." He hadn't called Dukas by his first name before.

"You gonna do the filing?"

"There's that nice girl. Let her do it."

"That nice girl lives with me, as you well know. If Washington knew she was here as a favor to me, they'd shit bricks—as you well know also—so I'd *like* for her not to work here." He sighed. "Okay, maybe I'll bring her in one more day." He didn't really care about what Washington would do. What he cared about was not building a debt of gratitude to Leslie—along with everything else.

Near Ambur

"This our turn?" Djalik asked, slowing for a paved road.

"Stop." Harry had his door open before the vehicle came to a halt. He got out on the road and reached into his

207

rucksack for a pair of binoculars. Alan slid over to his side and started comparing the ground around them to the elevations on the map.

Alan could see that Harry was making Fidel restless by standing in the road.

"If we're going to stop for more than ten seconds, we should check out the scrub," Fidel said, his hand on the door release.

Djalik just nodded.

"Hey, man, it's your ass, too."

Djalik nodded again.

Harry was looking up the paved road toward the high ridge. "I think I can see buildings all the way up the valley—concrete, like big apartment houses."

Alan nodded, looking at the map. "Should be four klicks south of here. The hills look right. Can you see the switchbacks in the road?"

Harry grunted. "Want a look?"

"I have two eyes," Alan said gruffly.

Harry gave him a smile as he handed over the binoculars, and said, "Don't linger, bud. We have got to move."

Alan took them, heavy, expensive Steiners, and tried to follow the road up the gradual ascent. He could see where the road vanished between two hills, and he could see some sharp angles way off in the haze of the day that might be buildings.

He hung the binocs around his neck and climbed up on the car, moving carefully to avoid putting the weight of his body on his left hand where he was missing fingers. *Quite a collection of cripples*, he thought. Once he was up, he panned around, moving his feet so as not to lose his balance while he looked at the horizon. To the east, the fighting was obvious with magnification; the line of shell bursts had moved past the road on which they had come up. To the north, he could see a town.

He saw a glint of metal. No. Glass. The information percolated through his brain, and then he realized that he was seeing the reflection of another pair of binoculars. *Or a scope*, he thought. He tried to look uninterested and continued sweeping. Without taking the binoculars off his eyes, he said, "There's a guy with optics watching us from that place where the road goes between two hills."

"Come down," Harry said. He gave Alan a hand. Harry was fidgeting, anxious, and Alan noted that Harry looked at his watch every few seconds.

Djalik was watching the ridge. "Give me a look?" he asked, and Alan handed him the Steiners. He could hear Fidel moving cautiously through the brush to the north of the car.

Djalik crossed the road, the binocs hung around his neck, and climbed a tree as if he was climbing a ladder one-handed, and in a minute he was straddling a limb and peering up the ridge.

"Another checkpoint?" Alan asked.

"Probably. I'm looking forward to telling the dynamic duo that we're going up anyway," Harry said. "We have got to get going, Al. *Now!*"

Alan turned to see Fidel trotting back from the road they'd come on, his shotgun at the low ready. Alan said, "Ever hear a woman say that her husband was a great companion as long as there weren't other men around?"

"My first wife used to say it about me." Harry gave a grim smile.

"Yeah. I think it's truer of SEALs. Alone, they can be quite nice."

Fidel came back. "Been traffic through here today. Tracks, people on foot in the brush, cigarette butts, some shit. Not in a few hours."

Djalik came back, too. "I think there's a vehicle up there, and men. Maybe two groups, one at the checkpoint and one farther up the ridge. Been some fighting, too; I can see bodies way up the road and some new earth just turned, like a bunch of shells hit."

Fidel nodded at Djalik with an I-told-you-so air. "We go up there, we're driving right back into the war. Somewhere up there, someone is going to have a whack at us. Capisce?" He took a breath. "I know that we're chasing nukes, and I know you two cowboys are going. So I want to tell you what we're going to do. When the first shot is fired, Commander Craik and me are going to bail out the left-hand side of the car. Mister O'Neill and Djalik will bail from the right. We'll move and fire in support of each other, remaining in communication. I think you guys should get water and ammo and put them in your bags now, because if we get shot at, it's just a matter of time before they blow the vehicle. Right?" He looked around, his eyes accusing. "One shot from that fifty cal at the last block would have brewed this tin can up. One grenade. One RPG. And then we're all dead, because we have no backup vehicle, no helo, no medevac. Nada. Okay?"

Alan put a hand on Harry's shoulder, primed for Harry to explode, but Harry didn't. He looked back at Alan, then at Djalik, who nodded. "Okay, Chief," Harry said. "No point in ignoring the experts."

Alan said quietly, "This had better be worth it."

"Amen, brother," Harry said.

Djalik put the Land Rover in gear and turned on the pavement. "Here we go," he said.

Trincomalee

Evan Soleck walked around his plane with extra attention, running his hands over the control surfaces, getting his nose down next to the landing gear struts where hydraulic fluid could leak, personally checking the chaff/flare load out under the belly of the plane, even though the check cost him some skin off his hands. They had so few maintenance personnel that he wanted to check *everything*. And he was flying in harm's way, with a crew of strangers flown out from Bahrain, aircrew who had been on the staff of Fifth Fleet in jobs from intel to targets to ASW.

He climbed up into the plane and started the auxiliaries, got the air-conditioning going, and began leafing through his kneeboard cards, already a day out of date. He was just sorting the useful ones from those already knocked to hell by the fire on the *Jeff* when a flight helmet emerged from the back end.

"Hi!" The woman wearing the helmet looked clean and eager. "I'm Nelly Garcia."

The natural consequence of putting Guppy on the flight sched as a lead pilot: a new copilot. Soleck noted that she was wearing the new, slick gray helmet usually issued to fighter jocks, and that she had a Palm Pilot thrust into her flight suit where most guys carried a kneeboard. She looked vaguely Hispanic and was attractive, even in an ejection harness.

"Evan Soleck." He reached out, shook hands. "Glad to have you aboard. Know what we're doing tonight, Nelly?"

"Giving gas to the CAP. That's what the flight sched at the hotel says, anyway."

Soleck had his copy of the schedule out, noted that Garcia was his copilot, not the TACCO. "Yes and no. We're going to carry a full load of gas, but we're going to go up high once we've given it and try to get a radar duct that will get us a look at the Indians up north of the BG."

She gave him a big grin that showed a lot of even, white teeth. "Cool," she said. "This going to get me some green ink?" Green ink in your flight log meant combat time.

Soleck gave her a thumbs-up.

She pulled at her seatback, checked the spreader pin, and then sat, her Palm Pilot already in her hand. "I've got freqs for the BG on this. And I did a little diagram to show the missile engagement zone and the fighter engagement zone around the *Jefferson*. I can input it straight to the computer once we have the back end up and the ship in the link."

"You supposed to put classified on that thing?" Soleck asked, feeling pompous and ungenerous. He was impressed as hell. Computer nerd was his middle name and it had never occurred to him to make downloadable sub-routines to support the ancient software in the plane.

She gave him a grin, wrinkled her nose. "You gonna tell on me?"

Fifteen minutes later, they were airborne for six hours of flying and giving gas over the BG, and then another hour of what Soleck hoped would be an uneventful look for what was left of the Indian battle group.

19

Near Ambur

The sound of shots, loud and close, and Fidel yelled "Out!" and they were on the road, Alan clutching his bag and the carbine. He rolled off the tarmac, fell in a heap through a mass of vegetation and landed on his back in water. The landing stunned him, and he wrenched his back, but he was conscious that there had been shots hitting the road around him, and he was aware that Fidel had bailed on the same side.

The water was only a few inches deep, muddy, running over sand and dirt, and he sat up, grabbed a branch and pulled himself to a crouch, his back screaming all the way. A few feet above him, he could see clipped bamboo shoots coming down where bullets were passing through the brush. The sound of fire was continuous. His adrenaline peaked again, his back was forgotten, and he was moving up the streambed, "Chief Fidelio!" he shouted.

"Here!" Fidel answered, almost directly above him. Fidel was crouched over his shotgun, firing carefully. He crouched down in a ball to get his head below the level of the gully. "Ambush." He had an I-told-you-so look to him. "Wrong weapon for this," he said.

Alan crawled up next to him and raised his head cautiously. A burst of firing flung up gravel on the road, a long line of tracer burned from in front of them, and then a flash of fire across the front at a different angle left streaks on the inside of Alan's eyelids as he ducked unconsciously and missed the Land Rover blowing up. The hood landed in the brush just to his right.

"RPG," Fidel said. He fired, the sound of the shotgun lower and louder than the rifles and machine pistols.

"How many?" Alan asked.

"No more than five guys. Lucky we weren't in that thing." He sounded pleased with himself.

"I'm going to follow the gully up. See if I can work around them." Alan felt his back twinge again and cursed to himself.

Fidel crouched again. "Gutsy. There's a guy on our side with a rifle. The other bad guys are across the road. Can you manage that carbine?" Ignoring any response, Fidel wrapped the weapon's sling around Alan's mutilated left hand. "Better than nothing."

"Thanks."

He let himself slide back down the wall of the gully into the red-brown water. With a little difficulty, he got the sling under his elbow and found that, despite his missing fingers, he could keep it steady now. He cocked it, embarrassed that he hadn't before, leaving the safety off. Then he started moving carefully, his head up. The water and the constant firing overhead muffled any noise he made. He had time to wonder if he had done the right thing bringing them all here, time to feel his back and his age, and then there was more firing, a sustained burst not very far ahead and above him, and he was focused on the moment.

Silence. All the firing stopped abruptly and he hesitated, crouched behind a bush that hung over the stream. He waited, ears straining to hear anything over the gentle, deceptive mumble of the water.

Boom! Fidel's shotgun. He moved again, his confidence in the cover of his approach ruined, his carbine following every sound he thought he heard. A pile of rocks from the grading of the road made a bend in the embankment to his right and he eyed them warily, his eyes and the muzzle of his weapon scanning them while his brain screamed for him to look off to the left. He flicked his gaze there, his muzzle trailing his sight line and he saw movement, something khaki, a face with heavy black eyebrows just registering surprise and his muzzle came up, sight picture and the other man fired first, *bang-bang-bang* and Alan kept his focus on the sight picture, squeezed the trigger—*bang-bang*—deafening him, and the man was down, hit with both shots, and Alan was moving, conscious that his back burned an entirely new way, right across the shoulder blades. And then he was looking down at the man, who was clearly dead. One shot in the center of mass and another through the base of the skull, a shocking sight. Alan knelt, opened the man's shirt, found the golden key he had expected, felt relief and a wave of nausea, then anger.

Two short, high-pitched bursts of fire from the road. Alan was on the wrong side of the ditch now and almost out of the gully, aware that the other man had been hunting him the same way he had been hunting, both seeking to outflank the other. He ran along the shoulder of the gully for a low mound of gravel, conscious that he was running in the open. Someone fired, and gravel hit his face and hands. He sighted down the carbine, saw three of them crouched, two changing clips, the third aiming at him, and he fired, hitting nothing but forcing all three to scramble for cover. The shotgun roared, there was a burst of fire, and they were down in a thrashing of arms and legs.

Screams, a single shot.

Silence. Or rather, the absence of the level of sound that the firefight had produced, so that Alan could hear the remnants of their car burning on the road and the sound of Fidel moving in the gully. Alan looked down from his gravel mound carefully and got a thumbs-up from his chief. He rolled back and the pain took his breath away. When his vision cleared, he saw Djalik crouched over the body and Harry using the far side of the berm for cover, now carrying an Indian Army AK-74. Fidel was looking up at him from the base of the gravel pile.

"You okay, sir?" he asked. He sounded concerned.

"I wrenched my back." Alan sat up a little, carefully, the pain already less. Fidel crunched up the gravel pile and shook his head.

"That's no wrench. You got a graze, a deep one, right across your shoulders. Lie still, let me dress it. Fuck, looks like a trench. Lucky it didn't clip your spine."

He sprayed Alan's back with a can from his rucksack.

"You got the wound full of dirt, sir." Fidel chided him. "Clean enough now. I put some gunk on it. Can you move?"

"Yeah." *I got up here, didn't I?* he thought, but as his adrenaline left him, he felt weak, almost in shock. The sight of blood under him scared him. He wondered about shock, felt his vision tunnel.

"Hey, stick with us, skipper." Fidel sounded happier than he had in two days. Alan could hear Harry talking, heard him say something about getting on. "Can he be moved?" he heard distinctly.

"Give me a minute," he called down. His breath was returning, and his vision cleared suddenly, as if it had been turned back on.

"Welcome back," Fidel said. His pinched face sharpened as Alan's focus returned.

Harry appeared beside him. "Djalik's watching the road. He thinks he saw a reaction at the checkpoint; this was probably their ambush." He looked south, up the ridge, shading his good eye, and then crouched down. "I think we're screwed, Alan. The four of us couldn't fight our way up this ridge even if you were in perfect shape."

"You want to go back?"

"It's going to take all evening just to walk back to the plane."

They looked at each other, each seeing the same thing: fatigue, unaccustomed defeat. Alan flexed his shoulders, painful even through the numbness but serviceable.

"How sure are you we can get to your guy through this village?"

Harry shook his head. "It was a long shot, at best," he said. Then, bitterly, "I hate to give up."

Alan looked over at Fidel, but his gaze was concentrated on the ground to his left.

"Want to try—" Alan began, but his words were drowned in a burst of fire, first from Djalik and then a heavier reply.

"Moving in the bamboo," Fidel said, lying full-length on the gravel next to Alan. "Not close. Can I have that rifle, Mister O'Neill?"

"Harry," Harry said, passing the gun. Fidel moved the rifle's muzzle over the lip of the gravel and worked it back and forth, seating it firmly in the stones. He fired a single shot, put his hand up to the sight, did something, and fired again. There was return fire, so inaccurate it didn't even throw up more gravel. Fidel grunted in satisfaction, changed his body position, and fired. This time, there was a cry well up the ridge, and a burst of return fire that was more accurate but showed Alan the enemy. He aimed at the area, watched it until his sighting eye began to twitch and his maimed hand burned from the pressure of the sling and let out the breath he was unconsciously holding. Something moved and he fired, realizing after he pulled the trigger that he hadn't really aimed.

Fidel fired again. "Got him," he said.

Djalik fired from across the road.

"How much ammo do we have?" Alan asked Harry.

"Not enough to take on a fucking company of infantry," Fidel said cheerfully.

"I think it's time to go," Harry said. "Best I can think of, we go downstream along the road until the first hairpin, and then climb down to the main road. We'll be in dead ground by then."

Fidel fired again. "Cocksucker. Do that weak-ass shit again," he mumbled to himself and then fired, grunted with satisfaction.

Alan fired carefully at movement in the bamboo.

Silence. At Alan's side, Fidel moved his sight picture fractionally. "They moved back," he whispered.

Alan looked at Harry. Harry was doing something to his rifle; across the road, Djalik was motionless on the berm.

There was a volley of fire way off to the right and higher on the ridge. Alan looked that way, saw movement, lots of it.

Harry saw him looking, came up to his vantage point and handed him the binoculars. Alan brought them up, lost his target, found it. Men in shorts, little men, darker camo. They were firing at something higher on the ridge, almost directly above Alan and half a kilometer away, people Alan couldn't see. He saw the dark camo men begin to unfold into a loose line moving across the hillside, firing as they moved, section rushes supporting each other. They had at least one light machine gun, and it began firing steady bursts.

"I think they're Gurkhas," he said, his voicing rising with excitement.

"Really?" Harry gave a short, sharp bark of laughter. In a fake-Brit accent, he said, "I say, old boy, it's like the end of *Gunga Din*." He added, "The movie, not the poem." And then, later, "I've always wanted to be rescued by Gurkhas."

Alan handed him the binoculars. Harry looked. "Well, they're Gurkhas. I see them often enough in Bahrain. Sure they're on our side?"

"I don't think they'd be susceptible to the Servants. But what really counts is that they're shooting up the checkpoint above us."

Harry gave a nod.

Alan slid down the gravel and shouted across the road. "Djalik?"

"Roger!"

"See the movement up to the right? Two o'clock?"

"Got it."

"We think they're friendly. What's out there?"

"Nothing. I think they pulled out five minutes ago."

"You okay?"

"Oh, this is great. I—" Djalik's further sarcasm was lost as he fired straight up the road.

Harry grabbed Alan's shoulder, making him wince. "Those Gurkhas are pushing the bad guys right down our throats."

Fidel flicked his head to the right, took in Djalik's fire and the return fire from the road. He got back down behind the sights of his rifle. "Djalik's kinda lonely down there," he said.

Alan gathered his bag under him and rose to a crouch. "I'll go."

"Get some, skipper," Fidel mumbled, and fired.

Alan heard Harry fire the shotgun and he dropped down into the gully, powered up the far side and threw himself down at the top, his carbine pointing up the road. He saw movement, camo, heavy moustaches, and he fired, fired again, and then he was changing clips, searching the bag for another, jamming it in the receiver and forcing himself to get his head up over the edge and not stay in the relative safety of the fetal position. Muzzle steady, firing. Shots from Djalik, a shout from Harry, shots from up the road. Load. Cock. On target. His world was a cone of movement and fire in front of his sights; he was aware that his carbine was too hot to touch and he had just one mag left, and then he was firing again.

Fifth Fleet HQ, Bahrain

"Spill it, Shelley. You're ruining what's left of my digestion, standing there." Pilchard wiped his mouth with a napkin. He was eating at his desk, a desk he hadn't left in twelve hours.

His flag captain had two message sheets in her hand and her expression wasn't happy. "I have a protest from Captain Lash on the *Fort Klock*, saying that he didn't request an overflight of the Indian units and feels that he's being manipulated. It's strongly worded, sir. And I have a message from Madje, that's Rafehausen's flag lieutenant, saying that Rafehausen requested the flight personally and signed off on the message. This is serious shit, sir."

"Thanks, Shelley. Leave 'em for me." Pilchard took a bite out of his pizza.

"That recce flight may already be airborne." Captain Lurgwitz was fidgeting with her clipboard. "You want it recalled?"

"Nope." Pilchard chewed for a moment, reading Lash's message. "Fuck him. Rafe's worth ten of him. Thanks, Shelley."

She paused in the doorway. "If Rafehausen's injured—" she began, but Pilchard just waved. He put a note on a big legal pad. "When I've got a second I want to send Hawkins on the *Jefferson* a P-4. Don't let me forget, okay?"

"Roger that, sir."

"Thanks, Shelley," he said again, and she was dismissed.

Near Ambur

Alan had no targets. Nothing moved on the road, and he could hear nothing in the brush except the thrashing of a badly wounded man and a rustle in some deep grass off to his left where another was crawling away. Alan rolled on his side, reached in his bag and pulled out his water bottle. He noted that his pistol was lying on the embankment beside him, ready for use; he couldn't remember drawing it. He ejected the magazine from his carbine and checked it—four rounds left.

Fidelio was climbing down the gully wall behind him. Alan turned back to the road and heard a burst of gunfire and a shout, another shout, a single cry repeated from several positions. He motioned behind him with his right hand, hoping Fidel could see him—*get down*. Four rounds.

Right in front of him, just twenty yards away, two hands appeared, and then a head. The man was facing the other way, kneeling with his hands up.

Fidel appeared silently, inching his way into position next to Alan. Alan pointed at the kneeling man. Now there was another, just visible farther down the road.

"What the fuck?" Fidel whispered, bringing his rifle to bear on the road.

"How's Harry?"

"He's solid. Nothing up there. I thought you might be dry— came to help."

"Thanks."

Someone to the north of their position yelled a long phrase, words well spaced out and distinct. One of the men kneeling in the brush answered, his voice shrill, nervous, and afraid.

"The Gurkhas?" Alan whispered.

"Like that," Fidel said, ambiguously.

"Cover me," Alan said.

"Hey, what the fuck, Commander!" Fidel barked as Alan clambered to his feet. His back really was bad.

"Anyone over there speak English?" Alan called. He was standing at the edge of the road, still partially covered by a stunted pine tree and some brush.

"Miracle you've lived this long," Fidel muttered. He actually had a hand on Alan's ankle, as if to pull him down.

One of the men with his hands in the air turned to glance at Alan. At the same time, two soldiers in darker uniforms

221

emerged from the scrub farther to the north, their rifles aimed at the high carry, swinging back and forth, and began to move slowly toward him. Behind them, boyish voices called, and Alan heard a whistle in the distance, and the sound of a vehicle. One of the dark-clad figures called something and beckoned, his partner still watching over the sights of his rifle. The men with their hands in the air got to their feet and moved to the road.

Bang.

One of the surrendering men fell clutching his guts, his feet beating rhythmically on the tarmac. The other threw himself flat. Both of the dark-clad men went prone and fired. Something clipped the tree next to Alan, and he felt and heard a *vzzt* just under his nose. Fidel pulled his feet from under him and he went down face-first on to the dirt. He scrambled, crawling backward faster than he would have thought possible, his back pulsing, until his feet went over the edge of the gully.

Alan recovered his carbine, rewound the sling on his left arm, and prepared to fire his last rounds.

"That was smooth, Commander."

Alan thought of replies—angry, sarcastic, apologetic—and bit them back, stared over his rifle in silence. He heard the vehicle again, moving, changing gears. Well off to Alan's front, screened by the brush on the far side of the road, a man moved through the brush, and Djalik fired, paused, fired again, and the noise stopped, became thrashing, and gradually stilled.

The only sound became that of the wind in the bamboo and the grass, the chuckle of the stream at their feet, and the distant noise of the vehicle. He waited, sweating, trying to ignore the pain in his back and his hand, and the fatigue that felt like the onset of old age.

He looked at his watch. The second hand was still moving, so it was running, but it said that less than fifteen minutes had passed since the start of the shooting. That didn't seem possible.

"I see a car," Harry called down.

Alan lifted his head. "Djalik?"

"Roger!"

"Report?"

"Nothing moving over here, sir."

Chief Fidelio nudged Alan. "Bastard shot his own buddy for trying to surrender. Djalik wasted him."

"Yeah. Can I have your permission to try standing again?"

"I'd wait for those little guys." Fidelio jutted his jaw expressively down the road, where the two prone Gurkhas had risen to a crouch and were preparing to move forward again. Behind them, others moved, only their hats visible above the grass. The whistle sounded again, and the two moved briskly down the road, now obviously covered by their friends. As they reached the man who had been shot, both crouched; one searched the body while the other aimed his rifle to the east.

A Land Rover Defender crested the rise in the road and halted in line with the helmets in the grass. Two men started forward, clearly officers, one wearing riding boots. The helmets in the grass rose to become distant faces, shoulders, visible rifles, a whole line of them, and they began to move forward. One of the officers asked something in an interrogative shout; one of the Gurkhas on the road pointed toward where Alan was lying.

Alan squinted at Fidel, who managed to give the impression of a shrug without moving the muzzle of his rifle by a hair, and got to his feet.

"We're friends," Alan called.

One of the pair by the corpse acknowledged him, pointed north toward the advancing officers. Both Gurkhas moved into the tall grass on the other side of the road, working toward the prone figure. Alan could see Djalik now that he was on his feet, and Djalik was aiming at something with intense concentration.

After a hesitation, the Gurkhas vanished behind the clump of brush where Djalik had fired. By the time the officers came even with them, they were leading the wounded prisoner out of the grass. One of the officers stopped. The other came on fearlessly.

"Hello!" Alan called.

"Good day," the booted figure replied, still coming forward, tall, upright. He didn't stop until he was extending his hand to be shaken. "Major Rao, Indian Army. Anyone hurt?"

"Commander Alan Craik, United States Navy," Alan replied automatically, clasping the offered hand. "I won't know until I see the rest of my men."

"Spot of trouble?" Rao said. He had a heavy black moustache and tanned skin over eyes so dark they might have been black, and his smile was grim. He had dust all over a very smart uniform, and, up close, Alan could smell his sweat and see that the holster of his pistol on its shining Sam Browne belt was unlatched and ready for use, the magazine pouch empty.

Dignity required Alan to keep his shoulders just as square, meet the dark eyes, and smile back, although his immediate desire was to sit in the road and slump, or maybe simply sleep. "Nothing we couldn't handle," he said, trying to match the tone of "spot of trouble." But that seemed ungracious, inaccurate as well, and he added quickly, "We are grateful for your help."

The dark eyes were studying him carefully, perhaps too carefully. Alan shifted under their regard. He had to resist the urge to step away. But suddenly the major smiled, his whole face lighting up. "Ahh. You are the man in the picture."

"What picture?"

"I'll show you. Do you want to gather your men?" Rao looked past Alan, saw Chief Fidelio for the first time only a yard away with his rifle pointed full at the major's chest, and gave a slight start that made him seem more human. He stepped back, nodded at Fidel, and looked at Alan. "I fancy we're on the same side."

Alan watched the Gurkhas with the prisoner; saw them dragging bodies out to the road. Djalik was still watching them.

"I think we can at least say we have the same enemies, Major. Show me this picture, and I'll call the rest of my men."

Major Rao took a laptop from the back of the jeep. When he switched it on, the Windows start screen was immediately replaced by the Servants of the Earth animation.

"I found this when we took their checkpoint up the road," he said, pointing north. Then he moved his finger around the pad, clicked, and held the open screen toward Alan—it displayed a crisp photograph of Alan Craik with "Kill on sight" in English and a writing that Alan couldn't decipher.

"It says 'shoot on sight,'" Rao said at his shoulder. "In Urdu and Hindi."

"I've seen it before."

"Any idea why they want you, Commander?"

"Yes."

Rao studied him, and then nodded. "And it's not my business. Very well. Want to tell me why you're here? I'd be willing to help, up to a point."

"We were headed south, to the housing complex up the valley."

Rao lit a small cigar, took a drag, and then looked at Alan. "Hmm?" he said.

Alan didn't want to play games, and answering questions wasn't going to get him anywhere. "Mohir," he said.

"I can get you there," Rao said. He took another drag on his cigar, looked at Alan again. "Very well, Commander. We'll go together." His attention drifted away at the sound of a choked scream over Alan's shoulder.

Alan turned to see that all of the dead had been gathered on the road. Thirteen corpses were lying neatly in a row, already covered in flies. Two short corporals were beating a wounded prisoner.

"I don't like that, Major," Alan said as he walked up to the jeep. He pointed at the beating.

Behind him, Rao spoke to one of the Gurkhas. Their officer came up at a trot.

"We could take that prisoner off your hands, Lieutenant." Rao was clearly speaking English for Alan's benefit.

"Of course, Major. I should have known you'd want him."

"Can you spare me a vehicle and two guards for him?"

The lieutenant looked pained, but he nodded. "Yes, sir." Then he turned to Alan. "You held them with just four men, sir? That must have been wonderful."

Alan nodded, his mind already on other things. *Wonderful.*

Harry and Djalik tossed their guns into the back of Rao's vehicle. Fidelio waved at one of the Gurkhas, who waved back.

Harry climbed into the back, grabbed Alan's arm. "Bud?" His eyes flicked over to Rao and back. He raised his eyebrows.

Alan shrugged. "Only game in town," he said.

Harry nodded. "If we make it to Mohir—"

Alan nodded, his hand on the door of the Land Rover's cab. "Yeah?"

"Keep the good major busy. Okay?"

Alan smiled and climbed into the front. Rao fumbled with the clutch before starting the engine. Under the cover of the first roar, he said, "I might have forgotten the prisoner, Commander."

"Call me Alan."

Harry leaned forward over the seat and shouted over the engine, pointed. "Mohir. Those concrete buildings just up the ridge."

Rao nodded and smiled a knowing smile. "Exactly."

Then they were rocketing along the tarmac, the grass a blur, headed for the village.

It wasn't so much a village as a massive prefab housing complex surrounded by a more traditional, if poorer, set of huts made from packing crates and the refuse of the building project. The prefab housing was neat, clean, and twenty storeys high, and every balcony had plants in profusion, with flowers growing off the roof and around the sheer concrete walls on either side. Four of the towers stood around a central square, contrasting with the squalor of the market in the middle and the rows of huts on either side.

Rao drove them up the main road, past a modern petrol station and two restaurants and a seemingly endless row of plywood tea shops and into the square. Carpet-roofed booths ran in disorderly lines around the square and across it, with kitchen wares, chickens, baby clothes and detergent, spices, electronics: anything that the householders in the high-rises might need. In the center stood a tea shop with a flowered trellis and some pretensions to gentility.

Many of the stalls were empty. There were no children and few women. Men stood in clumps, and every eye in the market watched their arrival.

Rao pulled up opposite the first concrete building. "Police station on the first floor," he said.

Two bodies wrapped in PVC tarps lay on the sidewalk outside, guarded by a constable in a chair with an old FN rifle across his lap. The crowd flowing around the stalls didn't afford them any space at all; a little girl hopped over one of the corpses as Alan watched. The constable didn't trouble to shoo the little girl away.

As Rao approached him, he stood to attention. They exchanged greetings, the formalities of rank and service. Alan stayed in the car, glanced back to see that Harry had stepped down, walked back, and was talking to Djalik through the window of the other vehicle.

"You're worryin' too much, skipper," Fidel said. "If these guys wanted us dead, we'd be dead. And Gurkhas—they're special. Like Special Ops special. Not the kind to take part in a mutiny."

Alan grunted. He was suffering post-combat depression; mostly, he wanted to sleep.

Rao came back to the jeep. "They had an attack this morning. The head constable shot one man and the terrorists shot a bystander. They have another prisoner, caught attempting to destroy a water tower."

Alan nodded. "Can we interview him?"

"Commander, could you give me some idea of why you and three other Americans are so interested in this?"

Alan sighed. "I thought we'd get to that eventually." He turned so that his back was as comfortable as possible and so that he had the powerful sun behind him and in Rao's eyes. "I'm an intelligence officer."

Rao pursed his lips. Later, Alan wondered if he had almost laughed. "Yes?"

"I was involved in a joint exercise with the Indian Army and Navy—"

"Lord of Light. I know it."

"—when a mutiny, a coup, call it what you will, broke out. One of my people was killed. I got in touch with my admiral, who asked me to find out why the lights had gone out and what was happening."

Rao nodded as if this were the most natural thing in the world. "And your friend? The black man?" Rao looked around suddenly, stiffened. "Where is he?"

Alan didn't need to turn his head to know that Harry had wandered off. "I think he went for tea. And to get me a clean pair of shorts." Alan pointed at the wreckage of Harry's spare shorts, which were filthy and still too big. Rao made him feel underdressed.

"It looks like a good market," Rao ventured. "When it's open. These people are frightened."

Alan nodded. "So can we see talk to the prisoner? And maybe the one your guys picked up?"

Rao shrugged. "Of course."

Harry worked his way through the market, with Djalik, obviously armed, a few paces behind him. The two of them created a zone of increased tension wherever they went. When Harry stopped at a stall, he was inevitably the only customer. When he moved along the market, other customers fled like shoals of frightened minnows. Short of wearing a sign, he couldn't have been more conspicuous.

He bought things mechanically: a canteen, some clothes for Alan, a candy bar. He was trying to cover his presence in the market and it seemed like a waste of time because there was *nothing* two armed foreigners could do to look safe and natural in the surroundings.

He abandoned the attempt and made for the tea shop, framing a prayer. His prayer was answered before he had it fully in his mind: a big man in a dirty coverall sitting under the single fan with a book open. He had a broad face and narrow-set eyes and a permanent scowl. *Lottery Ticket*. His exhaustion showed in deep pouches under his eyes.

Persian Rug had a number of sub-assets. One was Lottery Ticket, a middle-aged industrial electrician who specialized in the installation of security systems. He was employed at Ambur and had filed good reports, albeit for large payments, and Harry had activated his meeting sequence that morning with his cell phone. When he saw the big man, his fatigue vanished. *Yes.*

Harry was in a hurry and he didn't have time to waste on the endless safety formulas of espionage.

"You made it," the big man said. He looked around, shifted, looked around again. "I—uh—we—"

"No time," Harry said crisply. "Next meeting will be on the same system."

Djalik sat down in the doorway, his rifle obvious. In effect, he closed the tea shop.

"Do you have something for me?" Harry asked.

The big man put a cheap plastic shopping bag on the stained Formica table.

"I have a great deal for you. Here are some photographs. This is a video on a disk you can play on this camera."

"We have to hurry, I must be blunt. How did you get this?"

"I am the contractor for the whole facility, yes? I can go anywhere. I downloaded the feed from the security cameras after I received your call."

"You have been to the plant this morning?"

"I did the download remotely." The man's nerves were briefly replaced by smugness. "I installed the system. I left a back door?"

"How much?"

"Five thousand dollars."

Harry took off his belt, opened it, and placed on the table five thousand dollars in one hundred dollar bills. It wasn't the time to be careful with money.

"Listen, there's more. I can see on the feed that someone else took over the cameras during the attack. They went off, and then came back on focused on different targets. It was as if—" The agent paused, looking at Harry for some reaction, fearing he wouldn't be believed.

"Yes?"

"As if someone else could run all the computers on the site. You'll see it too; just after the attack starts, lights go out all over the facility. Pumps run, or stop, almost at random."

"Is that in a report?"

"No." The big man put the money in his pocket with a

glance at the tea-shop waiter, who was busy serving Djalik.

"Who were the attackers?" Harry extracted the first disk and the digital camera from the shopping bag.

The big man shook his head.

"Were you on site when the attacks began?"

"Yes."

"Think. Can you tell me anything else? What did they target first?"

"It's on the feed. First they hit security stations, then the turbines and an old storage bunker."

"What storage bunker?" Harry snapped.

"The Building Thirty-seven complex," the big man said.

Harry covered his alarm by looking at the controls on the camera. There were dozens of streams of video, more than he could run in the time he was allowing himself. He had almost lost his breath when the agent mentioned Building Thirty-seven. *Building Thirty-seven*, he thought. *Potential nuclear weapons storage.*

The agent shook his head. "I don't know who they were. No idea. Never saw them myself; as soon as the shooting began, I ran. By midnight, there were Indian Army units all over the facility, fighting other units outside. No one wanted to deal with the workers, so I just joined them and we all walked through the lines. It was chaotic. Indeed, it is still chaotic."

"Is Building Thirty-seven on the feed?"

"Of course," the big man said. He pointed at the video camera. "Do I have the contract for that building? No. But twice last year you ask me about it, yes? So I placed a new camera on Building Forty-four that covers the entrance, yes? And just happens to show the entire Thirty-seven complex, as well."

Harry nodded, smiled. Lottery Ticket was venal, even mercenary, but he knew his stuff.

"They took something out of that building; it's on the feed." The man twitched. "In a helicopter."

Harry's smile froze. Harry forced himself to exhale. "Has anyone ever mentioned what goes on in Building Thirty-seven?"

"Never. But it is all military. I'm no fool." The man made a motion with his hands, a mushroom cloud. "Yes?"

Harry shrugged. "Can't say."

Lottery Ticket shrugged, too tired to argue the point. "You are pleased?"

"Very."

"Bonus?"

Harry reached back into his belt. His hands were shaking.

Alan drank bad coffee from a paper cup, hunched on a stool, unable to understand a word of the interrogation in front of him. The surroundings were oppressive: a dirty basement office that smelled of mold and sweat and human fear, with two filthy cells and an overflowing toilet. His back ached, and the stool ensured that he couldn't make it comfortable. The coffee was thin and bitter, and he was deep in reaction to combat. His body was tired, empty of the surges of adrenaline that sustained him, and his mind refused to leave alone the fragmented images of the fight.

"He will tell us nothing beyond the name of his unit," Rao said. "I can't even make out whether he was a member of the cult or simply obeyed orders." Rao sighed, shook his head. "This is a rotten business."

"What about the other guy?" Alan nodded toward the man captured that morning by the police. "He was trying to blow the water tower, right? He has to be a member."

"He's a local worker, a migrant from the north who cuts cane. He brags that he is a member, but I cannot get out of him who ordered him to attack the tower. He says it was the earth herself, or Shiva, or the like; a senseless mix of Hindu and politics."

The head constable stood by with a tea tray, watching Rao for any sign of approval.

"Is the tea any good? The coffee is awful."

"Try it. Not bad at all. Tea plantations all over the hills, quite close."

"Yeah?" Alan slid off the stool, poured the rest of his coffee into the toilet, and held the cup out to the head constable, who poured him some from a chipped brown pot. Just the smell helped, and Alan took a deep waft before a sip. Better than the coffee, at any rate. The smell of tea cut through the oppressive reek of the cells and the toilet. "Think any of the locals would know anything? Somebody who was at work yesterday and made it home?"

Rao spoke rapidly to the policeman, who put the tray down, saluted, and went up the concrete steps to the market. "Not a bad thought. I was too focused on the prisoners."

The head constable returned, saluted, spoke. Rao heard him out. "Quite a few workers came back last night. They were released by the gate guards and passed through our lines, apparently." He sounded as tired as Alan felt. "If I had only been here."

"Can we interview them?"

"There might be a hundred of them." But Rao was already getting up. "It will get us out of this stinking basement, anyway." He gave orders, a long, steady flow, and took Alan by the elbow as if Alan was old or infirm. "This is a grave matter, Commander. But the boy knows nothing. I think he was obeying orders." Rao looked at him, less assured than a moment before, almost haggard. "To be honest, it frightens me. Civil war, perhaps. I feel so blind."

Fidelio waved a med kit at Alan. "I want to change that dressing and get a look at that wound, sir."

Alan winced. "Okay." He was almost asleep in the sun, and he stretched painfully. On the far side of the car, Rao

233

sat sideways on the driver's seat and questioned a small crowd of power-facility workers.

"Whoa, skipper. Mister O'Neill looks pissed." Fidel leaned forward.

Alan saw Harry in the rear-view mirror and turned his head. Harry looked grim. He had an armload of paper packages wrapped in string, a heavy plastic shopping bag, and Djalik, at his shoulder, had more.

"Got you some clean clothes, bud. You still a thirty-two waist?" Harry was holding the packages out to him. "The bush jacket's great. Look at it."

"Close enough," Alan said, and tossed the clothes on the seat.

"Look at it," Harry said again, with more emphasis.

Alan reached for the largest package. He flipped open his folding knife, cut the string and unfolded the paper. It was a khaki jacket.

"Come on, man! Look at it."

Alan looked at it. It was very well made, with cloth tape sewn in minute hand stitches down every interior seam, and a broad arrow stamped on the inside pocket.

"I need to get my dressing changed."

Harry nodded, already impatient. "We've got to get out of here."

Alan had endured the police office again long enough for Fidel to change the dressing on his wound. When Fidel, with a surprisingly gentle touch, was done, Alan changed into a pair of cheap green shorts, the boots, cotton socks, and a T-shirt, with the bush jacket on top.

Outside, Djalik was wolfing down a plate of biryani from a stall. He waved at two more plates on the hood. The smell stirred Alan's hunger, and he used his fingers to shovel the rice in. Rao was talking to Harry.

"Major's going to run us back to the airfield." Harry smiled at Rao, but the smile was thin.

Alan thought that Harry was as keyed up as he'd ever seen.

Rao excused himself. "I need to piss like a racehorse," he said and headed down into the police office.

Harry scooped the last of his rice with a piece of naan. "He's a spook."

"No shit," Alan said. "I like the jacket."

"He's offered us a place to stay. The bunch of us, even the plane. Thirty miles, over in the hills to the south."

"Wants to keep an eye on us."

"Just so. But I want to keep an eye on him, too."

Harry leaned over and spoke quietly. "I have a lot of stuff we need to go over. A lot. We need a place to stay. Let's do it."

"Get anything?"

"Yeah. I met my guy. He handed over a disk. I won't know, and I won't know what they prove till I can go through it. It's killing me."

Alan smiled for the first time in hours. "Buddy, four hours ago we were all going to die on the road trying to get here."

"Good point." Harry leaned closer to whisper. "My guy says that somebody took the nukes. In a chopper. Says it's on the disk."

Rao came up, looking cleaner. "In two hours, you will be enjoying the best food in Tamil Nadu."

"We will?" Alan asked. His appetite had just deserted him.

Bahrain

Henry, aka Enrique, Valdez, also called Bobby by a few people who had known him in the Navy, was a slightly plump Latino with a build like a fireplug, a ready grin, and a genius for computers. Harry O'Neill had hired him away from another company when he had needed somebody to set up a computer-security wing, with the result that Valdez now made more money than many corporate executives. Now, he was sitting in front of a computer, but he was looking sideways at a woman named Mavis.

"Whaddya think, Mave?" She was on a computer networked to his, and they both had up on the screen some stuff sent them from India by some Navy jg named Ong.

"I think it looks like an all-nighter." Mavis had auburn hair and green eyes and freckles the color of the palest autumn leaves, plus an Irish accent that came and went with her own self-mockery. Being Irish was, for her, a joke. Harry had got Mavis away from the National Security Agency because Valdez was nuts about her and had said he wouldn't come to Bahrain if Mavis didn't come, too.

"Encrypted," Valdez said.

"No shit, Sherlock, what was your first clue?"

The screen was filled with rows of numbers, letters, and symbols. None of it fell together to mean anything.

"Well— I say let's run Edgar on it." Edgar was Valdez's own decryption program, named for the author of *The Gold Bug*.

"Rickie, that's just your ego!" "Rickie" was her corruption of Enrique. "You've got an ego bigger than your ding-dong, man."

"Impossible. Anyway, if I don't run Edgar now, I'll just have to run it later, right?"

"To satisfy your ego, exactly. Okay."

"Tell you what, I'll run Edgar, you run something else."

"Is this a test? Are we having a race here?"

"We're trying to save time, Mave. Harry thinks maybe this'll tell us what's going down in India."

She was punching keys. "Harry in India?"

"You're not supposed to ask that."

"Oh, sweet Christ, you and compartmentalization—!"

"It's all because you're a woman. Women blab."

"Ha-ha. I can always go back to Dublin, you know. Did I tell you I got an offer from one of the German companies?"

They were both booting up decryption programs while they talked. Valdez finished first and sat there, pinching his plump upper lip between thumb and forefinger. "We're not going to crack this in one night. Whoever did this is good."

"We're also good—better than good." She sat on his lap. "What are we going to do about dinner?"

"Anomalies, that's the best we can hope for. Maybe as a way in."

"Anomalies have too many calories. How about we take off for the Tamarind and eat while this shit runs?"

"How about we do that." He put her off his lap and got up. From the door he looked back at his computer screen, which was dark red except for a yellow rectangle in the middle on which, he knew, were the words "Edgar Is Working" and, below them, a bar graph of Edgar's progress in green, on which the thinnest possible slice showed at the far left.

A long night.

South of Chittoor

From the air, the Serene Highness Palace Hotel looked like a pink fantasy rising out of a brown plain, its air of unreality reinforced by the blue of water and a fringe of brilliant green, as if it were an oasis. Behind the big pink building, a swimming pool was a blue-green sliver, and next to it a green one was a tennis court. A few hundred feet away, a single tarmac airstrip ran like a piece of black tape stuck to the flat land.

"No road," Djalik muttered.

"Dirt road," Fidel said. They were sitting together, both trying to see out the same window. "See, behind Disneyland there?"

Indeed, a dirt road curved from the towers at one end of the pink pile around the green trees and then off to the west.

"What kinda classy hotel gets reached by a dirt road?" Djalik growled.

"We're not coming by dirt road." Both looked down as the plane tipped and Moad took them along the airstrip on his way to turning back for an approach. "What kinda hotel is only reachable by air?"

Fidel sat back and snapped his seatbelt together. "We spent more fucking time going up and coming back down than we did getting from point A to point B."

"Yeah, but point B looks kind of interesting."

Moad banked again and turned, banked and turned in a longer arc and then they heard the wheels come down, and the brown landscape was fleeting by under them, marked now by green-brown scrub, a field of just-harvested sugarcane, and a village seemingly made out of the earth it stood on. And then they were down.

20

Over the Indian Ocean

Fourteen thousand feet over the Indian Ocean, six hours after taking off from Trincomalee and lighter by sixteen thousand pounds of fuel, Evan Soleck knew the names of his crew and felt he had lucked out in the lottery of random assignment. He'd never flown with two women in his crew, but in addition to Garcia, he had LTjg Dothan, a nugget TACCO fresh from the RAG in Jacksonville, who had a degree in aeronautical engineering and a mile of enthusiasm. Her lack of experience was balanced by Master Chief AW Simcoe, who had been the work-center supervisor for the ASW shop at Fifth Fleet and had twenty years in S-3s. By the time they'd made their last scheduled tanking run, they had the computer singing along in the back, with Garcia's additions in an overlay and a working datalink with fixes on every ship in the US battle group. Now it was time to have a look at the Indians.

"Okay, folks. I'm going for altitude; I'll try and get up around thirty-two thousand before we turn north. You can start the radar anytime you like. Don't be shy about asking me to maneuver for a duct or whatever. We've got plenty of gas and all the time in the world. Master Chief, have you got AsuW on the *Jefferson*?"

Garcia cut in. "I've got the freq in radio two, ready to rock."

"Want to leave me some work, ma'am?" Simcoe said with a deep chuckle. And after Soleck had climbed another thousand feet, he said, "I got LT Madje, the TAO."

"Just keep him informed as we put stuff in the link. Garcia, put the CAP freq in one. I'd hate to find an Indian fighter up here all alone."

"Roger that." She played with the radio and then gave him a nod.

He cycled his comms to the radio. "Racehorse One, this is Oats, over?"

"Roger Oats. Got you." That was Rose Siciliano, flying CAP. *Small world*, Soleck thought—she was already back from Colombo, hot to trot. "Racehorse One, I'm climbing to Angels 32 for a look around as briefed. Copy?"

"Roger, Oats. I'm going up high to cover you. Racehorse Two will stay low. I'll need to hit you again before I head for the barn, over."

"Roger, Racehorse One. I have three thousand in reserve to give. Out here."

"Racehorse One out."

They continued to climb into the night.

The Serene Highness Palace Hotel

The runway was as black as if it had never been used; near its eastern end, it had a taxiway that led to three parking pads, the most easterly of which put the aircraft's stairs practically in the shade of the ring of trees.

"Wow!" Benvenuto said when he came out of the plane's doorway. "Wow!" For a kid from the edge of the Adirondack State Park, the former palace of His Serene Highness, the Maharajah of Baipurjat, was a lot to take in. Its towers rose four storeys against an evening sky that was itself turning from lavender to cobalt; the towers, caught by the setting sun, were magenta. Lower down, the stone was paler but still pink. Arches and pierced screens and balconies marked its façade, with carvings so intricate they couldn't be taken in from that distance.

"Nice," Harry said as he stepped out, gently shoving Benvenuto along.

Alan, caught by a back spasm, was helped down by Fidel and Djalik and didn't pay much attention.

By the time they were down the steps, an ancient stretch limo had pulled up, behind it an even more ancient Land Rover. Indian servants in white turbans, orange shirts, and red pants piled out until they outnumbered the people from the airplane, and at once luggage began to disappear into the Rover. A tall, bearded man in a uniform that could once have belonged to the dressier formations of the Raj held open the limo door.

"Hey, we can walk," Djalik said, "it's only—" It didn't matter what it was only. They were going to be driven to the hotel door whether they liked it or not.

In fact, it was a hundred and sixty feet away.

"Wow," Benvenuto whispered when they were inside.

The entrance foyer was thirty feet high and at least a hundred feet long; one-storey red pillars surrounded it at ten-foot intervals, creating the effect of a kind of cloister with, in its center, a pool of blue water among living trees inside a golden cage, within which parrots flew from tree to tree and croaked.

Standing with his hands folded in front of the cage was a small, brown, white-haired man in a blue business suit. He was smiling, and the smile lit up his face with what seemed to be real pleasure. Next to the newcomers, a larger, younger man, also in a suit, said, "If you will, please? His Serene Highness has made an especial effort to greet with you."

The rest let Ong and Harry go first. The others formed a kind of human herd behind them, as if for defense. Alan brought up the rear, carried on their cross-gripped hands by two turbaned men who refused to put him down.

241

"His Serene Highness, the Maharajah of Baipurjat."

He greeted them as, for example, the prime minister of a country only slightly less important than, let's say, Sweden might expect to be greeted. He gave a little speech about the palace (never called by him "the hotel") and about Baipurjat, which until independence had been one of those separate principalities that the British had made theirs in exchange for a large annual stipend, and which was now absorbed into the state of Pondicherry. "We are no longer a principality," he closed, "but we wish to entertain you with what we hope you will find a princely hospitality. What you do not see, demand; what you do see, command." He smiled and looked over the others' shoulders at Alan. "My personal physician is waiting for you in his office, Commander Craik." He turned to the younger man who had brought them forward. "Adeeb, if you will show him the way—"

And Alan was carted off while the others were shown to their rooms.

Which were about the size of basketball courts.

The bathrooms were about the size of squash courts.

Room phones and televisions were unknown.

If they had recognized the signs, they would have understood that the palace's life had been arrested at about 1939, but only Harry knew what the porcelain faucets in the baths, the toilets shaped like swans, the brass lamps, meant. No matter: they were giddy with the charm of the place.

Alan had a brisk examination from the maharajah's medical man, who was short, plump, oily, and efficient. "Nothing serious. Bed rest will have you tippy-top in three or four days." He held up a plump hand. "You are about to tell me you do not have three or four days. Of course not! Not only the times we live in, but also this wretched disturbance that has left us without electricity. Therefore, half an hour in a piping hot bath, followed by a good night's sleep and a touch of medication, and you'll be ambulatory." He shook out pills from an old-fashioned bottle. "Muscle relaxants. Take one with water now, one every four hours thereafter, never more than one, and stop taking them three or four hours before you plan to drive an automobile." He poured a glass of water from a pitcher. "As for the gash on your back—a bullet? challenging life you lead, I shan't ask why, although I shall have to file a report with the local police, but you'll be long gone before they get it—it's been well tended to and I don't intend to meddle with success, other than what I've already done with topical antibacterials. You take aspirin? Of course you do! Two every four hours; don't take them with the muscle relaxant if you can help it, but alternate."

"I need to keep my wits about me," Alan said.

"You need to *sleep*. The bath and a bed will do that. As for the medication, nothing there will affect your mind."

Alan started to ask about payment, and a raised hand stopped him. Minutes later, he was lying back in a bathtub that represented the very best of 1930s technology.

Over the Indian Ocean
At twenty-four thousand feet, the plane moved sluggishly, the rate of climb down to a crawl, and Soleck had to watch his speed. He had spiraled up through the night air, describing an ever more gradual clockwise corkscrew as his turbofans had less air to bite. Somewhere above him and a little to the east was Commander Siciliano in her F-18, her position noted on his datalink.

"Back seat's got something," Garcia said over the intercom.

"Want to take the plane?"

"I thought you'd never ask."

There was just a hint of the acerbic to her response, and Soleck realized he'd had the controls for two hours. *Oops, I'm the mission commander. Time to command.* "You got her."

"I have the plane," she said formally.

Soleck eased back in his seat, stretched, and switched his comms from front-seat-only to cockpit. "You guys have hits?"

"Just putting the first one in the link." Master Chief Simcoe grunted, cleared his throat noisily. "Probable Delhi-class destroyer, course SSE, speed nine knots, radiating Top Plate. Probably has us on his radar and on ESM."

"You going to image him, Master Chief?" Soleck was looking at his own screen.

"Ms Dothan's got the ISAR warm."

"Go ahead. Anybody know what a Delhi-class *looks* like?" Soleck asked. For once, he didn't know himself.

Simcoe grunted again. "I've got a length and a radar set. Both match. Best I can do."

"Holy shit," Dothan said. "Look at the ESM."

Soleck switched screens. The ESM was lit up like LA viewed from Hollywood, hits spread across the screen, representing eighty miles of ocean. Soleck could just see Dothan, her head down over her console, her fingers flying on the keyboard. The two backseaters were silent except for muttered words.

"Kashin." The Kashin-class was a slightly dated Russian destroyer design with a Big Net air-search radar easily identified by the S-3's system.

"Another Kashin." Dothan murmured seconds later.

"Godavari!" Simcoe said with triumph. "Don't see that every day."

"They weren't up a minute ago. What got 'em stirred?" Simcoe asked.

"We did," Soleck muttered. "Picket ship rotated once, saw us, and told somebody."

"Wow," Garcia said. "This is real."

Off the Indian Coast
Captain Alex Fraser of the Canadian corvette HMCS *Picton* stood in the darkness of his blacked-out bridge wing and

sucked on his unlit pipe. His ship had been at action stations for thirty-six hours. So far the men were holding up well. The sea was relatively calm, with the monsoon blowing gently over his shoulder and frustrating his occasional attempts to relight the pipe.

A sailor leaned out of the hatch. "Sir? Plot would like a word. Launches in southern India."

Fraser gave up on his attempt to smoke, tucked the pipe in his breast pocket and went in to the bridge, dogging the hatch behind him. He picked up a phone.

"Captain," he said. He listened for a few seconds and said, "Got it. You're sure? Very well. Thanks, Doug." He hung up. "Petty Officer Lawrence? Get me Captain Lash."

Over the Indian Ocean
"—two pos bandits launching southern India pos intercept of Oats ETA seven minutes, do you copy, Oats? Third pos bandit course un-ID." Even through the digital encryption and the static, Alpha Whiskey sounded nervous.

Soleck noted the two new symbols on the link. "I copy, Alpha Whiskey. Break, break. Racehorse One, you copy?"

"Roger, Oats. Three pos bandits heading our way." Commander Siciliano sounded bored. Soleck couldn't help thinking that she was really a helo pilot with a couple of hundred hours in F-18s, all with NASA, and none of it combat training.

As he watched, the screen's air symbol on the lead pair of bandits pulsed and moved suddenly, indicating that one or both of the planes had radiated a radar and been caught, and the information in the link had updated their position from predicted to real. Soleck put his cursor on the symbol. The last time he had looked at it, it had said, "UNID." Now it said "MiG-29."

Rose watched the three bandits on her screen while she turned her plane to the east. They were below her by several thousand feet and hadn't climbed since the last update. It was probable that they knew she was there, knew where her wingman was. She flicked her eyes over her instruments, noted that her fuel state was not great, looked at the indicators for her missiles, which showed that she had nothing aboard but a pair of Sidewinders. Sparrowhawk medium-range missiles would have given her a head-on superiority that no Indian plane could match, but the only two Sparrows were on Donuts's plane, and Bahrain hadn't sent any more out yet.

On another level, she confronted the notion that she was about to engage in air-to-air combat. She wasn't afraid. She *was* flooded with adrenaline, and that made her remember that she was three months pregnant and thirty-eight years old. She wondered what effect a load of adrenaline and some high-g turns would have on a fetus. *On her daughter.*

Win first, she told herself. *Live. Then worry about the baby.*

The bogeys were two hundred miles away and now it would all happen very fast. And she had to let them make the first move—not a winning strategy in jet combat. She called her wingman. "Racehorse Two, ready?"

"Roger."

She put her nose on her possible adversaries, activated her radar. *Here I am. Want to dance?*

USS *Thomas Jefferson*

Sitting in the TAO chair, alone with a crisis, Madje didn't hesitate to order a runner to get Captain Hawkins, even while his gut told him that this would be over before anyone could come through the hatch and rescue him from the decisions he was about to make. He felt tempted to shout, *I'm a fucking two-bar!*

Only fifty miles to the north, the ocean was crawling with Indian ships, and it was clear that they were still fighting with each other. He *thought* that the new action had been provoked by the appearance of the S-3's radar and the subsequent mass illumination of air-search and surface-search radars, as if someone had shown a light in a dark basement and the cockroaches had gone to war.

"Racehorse One has her radar on."

"Bogey One turning to 040."

Madje thought, *If one of those planes fires a missile, we're at war. Jesus, we're probably already at war.*

"Tell Oats to get down on the deck and get out of there," Madje shouted at his AW officer.

"That's Alpha Whiskey's call—"

"Do it."

Over the Indian Ocean

The two planes coming at Rose turned back east, declining the engagement. As far as she could tell, they hadn't launched missiles. She turned with them, the g-force just nipping at her head and hips, keeping her plane's nose hot and on them. They were less than four miles away; the engagement was moving faster than she could consciously follow, her hands and senses seeming to act of their own volition. No thoughts of a baby now; just the turn, and her ear waiting for the tone that would mean a missile launch.

"Where's that third bogey?" she asked.

USS *Thomas Jefferson*

"—third bogey?" Racehorse one asked, her voice loud in the silence of CIC.

If Commander Siciliano didn't know where the third bogey was, that meant it was *very* low, lost from her radar in the wave clutter. Madje groaned. Lash was keeping the battle group in EMCON, putting the enemy in the dark but severely limiting their own information.

"Captain Lash? This is TAO *Jefferson*." Madje drove straight on. "The top bogeys are radiating. They know where we are, if it's us they're after. Request permission to radiate. We need to locate the low bogey."

"Negative, *Jefferson*." Lash's voice was calm and careful.

Madje heard somebody scrambling over the knee knocker, and then Hawkins's voice came from behind him. "Screw him. Radiate!"

The plot on the JOTS showed the far-on ring for the possible location of the third bogey as intersecting the *Jefferson*.

The third bogey *might* be hostile.

The third bogey *might* have located the battle group.

The third bogey *might* be less than a mile away. Or on top of them.

"Belay that," Madje said, struggling to keep his voice even. He thought Lash was wrong, but he was trained to obey. He obeyed. "Captain Hawkins? Do you wish to relieve me?"

Hawkins put a hand on his shoulder but said nothing.

The digital engagement clock moved relentlessly forward. The far-on circle swept over the *Jefferson*.

Over the Indian Ocean

"Bogey One broke left. Have you got him?" Rose called to her wingman. Her radar was no longer on Bogey One; she was following Bogey Two.

"Roger, Racehorse One. Bogey One is headed for the deck and I'm on his six."

Rose's prey began to dive as well. The MiG-29 went to afterburner, the streaks of his engines just visible against the high-altitude star field. Rose flung her head back and forth, looking for the S-3, whose altitude she was going to pass through in seconds. On radar, it looked very close indeed.

"Break, Oats, this is Racehorse One descending rapidly. Can you see me?"

"Got you, Racehorse One. I'm turning west."

The Indian fighter was turning slightly west, as well. Rose

swept her thumb over her missile release, tensing for the moment. She had a tone, steady in her ears, but waiting for the other plane to fire wouldn't save Soleck if the S-3 was the intended target.

Where's Bogey Three? she asked herself again. She pushed her nose down and watched her radar. *Who's the target?* Her adversary was powering away from her in his dive, probably too late to launch at the S-3 this pass, and she kicked in her own afterburner, already calculating her fuel consumption and what the S-3 had to give her. She could make one more turn, one more long burn, and then even the gas aboard the S-3 wouldn't be enough to get her home. Racehorse Two was in the same state.

Soleck could see the scene on his datalink—five planes descending in the same volume of airspace, with Commander Siciliano at the top of the stack and the lower Bogey at the bottom. As the second Indian plane blew past him and lost the angle to shoot a missile, Garcia leveled off and banked to the east as hard as the plane could stand, a turn as sharp as any break over the island when she was going for a shit-hot landing. The heavy aircraft stood on one wing, and the fuselage, older than LT Dothan, groaned, and then they were a thousand feet above the action and safer by the second.

"I think I've found Bogey Three," Dothan said.

"Bogey One is firing!" Racehorse Two said. Rose's thumb slid across the missile release switch.

Bogey Two was right on Racehorse Two's heels, with Rose just behind.

"Weapons free," Alpha Whiskey called. But the Bogeys were past the S-3, and whatever Bogey One had fired at wasn't a US plane. On her radar, her steep dive gave her a new angle and she saw Bogey Three at last, a new contact at altitude zero, wavetop height, headed north at Mach One.

"Belay that!" she called. "Bogey One is shooting at Bogey Three. Racehorse Two, turn west to 270 and look for Oats at Angels one two, over."

"Roger, Racehorse One." Racehorse Two sounded disappointed. Rose had time to wonder if she had made the right decision, and then she started her turn.

USS *Thomas Jefferson*
Madje watched the two F-18s breaking off to the west. He turned to his comms officer. "Call the beach and get them to launch the alert at Trincomalee. Racehorse has got to be out of gas."

"Aye, aye, sir."

Hawkins gave him a nod. "Where's Bogey Three headed?"

Madje was watching the screen, now updated with the data from the S-3. Sixteen Indian ships were within three hundred miles, and eight of them had fire-control radars active. He could imagine the missiles launching from decks and the sound of the guns. And the fires. Ships would be burning.

"It wasn't us, anyway," Madje said, reaching for his coffee. It had been the most fatiguing three minutes of his life.

"Could have been," Hawkins said.

Over the Indian Ocean
"Holy shit," Garcia said. "Holy shit."

A flash lit the horizon and the interior of the plane, and then a plume of fire climbed out of the sea.

"What was that?" Simcoe said from the back seat. "Something hit that Delhi Class?

"There was a big flash," Soleck said.

"The Delhi just went off the air. She's not rotating anything. I'll look on ISAR."

Soleck watched the two F-18s forming up above him. They would both need gas to get home. "Ms Dothan, can you get the FLIR deployed?"

"Roger that."

"Whoa. She's going. Gone. She sank." Simcoe sounded shocked.

"Just like that?" Soleck asked. "Sank?"

"Gone. Bow first. Not even a return."

"Bogey Three flew into her," Soleck guessed. "Got to be."

"Holy shit," Garcia said again.

Soleck glanced at her as she completed her turn, and flicked his intercom to front seat only. "You okay?"

"'Course I'm okay. Don't be a dick."

Soleck thought she sounded rattled. Her hands were moving around a lot.

Soleck leaned back and stretched his hands, glancing at her again. Then he started calculating fuel.

USS *Thomas Jefferson*

The voice of the TACCO in the S-3 sounded loud as she reported the death of the Delhi-class destroyer. The Combat Information Center was silent.

"That could have been us," Hawkins said again. "And if the Canucks miss one, we won't even know he's coming."

Madje watched the screen, sure that the mutineers had just scored a victory. Only the mutineers used airplanes as guided missiles. And it proved to him that what had happened to the *Jefferson* was not an accident. But he didn't have the energy to discuss it with Captain Hawkins or to listen to the older man spin it. He looked at his watch and realized that he still had two hours left before he would be relieved.

The Serene Highness Hotel

A modest dinner was available in what was called "the observatory." There, under a glass canopy—somewhat filmed with time and dust, a few panes cracked, none broken—a table had been laid out with platters of Madras and Bengali foods in quantities that would have better suited a regiment. One of the turbaned servants carried a plate, prepared by Harry, to Alan's room; the others, newly bathed and changed, bore down on the food. By then, they realized that they were the only guests in the hotel.

In the middle of the meal, a figure appeared in the arched doorway.

"Well, well," Harry murmured. "My favorite soldier." He got up and crossed the space, his hand out. "Major Rao."

"I turn up, you see, like the bad penny."

"I thought you might."

They sat together and talked about nothing (cricket versus baseball, the decline of the tiger population, Bollywood films) and probed each other's defenses—and got nothing.

"Charming man, Major Rao," Harry muttered to Djalik after dinner. "A real professional."

"A real professional what?"

"Guess."

It was dark above the conservatory glass by then, a few stars and a brilliant moon managing to penetrate the film. The party broke up, people wandering away, Ong following her small, quite pretty nose down one corridor and then another until she came to a set of French doors, which she of course opened to find a room lit only by the moon—in its beam, as if it were a spotlight, a grand piano. She sat, struck two chords, and a servant appeared with a hurricane lamp that he put down next to her before he rushed out, to return with another man and, this time, four lamps.

Ong revealed to the night that she could play jazz piano. Her hands were too small for stride, but she could play a wicked Fats Waller bass, and she launched into "Sweet Georgia Brown" as if she was going to knock the walls down. When she stopped and looked around, the Maharajah was standing there.

He grinned. He was holding a clarinet. "'Sweet Georgia

Brown' again," he said. "And-uh one, and-uh, two, and-uh—"

He could wail. He was an old-fashioned jazz fan, more Preservation Hall than Plugged Nickel, but he could wail! Panting slightly between sets, he said to her, "You are quite excellent! You are professional?"

"I minored in jazz in college."

He frowned, perhaps remembering Cambridge. "And uh-one, and uh-two, and uh-three—"

Benvenuto and Clavers came in and began to dance. Three waiters brought in more food and drinks, and Harry wandered by, then Djalik, and they danced together briefly, Harry reminding the other man of a famous general's line to the then secretary of state under the same circumstances, "Don't ask, don't tell," as they two-stepped through the moonlight.

Alone in a bed big enough for four, Alan woke. The doctor had been right—hot water and muscle relaxants and a bed, and he was out of it. Now, lying in the warm, scented dark, he heard the distant sounds of music. Jazz. Some bastard on a clarinet.

"Some people have no consideration," he said, and pulled the pillow over his head and was instantly asleep again.

21

Approaching Trincomalee

Soleck was in the pattern for Trincomalee, flying on fumes, when Dothan spoke up from the back.

"I've got an interesting signal."

"We're going to be on the ground in ten minutes."

"I got an anomalous radio signal from just off the west coast of India."

Soleck handed the plane over to Garcia, who was already in contact with the tower. Then he brought up his ESM screen. While he watched, the signal was received again and the location resolved from a vector to an oval area of probability that covered sixty miles of southern India and a stretch of coast.

"Could be a fishing boat."

Master Chief Simcoe spoke up. "That's the new Indian comms suite. There aren't many out there."

"What has them?" Soleck asked, watching Garcia fly.

"The new Delhi-class, the Krivak refits, and all their new-construction Kilos."

"You going to make me land this from the right seat?" Garcia asked. Soleck wasn't sure they were going to be friends, and he couldn't figure where he'd put a foot wrong. He liked *her*.

"I've got it," he said, and took the plane. "Dothan, you'd better call your radio signal in to the boat before I land."

"Roger."

He heard her make the call, heard the tired-sounding voice of the TAO on the *Jefferson* respond, but his mind was on the runway, which blurred under his extended landing gear until he had covered half of it. Gently, he touched the plane down, rolled out to the end, and turned straight into the big, white hangar they now called home.

"That was great, everybody. Thanks." Soleck wanted to recapture the upbeat moment when Garcia had turned away from the descending stack, the excitement of their tracking all the Indian ships. He was full of energy.

Garcia pulled off her helmet and scratched her head. She had a lot of hair, and it went every which way. She turned to Soleck and stretched, smiled broadly, her face alight. "It was excellent."

Dothan laughed from the back. "That was my first operational flight."

"Debrief with LT Shawna at the hotel, okay, Garcia? Nelly? Hey!" He tried to shout over the auxiliaries. She had unplugged her helmet cord and was out of the plane before he could grab her.

"I'll get it, sir," Simcoe said.

"Thanks, Master Chief. See you at chow."

He found that he was alone in the plane, a maintenance guy looking up at him curiously from the ground. He gave a wave and started to gather his gear. He knew they had done really well. It had been a big mission for him—his plan, his command. But it was over more suddenly than he had expected.

Soleck climbed down out of his silent plane and stopped to talk to the crew chief who was already under the fuselage. Commander Siciliano appeared under the wing.

"Nice job, Soleck," she said, and punched him in the arm. "Tell your crew that was shit-hot."

"Thanks, ma'am." Soleck could tell she was happy, assumed

it was just the same feeling he had magnified by more responsibility.

"You tag all those contacts?"

"Yes, ma'am. We passed them on link to *Fort Klock* and over the radio to the *Jeff*." He found himself walking next to her, headed for the hangar. "Were they, uh—going to shoot?"

"Yeah, Soleck, I think they were. But they didn't, and we're all home again."

Soleck turned for the van that would take him back to the hotel.

Rose walked across the apron to the hangar, resisting the urge to pat her stomach. *All home again*. So far, so good.

Bahrain

Dukas didn't get home until half-past nine, but Leslie had the pizza assembled and waiting to go into the oven, just as she'd said. Dukas had lived with other women for various lengths of time, never very successfully; Leslie certainly was the best of the lot—better than he deserved, he thought sometimes.

He kissed her, taking that tenth of a second too long to get to it that meant he was debating whether or not he should. She kissed him back with a lot of enthusiasm, although he knew she must have got the hesitation, knew what it meant. *Uncommitted Dukas, going once again through the question of what this woman is doing here.*

"Hard day?" she said.

"Yeah, yeah, sort of. You were there, what the hell." They had a house in the international section of Manama, in a development put up in the seventies by some hot-to-trot Saudi with Palestinian workers who had done all the work while he'd taken all the money. Leslie had moved into it and changed nothing, living, he thought, on the surface of his taste, his life.

She'd put the pizza in the oven when she'd heard his car. Now, the rich smell of tomatoes and cheese spread through the kitchen. They looked at each other, two people with nothing to do for nine minutes. Dukas sat on a tubular-steel chair and patted his knee, and she sat on his lap.

"Wanna neck?" she said.

"Not if it means burning the pizza."

"I was hoping you'd tear off my clothes in a fit of passion and we'd fuck while the oven caught fire."

"Food first."

The trouble was, he liked Leslie. The trouble was, he didn't love Leslie. Or he didn't know what loving somebody meant, and so he didn't know whether he loved her or not. The trouble was, she loved him and knew it and said it. The trouble was, being loved was for him a weight she had hung around his neck like the young arms that now encircled it, like the weight of her body on his middle-aged legs, on his irrepressible erection, which didn't share his doubts about her.

"You glad to see me, or that a flashlight in your pocket?"

"I teach you these jokes, they keep coming back to haunt me." He had his right hand on her left breast, more than a little interested. "It's actually a Louisville Slugger, the Mickey Mantle model."

"Dream on." She kissed him; the kiss went on; he got more and more interested. "Food first," she said and slipped off his lap.

Housing for somebody at his level in Bahrain was luxurious by the standards of what he could afford in Washington. They had everything that most people in the Middle East didn't have—air-conditioning, refrigerator, electric stove, terrazzo floors, a Filipino maid who came in by the day, two cars.

"Know why they hate us?" He said it often. By "they," he meant the four-fifths of the world that was neither American nor affluent. Tomato sauce ran down his chin; he gulped wine and touched her upper lip to remove a speck of cheese.

"Because we're us." She had heard it often, too.

"Because we're fucking conquerors. Everywhere we go, we set up these compounds and live in them and don't mix and flaunt what we are in front of people who could live for a year on what I make in a day."

She poured them both more wine and smiled at him. She had lost twenty pounds since he had first seen her in Washington; she still wasn't really pretty, but she had good eyes and a look of intelligence and humor and enthusiasm for being alive. "What are we supposed to do—give our money away and live in a tent?"

"Don't be a smartass!"

She picked up both glasses of wine and headed for the bedroom. "Just kidding."

He was thinking about chocolate ice cream, and then he saw her buttocks disappear behind the archway, and he decided that he could get the ice cream later. *And here I go again.*

The trouble was, he liked having Leslie around.

Most of the time.

Bahrain

Enrique, aka Henry, aka Bobby, aka Ricky Valdez was again slumped in front of his computer. Edgar was still running, and Edgar was still getting mostly nowhere. Whatever was encrypted in the stuff they had, it was like rock.

And Edgar was also unhappy because something kept nibbling at Edgar's pants. Every time Edgar found that his pants were being nibbled at, he swatted the nibbler and went back to work, and then the nibbling would start again.

"Hey, Mave."

"Yeah, what?" She sounded truly pissed, truly premenstrual-tension, get-out-of-my-face, I-hate-you pissed. Except that she wasn't premenstrual and she loved Valdez. What she hated was computer shit that didn't go her way.

"Bad, huh, Mave?"

"Oh, shut up."

"What I'm going to do, I want you to shut down what you're working on, and I'm going to send you a page. Okay?"

"Why should I be the one to shut down?"

"Mave, this isn't a fucking contest!"

"You just want to show me what wonderful Edgar has accomplished and I haven't."

"Will you please shut down your—"

"Oh, shut down this!" She hit some keys. "What I think, Rickie, if you turn your back on this shit, it's not going to kiss your arse." She put a CD in the drive and hit keys and waited and then said, "Okay, send."

Thirty seconds later, he said, "What you see?"

"I see that, contrary to me expectations, dearie—" she fell into her stage Irish when she was sarcastic—"Edgar's got no more sense of what's happening than Finn MacCoul had tits."

Valdez leaned over her chair. With the tip of a pencil, he pointed to a set of three characters. "What you think of that?"

"I think it's the initials of a heavy metal group. Jesus, Mary, and Saint Joseph, Rickie, I don't think anything! It's noise!"

Valdez reached over her and punched a key. The characters he had pointed at turned red, along with a dozen other clusters on the screen.

"Oh, me beating heart!" she cried. "It's magic. What has Edgar done?"

"Edgar's isolated an embedded program that's differently encrypted. It's scattered through the rest of the crap, but I guess it comes together when it gets the right order. Plus, Edgar's giving off signs that part of it's a worm."

She hit keys and the screen disappeared; in its place, a

deep blue screen carried a box with the message "Your computer is under attack and recommends immediate quarantine of the program that is running."

She looked up at Valdez. "It didn't do that to me before."

"Edgar triggered something. I keep getting the same message, over and over."

She looked at the screen, tapping the knuckle of her right index finger on her lips. "I tell you what let's do, Mister Babbage. Let's put it on some spare piece of hardware and let it go berserk."

Valdez raised his eyebrows. "Might ace the drives."

"Well, it's Harry's money." She took the CD she'd stored the material on and took it into the next room, Valdez following her; there, they isolated a desktop that had been the sensation of the world two years before and was now semi-obsolete and booted it up.

"Okay?" she said.

"Do it, do it."

She put the CD into the B drive. The computer whirred; the screen filled with the same indecipherable symbols, and then the screen turned orange. *Only* orange.

Mavis hit a key, then three keys together. She typed in an order. Nothing happened.

"Fried," Valdez said.

"Holy Jesus, that was *fast*."

Valdez tried Edgar on it The computer whirred, and the screen turned red, and the message "Edgar is working" appeared.

For three seconds.

And then the screen turned orange.

"It ate Edgar!" Valdez cried.

"If I was still a Catholic, I'd cross myself."

Valdez, who *was* still a Catholic, crossed himself and said, "That's for both of us." He typed instructions into the computer and got nothing. Whatever they'd put in there had gone through Edgar's defenses like spit through a screen.

"Okay, so now we know that if it can take over the operating program, it owns the box. Okay." He looked at the screen for several seconds and then muttered, "Okay," again.

"It's about as okay as having the thing from *Alien* living in the cellar."

Back in their own room, he said, "I'm going to keep running Edgar for a little while; you run the other disks to see if they're any different."

She loaded the other materials on a CD and put it into her computer. "What I like about you, Rickie, is you're masculine without being bossy, you know?"

"I just meant it as a suggestion, Mave."

"Yeah, I have a suggestion for you in return, love—stick it up, will you?"

He was watching Edgar get his ass nibbled. "What I like about you, Mave, is you're so meek and mild."

"Latino prick."

"Irish bitch."

They watched their computers for a couple of minutes and then she said, "Come over here. That's an order." Valdez scrambled over, stood behind her, and she reached around and grabbed for his crotch, giggling.

"Mave, be serious! I thought you had something."

"I do. Want some of it?"

"Aw, Mave—"

She hit a key. "Look." An animated cartoon ran with promos for something called the Servants of the Earth, followed by a brief speech of welcome and encouragement on video, after which a title appeared, "The Book of Wisdom," with a menu of choices for every day—personal crises, absent friends, parties, dangers, religious feelings, and sixteen other categories. Mavis highlighted one and brought up a set of pithy paragraphs, full of what apparently was wisdom, on the subject of sex. *What is the good of living as if your organs of sex are your enemy? The wise person lives as if sex is another door through which to walk into reality. But it is one door in a room that has many doors, and we must open them all.*

"I think that means that fucking's okay," Mavis said, "but don't make a career of it. Better than what my mother tried to teach me."

"What else is on it?"

"Nothing. Three of the others the same. *Not* encrypted. Pretty pictures, terminal cuteness, a lot of wisdom and the motivational speechifying."

"What about the last one?"

"Haven't looked at it yet. I just wanted to get you over here, you gorgeous hunk of virility, you. I thought we might open the door of sex and see what reality looks like." She hit a key. "Actually, I just wanted a change." The same animation came up, the same logo. Then there was a picture of a man and the words "Kill American on sight."

"Holy shit!" Valdez muttered. "That's Al Craik."

Then the screen went to encrypted data.

"Do your Edgar bit and see if the worm is here."

Valdez put in an Edgar disk, and Edgar went to work and found that nobody was trying to eat his shorts.

"No worm. Ver-ee in-ter-es-ting!"

She cycled through the encrypted data and found a few unconnected pieces in clear—a clock, currently running; what seemed to be a weather report; two incomprehensible pages of text, in clear but in a language they couldn't read.

"The jg, what's his name?—Ong—said this crap was on USB keys. He also sent it to NSA for decryption, which means they ought to have it in no more than three years or so. The truth is, you and I aren't going to break it."

"You amaze me. The Great Valdez?"

"I amaze myself. Trouble is, see, Mave, the clock's running.

That shit about Al Craik is a wakeup call, no kidding. 'Kill on sight?'" He shook his head.

She rolled her chair along the table to look at his screen. "What I think is, this mess needs a trigger, and until it has the trigger, it's going to stay just like that."

"Yeah, right, okay. What's the trigger? Like, how were those USB keys to be used?"

Valdez typed and brought up Ong's cover message. He scrolled until he found "...largest program was located on a USB key that was attempted to plug into a JOTS terminal."

"A JOTS terminal," he said.

"And what might he be when he's home?"

"Oh, the JOTS is a system for locating ships and airplanes. Comes up as images on a screen, incorporates data from all sorts of links—you can zoom in and out, see what's going on pretty much worldwide—who's where, all that."

He was scrolling on, reading scraps, hurrying on. "It would be nice to know what happened when the thing was plugged in." He glanced at her, put his hand on her leg. "It didn't come up encrypted code, you can bet your sweet ass."

"Flatterer—a body'd think you were Irish."

"Well, it wouldn't—would it?"

"Not if you meant it to do something. It might not show anything, you know. If the worm that ate Edgar is as tough as it looks, then it might go right to work and do whatever it's supposed to do." She put her hand over his. "Like suck the guts out of your JOTS?"

Valdez stared at the screen. "There's an awful lot of code there, Mave. I say that's something to be *down*loaded."

"*Into* the JOTS."

"Where else?" He thought about it. He turned her hand over and held it, palm to his palm. "Maybe the JOTS itself is the trigger?"

"Oh, clever man! Of course! You put it into the USB port, it looks around, the first string it hits tells it—Go! I mean, it could be the first string, that isn't impossible. It could key on the matrix, couldn't it?"

"It could key on the operating system. JOTS is unique." He kissed her fingers. "I'm going over to Fifth Fleet."

"Because they've got a JOTS," she said.

"If they haven't, the Navy's in big trouble."

"And what about me?" she said.

"Can't get you in over there, Mave." He smiled, trying to placate her. "You don't have a clearance."

"And you do, I suppose."

"I'm on a list."

"And I'm not? What list is that, then?"

They had a fight, of sorts. She kept saying, "What list?" and he kept saying, "Ask Harry," and she finally screamed at him, "Harry isn't here! I'm asking you!" and Valdez went off to Fifth Fleet feeling worn out before his night had really started.

22

USS *Thomas Jefferson*

One patient in the ship's hospital had been there for more than thirty hours before intel figured out that he was LTjg Collins, the TACCO from the missing S-3 commanded by CDR Paul Stevens. In the chaos after the Indian Jaguar had hit the flight deck, nobody knew for sure how many or which planes were missing, whether they'd burned on the deck, been pushed into the sea, or gone down somewhere. Then they sorted that out, and at some point the TAO and the squadrons knew about Stevens's plane, but intel didn't make the connection. And then it had taken a yeoman hours to identify Collins, whose ID had been ripped off in the crash. Because of the deck accident, his squadron-mates were scattered, and something as simple as a flight sked had been impossible to find. Even after they knew that the man found in the water was from Stevens's aircraft, it took time to find somebody who knew that Stevens himself was too old to be their mystery victim, somebody else who knew that Goldy was a woman. Finally, they had come up with a kid from the squadron who was at that point helping damage control near the number two elevator, and he described Collins for them. That is why, thirty-three hours after the Jaguar had hit the flight deck, intel had finally been able to make the connection.

The ship's hospital had pushed out into nearby spaces as

the wounded had come in from the accident. Even then, it was too small, and an auxiliary had been set up on the O-3 level, where they were sending the less seriously injured. As well, choppers were going back and forth among the *Jefferson*, the *Fort Klock*, and the gator freighter *Mindanao*, ferrying wounded who had already been through trauma care and stabilized.

The wounded kid from Stevens's S-3 was considered too critical to move. He lay in a ward assigned to the most serious cases—the one, in fact, where Admiral Rafehausen also lay.

At 2314 Local, the flag intel officer and a yeoman appeared in the hospital. They sought out the medical captain in charge, a weary, harried-looking man in a surgical gown who was still wearing gloves, and the flag intel officer said that they knew who the wounded boy was and they wanted to talk to him.

The captain muttered to somebody else, stripping off his gloves as he talked. His shoulders sagged. A nurse said they had a burn victim waiting for him in the operating suite. The captain looked at a list, rubbing his eyes. "You can't see him. He's critical." He handed the list back to another nurse and headed out.

"Sir!" The flag intel officer turned back. "This is critical, too, sir. We have to know why that aircraft went down. Another pilot thinks he saw electronic evidence of hostile activity."

"That man's sedated. He's got a nearly severed fourth vertebra; if it goes, he'll be permanently paralyzed or dead. I'll call you when he's out of surgery and we deem him ready to talk to you."

"Sir!" The intel officer turned again, this time with real anger. "I have orders from the acting commander of the BG. I'm to talk with the man. He's to be allowed to talk to me."

The surgeon put his hands on his hips. "You want to kill that boy?"

"We may be facing a war, sir. I *have* to talk to him."

The surgeon lost it. "He's sedated!" he screamed.

"Can he be waked up? Some kind of antidote?"

The surgeon stared at him. Abruptly, he turned to the nurse. "Take this officer to Doctor Fernando. Tell Fernando to contact me in surgery." He turned back to the intel officer. "If the boy dies, I'll report you for manslaughter." He jerked his head. "This worth your career, Commander?"

Doctor Fernando was a plump, exhausted man in a surgical gown, booties, and cap, a mask hanging at his throat like a bandana. He had large, almost feminine brown eyes with long lashes, under them the dark circles of extreme fatigue. He heard out the intel officer's story and then checked the young man's record. "You got a name for him? We've got him as one of our thirty-seven John Does."

"Collins, Hampton. LTjg, Squadron VS-46."

Fernando was muttering to himself as he read—"concussion, probable cranial swelling, contusions—six broken ribs, broken right leg—"

"The ID is tentative until you guys check him against the records."

"Yeah, yeah. So, what d'you want from us?"

"I want you to wake him up."

Fernando started to say something like "No way!" and then saw the seriousness on the intel officer's face, and he muttered, "Dangerous." He tossed Collins's chart on the hospital desk. He rubbed his forehead. "You want information from him, right?"

The intel officer nodded. Helpfully, he said, "I'll ask as little of him as humanly possible."

"Well, you may ask his life, is all. See, this man has likely cranial swelling and what laymen call a broken neck; awake, he may be incoherent, and the slightest movement, and he pops the rest of that vertebra, and there goes the spinal cord. You know what happened to Christopher Reeve? The actor?

That's one likely outcome. Worst case, that happens, then he goes into coma, vessel ruptures in the head, and he dies. You wanta risk that?"

The intel officer hesitated, then nodded. Fernando said to a nurse standing behind the desk, "Get me an anaesthesiologist—McCracken if he's around. Or wake somebody up—McCracken, if possible." He turned back. "McCracken's the best. This is going to be tricky." He shook his head. "Tricky."

Twenty minutes later, they were standing around Collins's bed. Dr McCracken had in fact been yanked out of his rack but showed no resentment as he immediately went about his business.

Collins's neck and head were in a rigid stainless-steel brace that surrounded them like some arcane torture instrument. One leg was in a plastic splint and was slightly elevated. Despite what he'd been through, however, his face had no bandages and looked quite normal, quite peaceful.

"He's sedated," Fernando said. "He was stabilized when he came in and now we're holding him. Believe it or not, he isn't one of our most critical cases. It's the burns are the worst. Anyway, vertebral surgery is tricky, really tricky." He looked at the anaesthesiologist. "What'd you think?"

"I want to bring him out and be ready to put him under again absolutely as quick as possible. If we hold it to thirty seconds or so— His blood pressure's elevated because of trauma; we can't put it up even more." An IV ran down to a heparin lock in Collins's arm, with another plastic joint partway up the tube where a syringe could be put in. McCracken already had three syringes laid out on a tray. "We'll try." He glanced at the intel officer. "Any time."

The intel officer nodded. Fernando nodded. McCracken eased a needle into the IV and injected colorless fluid, his eyes on an electronic monitor by the bed.

Collins's eyelids fluttered.

Fernando nodded to the intel officer.

"Collins? Lieutenant? Can you hear me?"

Collins's eyes were open now. Perhaps he tried to nod, because the eyes suddenly swung around, left, right, up, trying to find why he couldn't move his head. "Wha-a-a-?"

"You're in the hospital, Collins. You're okay. You're going to be okay. You were in Commander Stevens's aircraft. The aircraft went down."

The eyes widened. "Sub! The sub—shot us down." The voice became panicky. "Where are the guys?"

"A submarine fired on you? Collins, is that what happened?"

"Submarine! I caught it on the link—we laid down a line—caught it and Skipper said we'd go active t' scare them—and it surfaced and shot—shot— Where are the guys? *Where are the guys?*" He started to scream.

Fernando jerked his head at McCracken, and a second needle went in and instantly, it seemed, Collins's eyes closed and his screams stopped. "That's all you get," Fernando said.

"I need details! He was talking, godammit—!"

"His blood pressure's going up." Fernando's voice was level, calm. "We're all doing our best with what we're given here, Commander. That's all you're gonna be given—do your best with it." He turned the intel officer away from the bed. "Out, okay?"

Behind them, McCracken was saying something to a nurse and somebody else was running toward the end of the ward.

Bahrain

Late at night, Fifth Fleet headquarters should have been a quiet place. A flag desk would normally have been manned by a duty officer, as would desks in the principal departments, but the place would have lacked the sense of life that marked it by day. Now, however, the times were far from normal, and a tense activity was evident in lighted offices and hurrying figures with permanent frowns; the smell of coffee and a boombox playing somewhere suggested an under-layer of activity. The flag captain had finally persuaded Admiral Pilchard to go home after thirty-two hours without sleep, and he had dragged himself off an hour later, but duty officers were bunked down in the duty room and others had brought in sleeping bags and pads and were sacked out in cubbyholes all over the building. Most of them thought they were waiting for a war to start.

Six years in the Navy made Valdez sensitive to such activity. He moved through the Fifth Fleet spaces a little warily, nonetheless, because he was a visitor and an outsider now. Seeing people asleep under desks and on tables in the cafeteria told him how tight things were but didn't change his own status.

A Marine guard had led him to the intel spaces and hadn't left until Valdez had been signed in there. Now, Valdez was wearing an ID badge that said visitor not to be left unaccompanied, which he had been enjoined to wear "at all times, by which we mean *at all times*, sir!" by a Marine sergeant. Valdez had grinned at being called "sir" by a sergeant but hadn't got a grin back. Now, Valdez was facing a tall, skinny lieutenant-commander with prematurely gray hair who stuck out a hand and gave him a smile of uneven teeth. "Lieutenant-Commander Lapierre." Al Craik's assistant in intel.

"You're ex-Navy, I hear."

"Only a PO1, sir."

"They're the ones who do all the work, right?" Lapierre was never going to win any beauty contests—in fact, there was something of the central-casting idea of a hayseed about him—but he looked like a guy who was absolutely what you saw—no bullshit.

"Okay, you know what I got?"

"That I *don't* know."

"Okay, I got an encrypted mess of doo-doo that was sent to me from India by a Lieutenant jg Ong. You know this guy Ong?"

"It's a she, not a he, Mister Valdez."

"It makes me nervous, people call me 'mister.' Most people just call me Valdez. I got this data from *Miss* Ong, okay. She said it was on something plugged into the USB port of a JOTS terminal when Mister Craik 'intercepted' it, whatever the hell that means. You know anything about that?"

Lapierre shook his head. "We didn't discuss that."

Valdez nodded gloomily. He realized he was tired, and he was worried about just how angry Mavis was. "Can we move this right along?" he said.

"Be my guest. What d'you need? A computer?"

"I need a JOTS repeater."

"That we got."

"It's gotta be isolated from the system—one hundred percent isolated. I don't know how to do that, not my kind of electronics, and I haven't got the time to go through the manual and find out. I want somebody really knows what he's doing to isolate it and then guarantee to me that's it out of the system."

"What are you going to do with it?"

"Maybe I'm going to fry it; we'll see." He told Lapierre about what he and Mavis had done with the encrypted data. "My respect for Indian programmers went up about one thousand percent."

While they got somebody out of his rack in the enlisted barracks to deal with the JOTS, Valdez talked to Mavis on the telephone, an embarrassed chief leaning in the door because Valdez couldn't be left alone. She'd already been asleep; contrary to his fears, she was glad he'd called. And so it went: they had a common passion for computers that was stronger than either one's anger.

The JOTS specialist was an African-American PO1 named Markey who spent about forty seconds at the device and said it was okay, good to go, he was outa there.

"Guarantee?" Valdez said.

"Hundred percent, m'man—do your thing."

Lapierre leaned in between them. "What's the worst could happen if it isn't isolated, Valdez?"

"If I knew, I wouldn't have to be here, but what I think is, it could maybe seize or destroy the entire JOTS system worldwide."

PO1 Markey looked at the commander, then at Valdez. "I think I'll just have another look at my machine here," he said. This time, he took five minutes and turned to them, shaking his head, less cocksure, but saying that he'd checked every goddam thing he knew, and unless he cut off the electrical supply, he didn't know how he could isolate it any better. "What you got on that disk, anyway?"

"I wish I knew."

Valdez had to download the disk to his own laptop, which was already as well protected as the computers back at the office had been, and then download from there via the USB port to the JOTS. When he was ready, he said, "Okay, this is apparently what somebody was about to do when he was 'intercepted' by Commander Craik. You guys ready?"

Markey had stuck around, for all that he, like everybody else, was dying for sleep. He looked at the laptop and winced. Lapierre gave a toothy grin. "Shoot."

Valdez hit a key.

"Holy shit!" Markey, who had been leaning on the JOTS, swayed away from it as a complex image came on the screen. "Well, it didn't eat our lunch, anyway."

"What've we got?" Lapierre said.

Valdez was peering at the screen. "You guys tell me—what *have* we got?"

A voice behind them said, "It's the fleet exercise startex configuration." The speaker was a female chief, intel. Not cute, Valdez thought, but a really bright lady. Nice legs. *Big* headlights.

Lapierre was looking at the JOTS. "Yeah, it *is* the startex layout. There's the *Jefferson*—the *Klock*—these are Indian ships over here, right. Pulanski, you're good."

The female chief said, "We worked on the thing long enough, we oughta recognize it." She turned to Valdez. "Heather Pulanski, I worked for Lieutenant jg Ong. We did a lot of the preplanning."

Valdez made nice-to-meet-you sounds, but his attention was on the JOTS. "You think Commander Craik 'intercepted' some Indian who all he was going to do was bring up the startex configuration?"

"No Indian personnel were supposed to, like, touch the JOTS," Markey said. "I was there when we did the rules. Very big on 'You touch, you lose your fingers.'"

"We gotta see if this thing is real-time or what," Valdez said. "There's a ton of data in there—more than you'd need for this image. Maybe it's got the whole exercise on it." He picked up his laptop. "Can I have an office where I can be secure? I need an internet connection and a STU. I gotta talk to my boss."

Lapierre hesitated only a fraction of a second. "My office is down the passageway. Uhh—"

"I know, I know, you gotta hang around because I might steal the silver." A couple of steps along the way, Valdez turned back. "I need for somebody to watch that thing and see what changes. Anybody?"

Both Pulanski's and Markey's hand went up.

"Call me pronto if it explodes or anything."

USS *Thomas Jefferson*

As Captain Hawkins read the P-4 from Pilchard, his face went through several changes; first extreme concern as he accepted the message from a runner; then pleasure as he read the first few words, relief as he read the next sentence, and a return to concern, all in a few seconds like an actor practicing expressions.

HAWKINS—APPROVED RECCE FLIGHT DESPITE PROTEST FROM LASH. EXPECT TO SEE RESULTS ASAP. UNDERSTAND RAFEHAUSEN STILL CAPABLE OF CALLING THE BIG SHOTS. BETTER BE RAFEHAUSEN NOT YOU. REPEAT, BETTER BE RAFEHAUSEN NOT YOU. PILCHARD SENDS.

He turned the command chair through ninety degrees, crumpled the P-4 in his hand and stuffed it into the pocket of his khaki trousers. "AsuW? You got a picture?" He waved at the F-18 pilot manning the anti-surface warfare module.

"Yessir. With Supplot and the ASW module, I've tracked and mapped every contact raised by 703; and I've correlated to data from Supplot and our own ESM folks. I'll have it on hardcopy in a minute."

"I want an e-copy I can pass to Fifth Fleet. You ready?"

The F-18 pilot went back around the corner. Hawkins tried to remember his name—Miller? Schiller? He was missing the name tag on his flight suit. He came back with a floppy. "It's all there, sir."

O'Leary emerged from the ASW module with another floppy. "You know about the sub?"

Hawkins looked back and forth between them. "Mister Madje put it in the log. Anything new?"

"No, sir. But everything we do know is here for Fifth Fleet." O'Leary gave Hawkins a second floppy.

Hawkins turned his chair and put both in the hands of his message geek. "Get those out to Pilchard, red hot."

"Aye, aye, sir."

Bahrain

Valdez called the satphone in Harry's aircraft and got the pilot, Moad, who said he'd have to get Harry, who had to be waked from a deep sleep and wasn't happy.

"You need to talk to Al Craik," Harry said. "You could have asked for him in the first place."

"I work for you."

"Worse luck for me."

Craik sounded even worse than Harry did, his voice a dry croak. Still, he was there. Valdez told him about the stuff from Ong and plugging it into the JOTS, asked if it meant anything to Craik.

"You downloaded the stuff, you got the *startex* picture?"

"So they tell me." Valdez waited for enlightenment; nothing came. "What happened when whoever it was plugged his thing into the JOTS where you were, Commander?"

"The JOTS blinked. Then I had a wrestling match with him; that's all I saw."

"And it just blinked? The picture didn't change?"

"It was only a second, because then we had a fight and then another guy started shooting."

"We're letting it run, see what happens." Valdez waited for some comment from the clearly exhausted man on the other end. "See, I'd like to know at least if this is a picture of the actual start of the exercise, or is it a picture of the Indian *idea* of the start of the exercise—you follow me? What I mean is, did this guy mean to insert their idea of the exercise into the JOTS, or did he steal what was already on there?"

"Well, hmm— Listen, look at it again and see if it's got a Canadian frigate over against the Indian coast—about, um, 070 from the carrier, as I remember. If it's there, then that's not an Indian image, it's what we had up on our screen, because that frigate was hidden, and I don't think the Indians were on to it. If the frigate's there, I don't know what to say—maybe they wanted to steal our data so they could win the exercise?" He added, as if to himself, "You don't shoot people over an exercise."

"I'll check for the frigate."

Valdez went back and checked the JOTS and had himself

double-checked by Markey and Pulanski. There was no Canadian frigate.

"Okay, it's Indian and it's their idea of startex, then," Craik said. "I don't get it."

Valdez thanked him for his help and apologized for waking him up.

When he went back to the JOTS, three of the Indian ships had moved.

"Gonna be a long night," Markey said.

23

Trincomalee

The chartered 747 rolled to a stop two hundred feet from the darkened terminal, and the engines whined down, and, in the silence, men coughed and shuffled their feet, and overhead doors banged as weary sailors pulled down bags. Mary Totten was the only civilian female; she thought there were five or six other women among the couple of dozen people headed for the Navy's makeshift det in Sri Lanka.

"Wait, Bill," she said. Caddis was trying to climb over her. "Just sit down."

One good thing about Caddis—the only good thing so far—was that he did as he was told. When, six minutes later, she said "Now" and stood, he dutifully pulled himself up and helped her get their luggage out of the plane.

By the time they got out—the last ones off the aircraft—everybody else was lined up in front of a bus parked just beyond a chain-link fence. The bus's headlights and a sickly glow from its interior provided the only light. Hot, sticky blackness folded around them.

"City center?" she said to the last man in the line.

"I guess. I just go where I'm pointed."

She went along the line, asking where the bus was going. At the head, the bus driver, a small man with glasses that flashed in the light from inside, was flinging luggage into the well.

"Trincomalee?" she said.

"US Navy, Cosmopolitan Hotel."

"Is anybody here from the Navy?"

"Cosmopolitan Hotel, everybody Cosmopolitan Hotel."

"Duty officer?"

He said the name of the hotel a couple more times, and she turned away.

Bill had a huge rolling duffel, a shoulder bag, an overnighter, and a plastic shopping bag from the Bahrain duty-free shop.

"You carry yours, I'll carry mine," she said. She had the smallest size of rolling suitcase and a folding suit bag. *When in doubt, buy it when you get there.* "Let's go, Bill."

"We're not going on the bus?"

"We are not going on the bus."

She headed off into the darkness on a tarmacked road that paralleled the taxiway. She could hear Bill stumbling along behind her, his duffel rumbling over the rough pavement, his breathing labored. She wondered why she had brought him and reminded herself it was because of his brilliance and technical knowledge.

All that man Dukas had been able to tell her about Trincomalee was that they'd managed to rent an old hangar, and that the hangar was the last one in a row "beyond the terminal."

She kept on walking.

It was dark. As in *dark*.

The Navy det hangar was indeed the last one, and the only way she knew she was there was that she could see the silhouette of palm trees where any building beyond it should have been. Sweat was pouring down her sides and running into her eyes by then, and she was mad as hell.

Striding toward the black maw of the hangar, she recognized a couple of airplanes as being unquestionably military.

She was not big on aircraft ID, but she satisfied herself that they had some long skinny ones and some two-engined fat ones.

Somebody was snoring inside the hangar. She shouted and the snoring went right on. Moving into the darkness of the hangar itself, she tripped over something hard and fell on one knee. "Oh, go*damm*it!" she cried.

Bill's voice piped from far behind her. "You okay?"

"Oh, shut up." She pushed herself up, sure that she'd torn her chinos and was bleeding. She probed the thing on the floor with her toe, found something about three feet long, round, and hard. She made her way along it and only just in time saw a flicker of light to her right: she was about to walk into an airplane that, except at that one spot, was blocking some feeble light source within the hangar. She worked her way out along the wing, then ducked under it and saw a small, bare bulb ahead of her.

The bare bulb stuck out of the wall next to a pay telephone. Taped to it was a hand-written sign: "To call duty officer dial 647-898. Coins in slot."

Well, that was thoughtful of them. She didn't have Sri Lankan coins, of course. She felt in the slot where coins should go. No coins. They didn't mean that slot; they meant the slot where the change came out. Lots of coins down there.

She tried one, got nothing; tried another and then another and suddenly had a dial tone, which took her to the Cosmopolitan Hotel, which took her to a sleepy young man named Soleck.

"Duty officer Lieutenant Soleck speaking, sir."

"Lieutenant, I need to talk to your CO."

"Commander Siciliano's sleeping ma'am. Can I help you?"

"I need transport to India."

There was a pause, in which she thought she might have

heard a muffled, perhaps ironic, laugh. She ID'd herself, and he seemed to expect her; he asked where she was.

"I'm at your goddam hangar, where do you think I am?"

"You come in on the flight from Bahrain? Weren't you supposed to come to the hotel?"

"I don't want a hotel, Lieutenant, I want a flight to India!"

He sighed. "Ma'am, with all respect, this det isn't here to provide transportation for *anybody*. We got a bunch of really tired pilots who're trying to keep enough aircraft airborne to give CAP cover to a very important ship. Anything else, I'm really sorry. You'll have to talk to Commander Siciliano."

"When?"

"Tomorrow."

"Who's second in command?"

"He's in the air right now, ma'am."

"Lieutenant, you get your ass out here *now* and arrange transport for me, or heads are going to roll!"

Was he thinking that over? Was he going to dig his heels in? He sounded as reasonable as could be when he spoke. "Well, say twenty minutes to get dressed and get downstairs, half an hour to find a taxi—it's about an hour out to the field—well, I suppose maybe in a couple of hours, ma'am. I hate to think of you out there all alone while—"

"Oh, fuck off!"

Sri Lanka was connected to the Indian mainland by a bridge, but she knew the bridge was currently closed at both ends. No point in looking for the local rent-a-car.

Fucking Navy, she thought. She plunged into the darkness of the hangar.

Bahrain

At two in the morning, Valdez was dozing in an armchair when Lapierre shook his shoulder. Valdez came to with a crick in his neck and a pain in his lower back. "What'd it do?" he said. He thought there had been a major change in the JOTS.

"I just got a message from the *Fort Klock*. May mean nothing, but—" Lapierre sat down next to him, leaned forward as if he wanted to tell a secret. "A guy they picked out of the water yesterday said his plane was shot down by a *submarine*. This was right about startex. TAO on the *Klock* had a report at the time from somebody in the air that he thought he saw enemy activity and a weak signal that could have been this guy in the water, plus an F-14 got fired at in the same area. Somebody with a brain in intel plotted that and put it together with the guy's story, and they think there was a sub there."

Valdez leaned over the JOTS. Markey was sleeping on a chart table across the room; Pulanski had disappeared.

"This sub," Valdez said. It was still on the screen in, if he remembered correctly, its same location. "Sub shoots down a US aircraft, no way it's gonna be in the same location—" he looked at his watch—"nearly two hours later. This thing's been running; it's got changes, but the sub hasn't moved. I don't get it." He put the cursor on the submarine and got the message *Last known location*.

"The JOTS doesn't show you where things are," Lapierre said. "It shows you where people *report* things are. You with me here? And you have to understand, what Commander Craik had was the *referee's* JOTS. That means that his was the only one that would have shown everything—including that sub. The Indians' repeater showed only the Indian ships at startex, and then, if the exercise had gone forward, they'd have added the US ships and aircraft as they located them. Same with the US side—the US admiral's JOTS would have shown the US side only."

"But Commander Craik could see both sides."

"If the sub moved during the exercise and reported its position, his JOTS would show it."

"But—if our ASW didn't find the sub, and it didn't report a new position, it would still be there on the referee's JOTS

in the same place as, just like it says, 'last known location.'"
Valdez squinted at the screen. "What if the sub moved but
we didn't find it and it didn't report its new position?"

"Then it would show in its original position."

"But Jeez, wouldn't the BG have run ASW to locate it as
soon as they knew their plane was shot at?"

"But the *Jefferson* had the accident. Their ASW effort never
got underway." Lapierre slouched back in the chair, neck on
the chairback, long legs stuck out. "I need to talk to the
TAO." He was staring at the ceiling, obviously still working
it out. "What it looks like is, there's an Indian submarine
running around on the loose out there."

Valdez looked at the JOTS. "I don't get it." He straightened, made a face as he ran his tongue over his front teeth.
They tasted like something that had been in the fridge too
long. "I gotta call Commander Craik again. He'll love it."

He started for Lapierre's office and turned around. "Hey!"

Lapierre raised an eyebrow as the least energetic way of
asking what "hey" meant.

"What if the stuff the guy plugged into the JOTS changes
the positions when you put in data from the links? I mean—
what do I mean?—I mean, what if that program was meant
to seize the JOTS and *change* the data from the links? So that
no matter what people reported and no matter what, let's
say, our ASW found, the JOTS showed something else?"

Lapierre stared at him, then unfolded his long body. "Well,
let me try to input some data."

Valdez started out again. "I'll call Commander Craik."

The Serene Highness Hotel
Alan made his way through the shabby, beautiful corridors
of the palace, his left hand on the small of his back, wondering if he dared take another muscle relaxant now. Moad
padded along ahead of him, his feet covered in soft-soled
moccasins.

Outdoors, the night was wetly warm, sweet with the scent of something in flower, under that an odor of something spoiled, acidic. A bird screamed distantly; another, softer, trilled nearby.

The plane was pulled up on a pad near the palace, lights inside making the portholes look like a row of buttons. Alan hauled himself up the ladder, feeling the pain of the bullet crease on his back, the lower, burning sensation of something muscular. *Getting too old for this.*

"Yeah, Valdez."

Valdez's voice was tinny over the secure connection, almost a whistle. "Somebody aircrew from a plane yesterday, start of the exercise, was in the water and got picked up and taken to the *Jefferson.*" He gave Alan the coordinates. "He says his plane was shot down by a sub. Location checks out with an Indian sub on the startex plot in that data your jg Ong sent me. What I need to know is, does it check out with what you remember of startex?"

Alan could call up the JOTS layout as he had seen it before all hell had broken loose—he had stared at it long enough, waiting for things to start. He knew precisely where the sub had been. Still—

"A sub shot down an *aircraft?*"

"That's the story."

Would have to be something slow and low, maybe an S-3. *Christ, Paul Stevens was down there—I had a fight with Rafe about it—then he told me yesterday that Stevens got shot down.* "Yeah, it checks. Listen, Valdez, put Lieutenant-Commander Lapierre on."

He fired questions at Lapierre, who answered yes to all of them: Had he informed the admiral or the chief of staff? Had he informed the BG? Had he messaged the TAO for any new data on the sub?

Then Alan told Lapierre exactly what he wanted to know next. Getting answers meant Lapierre's staying up the rest of the night sending messages to the BG, to NSA's satellite-photography arm, and to the WMD Center at the CIA. Lapierre was no happier about the idea of staying up than Alan had been about climbing out of a wonderfully comfortable bed, but he merely groaned once and said, "Will do." Alan could picture that toothy, Mortimer Snerd grin.

"One more thing," Lapierre said when they were done. "Valdez suggested inputting new data into the JOTS while that program you guys sent us was in place. News flash, Al: you can input data to reposition the Indian ships and they show the new positions on the screen okay. *All but the sub.*"

Alan thought about that. "So even if the *Jefferson* hadn't been hit and they'd been able to launch their ASW—" he was thinking it through—"and even if they'd found the sub and put it into the link, it wouldn't have shown on my JOTS." He thought some more and then repeated, "On *my* JOTS. Question is, Dickie, would the new data have shown on everybody else's JOTS? I mean, was that what the whole thing was about—to hide the sub from *everybody*?"

"Oh, shit."

He thought about what it meant to have every JOTS screen with a glitch that kept a submarine from showing. "Oh, shit, indeed," he said. "You better wake the admiral."

Then Alan went into the hotel and waked Ong and Benvenuto and told them it was time to go to work, and he walked back through the darkness to the plane. And he decided that, no, he couldn't take any more muscle relaxants, but, yes, he could risk a couple of aspirins. And then, at last, he did what he'd wanted to do since he'd got out of bed: he curled up in a passenger seat and tried to sleep while he waited for the machines of intelligence to grind.

Outside, an animal that sounded to him like an African leopard coughed.

Bahrain

Ray Spinner had got a Canadian nurse he'd been pursuing for three weeks into the sack, and he was now lying awake wondering how come a really cute woman was a really bad lay. It didn't occur to him to wonder if he was perhaps a little less stimulating than a good vibrator himself.

She was lying beside him, exhaling the last fumes of expensive cabernet. He'd had to dine her, wine her, and bullshit her for two hours before he could get her pants off, and, while even bad sex is better than no sex at all, shouldn't there have been a better payoff for all that time and money? She didn't even seem to enjoy giving head, which in Spinner's view was a serious defect in a woman.

"How was it for you?" she said sleepily.

"Fan-fucking-tastic!" Lying was easy, also cheaper than cabernet. Maybe he'd want her again sometime. "I didn't know you were awake."

"I've been lying here. Thinking."

In Spinner's view, "thinking" was something he didn't want women to do, so he didn't ask her what she was thinking about.

"Want to know about what?" she said.

"Oh, absolutely."

"I was thinking I'm starved." She sat up. Light from the window shone on her. She had a really great body. Really great. But she didn't do much with it. "Let's eat."

Well, there went his chance to sneak out while she was still asleep and finesse all the morning-after crap. *Was I really good? Was it really good for you? Was it really, really good? On a scale of one to ten—*

She pulled on a robe that had seen better days—another thing about her, she wasn't what he'd call fastidious—and headed into the kitchen. Spinner, in pants and shirt, no socks or shoes, followed, kissed the back of her neck as if he was still turned on, and sat down when he got about the response

285

he expected—on a scale of one to ten, something with a decimal point. She was already throwing eggs into a bowl. Going to wow him with her ability to cook. If she thought he was cruising for a wife, she was crazy.

"—so what could I do but stand there, this guy's kidney in my hand—" she was saying. Her idea of conversation had a lot to do with talking about her work. So did her idea of simile. At one point she had said, "I was about as welcome as a colostomy bag." Really, she had no taste, along with everything else.

She scrambled the eggs and made ranch toast and put out three kinds of jam, and when he asked her if she always ate a breakfast like that, she looked hurt. *Time to go*, Spinner thought, but then she was talking again, on and on, and he munched his way through the food and pretended to be interested and said Mmm and No Kidding and Wow.

And then she said something interesting.

"Who?" Spinner said.

"I'm not supposed to tell, really. The new head of the NCIS office. No kidding."

Spinner's ears were like a computer program that pinged on certain search terms. They had pinged on "NCIS." He didn't give a shit really about NCIS or what it did, but he knew that it was on the fringe of intelligence, and getting inside gossip about it just might be useful to a man with his connections.

"His girlfriend's pregnant?"

"Mm-mm, tested positive and then she comes back and asks about an abortion, and we had to tell her that armed-services personnel no longer get abortions paid for since the new administration, and she goes, 'I'm not armed-services personnel, I just live with somebody.'"

"I don't know how you feel about it," Spinner said, "but I think that the taking of innocent life is disgusting and immoral." He really meant that, as a matter of fact. And he

286

meant it even more now that there was a conservative in the White House, where his father had said it might do him good to think the right things.

She looked at him and then at the forkful of egg she had been about to put into her mouth, and then she shrugged and said, "Don't become a nurse, okay?"

Spinner had the feeling that she was belittling him. *She* was belittling *him*. "Life begins at conception," he said.

She did an odd thing: she raised an eyebrow—one, not both, something he hadn't seen her do before—and said in a voice he'd never heard from her, "Majored in science, did we?"

Spinner wasn't going to sit there and be belittled by a fucking *nurse*, for God's sake, by a fucking *log* who lay there and didn't have any more wiggle in her ass than a fucking concrete *block*. On the other hand, he didn't want to lose the story about the NCIS, so he bit back the lecture on the sanctity of life and said, as if she hadn't shown him what a dork she really was, "So, the head of the local NCIS office knocked up his sweetie?"

"You didn't hear it from me." She gathered up the plates. "More coffee?"

"I really ought to go." He meant it as a punishment.

She didn't object as much as he thought she should.

Trincomalee

Mary Totten had stormed back through the dark hangar, barking her shins on hard, invisible objects. She'd have missed Bill Caddis if she hadn't fallen over him and his baggage, which formed a round, soft pile directly in her path. She dropped her bags on top of him, ripped a pair of running shoes out of it and jammed her feet into them. "You stay here!" He grunted and didn't wake up.

She jogged back up the access road she'd just walked down from the terminal. It was a little spooky, running over uneven

287

asphalt in the dark in a country where they might have God-knew-what wildlife running around a deserted airport. Once, something went scurrying away ahead of her, but aside from boosting her heartbeat into near-max, the incident was harmless.

There were no, count them, *no* air charter companies along the road at Trincomalee airport. None on the side of the terminal she'd first gone down, none on the other side. And no lights. And the bus was long gone.

She jogged back down to the Navy hangar and felt her way to Bill, who was still asleep on the pile of bags. Mary wrestled her laptop out of her suitcase and sat down on some of Bill's luggage and typed in "Trincomalee air charter."

Fifteen minutes later, on her third try at the phone numbers she'd taken down, she got somebody who spoke English and who thought that for enough money he could come to the airfield and he could perhaps fly her to India, if, perhaps, the money was enough, because India was closed, did she know that, yes?

It took him an hour to get there.

It took them fifteen minutes to negotiate.

It took him two hours to get a single-engine Cessna 180 checked, gassed, and ready to fly.

With Bill sleeping in a rear seat, they took off into a still-black sky where dawn was only a promise at the eastern edge.

Day Three

24

The Indian Ocean

In the light of dawn, a naval battle group is visible from space. It's not quite visible with the naked eye, but aided by a satellite you can see the black speck of the carrier and the contrasting white V of her wake if the sun is up and the sky is clear. Her immediate escorts with their own white wakes stick to the carrier like a flock of disciplined gulls—the Aegis cruiser and perhaps one of the new Aegis destroyers; the supply ship; the gator freighter carrying a battalion or more of Marines. Farther out, the satellite will show you the radar picket ships and the anti-submarine screen. The first are widening the radar horizon of the group, offering their hulls as a sacrifice to a potential threat in order to protect the carrier from surprises. The second are clearing the path of the carrier so that no hostile submarine can deploy a torpedo.

USS *Thomas Jefferson* is making almost seven knots as she heads SSE. Most of her escorts are drawn tight about her. With the exception of the Canadian frigate HMCS *Picton*, her most distant picket, USS *Lawrence*, is only twenty-five miles north of the carrier.

From space, the *Jefferson* looks as she does every day of her operational cycle.

Distance is deceiving.

North of her and her little flock of white Vs are two different flocks. The nearest white V is only thirty miles north of the *Lawrence*, but over the horizon and thus invisible to the carrier through most of the electromagnetic spectrum. On the *Jefferson* and the *Fort Klock*, however, they have computers and displays that show the last location of this ship—twelve hours ago. Her loyalty is unknown; her position, based on her last recorded course and speed, is a far-on circle of possibility, like the path of an electron.

She is the southern radar picket for five other Vs.

North and west again, there are only two Vs. A third ship is visible from orbit even without a satellite because of the plume of smoke that rises from her to the heavens. She does not have a wake.

The Serene Highness Hotel

Ong and Benvenuto were in touch with Valdez and Mavis Halloran by e-mail, and the four shot messages back and forth as the dawn came on. The first day-birds stirred—a peep here, a shriek there—and the eastern sky changed from black to deep blue to lavender, turning the landscape from gray to mauve, and its first details appeared—a tree, a building, a moving woman.

As the sun's rim just touched the horizon, Valdez and Mavis broke the encryption in the USB key and e-mailed it to Ong.

The palace stirred.

Eleven women straggled to a rear door from the houses beyond the runway. Something metallic clanged, and a female voice was sharp against the bird sounds; a brief argument exploded—shouting, sudden silence. Pots and dishware clinked.

Twenty minutes later, three turbaned men carried chairs and tables out to the blacktop near the airplane, then disappeared and returned after another ten minutes with two oversized teacarts that bounced and tipped as they came along the cracked concrete beside the palace. They carried a coffee urn, covered dishes, cutlery, English jam jars, sugar bowls, milk jugs, plates of cut-up mangoes and papayas and bananas, a silver toast rack configured like a snake whose coils held the slices, breads, freshly baked muffins, and, a jarring note, four kinds of commercial cereals in their unopened boxes.

"What, no porridge?" Harry O'Neill said, having strolled out the front door as the carts came up the walk.

"Coming, sir," one of the turbaned men said. A silver chafing dish was coming along the walk, a pair of legs below it and a turban showing over the top.

"What you do not see, demand; what you see, command," Harry murmured. "Coffee!" he snapped. He was wearing white linen shorts and a short-sleeved Madras shirt, well-worn and -bled, his eyes, good and bad, hidden behind sunglasses.

"Sir!" The coffee appeared; cream and sugar appeared, were waved away. Harry carried the cup up the aircraft steps, its aroma turning Ong's and Benvenuto's heads from their laptops, and back through the aircraft to the seat where Alan lay curled. Harry passed the coffee under Alan's nose.

The eyes opened.

"Jocund day stands tiptoe on the misty mountain-tops," Harry said.

Alan groaned. "Where's your turban?"

"Drink and awake, *effendi*. The caravanserai's a-move."

Alan moaned and straightened in the seat. He took the cup and drank and gave a long, pleased sigh.

"When you're feeling human, join me under the banyan tree and we'll talk business." Harry went back up the aircraft and down the steps.

USS *Thomas Jefferson*

"You going off watch, Lieutenant?"

Madje relinquished the TAO's chair to his relief. He saw

the ASW watch officer leaning through the hatch and dragged himself over. "Yeah." He stretched as far as the low overhead would allow him. "Need something, Warrant Officer O'Leary?"

"Want to toss this over the side on the way to your rack?" O'Leary held up a four-foot-long tube.

Madje wondered if the guy was having him on. "Over the side?" he asked dully. He'd been on for six hours, watching the remnants of the Indian fleet to the north on ESM as they tried to stay alive. He had watched the battle between loyalists and mutineers through passive sensors. That's us, he thought. Passive. He was almost over his bitterness that they weren't helping the good Indians.

He was also wasted with fatigue.

O'Leary barked a laugh. "Sonobuoy, Lieutenant. I'd go up and toss it in myself, but I'm alone here."

Madje took the tube and looked at it without any comprehension.

"Just open the cap, pull the buoy free and toss it clear of the rail. Think of it as your dues for drinking my coffee."

"Roger that," Madje said. He took the tube carefully. "Damn, Warrant, are we that desperate?"

O'Leary opened his mouth, thought better of it, and grunted.

Madje winced. In other words, yes.

The Serene Highness Hotel

Five minutes after Harry had left him, Alan came down the Lear jet's folding steps; by the time he reached the ground, a turbaned man was standing there with fresh coffee. Alan crossed to a table where Harry was sitting alone, noted Ong and Benvenuto at another. Alan could smell steak, eggs, toast. "No bacon?" he said as he eased into a chair.

"The maharajah is Muslim. No meat of the pig."

"Well! There goes one of their five stars."

Harry was eating Weetabix. When Alan said something about its being soggy, Harry grinned. "Weetabix is an acquired taste. Soggy is part of its charm." He wiped his mouth. "Djalik was up on the roof and found an antenna array under a permeable dome." He pointed up with his spoon. "Invisible to the eyes in the sky."

"You're trying to tell me something, I'll bet."

"I found a bug in my room. Valuable antique—Soviet, circa 1970. Not worth piss-all with the electricity off, but a few deep-cell batteries would keep a whole palaceful of them running for a week. Feed yourself, bud; there's work to do."

Alan filled a plate at the buffet, and one of the turbaned men insisted upon taking it from him and putting it down on the table with cutlery and a snowy napkin. When the man was gone, Harry said, "Safe house."

"You think?"

"Mmm." Harry was now eating chappatis and some sort of savory vegetable stuff with rice, using the chappati to pick up the vegetables and carry them to his mouth, licking his fingers after each load. "My guess is it's some branch of Indian intel, probably mil spec because of the old Soviet stuff. *Not* the Servants of the Earth, because they'd have the latest and coolest." He wiped his fingers on his napkin. "I wonder if I could bribe the cook away from the maharajah and take him to Bahrain." He belched. "If that's breakfast, when's lunch?"

"Major Rao sends us here; it's an intel safe house; there-fore—"

"My guess is that Major Rao is not just Army intel, but RAW, right." RAW—Research and Analysis Wing, the most secret level of Indian intelligence. Harry put his palms on the table as if he planned to push himself away from it. "I think it's time to put our cards on the table and have Major Rao do the same, We need all the help we can get, and so does he." Harry pushed himself back. "Fruit—time for fruit—"

A turbaned man appeared with a bowl of fruit.

Alan told him what he had learned overnight from Valdez and Lapierre. "I've asked for info on nuke delivery systems from the Agency WMD Center, but we haven't heard zip. 'Urgent' is not in their vocabulary." He spread black currant jam on a triangle of toast. "Valdez broke the decryption on the gold keys and sent what he called 'protocols' for the Servants of the Earth sites, which has Ong and Benvenuto all excited. They spent the night looking for data on the Servants technical capabilities. Seems they're into a lot of stuff."

"Like arming submarines?"

"Like owning companies that bid on military contracts. I told Ong to dig for connections with the Indian Navy and submarines." He shrugged.

Harry sucked at something between two front teeth and signaled for more coffee. "I compared the video that my contact got from the Ambur security cameras with the builders' plans. The helicopter that left the place was heading about one-ninety or two hundred when it left there."

Alan shrugged again. "I asked Lapierre to get satellite imagery of both coasts and put a photo analyst on it looking for something that screams 'submarine.'" He waited while fresh coffee was put in front of him. "When are you going to put the bell on Major Rao?"

"I'm not—you are." Harry looked at his watch. "My supposed Agency control is going to bop in here any time— rent-a-plane. My cover is pretty thin, at best, Al, but I'd rather not get naked for Major Rao." He picked up a tote bag from the ground and handed it across. Inside were the videocam and the disks from Mohir. "Show him the stuff with the chopper. It's in the mini-cam."

"Your cover story's pretty thin."

"You can't be too thin or too rich." Harry stood. "I'm going to mosey out on to that runway with Djalik and an umbrella and wait for my control. You got a better idea?"

"You black guys have all the fun."

"We be made fo' fun."

Harry strolled away. A few minutes later, Alan saw him and Djalik as watery miniatures in the heat shimmer already rising from the runway. A golf umbrella rose above their heads, but almost at once two hotel servants trotted out with chairs and a table and a beach umbrella.

USS *Thomas Jefferson*

Madje stepped through the hatch and blinked at the first rays of the rising sun. The sea showed dark turquoise. The port-side ladder was a twisted wreck, and the stanchions and chains were gone, so he had to pin the cylinder to the buckled catwalk with one hand and climb down while the sea rushed by, forty feet below his legs.

"Hey! Dickhead!" Someone above him was shouting.

He pulled the cap off the tube, turned it out over the water and watched the buoy slide free and fall. He didn't even see the splash, lost in the blue-green turbulence of the hull.

"You!"

Madje looked up at the deck. A man in a red turtleneck and a white deck helmet stood over him, hands on his hips. "Get off the fucking catwalk before you get yourself fucking killed!" the man yelled, and added as an afterthought, "Sir!"

In fact, Madje was feeling the catwalk giving under his weight. He reached up, grabbed the edge of the buckled deck and struggled to pull himself up. Two tattooed arms grabbed him under the armpits and hauled him on to the deck.

"What the fuck are you doing on my deck without a float coat?" The man pushed his face within inches of Madje's. "Sir?"

Excuses bounced around in his head like balls on a handball court. "I wasn't going on deck, Chief. I'm the flag lieutenant, Chief. I was doing a guy a favor, Chief." He hadn't been so rattled by being in the wrong since AOCS. "No excuse, Chief," came the old answer.

The Chief smiled. "Can you cross the fucking deck without falling off?" he said, but not unkindly. He pushed Madje toward an access hatch on the starboard side. Then he turned and bellowed at someone else. "You saving some of that fucking nonskid to eat, Glock? Get it all on the deck, you fat fuck."

Madje left him and started across the deck and then stopped, still blinking in the morning sun. The deck was covered in work crews, dozens of them, hundreds of men and women working in a melee of shouts and a riot of flight-deck jerseys. Teams in a line across the deck were laying steel plates over the damaged areas and cutting them to shape, welding them down, their arcs clear and blue in the new light and hissing like high-powered static. Behind them waited crews carrying more steel plate, and more. Because the main elevator was wrecked, they were carrying them up through a hatch that had been cut in the deck, with a new ladder well descending into the darkness of the hull.

Behind the welders were teams with grinding equipment, finishing the edges of the deck plates, and behind them came a phalanx of sailors with long-handled brushes and buckets of the thick black mixture that, when it set, made the flight deck safe to cross. Nonskid. The whole effort was moving from the bow aft, and Madje could see that the bow already had stripes and spot markings laid over the nonskid. From frame 100 forward, *Jefferson* was operational, except for cat three, which had born the full force of an explosion.

He walked to the new ladder well and waited for another team to pass him with a deck plate that must have weighed two hundred pounds. Off to his right, two teams of welders were bracing the twisted base of the superstructure with metal beams. The top thirty feet had been cut away, left to sink somewhere in the Indian Ocean. The missing height and the lack of antenna arrays made the carrier look bald, but just forward of the island a swarm of electrician's mates were installing cable and antenna dishes: one team soldered under the supervision of a warrant officer with a cable chart while another team was installing cable ducts to cover the wires.

Madje drew a big breath and realized he was grinning. He knew, intellectually, that carriers went to sea loaded with material for self-repair, but it was a stunning thing to see how quickly it was done, or the impact on the damage of hundreds of trained hands. He paused to watch the crew coming up to move the huge deck plate into position and realized that he was in the way; this was no place for an observer.

But before his head hit the pillow in a borrowed rack deep in the bowels of third deck, another team had the plate welded in place, and a third team was grinding it level. The *Jefferson* was not done yet.

The Serene Highness Hotel

Major Rao joined Alan as he was finishing breakfast. He was having tea and the same vegetable dish that Harry had had, plus an array of small metal bowls with which a servant surrounded his plate. Alan saw yogurt, something bright green, two reddish things he supposed were chutneys, three unidentifiables, and a dish of dried fruits and nuts.

Both of them were deliberately cheerful. Rao asked about Alan's back, professed delight that he was feeling better. Alan admired the food and waited through Rao's explanation of what was in each of the metal bowls. Then the conversation ran down.

"I wonder if we have something in common," Alan said. Not one of his best opening lines; he still felt drugged.

Rao, in the midst of putting food into his mouth, looked up.

"A common interest," Alan said. He took the videocam

out of the bag and handed it over. "Push there to start it. There's some interesting imagery in it."

Rao, who ate with a fork rather than his fingers, put his utensils down on his plate, wiped his hands, pressed the switch. He looked at the two-minute segment that showed Building Thirty-seven and the helicopter taking off from it and asked to see it again and then sat there without eating and played the segment not once more, but three times.

"Building Thirty-seven," Alan said. He waited. "The helicopter is an old but serviceable Soviet Mi-26. Maximum load twenty thousand kilos."

Rao put the videocam down, raising his eyebrows as if in question. "Where did you get this?"

"How many nuclear devices were stored in Building Thirty-seven?" Alan said. Bang, no subtlety—he wasn't up to subtlety just yet.

Rao had picked up his fork as if he was going to eat, but he began instead to trace patterns with it in the gravy on his plate. "That is a startling assumption," he said. "Which I might be more willing to explore if I knew—knew the bona fides of that tape."

"I'm an intelligence officer." He told Rao about the exercise and about the violence at startex and the flight through the Mahe naval base. Then he shrugged. "An agent provided the tape."

Rao nodded. "*That* is why your photo was on the laptop with the message to kill you on sight!" Rao nodded his head. "Rather persuasive bona fides."

"I was ordered to find out what had happened to the nuclear devices stored in Building Thirty-seven."

"Very nice to have a friend with a Lear jet."

"Very nice to have a rich friend, yes." Alan gestured toward the palace. "Very nice to have a friend with a palace."

Rao was still making patterns in the gravy. "Not my friend, I'm afraid."

"With an antenna array on the roof and bugs in the rooms."
Alan put his forearms on the table. "Are all the servants
trained intelligence people?" When Rao didn't answer, Alan
said, "Is the maharajah a senior intelligence officer?"

Rao smiled but did not look up. "The maharajah is my
uncle."

Alan waited. Rao picked up a little of the food with the
fork and ate it; he seemed to have trouble swallowing this
time, and he sipped tea and looked away and didn't say
anything. After a while, he picked up the camera and looked
at the video again.

"It's an original security-camera feed from Ambur. That's
all I'm prepared to say. It's genuine. Your turn. How many
nuclear devices were there in Building Thirty-seven?" Alan
leaned forward.

Rao looked across the runway where Harry and Djalik
were sitting. A sudden silence fell, as if all the birds and
insects had at that moment decided to shut up. In that abrupt
quiet, the faint sound of a piston engine reached Alan's ears.
He searched for the airplane in the southern sky. Rao, too,
searched and apparently found it, and, as if the coming of
the airplane meant the arrival of some weight that changed
a balance, he said, "There were three nuclear devices in
Building Thirty-seven." He put his hand on his teacup but
didn't lift it. It was trembling, but his voice was steady. "The
question is, how many are there in there now?"

"What'd Rao say?" Harry said.

Alan told him. "He wants to work with us. He's Indian
Army intel—or that's his story, anyway. I think he's Research
and Analysis Wing, like you said. I think this whole set up
has RAW written all over it. He says he's pretty much on his
own because he's lost touch with New Delhi."

"Out there on a shoeshine and a smile. Well, well." Harry's
grin was broad below the sunglasses. "How many nukes?"

"Three."

Harry made a ticking sound with his tongue. "Make a bit of a mess, three nukes. Warheads?"

"He says not configured. But I'm not sure I believe him. Anyway, the submarine stuff blindsided him. Apparently, what his people were afraid of before he lost touch was that the nukes would either be turned on Pakistan or sold out of the country. Now he can see the headline—'India Nukes US Battle Group, Massive Retaliation to Follow.'"

"With two nukes left to make more trouble with, right. Well, is he going to play team ball?"

"He says so. How about your Agency control?"

"She's a handsome bitch on wheels. At least she got on the WMD Center in nothing flat. She says if we don't start to get data from them in fifteen minutes, she'll kick ass at the DDI level."

"You tell her she's under my command?"

Harry nodded.

"What'd she say?"

"Nothing to what she'll say when she hears that Major Rao is part of the package, too."

25

The Serene Highness Hotel

Showered, shaved, and dressed in a crisp shirt and shorts that had appeared on his bed, Alan sat at the now cleared breakfast table with a cup of coffee. The truth was—the physical discomforts aside—he felt drained. He was still finding it hard to concentrate. Maybe it was the muscle relaxants. Or the heat. Or—wasn't depression like this? He tried to focus on a specific question to force his mind to work. For example—why, why, *why* had the Indians tried to do something to the JOTS? What had they been after?

He raised his cup to drink, and over the rim he saw a woman striding along the patio. Not Indian, therefore Harry's "handsome bitch on wheels." Alan watched her give a turbaned man a big smile and speak a word and then come striding toward him. "I'm Mary Brevard." She held out a hand. "I know who you are."

He smiled. "Always pleased to meet a friend of Harry's."

She grunted at the idea that she and Harry were friends. She said, "I guess you guys really got the goods. I've sent the video and everything I thought mattered back to my office."

He glanced around, but the patio was empty, the only motion the gentle swaying of the fronds of a banyan tree. "You're with the WMD Center?"

"I'm the *head* of WMD, Commander."

He stared at her, unable to say anything bright. "So—on paper, you're senior to me, Mary."

Behind her, a hundred feet away, he saw Fidel amble into sight and stand looking at the flat land, his hands on his hips.

She leaned forward. "I promised your admiral I'd take orders from you. That was the price of coming out here. But if there are nukes, they're mine. If there's intel on WMD, it's mine."

"If there are nukes, I think they belong to Major Rao."

"Who's Major Rao?"

"I think he's a senior officer in the Research and Analysis Wing of the Indian military. He's inside someplace."

"What the fuck is he doing here?"

"The hotel seems to be an RAW safe house. The maharajah who owns it is his uncle, he says."

"This could be a serious CI issue!"

He beckoned to one of the turbaned men. "Would you find Major Rao, please?" He waited until the man was gone. "Can your cover handle meeting him?"

"What the hell. I'm here 'declared,' which means that somewhere in Delhi a fax machine with no power should have received my passport and the Indians should accept my status and diplomatic credentials."

"What's your story?"

"I'm a diplomatic security officer come out from Bahrain to support you. I have a passport and creds to prove it." She shrugged. "If he's really RAW, he'll see through me in a second." She shrugged.

Major Rao came through a pair of French doors behind them. He smiled at Alan and gave Mary a long look, not all of it professional. She returned it with interest.

"Major Rao, Mary Brevard from the State Department." Alan saw Moad waving to him from the plane.

"Harry wants you!" Moad called.

It seemed a good cue to leave. "Would you two excuse me for a moment?"

He passed Fidel, who was putting together a breakfast, on the way to the plane.

Fidel glanced up, then away. "You okay?" Alan said.

Fidel dipped into a bowl of cut-up fruit. "I'll be okay." Putting it in the future.

"I guess I'll be okay, too."

Fidel looked at him then, a full, long look, studying his eyes. "You sleep okay?"

"They gave me pills."

Fidel let out a long breath. "I didn't sleep so good." He shut his lips together tight. He looked away from Alan toward the flat, alien landscape. He turned away. "Maybe I'm getting old."

Alan thought maybe they both were.

USS *Thomas Jefferson*

The incoming TAO took a slug of espresso from his thermos and, face grim, cycled through the screens of data that Madje had passed down to him to show the night's activity.

"God damn it, the mutineers got the *Betwa*," he growled to no one in particular. The *Betwa* was a well-handled frigate that had held its own since the first mutiny, repeatedly covering the withdrawal of other damaged ships with skill and daring. He flicked to the next screen.

An ensign assigned from the navigation department flipped through the message board beside him. "She hasn't sunk and we think a message that went out an hour back might mean she has her fires out." He handed the new TAO a message on yellow paper. He glanced at it. The ensign took a chance and said, "Maybe she'll make it."

The TAO looked at the kid next to him. He swallowed his first temptation to savage the boy. "Yeah, Ensign, maybe she will." He looked back at the screen where the JOTS was replaying the ESM cuts that showed the coordinated attack on the *Betwa*. "No thanks to us."

The Serene Highness Hotel

In the aircraft, Ong and Benvenuto looked exhausted, heavy circles under their eyes, sagging shoulders, but they were hard at it, their heads down over one computer. They didn't even look up as Alan brushed past, but continued a jargon-filled muttering about data streams. Behind them, a heavy man with pale eyes looked at Alan without interest and said in a voice too loud for the space, "You guys got anything out of the Delhi mainframes?"

Alan went on through to join Harry. "Who's the fat nerd?" he said.

"Mary's geek. All the social skills of a slug. You got a phone call from Lapierre—if he's still on." He got up and handed Alan a headset.

"You could have told me she was the *head* of WMD," Alan said.

"Yeah, I could." Harry smiled. "But you're a big boy." Harry slapped the seatbacks.

"Al Craik," Alan said into the headset.

Lapierre identified himself and began to brief him. He sounded exhausted. "Aircrew from an S-3 intercepted an anomalous signal last night off the south coast of India. All hell was breaking loose—still is, from what we can tell—but we think it's the missing sub. I say again, we *think* it's the sub."

Alan looked up at Harry. "Map?" he said. "Chart? South-west coast of India?"

Harry vanished. Alan scrounged a pen and an old receipt from the fold-down desk. "Give me the location."

"The footprint is pretty big, Al. Ninety by sixty miles. But it's centered on 09N 077E."

Alan read it back, grabbed a chart that Harry shoved at

him. He plotted a rough circle. "I got a town marked *Quilon*, right on the coast."

"That's right."

"Looks like a natural harbor, Dickie."

"But a hell of a long way from the battle group." *If it's intending to attack us,* he meant.

"Huh." If the sub had kept moving at five knots since it had shot down Stevens's plane, it could have given off the signal near Quilon. But why go there, as Lapierre said, if it was after the *Jefferson*? Why wasn't it shadowing the BG? "Got a theory, Dickie?"

"Admiral Pilchard is tearing out what hair he has left wondering if the BG needs CAP *and* round-the-clock ASW. Acting BG CO, on the other hand, wants them to have the lowest possible profile. Skivvy is that Washington is trying to tie Pilchard's hands on this and hope that the *Jefferson* makes Colombo without an incident."

"Incident" was a nice word for an attack on a crippled aircraft carrier.

"What's Washington playing at?"

"Uh—" Lapierre was one of those old-fashioned officers who believed that you never discussed politics, women, or religion. "I think they're 'disengaging' from what's going on in India."

Alan found himself wishing that he could do the same thing. He rubbed his forehead and forced himself to concentrate. "Okay—is the CAP still flying?"

Lapierre told him that Rose had got Sri Lankan permission for the CAP to fly armed out of Trincomalee, and that the planes there now had fuel.

"So the *Jefferson* has at least some cover. Okay, tell the admiral I said that we don't know enough yet to call off ASW coverage for the BG. I think he's gotta overrule the acting CO until we sort this out. Get an ETA Colombo for the *Jefferson* and plot possibles for that sub—like, it wouldn't take a genius to guess that the carrier is going to Colombo, so does the sub plan to intercept it someplace? And where would that be and how soon, because you for sure want to tell the flag the BG needs CAP and ASW until at least then. The question right now is, what's the sub doing down there near Quilon? There any kind of naval facility down there?"

"Our data says no, but a SIGINT report last year said that some kind of exercise was held there. NSG logged it as a special-forces landing exercise. From a sub."

Alan rubbed his nose. "From a sub. Huh." He tried to think it through, gave up for lack of information. It was all pie in the sky. "Any more good news?"

Lapierre laughed. Alan told him to get some sleep and ended the call, then sketched the situation in for Harry, who had flung himself into the next seat. Alan showed him the chart and Quilon and a roughly sketched-in track for the *Jefferson*. He put the pencil on a point several hundred miles off the coast. "BG ought to be here by now. That sub's a diesel. If it's really at Quilon, it's put itself in a worse position to attack with conventional torpedoes than it was three days ago."

Harry was lying back in the seat, his head on his left hand with the forefinger running up his cheek. "Maybe it's not going to use conventional torpedoes. Maybe it's picking up the nukes."

"To do what ? You can't fit nuclear torpedoes into a diesel sub; they're too big. And it's not missile-configured, either."

"Suicide mission? They'd only need to get within ten miles or so of the carrier."

Alan groaned. "Jesus, you have a gloomy mind." He stood. "I left your boss and Major Rao together."

"She's *not* my boss."

"Well, we're lucky that Pilchard made sure she's not *my* boss." He stood "You sit here and stay cool."

"Not for long. Power's low." Harry raised his eyebrows,

pointed a finger. "Time, bud." The temperature inside the plane, he pointed out, was climbing, and they would have to shut down the air-conditioning altogether or get a land line or more fuel, because the plane's auxiliary power was heading for zero.

Alan looked at the three working in the front of the aircraft "We'll have to get these guys indoors."

"No electricity there, either."

Alan raised a skeptical eyebrow. "A safe house without a generator? Somehow, I'm not convinced."

"Are you suggesting that that nice maharajah deliberately denied us electricity? I'm shocked—*shocked*!" Harry raised an eyebrow.

The White House, Washington

It was nearly midnight in Washington, and the President was in bed. As a result, he wasn't pleased when the director of the CIA called him to tell him that one of their officers, on the spot in India, had evidence that it was now certain that three nuclear devices had been stolen from a secret Indian government site. The President, who had no more interest in India than he had in girls' basketball, said that the Agency should pull together any evidence they had to show that the nukes were a threat to the United States and present it at the morning briefing. Then he went back to bed.

26

The Serene Highness Hotel
The Serene Highness Hotel of course had a generator. The maharajah's secretary explained that it had regrettably not been working when they had arrived, but, after the hotel mechanics had worked on it all night, it now functioned. Alan heard this speech through without cursing or breaking into derisive laughter, although he didn't dare look at Major Rao, who was resolutely not looking at him, either.

Rao had been persuaded that it was better to have Alan's computer people working on what had become their common problem than having them sitting in an airplane without power. It had taken Alan twenty minutes to convince him, and then Rao had had to go away (not to talk to New Delhi, unless he was lying about having no comm link). He had come back five minutes later to say that, yes, electricity could be provided. (Having been gone long enough only to check with some higher-up close by. Like the Maharajah, perhaps?) It occurred to Alan that Rao saw an advantage to bringing the three computer specialists in where they could be monitored. (Always trust your allies, right?)

A squad of turbaned servants was soon moving equipment from the Lear jet into a big, gloomy room several doors away from the music room. In the middle sat a full-size billiard table that made it, Alan guessed, the billiard room. The space was dark and ornate—carved, varnished wainscoting, green flocked wallpaper above it, and, over the enormous mahogany table, a lamp with a leaded glass shade whose light, reflected from the green felt of the table, made the room seem like an aquarium.

Now they were all in there for a briefing on what the geeks had found—a showered Ong, an unwashed Bill, plus Benvenuto, Alan, Mary Totten, aka Cindy Brevard, and Rao. Djalik and Fidel had the morning off to do R&R by the pool. Harry had exiled himself to his room to preserve what little was left of his cover.

Ong started the briefing. "We—Petty Officer Benvenuto and I—" she made it clear that Bill was not to get credit for this part of the operation—"have followed the money spent by SOE. All over India. We thought that the best strategy was to get a fix on their holdings. Petty Officer Benvenuto followed one of the money trails to Europe and another into an offshore bank in the Cayman Islands. Then we tried to focus on SOE holdings in India, and then—" She turned a page of her notes. "There are over seven hundred of them, and that's not counting front-company sub-holdings. Just for example, they own a cell-phone network, which is how they were able to communicate when everything else went down at Mahe."

"How much are they worth?" Mary's eyes were narrowed.

"Maybe ten billion. Maybe double that."

"*Dollars?*"

"Just their Delhi real estate's worth a quarter of that."

Benvenuto jumped in after a glance at Ong. "So when Bill—uh, Mister Caddis—arrived, we were facing this mountain of data and we were just staring at it. And he told us to follow the data stream. We didn't even know how, and he showed us. It's like a whole different level of computing. I didn't even know you could *do* that."

"Anyway," Alan said. "So you followed data streams from SOE-owned facilities and did a traffic analysis? And?"

Ong took over again. "The big bandwidth users were eleven IPs, most of them in the south of India. We correlated them to our list of SOE-owned facilities and got six hits. Three of them are located south of the Ambur facility, which was our indicator—that you think the warheads were taken south from Ambur."

Rao looked puzzled and glanced at Alan.

"One of our people analyzed the video of the helicopter and found that it was on a heading of about one-ninety." He didn't say that the person had been Harry.

Mary cut to the chase. "You've got us down to *three* facilities?"

Bill spoke without turning his head from contemplation of a fox-hunt picture. "Only one of them's important." He moved to his laptop and typed and swung the screen so they could see it. "See? Yeah. Cool." They found themselves looking at numbers. "It's *obviously* a big factory doing contract work for the Indian Navy. And it gets the bandwidth of a TV station, so they must use it to watch the whole place on security cameras—what else? *Now* do you see it?" He sounded both patronizing and dismissive. "And anyway, it's on the WMD Center's possibles list."

Alan heard Mary's quick intake of breath. He ignored her; if Bill had just blown a WMD Center secret to Rao, it was too late. "*Who* uses it? Uses *what*? And how do you know?"

Bill groaned. "*Servants of the Earth* use the *bandwidth* to let big shots at this set of IPs watch the action on the factory production floor!" The word *stupid*, as in *I just told you, stupid*, was left unsaid.

Ong was chewing her lower lip. She said, "He means that he thinks we've found an SOE site south of here that's a big assembly facility where they might be able to do something with the nuclear devices. Something connected to the Navy."

Alan winked at her. "Now you're talking." He changed his

tone to that of somebody speaking to a particularly spoiled child. "Bill, can you tell us *where* this facility is?"

"From the website! Don't you get it?" He was gesturing at his screen, which was still filled with numbers.

Ong pushed a map at Alan, a finger tapping a location. "It's about sixty miles southeast of here."

But Bill wasn't done. He gestured at Ong and Benvenuto with a sneer. "Oh, they can tell you *where* it is, oh, sure!" His voice rose with excitement, so that the next sentence came out in a squeak. "In half an hour, *I'll* show you *what* it is—on their own security cameras!"

Ong turned on him. "We got the protocols for their security-camera feeds from Valdez, not from you! They were in the embedded code for the keys, which Valdez and Mave cracked without your help, Bill!"

"Yeah," Bill said. "Yeah. *Whatever.*"

Alan shut them both up. "Bill, are you telling us that you can show us what their security cameras at this SOE facility are *seeing*?"

Bill made a *Mad*-mag Alfred Newman face. "Duh, I think he got it! Du-u-uh—"

Mary hissed, "Bill—" and Alan waved her to silence. "How soon?" he said to Bill.

"Half an hour. I've been saving the undecrypted data to disk. We'll be able to watch the feed from an hour ago and then live, too, once I use Valdez's software to decrypt, which we're downloading as we speak."

"Get to it, then," he said. "And I want to double-check your data on how you boiled all your choices down to this one. And Bill—" He smiled at Bill. "We'll have politeness lessons when this is over."

He took Mary aside and asked her to get on to the WMD Center at once and get overhead imagery on the site that Ong had shown them on the map. Then he started out to go up to Harry's room but thought better of it and went back to where Ong was leaning into her laptop. "Lieutenant," he said softly. "One little task, and keep it to yourself. See what you can find out on the web about our friend the maharajah, will you? In particular, any military background?" He tapped the table once and left her.

NCIS HQ, Bahrain

Bahrain NCIS headquarters comprised two double-wide trailers connected by a plastic tunnel that looked as if it had been designed by Doctor Seuss. The door was reached over a sandpit that maybe somebody had once intended to fill with concrete and that some earlier occupant, tired of sand-filled shoes, had covered with rubber-mesh mats from the Manama souk. The step from the mats up to the office level required strong thighs and loose pants; beyond it, nonetheless, the air-conditioned offices seemed almost pleasant. Or could have, if they had had a little color; against the brightness of the Bahrain sand and sun, everything dwindled into colors so pale that they looked as if they had been bleached. Leslie, who kept bringing stuff like artificial flowers to brighten things up, thought the fading was some reverse effect of the Bahrain humidity.

"Maybe curtains," she said, standing in the middle and looking at the windows, which were covered on the inside with Venetian blinds.

"Don't you dare," Dukas growled.

"How about a coat of paint? Like, a nice blue, with maybe yellow—"

"The NCIS budget doesn't run to decorating, plus the new SAC Bahrain is a skinflint and won't spend a penny on anything except the case load." As himself the new Special-Agent-in-Charge, Bahrain, he spoke with authority.

"Sometimes you're a disappointment to me, Mike."

"Life is hard." Dukas was looking over a new case that had come in overnight—two Marines were in the Manama

314

police station in "protective custody after an offense to Islam." He looked up at Leslie. "As long as you're working for free, couldn't you do some work?"

"I work for free, you're not grateful?"

"I'm grateful, I'm grateful; I just like people to work if that's what they show up to do." His head was down over his papers. She tiptoed over and put her hands on his cheeks, lifted his head and planted a wet kiss on his mouth. "You're so tough," she said.

"Jesus, Les, somebody might see!"

"Nobody's here; I checked."

With that, Rattner walked in. If he thought that that was lipstick that Dukas was wiping off with a used napkin, he didn't comment. Instead, he shouted, "Hey, place looks great—looka those flowers over there!" He threw a stapled sheaf of papers down on Dukas's desk. "Read 'em and weep, kid—I got the goods."

"Should I leave?" Leslie said.

"What, and take the life out of this place?" Rattner grinned. "Unless you'd like to file that crap on my desk—"

She headed for his desk.

Dukas was looking over Rattner's pages—Xeroxes of a telephone log. "So?" he said.

Rattner pointed at an entry highlighted in yellow. "We got him."

"Who?"

"Cost me two hundred bucks. I'm gonna put it in as transportation expenses, and you're gonna okay it." Rattner pulled a chair over. "Cell-phone call, Manama to Washington, within the window your CIA lady gave us. Number in Washington is a high-powered law firm. Greenbaum got on the FBI overnight, they dicked around and I thought were maybe going to the UN for approval, but a half hour ago they up and deliver the goods: there was a call from same law firm to an office in an executive building I need not name, two minutes after the Manama–Washington call. Recipient is an assistant to the National Security Advisor."

"Who's the leaker?"

Rattner grinned. He looked as if he wanted to say, "Guess," but he didn't. "Pilchard's flag lieutenant. His daddy's a partner in the DC law firm."

"You sure?"

Rattner pointed at the highlighted entry. "That's his cell phone. Guy's nuts, do a stunt like that with a cell phone."

Dukas was rubbing his hands slowly together, looking into the space beyond his desk and the waist-high partition that was supposed to define his office. "Okay." He kept rubbing his hands. "We got him—once. You said you thought you had a leaker a couple other times. Did you check—?"

"Near as I can tell, no; I already did the phone thing the other times, but we didn't have this tight of a window. The other times, maybe he used e-mail."

"Which would be on his computer. Maybe." Dukas frowned. "What'd you mean, Greenbaum got on the FBI?"

"It was on his time—three a.m, he figured it was okay if he wasn't learning to file. I had the night duty, I wanted help, I called him. What you gonna do, take away my gold star?"

"No wonder he didn't show up this morning. Still— You guys did good. Both of you." Dukas put one hand on a telephone and said, "When's Greenbaum coming in?"

"He's out trying to find something about this guy."

Dukas sighed. "Okay, so the only work that gets down around here today is the leaker." He fumbled through the papers on his desk and raised his voice. "Who the hell's got my base phone book?"

Rattner and Leslie moved at once, Rattner muttering, "Oh, jeez—" Both of them held out dog-eared Navy telephone books. "The office doesn't have enough of them," Leslie said.

"You guys took *my* phone book last night? Why can't you

put stuff back?" Dukas tried to looked stern and jabbed his finger at the phone with what pretended to be anger. Rattner winked at Leslie, who raised her eyebrows at Dukas, who looked disgusted. He would have said something, but a voice was in his ear and he said, "Flag Security Officer, please. This is Special Agent-in-Charge Dukas, NCIS, Bahrain." He put the phone against his ear, covering it with his hand, and said, "Anybody got anything to eat? It's way past lunchtime."

"Michael, it's barely eleven o'clock. If you'd eat a decent br—"

He waved her quiet and swiveled away from her. "Yeah, Lieutenant, Special Agent Dukas. I've got something to discuss with you but it requires going secure. Okay? Right. Okay, going secure."

Dukas leaned back. When his screen told him that he was secure and was, indeed, speaking to the office of the Flag Security Officer, Fifth Fleet, Bahrain, he said, "We've got an issue here. It looks like a person on your staff has been passing information to a contact in Washington." He didn't give the suspected leaker's name then but summarized what Rattner and Greenbaum had found. When he was done, the security officer said, "Can you tell me the person's name, Mister Dukas?"

Dukas looked at Rattner and actually winked. "The cell phone on which the call was made appears to belong to a Lieutenant-Commander Raymond Spinner."

A little silence followed. "I think that Admiral Pilchard had better hear this next."

"That's good; the admiral and I had a little talk last night about the problem."

"Yeah, um—I was in a staff meeting where, um, the problem was discussed with some, mm, forcefulness by Admiral Pilchard. I think he'll want to know about this at once."

"Should I hang by my phone?"

"Yes, sir, if you would. Or keep me informed of how you can be reached quick."

Dukas hung up. Rattner and Leslie had been working at different desks, but both looked up. Not that they'd been listening, of course. "I think the shit's about to hit the fan," Dukas said. "Who's going out for pizza?"

The Serene Highness Hotel

Harry had exiled himself to his bedroom so that he would at least appear to have no connection with the work. Alan found him there and told him what the computer people had done. "They've worked their asses off, and maybe they've hit paydirt. If Bill really gets into the security cameras, we'll know a lot pretty quick."

Harry murmured that time was a-wasting and said something about not seeing the woods for the trees.

"You want to stop talking in Zen and say what you mean?"

"The nukes are gone, pal. Even if you locate them, you think you're going to take them back somehow? Do you really think that the people who have India in chaos are going to fall on their backs and wave their legs in the air because you show up with five guys and a rubber-band gun?"

"You got a better idea?"

"Yeah—go for the monster's head." Harry sat up. "I've been lying here thinking about the whole *shmeer*. We should have been going after the people who run SOE from the beginning, not the nukes. I know, I know, I'm the one who pointed us at the nukes in the first place, but that's because I was being a good NOC. Well, now that I have time to think about it, I believe that was wrong."

"My orders are to find the nukes, and that's what I'm going to do."

Harry grinned. "Don Winslow of the Navy, ta-ta!"

Alan stared at him and then said, "You're not helping," and he called Fifth Fleet on Harry's STU and got Lapierre again. "Dickie, find out if anybody can put a SEAL team in here in twenty-four hours." He was thinking of how they would get the warheads back if Bill's wizardry actually located them.

Harry, who had closed his eyes, blinked open the good one at the sound of the word "SEAL." "Ask for about ten thousand of them," he murmured.

Lapierre was telling him that the battle group's SEAL team was ashore somewhere. Alan grunted. "Well, see what you can get me. Even fleet Marines. I may need them soonest." And he gave Lapierre a barebones account of what was happening. Lapierre said that the admiral had better get that from the horse's mouth, and in thirty seconds, Admiral Pilchard himself was on.

"What's going on, Alan?"

"I don't know yet, sir."

"You're paid to speculate, Al. Now, speculate!"

A violation of a basic tenet of Alan's idea of intelligence— *never speculate*. Except when you're ordered to. "*If* the nukes have been taken to a big factory or assembly facility, and *if* the place has the equipment and a clean room and the technical know-how—then I think they could be trying to put them into warheads. The Servants of the Earth have the money to afford all that—equipment, technical knowledge— plus, if they'd planned this way ahead, they'd have everything in place. But I don't *know*."

"If they put one of those nukes on an aircraft and fly it into the *Jefferson*, we'll lose at least six thousand men and a major part of the fleet."

"I was told the CAP is flying."

"Two aircraft. What if they send in a flight of twenty against us? Three nukes on three aircraft—that's a pretty good chance of one getting through."

"I don't think it'd be aircraft, sir. I think that the sub-marine—"

Harry's good eye was on the door; Alan looked and saw Benvenuto leaning in, one hand extended as if he'd just flung a pair of dice into the room, and his eyes wide as if he was looking for a seven.

"One moment, Admiral—" Alan looked at Benvenuto with a *This better be important* scowl. "Make it quick!"

"We're in! You can see right into the—the—!" He waved the hand. "The factory!"

Alan turned back to the STU. "Sir, may I call you back?"

Pilchard was not happy. "You better have a reason."

"Yes, sir!"

Then he was running down the red-carpeted stairs.

Bill was actually smiling. On his screen was a grainy, gray picture of a big space with pipes and conduits overhead and a vast floor crowded with machines. Even as Alan watched, the picture changed, and it took him several seconds to realize that he was looking at an entirely different space—smaller, uncluttered, brighter. A forklift drove across the line of vision. The pictures were eerily silent.

The feed was running on Ong's computer, too, so he leaned over and said, "Great job! You've all done a great job." He realized that his heart was pounding, and not just from the run through the palace. *They were looking into one of the Servants of the Earth's own factories through their own security cameras.*

He watched the feed again—an external shot now of a metal-sided building with windows high up, nothing moving. Then a shot of a loading dock. A corridor. Another corridor. Exteriors again, weedy spaces next to buildings, hurricane fences with razor-wired tops.

"Count the cameras," he said.

"We are."

"Any repeats yet?"

"No, sir."

On another laptop, Mary was watching the footage whose

digitals Bill had earlier put on disk and now decrypted—in effect, the history of the hour before they had got in. She was taking notes, jumping back and forth, manipulating the shots because they weren't live and going through them quickly because she was controlling the pace, not the live cameras' program. "Forty stations," she said. "About a minute a station, average, but it varies—forty minutes to go through the whole sequence live if somebody there doesn't override the preprogram."

The picture quality was poor but clear enough to show a big facility with at least two big buildings and a scattering of offices and support structures—a power plant, a vehicle garage with heavy trucks, and an office complex that might have been a separate building or might have been a top storey above one of the big work floors. And the exterior cameras showed long lines of razor wire coiling away like spiral mirrors in the white of the sun, and an industrial waste-land beyond like the surface of Mars.

And a gate with armed guards.

And no sign of the three nuclear warheads.

BBC World News

"And now to Ben Mackinnon in Mumbai."

"Thanks, Erin. The situation here remains terribly confused, with rumors everywhere but not much in the way of facts. There were explosions overnight here in Mumbai; I could hear them from my hotel. The concierge told me with some excitement that one of the big film studios had been hit, but I can't get confirmation of that. I talked last night to one old man who told me as absolute fact that the Americans have invaded along the southeast coast and that the Indian air force has sunk an American aircraft carrier. People on the streets seem to be thoroughly frightened still, and little wonder—the trains have stopped running, the telephone and electrical systems are down, the police can't control looting, and the reports of widespread mutiny in the armed forces are simply too many to be laughed away. Under the general nervousness is the real fear of war with Pakistan. This is a modern city accustomed to instant communication and abundant information, and, suddenly lacking both, it's a very sad, very nervous place. Ben Mackinnon, Mumbai."

The Serene Highness Hotel

Everybody was watching the live feed from the SOE assembly plant. Alan was leaning over Ong's table, whispering with her. "So what'd you find about our host?" he said.

She glanced across the room at Major Rao and whispered back, "The maharajah was a major general in the Indian Army before he retired six years ago."

"Intelligence?"

"I couldn't find anything about that. In fact, I couldn't find anything about his service after 1973 at all. It's like—"

"I know what it's like." Alan patted her table, because he didn't want to pat her shoulder or her knee. "Good job." He walked across to where Rao was watching a laptop, and, as he came up, Rao turned to him, pointing at the screen, and said, "You say this is a *Navy* project? *My* Navy?"

"The Indian Navy and the Servants of the Earth seem to have a cozy relationship." Alan shrugged. "Some of the Indian Navy, anyway."

Rao began taking notes. On the screen, a camera in a garage came to life. He could make out two heavy forklifts and an enormous dolly. "Mary!" Alan called.

"Son of a bitch," Mary said. She reached over Alan and started to type.

"This is live," Alan said.

"Yeah. We should be saving all the live feed."

The shot changed; the new place appeared to be entirely white—walls, floor, ceiling, the camera looking into it from a corner. The lights were bright and reflected off polished

322

metal surfaces. Alan heard Rao take in breath, and he felt Mary stiffen. She had already seen it on the old coverage and knew what it was, he realized. "That's a clean room, isn't it?" he said. There was no point in trying to hide it.

"I suppose."

No supposing about it. It was a clean room, the indispensably antiseptic and dustless space you needed for high-tech work. People were working in it, silent, oddly inhuman. They wore white coveralls with hoods and gloves and respirators. What they moved among were indecipherable shapes, mostly cylindrical, all gleaming.

And, as abruptly as it had come, the picture disappeared, to be replaced by one of a warehouse or garage, because part of a truck was visible.

And so was part of something else.

Rao touched the screen. He had to clear his throat before he could speak. "That's a missile, isn't it?" The angle made it difficult, but the long, brilliantly reflective tube did, indeed, look like a missile.

Mary leaned in until her nose was almost touching the flat screen. "It could be a missile." She sighed again. "Those are slings. It's hard to see, but that thing right there could be for moving it around. I don't know—" She paused and pulled at a length of hair that had fallen over her eyes. They all stared at the screen, Alan thinking what it would mean if the things were missiles, and if the three nuclear devices had come to rest in a place where there were a clean room and missiles.

The picture changed to a hallway with two empty office cubicles.

"Shitsky!" Still leaning over Alan, she began to click through options, opening up another video display and replaying the feed she had saved. Alan was conscious that one of her breasts was brushing his shoulder

The image of the garage returned. Now it was frozen and

had the slight distortion of video frames, but the truck and the missile, if it was a missile, were identifiable, so they had both been there more than an hour before.

Mary began humming to herself. She had seen the image before, then, when she was going through the saved data. "You should have told me when you first saw it," he whispered to her. He felt her shrug as she stretched across him. He pushed back and extricated himself; she slid in without comment. She laid a grid over the frozen frame and did something that brightened the image.

"Major? How long is an Indian license plate?"

Rao held his hands up and looked at them. "About fourteen inches."

"I need to know *exactly*."

"I'll go and measure one."

Alan heard the billiard room's door open. She reached for the satellite phone she had brought from the aircraft, another of Harry's useful toys in a country where the networks were down. "Before Rao comes back," she muttered. "Alan, this is a Tomahawk cruise missile clone. The Indians are building a *cruise missile*, and it looks like they stole the tech from us." She began to tap computer keys. "This is going to get sticky, Alan. Rao's not going to be very happy about our uncovering a secret missile program."

"I think it's as much a surprise to him as it is to us."

"And I've got a bridge I'd like to sell you."

"What if it's an SOE project?"

But she was talking into her phone. "Yancy, Mary. I'm sending you some pictures. From a factory floor in southern India. Coordinates as marked." She leaned toward the computer screen. "They're making a copy of the Tomahawk. Of course I'm not *sure*. I'm pretty goddam sure, though. Call the DDI." She became very brisk—Yancy was clearly a subordinate. She demanded immediate specs on the Tomahawk missile, with photos, capabilities, warhead space—the works.

When Major Rao came back in, she lowered her voice and talked faster, and by the time he had reached them, she was off the phone.

"Nine and a half inches," Rao said, holding his hands about that far apart.

Mary looked at him, laughed, laughed harder. Rao blushed. "Just my size," she murmured. Then she turned back to the computer and moved blue lines over the image until she had boxed the truck's license plate and the diameter of the probable missile. She stared at it and then hit a key, and the image vanished. She gave Rao a bright, perhaps flirtatious smile. "Major, can you start looking at the saved shop-floor footage and see if you find more of these?" She got up and pointed him toward her own computer a dozen feet away. When Rao's back was turned, she looked straight at Alan and nodded.

The message was unmistakable: they had been looking at a Tomahawk missile.

27

The Serene Highness Hotel

By noon, Alan was back on Harry's secure satellite phone, passing the first digitals to Fifth Fleet. When he was done, he asked for Admiral Pilchard again.

"We think they're trying to fit their warheads to some kind of missile. It looks to our WMD folks like a Tomahawk—"

"Wait one."

Alan could hear Pilchard talking and a ghostly, digitally encrypted voice reacting. Neither voice could be understood. They went on and on. He began to envision the phone as lying on Pilchard's desk, Pilchard called away—

"Sorry, Al. Had to deal with another matter—we think we've got that leaker. Okay—a Tomahawk. What're we talking about?"

"Twelve-hundred-mile range, sir. I need to have Lapierre find out if they could possibly launch one through the tubes of a diesel sub."

"To do what? The BG's way within that range already."

"Well, sir—" He thought of what Harry had said about focusing too much on the Navy. "If they got three nukes, maybe they have three targets."

Silence. An odd ticking sound, something Pilchard was doing with his lips or tongue. Thinking. Then: "The battle group's my first concern. Also yours."

"Yes, sir."

"What're the chances they're going to put these things on a ship or a plane instead of a sub?"

"No idea, sir. There's no naval base nearby, but, hell—"

"Okay. I'm going to see who's around who can take out this place you've found. Maybe it'll have to be the Air Force out of Diego Garcia. Frankly, I don't think I'll get the go-ahead to do it—bombing mainland India's not going be a popular idea in Washington—but we have to try."

"Sir, we don't know—"

"I know what we don't know, Commander! So do you! So get us more information and then we'll know, and then maybe I can move some of these politicians off their dead asses before the whole goddam theater blows up!"

Alan had never heard him quite like that before. "Yes, sir."

Pilchard's voice got less angry. "Your first priority remains the nukes—nail down where they are. Two, nail down whether they've been used to weaponeer those missiles. Three, find out what the hell they're going to do with them." He barked out a laugh. "Try to have it by seventeen hundred, could you?" He hung up.

Harry was standing by the window, hands in pockets. "Don't try to do it yourself," he said without turning around.

"Do what?"

"You know." He turned to face Alan. "These are serious folks. You and Fidel aren't going to take their nukes away all by your lonesomes."

"You're not playing this time?"

Harry came toward him and put his left hand on Alan's right shoulder so that they were side by side, as if he were going to walk with Alan's support. "You gotta know when to hold 'em, and know when to fold 'em, buddy. I told you before, I think you're following the wrong trail."

Alan went down the red-carpeted stairs, more slowly this time because he was frustrated and angry. The huge reception room was empty, the corridor to the billiard room empty, as well. The emptiness hardly registered on him except as a small anomaly, because always before, a turbaned servant was to be seen. He went silently down the corridor, his feet seeming to sink into the old carpet, and turned into the shadowed coolness of the billiard room.

Bill, Ong, and Benvenuto were at their computers, each with an electric desk lamp that made a little island of light. Clavers was in a corner working with paper that was spitting out of a portable bubble-jet printer. Separate from them in her own light was Mary. The only sounds were the soft fluttering of computer keys.

"Where's Rao?"

"Stepped out, thank God. Look here—" She had two different views of the missile on split screen. "I've ID'd three, possibly four of them in the old data, and we know for certain that one of them has been moved between the old stuff and the new. Plus—and this is exciting, Alan, but bad—I see something in the clean room that looks to me like part of a cradle for a nuclear device. I can't make out enough of it to be sure, but—" She ran her hand through her hair. Her eyes were bright with excitement. "I think they're putting the nukes into the warheads." She made a sudden movement to silence the objection she could apparently see coming. "No, no, don't say they can't have done it that fast. They've had at least twenty-four hours. *Listen* to me! If they've been planning this for months or years, then they had already engineered the warhead to fit the nukes ages ago! It's like this was simply the last stage of the manufacturing process. They aren't some ragtag terrorists stealing a nuke and then trying to find a way to jury-rig it into something; this was high-tech all the way. They can do it!"

But Alan was listening to a sound that was out of place. He couldn't identify it for several seconds and then he got it—a truck. A heavy truck. Moving away, and then another and another.

Trucks?

And he turned to start out the door and found that he wouldn't be going that way. The door was blocked by a large man and two smaller ones. With guns.

The billiard room broke into annoyed voices—not because of the men with the guns, but because the internet connection abruptly disappeared from every computer screen.

The lead man in the doorway was big, with a ferocious moustache, perhaps fifty, dark-skinned. His eyes met Alan's and he saluted and said, "Ex-sergeant major Khan, sir. Please—" The voice was almost pleading; Alan noticed, despite the hubbub, that the guns were pointed away from the people in the room.

Behind Khan, the maharajah was peering around his shoulder as if too unimportant or too shy to be noticed. Then, almost timidly, he pushed himself between Khan and a younger man and said, "Commander, my apologies, but I am afraid you will be confined to this room and its comfort room—" he meant the toilet, reached by a door near the far corner—"until they are able to release you. I believe it will be only a matter of hours."

Alan took in the guns—two of the men had Steyr assault rifles, Khan a machine pistol—and the fact that others were behind the maharajah. He felt instant rage, damped it down as futile, said, "Where are my other people?"

Khan looked sideways at the maharajah to see if he was going to answer and said, "Two out by swimming pool, no problem. Quite safe." Fidel and Djalik, lolling in swimming trunks—no place to carry a gun. "One upstairs restricted to his room. Pilot in aircraft. Everybody okay."

Alan looked at the maharajah. "Did you think we'd try to fly away?"

The maharajah looked pained. "I am so very sorry. We are doing this as gently as possible." And turned on his heel and left them. The two men with the Steyrs backed out, too, aiming the weapons at the floor with great care, and Khan slid out after them, keeping his gun, too, aimed away from the Americans. It was all very civilized.

The lock clicked over in utter silence.

"We've lost the feed!" Ong cried.

"They've pulled the cable." They had been using a jury-rigged cable that snaked out a window to the Lear jet. Alan saw the situation at once: Rao had taken a force off to try to retake the nukes; he'd cut them off the internet because he didn't want them doing something crazy like e-mailing Fifth Fleet for an air strike or a couple of cruise missiles.

He thought fleetingly of escape and dismissed the thought as foolish. *Where to? And how?* He looked around at them—Ong and Bill useless in a fight, nobody armed—and at the tall, narrow windows that lined the outside wall, to see, on the verandah outside, four more armed men. *If I had Djalik and Fidel and Harry and—and what? A Marine detachment?*

Benvenuto, standing now by his chair, fists clenched, said, "Why the hell are we prisoners?"

"Petty Officer Benvenuto, sit *down*."

Behind him, Mary had her hands on her hips, face angry. "Start downloading that stuff on the shop floor and the clean room to disk! If they come back to take the computers, I want the data in my pocket!"

"Good thinking." Actually, he didn't believe it was such hot thinking, but saving the data would give people something to do. "Lieutenant Ong, Petty Officer Benvenuto—get on it! We want everything showing the clean room, the garage, and the factory floor saved—compress it if you can. Let's go!"

"But we worked so *hard*," Ong whined. Her hands were trembling.

"If Rao grabs the nukes, your work will still pay off." *For India.* The bastards. "This isn't Stalag Seventeen and we're not going to start digging a tunnel."

Bill was grayer than usual, maybe in shock. His mouth moved, but no sound came out. Alan caught Mary's eyes and jerked his head at Bill, and she went to him and started to whisper, patting his shoulder. She came back and leaned her buttocks against the polished wood of the billiard table and muttered. "Man, did I guess that sonofabitch Rao wrong. We were *suckered!*" She shook her head.

"You ID'd the missiles and he figured he didn't have much time."

"Rao didn't take off until I spotted the missiles. I think he had suspicions of his own, and he waited for us to prove them. I know something about India, Al; there just aren't that many top scientists, and they all go to the same schools and they all marry each other. Rao wasn't surprised by what we were seeing until he saw the missile. Now, he wants to get the nukes *and* keep us from seeing the missiles up close."

"Would you do any different in his place?" Alan sat on the edge of the billiard table and crossed his arms. "Maybe we ought to be thanking him, not bitching."

He looked at his watch. They had been prisoners for thirteen minutes.

Mary passed the time by playing billiards. She leaned across the table, the tip of her tongue between her lips and her right leg cocked up over the corner, brought her cue in line with her shot, bridged her left hand, and suddenly looked up at Alan and gave a lopsided, ironic grin. *Playing pool while the* Titanic *sinks.*

Click.

Alan looked at his watch—eighteen minutes. "I'm a pool player," she said. "Never played billiards before."

Click.

"If I could see into the clean room for any length of time—" she said. She glanced up, then down; she had left herself a difficult shot. She slapped her hand on the heavy

331

oak frame. "Fuck, we were *that close*. Rao could at least have taken us along. You think he's there yet?"

Eighteen minutes and twenty seconds. The facility Rao was heading for was sixty miles away.

Click. "You want to shoot?" He had been holding a cue for no good reason.

In an hour and a half, Rao and a couple of truckloads of men would try to attack a defended factory to get three nukes that might wind up destroying an entire battle group, and he was being asked to play billiards! He threw his cue on the table. "No, I'm going to stop being a horse's ass and try to help Rao."

"You'd be helping a sonofabitch who—"

Alan hollered at Clavers, who was closest to the door. "Knock on that door and ask them to get the maharajah!" He turned back to Mary. "There's no point in standing around hitting little balls together when we could be helping the guy with the only real chance at those nukes."

He strode to the computers. Ong was making notes on a pad and Benvenuto was staring at nothing.

"Petty Officer Benvenuto, pull up the most recent data we have and start checking for security forces or other potential opposition to Major Rao's operation."

"Sir?"

"Bill!"

"Uhh?"

"Can you control the data stream? Is it possible? So we can choose which camera we look through?"

Bill looked at him. A flicker of interest showed through his daze. "Not without a connection to the net."

Alan smiled. "Just start thinking about how to do it—okay?"

"Yeah. Sure. Okay." Bill looked around, seemed to notice the other people in the room for the first time. "Sorry, I— Sure." Then he looked at his screen. "If their system is that way, we'd be screwed. But if it's controlled by remote—"

"Then it's SCADA," Alan said. "You do SCADA."

He turned then to see two armed guards and the maharajah, who was already standing, hands folded at his groin, a few feet in front of the others. "I think we should support our allies. Don't you agree, sir?" Alan said.

"I feared you would think we have not been behaving much like allies," the maharajah answered.

Alan walked toward him. "Your highness—General." The maharajah's right cheek gave a minuscule tic. "Whatever other agenda you have, we both want to neutralize those warheads." The maharajah's expression softened, an ironic smile just beginning to form. "I think we can help Major Rao, if you'll let us have the internet connection back." Alan pointed at the computers. "If we can take control of the cameras in the facility, we can let the major know what's happening—give him an eye. Maybe we can even blind the enemy's security by playing old pictures back to them—make them think nothing is happening."

"If you could do that, Commander—" The hands came up in a gesture of surrender. "However, I cannot have you communicating with your superiors."

"I'll give you my word. And you can remain in the room. Or put people in here to observe."

The maharajah looked at him, looked around the room, noting with a curious smile the lighted billiard table and Mary's cue, and then he turned back and called for Khan, and the two men talked in soft, low Hindi. Then he nodded at Alan. "I will take responsibility for the risk." No attempt now to disguise his being in command.

"Has Major Rao a map of the facility?"

The maharajah hesitated. "He has notes that he made from your computers. This was done so quickly—"

"But you *can* communicate with him?"

The maharajah stirred as if he was uncomfortable. "A somewhat antiquated system—we are not so high-tech as we might like—"

Alan was already with Ong and Benvenuto, explaining how they were going to make a map. "I want the whole layout—size of buildings, as near as you can figure; location of doors; layout of buildings with relation to the others; where the clean room and the garage are—everything. Think assault and defense—understand? As if you're setting up the attack yourselves and were going to brief it."

"We're *helping* them, sir?" Benvenuto looked as if he was going to break into tears.

Alan put a hand on Benvenuto's shoulder. "Pride goeth before a fall. Get to work."

They spent a half-hour comparing an overhead satellite photo with the calculations that Ong and Benvenuto made. From that, they put together a rough diagram of the facility.

Before they were finished, Ong whispered, "Bill says he's got it."

"You and Petty Officer Benvenuto zero in on the garage and the trucks. Go through the old data and the live feed and tell me anything that suggests change. Okay? *Anything.*"

He crossed to Bill. "What've you got?"

Bill waved at his screen. He hit a key and the shot changed; he hit another and it changed again: he had taken command of the security screens.

"Can they tell you're doing that?" Alan asked him.

Bill pointed to a smaller laptop. The screen was split into twelve sections, the view of a different security camera on each. He touched a key, and a different twelve appeared. "They got all forty pictures up all the time, maybe on a split screen or something. The preprogram cycles through, like we been seeing, and maybe that's on a big screen for them, but for sure it's on the feed going out to the IPs for their bigwigs or whoever to look at. Plus the security guys can bring up any screen they want, which is what I just did here."

"Great. See if you can *block* the security screens at the site and play the old data on them. Understand? So that their security people will see the old stuff and think that everything's fine. Okay?"

Bill stirred. "SCADA," he said.

"Sorry?"

"SCADA. I can do anything with SCADA." Bill sat like an idol, staring at his screen. "I'm great."

"Right. You sure are. Get on it, Bill."

Over Bill's head, he saw Ong looking at them. He raised his eyebrows and his shoulders a fraction. She smiled.

NCIS HQ, Bahrain

Dukas's phone rang and a voice asked him to go secure and then stand by for Admiral Pilchard.

Pilchard was on within a minute. "Dukas? Admiral Pilchard."

"Yes, sir."

"My security officer tells me you're on this goddam leaker. Run through it for me."

When he was done, Pilchard said, "Great to get a little good news for a change."

"Yes, sir."

"I didn't need some back-door kibitzer at the White House."

"No, sir."

"I want you to nail him."

"The only quick and sure way is what we call a poison pill."

"You mean feed him some piece of bullshit that he'll pass along. Great minds run in the same channels—I'm already on it."

"It would have to come from you and then be denied by you once he's passed it on."

"Yeah, and it has to be believable and it has to be disprovable after the fact. I'm in a meeting with my flag captain

335

about it right now. I'm going to call you back in no more than ten minutes and tell you what story we're going to pitch for him."

"Admiral, will you back me in going to JAG for a warrant to search LCDR Spinner's quarters?"

"Whatever. Call you back."

The Serene Highness Hotel

"How long?"

The maharajah checked his watch, a rather old Rolex, gold. "About half an hour more, I think."

Alan showed him the rough map they'd made of the facility. "I think it would help them to have this."

"We didn't send a fax machine along, I'm afraid."

"I can talk it through, sir."

The maharajah looked at Khan and made a sign, index finger tapping his right ear, then a bob of the head toward Alan. Khan stepped out of the room and came back within seconds with a headset.

"How are they doing?"

The maharajah looked away. "They are very hopeful."

Hopeful. Jesus. Alan had done incursions and worked the intel on others, and he knew that hope was your last resort.

"Hello, hello," he said into the headset. "Commander Craik here. Hello?"

"Hello, Commander. Rao here." The voice sounded amused, slightly uneven because, Alan thought, of the bouncing of a truck. "I'm sorry, Commander. About what we had to do, I mean."

Alan knew Rao wasn't sorry, would have done it again— so would Alan—and so he let the subject pass and said, "We've made a diagram of the facility, and I thought it would help you to have it. I can you talk you through it if you want it."

Silence, then a burst of chuckles, and then, "Yes, yes, of course—let me get a clean sheet on my clipboard—yes—?"

Alan glanced at his watch and bit back the urge to feel outrage at what he was reduced to doing. "I'll start at the northeast corner and move west and south. Got that? You'll be at the upper right of the map—right? Okay— The perimeter fence appears to enclose an area of at least six acres. It's metal mesh with razor wire on the top. There is at least fifty meters between the fence and the nearest building in the northeast quadrant of your map; that building is about eighty meters by—"

It took more than twenty minutes to do it properly. When he was done, Rao went back over several points and was quiet and then said, "Thank you." And, as if that was not enough—and it wasn't—"Thank you very much." He seemed to mean it.

"How far are you from the gate?"

"We think perhaps eight kilometers. Rather slow going here—people on the roads, much movement. Many of them have tried to stop us to ask for help. It is very difficult."

"Well—good luck."

"Yes. Quite."

Alan handed back the headset and avoided the maharajah's eyes, instead turning away to look at Ong. She beckoned him over.

"The trucks are gone."

That took a second to sink in. "With the missiles?"

"There isn't a shot that actually shows, you know, some guys loading a truck with something with a sign on it that says 'cruise missile,' but, yeah. We believe they loaded up the missiles and took off." She turned her head and shook her hair, and it brushed his face. "They're gone," she said.

Alan knew that Rao would have to go in anyway to be sure.

28

Greenbaum had come into the office while Dukas talked to Admiral Pilchard, and Dukas waved him and Rattner over. Leslie hung back and he made a motion at her, too. "We need your brains, Les. Come on."

"I don't want to compromise your case."

Dukas laughed. "Lady, if this works, Monica Lewinski couldn't compromise the case." Dukas rolled his chair back, put his feet on the desk. "Okay. Pilchard's going for a poison pill. What d'we need?"

Rattner and Greenbaum looked at each other. Rattner apparently signaled Greenbaum to do the talking, because he said, "We gotta cover his telephones, his cell phone, and his computers. He lives off-base, but treaty with Bahrain says Navy has jurisdiction over Navy personnel, so we get a warrant from JAG and we're good to go into his apartment and seize the computer there. Computer in his office is Navy property; we say grab it the moment he leaves."

"We think he'll beat feet out of Fifth Fleet HQ absolutely as soon as he can, once he gets the dope he wants to pass to his old man," Rattner said.

Dukas nodded, signaled to Greenbaum to go on.

"We think me and Rattner should be in the parking lot with a cell-phone scanner. If he comes out, we'll catch the

338

call. If he doesn't, he's gonna either use his laptop or his home computer, or he's gonna use his home telephone."

"You hope." Dukas was frowning. "He's gotta plug the laptop in somewhere to send an e-mail, right?" Dukas was not strong on computers.

"Yeah, modem."

"What if he goes to a cyber café?"

Rattner shook his head. "Too risky. Anybody on staff knows FBI's got the cafés covered like a blanket."

Greenbaum started nodding his head. "We can stop him at the gate. It's established in law—Marines can stop anybody, search anything, at a military gate. Also seize any suspicious objects."

"Yeah, but we want him to send the message *first*. The message is going to be the proof—he'll be the only one who has that information; if it gets sent, he's the leaker. If it gets reported to NSC, his old man's the contact, and we get double bang for our buck." Dukas pulled his feet down and leaned forward, his hands folded on the edge of his desk. He jabbed the air with a finger. "Pilchard's worried that when push comes to shove, he's going to get dicked by the White House. He wants to show them that they've got the problem, not him." He jabbed the air with a finger again. "Pilchard's a good guy." He looked around at them. "We're going to nail this sonofabitch." He looked at Greenbaum. "Good job. Now could you do some filing?"

The Serene Highness Hotel

After Alan told her that it looked as if the trucks—with the armed missiles—were gone, Mary Totten managed to hide from him the rage she felt. She thought he was an attractive, nice, stupid naval asshole who would be fine in the sack if you put a sock in his mouth but who was so focused on the Navy he couldn't see that Rao and the nukes were history. But she could: if the nukes were gone, they were gone, and Craik was pissing down the wind by helping Rao and the maharajah.

She crossed to Bill under the eyes of one of their Indian watchers and bent over him. "You okay?" she murmured.

"Me? Sure. I guess." He did look a little better. Using a computer made his blood flow.

"Bill, you and I have to move on. No, don't look at me. We're talking, that's all. Can you send an e-mail on the little computer in your lap? You can? Okay—send it to the office. Our office, Bill—the WMD office."

Bill looked scared. "The Navy guy promised the maha-who-ha guy we wouldn't send any messages."

"Bill—!" Her fingernails dug into his shoulder. "Address the fucking message!" She turned to smile at the maharajah, then to glance around for Alan, who was across the room. *Good.* "Okay, Bill, this has to go in clear. Okay? So here's the message. 'Lost all three contracts today.' Got that, Bill? Contracts with an *r*, not contacts—"

"I can spell 'contracts'!"

"It's better with the *r*, okay? All right, 'Lost all three contracts today.' Then, 'Sailors all screwed up here. Sailors—all—' Good! Then, 'Going after new customer CEO.' Great. Now hit send. Bill—hit send— No! don't look at Craik! Hit send, Bill—!" She raised her eyebrows at the maharajah, as if dealing with subordinates was just *such* a bore. "Oka-a-a-a-y, Bill. Now—I want you to find the main server that the Servants of the Earth are using. Okay? The one where the most of their traffic is going? I mean, if we locate the server, we're probably going to be close to their HQ, right?"

Bill's lips moved. Finally, after thus talking to himself for about ten seconds, he said, "Probably."

"Okay. Do a traffic-flow analysis. Can you do that?"

"My laptop's supporting SCADA seizure."

She looked down at the mini in his lap. "How about that one?"

"Oh— Well." He frowned. "I'd be doing two things at once."

"That's why I brought you along, Bill—because you're the kind of guy who *can* do two things at once."

Bill's eyes flicked sideways at her hair, which was brushing his face, then down at her breasts.

"Okay." He gulped. "But the Navy guy won't like it."

She showed her teeth. "The Navy guy won't know about it."

Radio Beijing

"The almost total collapse of the nation of India continues to be marked by armed clashes inside the country and by provocations along the border with China. As the military buildup on the border grows more intense, the People's Army has rushed troops and heavy weapons to the area to defend Chinese sovereignty.

"Nothing has been heard in thirty-six hours from the Indian Prime Minister. The state of emergency declared by chief of the armed forces Major-General Praba Ramasubu has not been confirmed by civilian authority. The strong possibility remains, therefore, that a military coup, coupled with a falsification of events to divert our eyes from the provocations along the border, is what has been engineered in India.

"Forward elements of the People's Army are prepared to resist to the death this outrage. Any movement across the border will be answered by massive force, up to and including what President Jong-Wu called last night 'ultimate weaponry.' Let renegade elements in India beware!

"The suffering people of India continue to groan under this burden. Food is now scarce in many parts of the country. Water systems have failed in at least six states. No major city has reliable electrical power. The computer industry, long the jewel in modern India's crown, has collapsed. Units of the army and navy continue to battle among themselves in a frenzy of self-destruction that may have been rigged by power-hungry nationalists at the top of the military order."

The Serene Highness Hotel

"They can see the gate," the maharajah said to the room. He held up a headset and Alan hurried over; the maharajah pressed it against his ear, and he heard Rao's voice say, "Ten seconds."

On the computer screens, the gate was seen from inside, four armed men standing about. On the road outside, figures—workmen or idlers—straggled toward it. Something grabbed their attention; several pointed, and heads turned toward the approach road. It was like a silent film without the music and without titles, strangely unfinished-looking, as if reality would become real next week when the other elements were added. Then a Land Rover pulled up at the lowered barrier and every door was flung wide. A dark stick figure came out of one of the gate buildings and was knocked flat by an invisible hand. The workers were already off the road, flat in the ditch or running across the fields of industrial rubble. One of Rao's men jumped back into the lead vehicle and, as the gate rose, drove it forward, the passenger doors snapping shut with the suddenness of his acceleration.

"They're in," Alan said to the maharajah, and he nodded as, on the screen, a heavy truck flew through the gate, accelerating all the way, the tires flinging gravel and dust. The maharajah, holding the headset to one ear, said, "They say an alarm has sounded."

Alan whirled toward Bill. "Are you feeding them that old footage?"

"Yeah, yeah—yeah, I'm doing it, I'm doing it—!"

Alan grabbed Mary. "You going to monitor the clean room?"

"You bet your ass!"

342

"Warn them of any resistance, any guards—anything!" He ran to Ong. "Can you pull up the *outside* of Building One while Mary's—? You sure? Okay—I want you to stay on the outside, more than one view if you can—we've got to know if anybody is moving toward it. We're the only early-warning system these guys have got!"

He raced back to Bill. "Can you show me the live feed and still block their security? I need to—" Bill was waving at his larger laptop. Alan saw a loading dock, doors, metal surfaces catching the late-day light. The Land Rover appeared far away at the left of the screen and slammed to a stop and two men spilled out the back; then it was accelerating again toward the camera.

The Land Rover accelerated around a short curve into a flat gravel apron between the back of the main factory building and the front of the garage, with a low shed making the parking apron a cul-de-sac. They knew of the shed only from the satellite photography because the security camera was actually sitting on it, unable to see itself. The Land Rover, however, was blocked by it; it spun in a controlled skid, stopped, and people jumped out. Far behind them, one of the trucks turned into the space between the buildings.

Before the Land Rover had stopped, Rao was out, crouched behind his door with a machine pistol ready. The driver was leaning over the hood from the other side, aiming past him, a heavy automatic rifle firing right across Rao's line of vision. In the silence, cartridge casings spit out of the weapon; Alan imagined their clatter as they hit the vehicle. The other pair from the Land Rover were running for a concrete wall to the right. Soundlessly, the vehicle's windshield dissolved inward. Rao looked up and to his right and aimed; his weapon bucked but there was of course no sound; casings scattered. Rao threw himself flat, shot one-handed, and began crawling backward under the Land Rover.

Alan jumped to Mary's computer. "What's going on in the clean room?"

"Nothing—goddam nothing."

He glanced at Ong's and Benvenuto's screens. Five men were trotting down the building's outside wall, weapons at port; Alan shouted for the maharajah and said, "Are these yours?"

The maharajah stared at the battle dress, the body armor, the helmets, and nodded with enormous vigor. "Ours, oh, yes—ours!"

They hadn't enough screens to know where all of Rao's people were or what was happening to them, and the lack of sound made it impossible to tell how much of a fight was going on. *The modern battlefield*, he thought. *The same old fog.* At the billiard-room door, Khan was on a headset with somebody, probably not Rao, because he was shouting at him. Alan went to him, put a hand on one arm; Khan held up his hand, listened, barked something, then barked something else at the maharajah in Hindi. To Alan, he said, "Truck three setting up perimeter to defend exit strategy. Truck two in support. Truck one and Land Rover in hot zone!"

Rao rolled to his knees, pushed himself erect and up the two steps to the shed. His driver's fire was pinning the shooters in the factory. Rao tried to elbow the double doors open, felt some give, threw his weight against them and then reached out to turn the knob, losing control of his weapon in the same motion.

The driver stopped firing, his clip exhausted.

The knob turned and Rao went through, off-balance and with his machine pistol hanging by its sling from his wrist. The interior was bright, and a man was standing a meter away. He had an assault rifle but seemed frozen. Rao swung his left arm and the pistol struck the man full across the face, snapping his head back and tearing a dingy handkerchief from his head. He grunted and fired into the floor reflex-ively, the rounds whining around the space like angry bees. Rao got control of the machine pistol and shot him.

Alan cycled Bill's screen-views to find the garage and got the right one just in time to see Rao, bent over, rotating with the machine pistol held ready to fire. Seen from above and at an angle, he was foreshortened and almost dwarfish. Alan in fact didn't recognize him but thought he recognized the weapon. A man lay twitching at Rao's feet.

Another figure in body armor and helmet came through the door behind Rao.

"They're securing the garage door," Alan called to the rest of the room.

The maharajah was standing behind him. "Is that my nephew?"

"Yes, sir."

"He is all right so far, then."

Other armed men joined Rao and he motioned them forward, and they disappeared from the bottom of the screen, seen almost from directly above as they flowed down it. Alan found another camera that showed the garage and the inside of the loading dock from the far end so that it looked up the interior and just caught a door, through which Rao and his men were coming. They came up the long garage by files, leapfrogging and covering each other, and Alan saw no sign that any of them fired a shot. The lead men came right down to disappear again at the screen's bottom, merely by then tops of heads with feet appearing and disappearing fore and aft.

Behind them, Rao came slowly, looking around, slowing, stopping. When he had looked back up the garage and seen, apparently, that it was empty, he looked up directly into the security camera and shook his head.

* * *

"Okay, you were absolutely right; the trucks are gone," Alan said to Ong. "Good job."

"Bad for our side, though."

"You could say that."

The maharajah was still watching Bill's computer. Alan joined him. Very little resistance had appeared after the first flurry of shooting; they had watched Rao and his men move back up through the garage, then suddenly appear on a camera covering one corridor of the main factory building, from which they had made their way up to the second storey.

"Khan says we have three injured so far," the maharajah murmured.

"It could be a lot worse."

He was switching cameras, trying to find Rao. He had last been seen crossing a factory floor toward a set of double doors.

"They're in the clean room!" Mary shouted. "I've got them—"

Alan cycled, cursing silently, and got it. They had four camera angles in the clean room, only one of them with a broad enough view to get most of the space. He found that one at last and saw that the double doors Rao had been heading for led to the clean room, for he was just coming in now. His outriders had already come through and were darting down the room, covering themselves behind big pieces of equipment.

"Like watching a bank robbery," Alan muttered.

They swept the room. They apparently found nobody.

It's over. He didn't want to say it aloud to the maharajah. *They were too late and it's over.*

Then Mary said, "Paydirt," and he looked at the screen again. Rao was standing on a table, directing two men to move something that the table was blocking from the security camera. Alan recognized it as the dolly Mary had pointed out earlier—a dolly holding a matte-black cradle two feet long.

"That thing's a *warhead* cradle," she said. "That sucker's *small*. We're underestimating these bastards."

And then things speeded up. Ong shouted, "Bad guys at the back!" and Alan raced to her and saw the grainy black-and-white of the factory exterior, men running forward toward an open door. They wore black body armor and French-style kevlar helmets.

"Khan!" Alan shouted. "Bogeys on the north side of Building One! Entering the building at the northwest corner! Tell Rao—!" He turned to the maharajah. "Sir, tell them— the building's being entered at the ground floor at the—"

And then there was shouting in Hindi and in English, and the men in the clean room suddenly burst into movement. They were running for the double doors, firing, crouching behind machines, and then they were coming back down the room as the doors exploded, dust and flash and smoke bursting on the screen; and Rao, who had been standing still on the table bent to get down and then straightened and raised a hand toward his head, but his head had already snapped back and to the side and burst toward the camera in a spray of black pixels.

Washington

An emissary from the Central Intelligence Agency—usually the director—briefs the President every morning. Brief was what he had learned to be, because the President's attention span was not of the longest. "Just give me the big picture," the briefer had become accustomed to hearing the man say. This President believed that his job was thinking big, and details were what he had all those other people for.

Now, it was well before the normal briefing hour, and the President was still in pajamas. "Our officer on the spot has reported that the attempt to recover the three nukes has failed," the director was saying. "There's now sound evidence that they've been loaded into clones of our own Tomahawk cruise missile and are somewhere in southern India."

"Can they hit America with those things?"

A presidential briefer has to have a poker face and a lot of patience. Now, he made his face expressionless and said, "The range of the Tomahawk is twelve hundred miles, sir." Would he have to say that Washington was farther than that from southern India? No, apparently not.

The President was scowling. "India isn't an American concern. And I don't appreciate being waked up in the middle of the night to hear about it."

"Sir, so far as we know, the nukes were taken by a terrorist group. They could pass them on to any of a number of other groups who *are* our concern."

"What'd they put them in the Tomahawks for, then? Don't give me that! When you *know* some raghead terrorist group that's got it in for *this* country has got a nuke, I want to hear about it! Until then—" He looked at his watch. "India's a State Department issue, right?"

"State's trying to find enough of the Indian government to intervene, yes, sir. But the government's fragmented—the president's in one hideout, half the parliament may be dead, the—"

"Yeah, yeah, yeah, you told me yesterday or sometime. Our position is that India's internal affairs are India's business. Have I made myself clear?"

"If they can move the Tomahawks around, they could hit Karachi. Even Islamabad." He waited, thought he'd better make sure he was understood. "In Pakistan."

"And?"

"The Pakistanis have nukes of their own; they'd retaliate at once. The Chinese have forces on the Indian border; they might well invade. The whole of Southeast Asia—"

The President threw himself back, banged a forearm on his desk, and rolled his eyes. "I don't seem to be making myself clear! It's your job to monitor stuff like that; I don't want to hear it! *We're not involved!*" He shifted his weight and looked again at his watch, laughed suddenly. "Maybe we should ask the guys who stole the nukes to do us a favor and lob one at Saddam Hussein, how about that!"

The briefer didn't say that Baghdad was at least a thousand miles beyond the missile's range.

Fifth Fleet HQ, Bahrain

Pilchard kept tapping his pencil on his desk, harder and harder. As he waited on the line, he began to drum the eraser on his mouse pad. Waiting for the Joint Chiefs of Staff to dance with politicians.

"Admiral?" His top boss, the Chief of Naval Operations, sounded hoarse. A really good officer with a long record as a fighter.

"Yessir."

"Admiral, that's a big *no* on deployment of a SEAL team on Indian soil. Don't even ask me to go back and talk about a B-52 strike."

Pilchard was still for a few heartbeats, trying to will those words unsaid. "Sir, with all respect, we're talking nuclear weapons here. Could be my battle group. Could be Pakistan or Iran. We're talking—"

"Save it, Dick. I *know*. The White House has something called *other concerns*."

"What *other concerns*? What comes above the deployment of nuclear weapons?"

"You want me to spell it out?" The CNO was talking too fast, his own anger too raw. "The White House says your nukes are all smoke and mirrors. They think the threat to the battle group is negligible and that any other action taken is quote not a matter for US intervention. Okay? I don't want to spin you up further, Dick; I'm in your corner, but I just got my ass reamed and I can tell you that this bunch has

349

already made up their minds and they are not going to budge one inch."

"What do you recommend I do, sir?" Pilchard looked down and found that he'd broken the pencil between his fingers.

"Jesus, Dick. What do you want me to say? Obey. Or—" The CNO hesitated. Pilchard could hear him breathing.

"Or walk into disobedience with my eyes open?" Pilchard was mutilating one of the pencil ends.

"I didn't say that, Dick." The CNO sounded as if, in fact, he was saying just that. In fact, he sounded as if he was pleading.

29

The Serene Highness Hotel

There had been no question of continuing the Americans' confinement after the failure of Rao's mission. The maharajah had called it off the moment he knew that the trucks were out the facility gate and headed home

Harry O'Neill had been praying when the release came. He finished his prayers, rolled up his rug, and strode out of his bedroom the moment Alan appeared and told him about Rao—along the silent corridor, down the stairs, across the huge lobby. He didn't head for the billiard room but went straight to the airplane, jumping up the stair, stepping over the cable that carried the internet hookup for the computers. He checked with Moad, asked if the plane was ready to fly, amount of fuel.

"Where we going?"

"I don't know yet. Gotta get out of here, for sure."

He went back into the palace and this time to the billiard room. Only Bill Caddis and the Navy enlisted man were there, the soft clicking of keys the only sound.

"Where's everybody?"

"Taking a break. We were locked in here. You hear about that, sir?"

Harry nodded. "You're Benvenuto."

"Yes, sir."

Harry sat down next to Bill, who acknowledged him by leaning in the other direction.

351

"Bill?"

"Huh?"

"I want you to do a traffic-flow analysis to find the SOE router hub."

Bill's head turned toward him. Bill didn't look good, Harry thought—pasty, pale, his muddy eyes like light bulbs without the power. "Been there, done that," Bill said. "Mary already asked me." He slammed a disk into its port and waited while a light flashed and something whirred. He handed the floppy to Harry.

"Thanks."

"Unh."

Harry then sat next to Benvenuto and asked him to pull up the data from the disk. He studied it, jumping back and forth, and then put the disk in his pocket and went out. By then, the others were drifting back

Harry found Adeeb, the maharajah's secretary.

"I'd like to see His Serene Highness."

"It is not, I am sorry, a good time, sir." The secretary hesitated. "We have had a blow."

"Is Major Rao dead?"

"It is not known for sure. His Serene Highness's physician has gone to meet the party on the road." The man shook his head. "The hospitals are full. Such a very sad time."

"I want a Survey map of western Uttar Pradesh."

"Maps, sir—we have driving maps, tourist maps—"

"You have Indian Survey maps. This is a military facility."

The secretary looked severe, then frightened. "I would have to ask His Serene Highness"

"The general, yes."

The secretary made a face as if he was about to blow a large bubble. He nodded his head very fast. "Yes, yes." He blew the bubble. "Please to come with me. He is at prayers. You are a believer, I think?"

Later, coming back with the maps, Harry saw Mary, who

352

signaled to him. He had things to do—most of all, he had places to go—but he went to her.

"We're getting out of here," she said.

"Indeed."

"If we find the router hub for the main SOE IP, I think we can maybe zero in on their headquarters."

"Good thinking."

"I'm dealing with the fallout from the mess that Rao made. You heard? They got shot up; everything was already gone. Thanks to God I'd already messaged the office it was a bust. Now we gotta *move*, man! Craik thinks he's going to save the world with a Navy plane. Christ. I've got to file a report on this fiasco and try to cover my ass with DC. Find out where Bill places the router hub and find a way to get us there—ASAP."

She started away. He put his hand on her arm. "You messaged the office *when*?"

"As soon as I figured out they were never going to get those nukes."

"Al Craik gave his word there'd be no messages sent."

"Oh, get a life! This is the real world, sweetie—I don't care if Commander Tightass gave his right ball! *I had a job to do and I did it!* And because I don't believe in *honor* and I don't believe in some sailor's *word*, the President of the United States is state-of-the-art on what's going down with those nukes. Now get off my ass and do your job!"

Harry smiled. He had a good smile; men and women both loved it. "I don't have a job, Mary. And as for the volunteer work I'm doing for your bosses—that's history. I'll finish this one, and then I'm out."

"Oh, for God's sake—! Why?"

Harry looked at her, gave a single, breathy chuckle. He hadn't told her he'd already seen Bill, had already located the router hub, had already found where they had to go. He'd thought of not taking her at all but decided that to do so would be merely childish. "I don't like being called 'Persian Rug,'" he said.

He went out to the plane and handed the maps to Moad. "We're heading for a place north of Delhi called Patiala. Find us a landing field that'll have gas. You can file a flight plan through the maharajah's secretary, and the old man'll see it's official."

"What'd that cost?"

Harry said, "One Muslim prayer. Did you know there's a little mosque on the far side of the palace? That's where he is. All by himself."

Coming out of the aircraft hatch, he met Djalik, who simply shook his head to show his embarrassment at having been detained by a damned swimming pool. Harry laughed. "I was having a nap." He patted Djalik's shoulder. "Check the weapons and get ready to roll. Make sure we've got food on board for five—twenty-four hours in the galley plus MREs." He looked at his watch. "Say—twenty-two hundred hours."

"Home?"

"Eventually."

Fifth Fleet HQ, Bahrain

From the time he'd hung up with the CNO to the time Al Craik called back for his final orders, Pilchard had gone through the motions of obedience. He'd alerted every ASW asset in his theater, called Sixth Fleet HQ in Naples and asked for the P-3 det in Sigonella to be flown into Bahrain ASAP, sent his own two P-3s to Oman and asked the ambassador to get the Iranians to let his boys fly out over the Indian Ocean without getting harassed.

It was all bullshit. The P-3s from Sig wouldn't get to him for twenty-four hours; the P-3s in the Indian Ocean wouldn't find a diesel sub in that vast sheet of water without direct aid from the Almighty.

But he went through the motions, aware that somewhere to the east of his career lay his duty.

And then Al Craik called.

It didn't take long to get to business. Craik had his answers—where, when, how. While they were talking, Lurgwitz, the flag captain, placed a shiny computer image on his desk. The code at the top said "CIA WMD," and the black object inside the analyst's white circle was labeled "Nuclear warhead transport cradle." Under that image was another, just as chilling; a crisp satellite shot of a surfaced submarine alongside a small pier, with the shadows of two cranes extending like the arms of a mantis over the hull. Pilchard lost Craik's voice for a second. Then he focused.

"—Quilon. That's where the sub is; there's imagery that she's pierside right now."

"I'm looking at it, Commander."

"I want to go after the sub." That was Craik. Focused on the job. Pilchard almost smiled.

"I sure wish the Indians had pulled it off." The words came out unbidden; Craik had already told him about the Indian attack and the cost.

"Yessir."

"Because if they had, I wouldn't have to be a fucking weasel. You ever known me to be a weasel, Al?"

"Can't say I have, sir."

"I have orders to take no action. You understand, no action, Commander?"

"Sir! For God's sake, we're talking nukes—"

"Stow it, mister."

Craik sounded puzzled. He wasn't political, and Pilchard had seen him do this before. This focus. Only the goals mattered to Craik.

Craik said, "All I need is your permission—"

Pilchard cut him off, angry at himself that he had to do

this, angry at the White House and the CNO. "You know the old saying, Al? Better to beg forgiveness?"

Craik tried again. "This is about nuclear weapons, sir. I think—"

"I think you have wax in your ears, Commander. I think you should consider how your boss has somebody *leaking* intelligence and how politicians often give *direct* orders if sailors ask them hard questions." Pilchard softened his voice. "Al, I'm not cutting you adrift. I've been ordered to avoid *any direct action*. I'll back anything you do to the hilt; you're playing for all the marbles. But if you ask me right out—" He paused.

Alan cut in, his voice hard. "I guess I'm slow on the uptake, sir. You're saying I'm the commander on scene."

"I'll back you to the hilt." *And then I'll be a civilian.* Pilchard thought he might be able to protect Craik. "I sure wish the Indians had pulled it off, Al."

"Yes. Sir." Craik was angry. "I'll get it done."

Pilchard nodded silently. "Out here," he said and cut the connection.

USS *Thomas Jefferson*

"Here are Captain Lash's orders. No change there," the TAO said, handing Hawkins a blue plastic folder. "We're to take no action and make no provocation, blah-de-blah. Loyalists lost another ship at first light, we think she was the *Betwa*. Bad guys have a picket about sixty miles north and west, and we think they've altered course and increased speed. Supplot's best guess is in the JOTS; I make them heading for the coast. About two hours back, the picket ship locked up one of our CAP Hornets with a SAM radar. Hornet turned away, nobody launched, but they all lit up and so our picture's more up-to-date than usual." The off-going TAO got up from the raised chair and indicated it. "Lash ordered the Hornet not to respond. Of course. She's all yours, Captain."

Hawkins could see at a glance that the TAO had aged during the period that the picket had locked up one of the CAP planes. The TAO's voice was a monotone; his skin was gray and dry, as if all the sweat had already run out of it. Hawkins flipped to a new page in the pass-down log. "We still doing this medevac run Lash cooked up?"

"Sorry—yeah. Air Ops thinks we'll be in helo range of Trin in about fifteen hours, so all the worst cases that can be moved go first." The TAO shrugged. "Is it just me, or does Lash want Rafehausen off the boat?"

Hawkins grunted, already leafing through a message board. He glanced up. "How's the deck?"

The TAO picked up a spiral-bound notebook from the stack of TAO notes and flipped it open. "We're open for helos. The deck is replated and sound all the way to the stern, or good enough to get by. Cat one is operational but has a steam leak they're trying to locate; right now they can only cycle it every fifteen minutes. Cat two ought to be up tomorrow. They've salvaged enough from the arresting gear to re-rig a wire; Air Ops told them to rig the three wire, and they'll get to it later tonight. No one thinks we can launch or recover with one cat and one wire, so—"

TAO's pass-down was interrupted by a slim petty officer third class from the comms shack. She slammed the hatch behind her and backed into Hawkins in her haste. "TAO?" she asked, unsure which of them was on duty.

"Shoot," Hawkins said.

"I've got a secure call from a Commander Craik, says he's in India. He asked for the commanding officer or Admiral Rafehausen." She waved a yellow sticky.

"Hit your rack," Hawkins said to his predecessor, already in motion. "I relieve you."

"I stand relieved," the man mumbled to an empty chair and headed for his stateroom.

The Serene Highness Hotel

Hawkins was on top of the situation and Alan didn't have to waste a word in getting to the point; he exuded competence, which Alan needed to hear. Having summarized his own message traffic, Alan got to the point.

"I think Servants of the Earth are loading those missiles into the sub. They could plan an attack on the battle group; they could have another target. I no longer think it's feasible to go after the warheads in India. The Indians tried and failed, and I don't have the resources. I want to go after the sub." Alan expelled a breath, took another one, and held it.

Hawkins's response sounded whispered. "Captain Lash is in command of the battle group."

"Roger. I've spoken to Fifth Fleet. Admiral Pilchard is willing to see this through." Alan chose his words carefully. "Captain Lash may be hesitant. All I need is a torpedo and a depth charge sent in to the beach at Trin."

Hawkins spoke louder. "We're fifteen hours from having the range to put a helo carrying a heavy load ashore, even refueling. And the last I heard, the Sri Lankans wouldn't let us land any weapons."

At the other end of the phone, Alan began to deflate. Fifteen more hours meant that the sub would have had almost a day to put the missiles aboard and sail away. He knew that once that submarine cleared the hundred-fathom line off the port, she'd be gone.

"I've got a different proposition for you, Commander." Hawkins's voice was quiet again but confident. "What if I could get the deck of the *Jefferson* open for one recovery and one launch?"

Alan rode the roller-coaster up again. "That possible?"

"If you've got a pilot who'll land an S-3 with no net and one wire, I've got a deck. Cat one is good for one shot every fifteen minutes. I'll have a three wire rigged by 2300."

Adrenaline surged. Alan recalculated it all—an S-3 to get

him from Trin, flight to the boat, get a torp loaded, get back in the air, rendezvous with CAP, press home. It was actually better for fuel and time than flying from Sri Lanka, five hundred extra miles every leg. Way better. Alan looked at his watch, tried to count hours. "If this is going to work, I'll be coming aboard about 0100 tomorrow. I'll take a torp and a depth charge and a harpoon and a rocket pod."

"And Admiral Pilchard's buying all this?"

Alan tried to keep the hesitation out of his voice. Hawkins was reputed to be a political animal, and he'd know what was happening at Fifth Fleet better than most. "Yes, sir." *Yes, sir, I have a blanket authorization not to inform him what I'm doing.*

"Okay." Hawkins paused, and when he continued, his voice was soft. "Better come in EMCON. Tell your pilot there's no needles and no *nothing* else. I'll do what I can to get an LSO and a ball and some cut lights. Have your pilot do a break and then take his time on a straight-in so we have plenty of warning, but don't call the boat. You understand me, Commander?"

Alan had to assume that he was now part of a conspiracy to keep his plane's landing from Captain Lash on the *Fort Klock*. Alan thought of an old CIA joke—*We're in a conspiracy to do our jobs.* "Roger that, Captain."

"The sea between us and the coast is crawling with SOE-controlled ships. They lit up one of our Hornets last night, so look sharp and stay south of us on your way in."

"They're east of you?"

"They're headed for the coast," Hawkins said. "At least, that's what our intel people think. They changed course a couple of hours back." Alan could hear the rustle of papers through the phone. He thought he had it all, now.

"Sir, can you give me their ETA if they were headed for the port of Quilon?"

"Wait one, Commander— 0700 tomorrow if they don't change speed. You there?"

That's when the sub is coming out, then. Alan thought he had the whole picture now. The SOE-controlled surface ships were moving to the coast to cover the departure of the sub. The sub would be vulnerable until it crossed the hundred-fathom line; after that, it could go anywhere. For all he knew, there was a tanker out on the ocean somewhere to refuel it.

"Captain, can you ask your intel guys to get me the latest imagery of Quilon? I asked for some yesterday; Dick Lapierre ought to have it at Fifth Fleet."

"I've seen it; Agency sent it from the National Reconnaissance Office. Got it. Anything else, Commander?"

"Yes, sir. How's the admiral?"

"Not as bad as we feared. You guys are friends?"

"I've known him since my first squadron."

"He may be medevaced to Trin tomorrow morning."

"I'd like to see him while I'm aboard."

"I'll do what I can. He was good today; he had some energy and he got a whole brief on the situation from me when I went off watch."

"Thanks, sir." Alan looked at his watch, counted twice. "I should be there in six hours."

"Good luck. Out here."

Alan unfolded himself from Harry's bed and closed the case carrying the encrypted phone. His head was full of plans—he needed a good chart of the western Indian Ocean; he needed stuff for his helmet bag; he needed to draw far-on circles for a lot of ships.

Harry was standing just outside the room, his bag in his hand. He reached out a hand, but Alan swept him into an embrace. They pounded each other's backs in silence for a few seconds.

"Take care of yourself," Alan said.

"You too, my friend."

And then Harry was gone, and Alan focused on the next step.

* * *

"Det Trincomalee, commanding officer."

The warm voice on the other end washed away Alan's fatigue. "Hey." He didn't get any further than that before his voice caught.

"You!" Rose laughed and then gasped. "You!" she said again.

A moment of static silence passed between them.

"I should have called—"

"No, me. Oh, shit, Alan—"

"You okay?" Even as Alan said the words, they sounded insipid to him, useless, a replacement for an hour of questions. Instead, they spent a minute talking about the kids that neither of them was with. And then Alan got down to business; he needed a plane, an escort, weapons.

Rose switched gears; professional, on the ball. "I have three S-3 pilots; two nuggets and Soleck. I'll send you Soleck. He's had his crew rest. One of the nuggets will have to learn to play with the big boys and girls. I'll put two Hornets on alert. I'm short on weapons—you know that, right? I have one Hornet with a full missile load and everyone else has Sidewinders and guns."

He still had a list in his hand. "Got any Harpoons?"

"No."

"HARM?"

She laughed. "What is this, Let's make a deal? I have one HARM. It's on one of the birds. I'll try and put it up for you. Anything else, Mister Craik?"

"I love you, Rose. Stay safe."

"It's not me I'm worried about," she said. "Wait! I've got something to say and it's stuck—Jesus." She almost sobbed. "This isn't the time."

Alan caught the change in tone; not the commanding officer, but his wife, with something. "It's never the time, Rose. Tell me."

"Now I feel dumb." She was choked; maybe crying.

"Damn it, Hon! Let's not play 'wait till your father gets home.' What's the matter?"

Silence.

"I'm—pregnant," she said, her voice rising and her words tumbling out faster and faster. "I'm three months pregnant and I didn't want to say in case I—miscarried—you know—again, fuck, okay? And I made two high-G turns and she doesn't seem to mind so I think she's going to stick."

"She?" Alan said, delight cutting through fatigue. "She?"

"Go get it done. Love you."

"She?" Alan said again. Then, "Love you both, Rose."

"Out here," she said finally, and the connection was cut.

Trincomalee

Rose put the phone down and shouted, "Donitz!"

"Ma'am?" Donitz was outside her office, wrangling with the flight schedule.

"Donuts, I'm taking you off this event." She was working out which planes to send, scribbling notes in pencil on a yellow legal pad. She glanced up.

Donuts stood there, arms crossed, deflated. "Yeah?" and, as an afterthought, "Ma'am?"

"I'm putting three pilots and two planes on alert. It probably won't go until 0500 tomorrow. You can take your own plane and 206 with the HARM."

"Yes, ma'am." He looked interested, maybe even excited.

"Al's doing something later tonight, maybe tomorrow. He wants a CAP to cover him. This is harm's way, and you're the best I've got. Okay? I'm pulling you off this event to keep you in crew rest for 0500."

Before she was done speaking, his arms uncrossed and went to his hips. "Oh," he said. He fidgeted with a ring on his right hand. "Oh. Yeah, I get it. I thought you were grounding me to do—you know. Paperwork." Donitz said "paperwork" like it was a dirty word.

"Besides, you've pulled Al's nuts out of the fire before. And you've shot down a MiG-29."

"Well—an Su-27. Maybe a couple." His grin flashed and went away. "Where's he going?"

"Indian coast. He's going after a sub that might have a nuke on it, Donuts. And the sub's going to have support."

"Do I get a brief?"

"I'll have somebody give you one when Al's on the boat. But the stuff about the nukes stays between you and me, okay?"

"Roger that, Rose," he said. "Al's goin' to the boat? Is the deck open?"

"They think they'll be ready to take him aboard by midnight local."

"Why can't we get some air power?"

"I gather that it's all still hypothetical and cat one is only up to full steam every fifteen minutes. If they get an open deck, this could all change." She looked over her notes, wondered what Alan would do if the deck stayed closed. "Who do you want as your wingman?"

"Give me Snot. I'm used to him. And he's seen a MiG before." Snot was in fact a veteran pilot now, with two cruises under his belt. He'd been in combat as Donitz's wingman before, when they had bagged two Su-27s in '99. The recollection made Donitz smile.

He headed out the door, but a hand caught at the frame and his head reappeared. "Thanks, skipper."

Rose smiled broadly and went back to work.

The Serene Highness Hotel

The Lear jet's windows were bright, and light flooded from the hatch over the folding stair.

"You could tell me I'm doing a great job." Mary had turned from the second step, thus to look down on Harry.

"I could." He made shooing gestures to get her to move

363

inside. She sighed too loudly and went in. Harry ducked his head to look under the plane at the glow of a flashlight. "All in. Close her up and roll when you're done." Moad grunted and went on with his preflight.

Djalik was forward in the copilot's seat doing something on a kneepad. Bill was in a club seat on the right side, already asleep. Mary was halfway down on the left, cheek on hand, eyes exhausted and pissed off. "Seat belt," Harry said.

"You're the flight attendant, too?"

"I push a drinks cart up the aisle soon as we're airborne." He leaned on the back of the seat opposite hers. "I'm tired of this operation, Mary. It's been screwed up from the beginning. We missed the big chance; I've left an agent supposed to meet me tomorrow and I'm not going to make it—it's crap. I don't like being a NOC and I don't owe you compliments for passing an intelligence coup back to Washington and violating an agreement a friend of mine had made. But I think I know where SOE headquarters is now, and the sooner I get there, the better. You don't like it, get off the plane."

"You'll do your job!"

It was Harry's turn to sigh. "I told you—I don't have a job. And frankly, my dear, I don't give a damn." He walked back to the double club seat at the rear and fell backward into it and stared out at the night. Seconds later, Moad came in and raised the stair and closed the hatch.

Harry looked at the lighted windows of the hotel, frowning at the illusion of pleasure, the reality of suffering in there. The plane started to roll, and he put his head back to sleep.

30

Bahrain

Rattner and Greenbaum were sitting in Rattner's Taurus in the Fifth Fleet HQ parking lot. It wasn't yet dark but it soon would be, and neither was happy about having to surveil Spinner once darkness fell. Between them, the cell-phone scanner blinked its array of LCDs and picked up the odd call—but not the one they wanted.

"He's coming out," Rattner said after they had been there for an hour. He was in the passenger seat, wearing a headset. He pressed a throat mike. "Two, you get that?"

"Got it." Dukas was in his own car near the base gate.

"Three?"

Leslie's voice sounded thin and far away, but Rattner heard her well enough. "Yeah." She was in a borrowed SUV about a hundred yards beyond the gate.

"He's been sitting on this hot piece of news for a fucking *hour*," Greenbaum said.

"Forty minutes."

"You'd think he'd be hot to pass it to Daddy." Greenbaum was nervous. Rattner chuckled, because Greenbaum had said he had done lots of stakeouts in his cop days and now he was as nervous as a rookie. "Well, what the hell," Greenbaum said when he heard Rattner laugh, "I want this to go down smooth—I'd like Dukas to think I can do my job, okay?"

"You pee?" Rattner said.

"Yeah, yeah. I told you, I've done lots of stakeouts. Anyway, I got an iron bladder."

"Wait until you're fifty." Greenbaum had an empty gallon jug in the back seat. He started to explain the strategies of over-fifty urination when a voice in his ear squawked, "He's coming out into the parking lot."

"He's coming out."

"I awready got him—see him, the tall guy, carries his head funny? I was in there this aft, got a look at him. Boy, do people hate his guts! We nail him, they're gonna take up a collection to buy us a medal."

"What'd they hate him for?" Rattner was watching Spinner pick his way among the cars as he headed for his BMW.

"He's a politician. Also sort of a far-right hard-on. Also makes remarks about the admiral, and Pilchard's a popular guy. Plus he can't stop telling them how important his old man is."

Greenbaum touched his throat switch. "Two, Three, he's at his car. He's getting in."

They watched Spinner settle behind the wheel. They waited for him to take out his cell phone.

"Make the call, you prick," Greenbaum muttered. "Make it—"

"Oh, shit."

Spinner's car backed out of its parking space and whipped past them.

The Serene Highness Hotel

The trucks came back after darkness fell. The maharajah was waiting outside in the warm, scented dark, his hands joined in front of him as if he were a host waiting for some late but much-loved guest. Khan waited with him. The secretary came out several times, murmured, went back. Alan, busy now with his plans, had only glimpsed the silent, waiting figures.

366

Now, feet pounded down the corridors, then a gurney, three servants running with it and men in loosened body armor running ahead and behind.

Alan got up and went out. The doctor who had tended his back was walking in the path of the gurney, but more slowly. He was wearing bloody hospital greens, tying a mask as if preparing for surgery. Seeing Alan, he stepped a little aside; their eyes met, and the doctor shook his head and went on. *Preparing to operate, even though it was too late.* Alan remembered the image on the computer screen. *Like Kennedy in Dallas. It was too late even while you were looking at it.*

The maharajah came last, alone. Alan stood back against the wall to let him pass, but the maharajah stopped and folded his hands together and remained there. Alan, embarrassed, moved, said, "I'm very sorry about your nephew, sir."

The maharajah inhaled deeply, exhaled. "He isn't my nephew, actually. He's my son." A smile flitted over the lower part of his face. "What the English used to call a 'by-blow.' But still—my son." He stared into the billiard room. "You will be leaving tonight, Commander?"

"If you'll allow a Navy plane to land here."

"Of course. But your friend with the aircraft—?"

"Has gone. Separately." Alan felt the need to say something that didn't sound as if they were abandoning him. "We're going after the Servants of the Earth in different ways."

The maharajah nodded. "They are appalling people. I don't even understand what they want." He paused, looked at the lights in the billiard room. "You and your people have behaved well. I want to thank you."

"I think we have to thank you, sir. For trying."

The older man said nothing. He was shorter than Alan by several inches, so he had to reach up to rest a hand on his shoulder. "Good luck." He walked away.

Bahrain

Rattner and Greenbaum were in the Bahrain mini-mall parking lot.

"Well, at least we learned that he's having KFC for dinner."

Spinner had parked below Colonel Saunders's benign smile.

But he didn't get out of the car. Then they saw that he had his cell phone held to his ear.

"The sonofabitch is doing it!" Rattner cried.

The cell-phone scanner winked and a male voice said, "—please. This is, uh, his son. Urgent, okay?" Rattner hit a key on the scanner to hold the frequency and said into his throat mike, "He's making a call—"

"He didn't want to call from the HQ parking lot!" Greenbaum hissed.

"You're smart, that's why we brought you along." Rattner turned up the volume. "Now shut up."

A female voice had asked the caller to hold, and then there had been crackling, prickly silence. Rattner was noting the frequency and the caller's cell-phone number; Greenbaum kept saying, "You sure it's him?" and Rattner nodded and took notes and made sure the tape recorder was turning.

"John Spinner speaking."

Greenbaum punched the air with a fist.

"Dad!"

"Hey, boyo. Good to hear your voice. I've got a client."

"I'll make it quick. I got something hot for you."

"Shoot."

They bent over the scanner. The tape recorder turned. Greenbaum shook his head as if he couldn't believe it—the poison pill was passing from son to father as if it was a Father's Day gift. The tale that the flag captain had told Spinner, in strictest confidence, was that Pilchard had ordered the *Jefferson* to change its destination from Colombo to Diego Garcia, another twelve days' sailing away, there to offload

368

all its aircraft. In Washington, Dad thought that was pretty juicy news.

Rattner was on the headset again. "Two, Three, acknowledge." When they had checked in, he said, "Our guy has made his call—repeat, he has made the call. Daddy ID'd himself, and we've got it on tape. Over."

Dukas's voice growled in his ear. "Stay on him. I want to know he's tucked into his little beddy-bye, then we trade off outside his place. Got me?"

"Yeah, got you, Two." Rattner looked at Greenbaum, who had his eyes on the KFC restaurant, into which Spinner had now disappeared. Rattner switched channels and checked with somebody at Fifth Fleet HQ and said to Greenbaum, "Security officer's already grabbed his office computer. Marines have orders to pull him over at the gate and keep him at least ten minutes and secure his laptop; by the time he gets home, they'll have his home computer. FBI bugged his home phone an hour ago."

"So what d'we do?"

"We sit and watch him scarf down chicken and then we follow him. Might be an interesting night once he realizes what's going down. Now put the fucking car in gear; our guy is leaving."

The Serene Highness Hotel

By 2130, Alan knew that Soleck was on his way from Trin. He had a route to the boat and a comm plan and some fuel figures that Soleck would have to re-do. By 2300, Soleck was only a few minutes out, and he'd planned what he could do; he'd calculated the enemy's moves as much as the data allowed; and now he was standing in the situation room, his butt on a billiard table covered in maps, watching other people work. He was done.

Ong and Clavers were typing away at intelligence reports based on the data they had gleaned from all the sources they

369

had found. Benvenuto and Fidel were choosing still images from the digital video and turning them into useable data files to attach to the reports. Whether Alan's next moves succeeded or failed, the reports would matter to the other men and women who would have to deal with the Servants of the Earth.

"Folks?" Alan said. "Can I have a minute?"

They all looked up; Ong's face in the soft light of a desk lamp looked older and harder. Benvenuto rocked back in his seat and stood as if to face a blow, and Fidel's eyes narrowed as he turned in his chair.

Alan cleared his throat and stood away from the billiard table. "I'm leaving. You people have behaved in what we call 'the best traditions of the naval service,'" he said. "I left a quick report on Ms Ong's computer, in case—in case I don't have time to write more." He thought about all the things he couldn't say, like *Some of you grew up a lot*, and *I underestimated you*. Not for the first time, he understood why most command speeches were bland, the real praise almost too harsh to say. Unconsciously, he spread his hands. "You were superb," he said. He looked at Ong, who smiled back, and then at Benvenuto, who was grinning so hard his ears moved. "We all have to keep going for a bit. Sometimes the end game is the hardest. It's easy to sag." *Who am I talking to? Me?* "LT Ong will be in charge of getting these reports out to the fleet. When you're done, get some sleep. By the time you wake up, Fifth Fleet should have some transports together to take you home."

He tried to smile at them all. None of them needed to ask where he was going. So he looked around, making eye contact one more time. "That's it, folks. I'll see you in Bahrain in a day or two." He felt tight with emotion and nerves. "Thanks." He picked up his helmet bag and pushed through the door, surprised to find his throat closed and his hands a little shaky.

Somebody came out into the corridor right behind him, and he turned, expecting Ong or Benvenuto. Instead, he found Fidel.

"I'll walk you down," he said.

"Sure." Alan didn't know what to say to Fidel, never did. So he walked along in silence with a fortune in ancient rugs muffling their footsteps and into the lobby.

"I'm headed to the kitchen," Alan muttered. "Coffee."

"Yeah," Fidel said.

Through the process of getting his thermos washed and filled by too-attentive staff, Fidel stood behind him in silence. Alan couldn't find anything to say, his thoughts either far away or inconsequential. Alan didn't turn, but the silence got to be too much. "Always hungry in planes, you know? And food is sleep—"

"Yeah," Fidel said, nodding hard. "Yeah."

Then they were outside, standing in the warm dark listening to the *whooost, whooost* sounds of Soleck's engines on final, and they still hadn't said anything. The S-3 appeared in a burst of light and motion, cleared the jungle at the far end of the runway and was down and taxiing before Alan could think of a way to say goodbye.

Suddenly Fidel grinned at him as if he'd found the answer to a difficult question. "How's your back?" he asked, his voice rising against the engine noise.

Alan nodded back. "It'll be okay."

"Ejection seat's gonna be a bitch. Eat some more of that ranger candy before you do the deed."

Alan nodded along as if receiving wisdom from a guru. In front of him, two more men in turbans used paddles and flashlights to taxi Soleck to the apron, and the sandwich carts began to roll to the plane.

Fidel reached up, put one hand on Alan's good shoulder, and took his right hand with the other one—not quite a hug, more than a handshake. "Stay safe, skipper," he said.

Bahrain

Spinner had been in a sweat since he had been stopped at the gate of the naval base after he'd called his father from the Kentucky Fried Chicken place. When two Marines had searched his car, he had warned them that they were in for real trouble, but they had gone on, and, when they said they were done, they had handed him a receipt for his laptop, which they had kept.

Spinner had made a stink. He had telephoned the three people he thought might help him—the flag captain, Shelley Lurgwitz, who hated his guts but had a responsibility to help him; the flag security officer, who had no reason to love him but had a responsibility to protect him; and a senior commander in the supply office who was impressed by his being his father's son. But nobody would help him, no way. People seemed, in fact, unaccountably cool.

Spinner's hands had trembled as he had driven away from the base, and he had almost had a fender-bender at the first intersection. After years in the Navy, he knew its politics but was ignorant of its ways. Still, he saw that the seizing of a personal laptop had serious implications.

The implications had got suddenly worse when he got to his apartment and found a warrant officer he'd never seen before waiting at his door with a receipt for his desktop computer. *From his apartment!* Spinner had come very high over the guy, but the warrant officer, who had been in the Navy longer than Spinner had known where to find his dick, introduced a shore patrolman with a sidearm and a warrant from Fifth Fleet JAG.

"Suspicion of violation of security," the warrant officer said, and he'd asked for—and got, because he and the SP both looked as if what they'd really like to do for amusement that evening was use Spinner as a crash dummy—his base pass, his passport, and all the cards that got him into all the places in Bahrain that were classified, restricted, interesting, or important.

Spinner had gone from the warrant officer straight to his bathroom and upchucked his Kentucky Fried Chicken. Then he had lain down, trembling. Then he had tried to call his father and was told that Mr Spinner was in a meeting and was accepting no calls at present.

So it was a while before he talked to his father, and only then because his father called him. And all his father said was, "Call me at Effie's on a public phone. Don't use your cell phone and don't use your home phone!" And then his father broke the connection.

By then, Spinner's eyes were red because he had actually wept. He had also soiled his J. Press boxer shorts, because Spinner had never in his life before been in a spot where he couldn't get to his father to be saved.

As weak and trembling as if he had the flu, Spinner stumbled down to his car and went looking for a telephone.

Over Tamil Nadu, India

The back end was up and running, and Alan ignored the good-natured prattle about the maharajah's hotel and dug up the datalink. Before Soleck had made his clearing turn to the north, Alan's plan was in trouble because he was tired and he hadn't seen a chart recently.

"Soleck?"

"Skipper?"

Alan was looking at the projected positions of the five probable SOE vessels en route to Quilon. His intended course, it now turned out, ran right through the center of their projected radar horizon. "You got a route to the boat?"

"Yessir, you passed it to Commander Siciliano."

"Soleck, I did that track before I could see the far-on circles on these hostile contacts. Look at the link."

"Holy shit," Garcia said.

"Whoa," Simcoe whistled.

"We've got to go all the way south until we're clear of

their envelope and any possible ground radar around Quilon and then head west to the boat. Do we have the fuel?"

"Give me a minute," Garcia said.

Alan was looking at his new route, which added an hour to their flight time. Nothing to be done about it now. "How low did you come in?"

"Pretty fucking low," Simcoe growled.

"Low-ish." Soleck sounded pleased with himself.

"Fuel to spare if you go high once we're feet-wet." Garcia yawned. "Tight if we're low all the way."

"I want to go high once we're clear of the coast, anyway." Alan looked at the link again. "I want to update these locations before we get to the boat. This is going to be tight all the way." *And I just lost an hour.*

"They've got a pretty tight EMCON going, sir," Garcia said. "We won't get a sniff of 'em unless something else stirs them up."

"We'll just have to radiate," Alan said, his mind already on other things.

"That's a non-starter, sir," Simcoe said beside him. He reached over and deposited a kneeboard card on Alan's working tray.

Alan read it in a second; a total prohibition on active forms of emission or any action that might provoke a hostile reaction. He flipped it over to see if there might be more. "This from Captain Lash?"

"Yessir." Simcoe again, his voice carefully neutral.

The front seats were silent; Alan wondered if Simcoe had cut them out of the conversation. He glanced under his elbow. Yep. Simcoe was smooth. Alan took a deep breath and let it out slowly. This was the moment, the first of a hundred moments he knew would come and yet wanted to shrug off for as long as he could—where his plans conflicted with other people's orders and he was placing his career and other people's careers on the line for a big risk with a lot of guesswork.

"I have orders from over Captain Lash." There. The first half-truth.

Simcoe's grin was visible even in the dark of the back end of an S-3. "Shit-hot."

No question whose side Simcoe was on.

They flew low over Tamil Nadu for an hour, the ground as dark as the sea, bereft of city lights or even the clustered glow of villages. As far as Alan could determine, Tamil Nadu was blacked out from north to south. The only exception had been a glow over the horizon to the west early in their flight.

"Lights are on at Quilon," Soleck said.

Circumstantial evidence. But it made Alan smile, nonetheless

Bahrain

Mike Dukas and Leslie were sitting in Dukas's leased Toyota when Spinner came out of his apartment. "He doesn't look so good," Dukas said. He didn't sound sympathetic.

"Won't he see us?"

"Doesn't matter."

They knew about Spinner's attempt to call his father, and, as they drove, Leslie was on their cell phone to an FBI agent about the call that Spinner had got from his father. "So he's going to a public phone now, right?" she said to Dukas.

"Good luck finding one in Manama."

"There's three in the souk," she said.

"Somehow I don't think Spinner will go into the souk. Especially at night."

They followed the tail-lights of Spinner's car for fifteen minutes, in and out of the business streets of Manama, silent until Leslie said, "His father said to call him at 'Effie's.' Who's Effie?"

"Somebody they both know. Maybe a sister, girlfriend, somebody they'd have to know pretty well. Dumb, to drag somebody else into it. But, like all smart people, they're pretty dumb."

It was another fifteen minutes before Spinner found a pay phone he liked outside a twenty-four-hour gas station. Dukas told Leslie to tell the FBI exactly where they were, and he pulled the Toyota right behind Spinner's car and got out. Spinner was trying to work something out with coins and the telephone and getting no satisfaction, and at last he stomped into the gas station and did some shouting and came out with what proved to be a phone card. By then Dukas was leaning on the phone's plastic enclosure.

"Do you mind?" Spinner snarled.

"Nope."

"I want some privacy, asshole."

"Hard to find these days."

"What the fuck?" He put his face close to Dukas's and tried to look terrifying. Dukas smiled in a way that *was* terrifying, so Spinner took a step back and shifted himself from Spinner the Dangerous to Spinner the Lofty. "Have you been following me?" he demanded.

"Yep."

"I am an officer in the United States Navy! Get the fuck out of my face or I'll call the shore patrol!"

Dukas held up his NCIS ID and badge.

Spinner swallowed. His face was deep red. Dukas had already figured out that he had been crying. "This is harassment," Spinner said. "I'll have your ass."

Dukas folded his arms and leaned against the telephone enclosure. After several seconds, Spinner used some more of his Real Navy vocabulary and jumped into his BMW and slammed the door. Dukas was slower getting into the Toyota, and when he got on the road again, Spinner's tail-lights were out of sight. Dukas accelerated and got the car up to ninety and held it there until he saw the lights far away in the darkness, and then he and Leslie trailed Spinner until he pulled into a complex of one-storey apartment buildings near the international hospital. Spinner was already out of the car, and he would have been impossible to follow except that only one apartment had a light on.

"Call the Feebs and give them the address."

31

Bahrain

Spinner was in the Canadian nurse's bedroom after almost having to use physical force to get by the front door. She hadn't been happy to see him, and she wasn't happy now, sitting in her kitchen while he locked himself in her bedroom and called the States, but she'd been delighted that he wasn't making a visit with romance on his mind. Well, fuck her.

"Dad, it's R—"

"You dimwit! You idiot!"

"Dad—!"

"Do you know what you've done? Do you know what the fuck you've goddam you *done*? Say something!"

"Daddy, Jesus—"

"Ben Weisel may just lose his position at NSC because of you, are you aware of that? Has it crossed your pea brain that a mistake like this could cost a lot of good people, a lot of good work, a lot of—a lot of *important projects*—could cost a lot? You've ruined us, sonny boy!"

"I didn't do it on purpose."

"Say, that's a comfort! Jesus Christ, I'd almost rather you had, then I wouldn't think I had a fucking moron for a son! You stupid sonofabitch, you fell for some jerk-off trick I wouldn't expect from a pro bono hack from Cowshit Law College! How could you fall for it? A story that even a goddam black high-school dropout would see through! Do you know how long it took the National Security Advisor to see through it? I'd barely put the fucking telephone down before Ben Weisel was back on the blower to me saying he was blown sky-high and what the hell did I mean, retailing phoney intelligence to him?"

"Well, you believed it enough to pass it on to him. Didn't you? I mean—"

"Don't you dare talk to me like that! Don't you dare drag me down to your level. You set me up. Is that what this was all about—you set up your own father? You sold me out, is that it? Say something!"

"Daddy—Jesus, Daddy—" Spinner was crying again. His father shouted some more and then began to run down, warming up a couple of times as his own rhetoric enraged him all over again, coming to rest at last at a level of cold rage and deep disgust.

"I will never be able to explain to you the depth of my disappointment in you, Ray. You've failed as a son and you've failed as a man. Failed not only me, but this country. I've tried to explain to you how vital it is that our people at the highest level get intelligence that can be relied on—intelligence that hasn't been altered and twisted by a lot of analysts with their closet-liberal mind-set. We thought we had a channel here direct from a source to the highest levels. We thought we'd achieved a breakthrough—intelligence without the interference of the goddam CIA. And you blew it." He cleared his throat and his voice got weary. "All right, what's done is done. You've failed. Now I suppose I have to save your ass. What's your status?"

Spinner told him about the seizure of his computers and about Dukas's appearance at the pay phone. "I think they're after me, Daddy."

"You do, do you. Well, Ray, I'd say no, they're not *after* you; I'd say they've *got* you. Do you at least have the brains to see what they did—get at me through you by sending this phoney message?"

"I got it from the flag captain herself."

His father's words became slow and enunciated. "It has in fact been denied in person by Admiral Pilchard himself to the National Security Advisor. And just in case you care about the effects of your stupidity, I've been told that there's a leak up there—people who've just been waiting to get at Ben Weisel, I suppose—and there'll be a piece in the morning's *Washington Post*."

Long silence. "I'm sorry, Daddy."

"Not half as sorry as you'd be if I wasn't here to save your buns, but I am and I'm going to do it if only to prevent an even worse mess. Now you listen to me, and try to focus both brain cells, because this is what's going to happen: I'll lean on some people in the Pentagon and I'll get you off any charge they're thinking of making. You're going to hunker down and say nothing and do nothing, and I'll find you a new duty station as quick as it can be done. In the meantime, take leave or do whatever the military does."

"I'd like something in California if you can swing it."

His father gave that a long silence and then groaned, "Jesus Christ—"

Outside in the parking lot, Dukas said to Leslie, "I'd certainly like to hear what they're saying." The FBI had been able to tell them that the telephone belonged to a Canadian citizen and was in use, but of course they couldn't tap it. On the other hand, they knew what telephone the father was using in Washington, and so in the morning they'd be making a visit to that address as well as to the owner of the phone Spinner was using.

"Would it be important?" Leslie murmured.

"Oh, probably, if we were going to trial. But my guess is we're not going to trial. That's probably what Daddy-O is telling Number One Son right now."

"Mike, you're so cynical."

"Stick around. You'll see." He got out his cell phone and dialled Admiral Pilchard at home.

Over Tamil Nadu, India

"Those were great sandwiches," Soleck said for the third time. They'd eaten all the cookies and drunk all the coffee, and the engines were straining to lift them to twenty-six thousand feet. The plane's motion was steady, so that inner ears began to believe that the angle of climb was normal and indeed flat. The darkness outside the plane was total in every direction; sky, sea, horizon, ground all one great void, like space without stars. Pilot hell.

"Skipper Craik showed me how to have a great wetting down," Soleck said. "Want to hear the story?"

"You ever going to let me fly this plane?" Garcia snapped. "Do I give a shit pardon-my-French about your wetting down?"

They were unaware that the cockpit intercom was still set to all seats. Alan thought they sounded like an old married couple, or like a couple of kids edging toward flirting. Not for the first time, he thought about the change in dynamics and paradigms brought by women at sea. Not worse, and probably better, but different.

"Hey! It was cool. Jeez, Garcia, give me a break, here. I've been up with Mister Craik before, and I—that is, he—" Just in time, Alan heard Soleck realize that any way he went with his explanation of why he was still flying the plane, Garcia was going to blow. "Never mind. I'm a jerk. You ready to take it?"

"Born ready," she shot back.

"All yours." Soleck met her tone and raised her one, from anger to indifference.

Kids.

"Coffee?" Soleck asked after a while, a clear attempt at a peace offering.

"That'd be nice." Garcia's voice was different.

They were silent for a while; next to Alan, Simcoe snored. Time passed as they approached the datum Alan had marked as the point at which he'd turn on their radar and start his conflict with the enemy and Captain Lash.

"Hey, Garcia?" Soleck sounded earnest.

"Yeah?"

"I'm not the enemy. I'm your pilot. Can you shit-can the attitude?"

Garcia laughed, a low, throaty laugh. "We'll see," she said.

Alan smiled in the back and turned off the intercom.

Trincomalee, Sri Lanka

Donitz looked at his watch for the hundredth time in an hour and stopped to run his hand over the leading edge of a wing. Siciliano said five a.m., but she wasn't sure; no one was sure, and he'd already had four hours of sleep. He looked at his Sparrows again, checked the safety pins, ran his fingers over the pistons in the landing gear and checked for hydraulic fluid leakage. He did everything he could think of to make the time pass, and that got him fifteen minutes.

Somebody moved in the lit space of the hangar and he thought it must be Snot, as eager to go as he was. He ducked under the tail of his plane and started toward the hangar, only to realize that it wasn't Snot. It was Siciliano.

"Rose?"

"I'd say that bird was ready to fly, Donuts."

"Yes, ma'am."

"I can't sleep either, but I'm going over to the hotel to pretend. There's a pretty good chair in my office."

He couldn't see her face in the dark, but she sounded as if she was smiling.

"Thanks. I—"

"I know. But you'll be better with some crew rest."

Over Southern India

The computer sounded a shrill alarm as the airplane reached a marked point on her course. Alan blinked, rubbed his eyes, and grunted.

"Back with us, Commander?" Simcoe asked.

"I want to radiate soon." He sat forward in his harness. "Master Chief? You know how to trigger the ISAR without radiating the surface search first?"

Simcoe's fingers were flying on his keypad. "Hmmm. Never done it." He made a little humming noise. "No reason why not, but you wouldn't get an image unless you hit something by luck. One in a million."

"I don't need an image," Alan said slowly, still looking at his idea from different angles. "ISAR looks like a targeting radar, right? So if we illuminate them with it, it should set off their ESM gear as a targeting radar."

"Could work," Simcoe said, grinning. "Worth a try. Way the hell better than just radiating all over the place."

"Which we can do anyway if it doesn't work. It worked on Iraqis back in the Gulf."

"I'm game, Commander. Radar's warm and on hold."

Alan looked down at his kneeboard, back at the datalink, calculating on the basis of hours-old data. If the ships were headed from their last location to Quilon and they hadn't altered speed, they should occupy a volume of sea located—there.

"You got ESM ready?"

"Shine the light."

In for a penny, in for a pound. Alan pushed a switch to ISAR and hit radiate. He counted to three and cut it off. His screen showed the random reflections of the powerful beam of the ISAR on waves and an empty ocean.

A hundred and ninety miles to the north, just a few miles outside of the narrow beam of Alan's radar, a passive sensor on a Krivak-class frigate registered the flash of the ISAR. The ESM system on the Indian frigate was simple and robust, and all the operator received was a small beep and an amber warning light. Had there been parameters on the system, the operator might have had a chance to wonder where the signal had originated. As it was, he assumed that loyalist fleet units had radiated a targeting radar, and he called the bridge.

"That's slick, Commander." Simcoe's ESM screen suddenly showed repeated hits on a surface-search radar at the edge of the radar horizon to the north. "Surface search. Krivak-class."

"Ms Garcia, turn to 270 and increase speed."

Garcia said, "Roger that." The plane banked into a turn, and then, "Soleck's asleep."

Alan had already switched screens to watch the ESM, where a second radar bloomed as a long green line, and then a third, all evenly spaced-out vectors. "Come on!" he said aloud.

The pitch of the engines increased as Garcia pushed more power through the turbines. At this altitude, there was no immediate tug at the harness, but they were moving off their initial bearing, trying to triangulate on their first burst of hits. Two vectors from identical transmitters gave a possible solution; three or four would give a fix.

"They've been fighting for two days. They've got to be on edge." Alan realized that he was talking to convince himself. *I've been fighting for two days, and I'm on edge.*

Simcoe grunted.

"That good enough, sir?" Garcia was eager—finally the pilot, not just the copilot.

"Excellent." Alan watched his screen, like a fisherman watching a pool.

"Will ya look at that?" Simcoe jabbed a finger at his screen as Alan saw the green vectors vanish, replaced by hard-edged diamonds.

"Don't transmit them into the link."

"Why not?"

"We'll be on the boat in an hour; we'll put them in by hand. If we were lucky, and I think we were, they emitted all surface-search radars; they don't know we're here. We put stuff in the link, we're emitting."

"Roger that." Simcoe watched his screen. "Got to put that one in the playbook."

"My skipper did it to Iraqi SAM sites in the Gulf War. They always lit up." Alan remembered it so well.

"Sweet. And these guys—"

"Are still looking for a surface contact. Whoa. There they go again!" Alan pounded his armrest with his right fist and felt a twinge of pain in his back.

"Course and speed!" Simcoe chortled. "Man, it's a jackpot!"

"And formation." Alan looked at the three ships in line astern. "I'll bet they've flank pickets and they couldn't see the beam. Whatever. That's where they are." He sat back, tired again, but a little closer to his goal. "Got a good tape in?"

"Sure."

"Record all this."

"Roger that."

"Garcia, how's our fuel?"

"We could go back to Trin if we had to."

"Take us down below the radar horizon, okay? Maybe twelve thousand?" Alan tried to do his equation. He couldn't. "Get below ten. What's our ETA?"

"Under an hour, sir."

An hour until the next bump. Soleck, who on his last cruise had had the lowest landing scores on the boat, would be putting them down on a crippled deck with a three wire and no net.

Bahrain

Dukas and Leslie were getting ready for bed when a phone call came from the Washington JAG headquarters. The watch commander who was calling told Dukas to stand by for an admiral. The self-righteousness of the man's voice told Dukas all he needed to know about what the admiral was about to say.

"Special Agent Dukas?" The JAG admiral's voice sounded unhappy. "You are to consider this an order, is that clear? Written confirmation will follow. Don't give me a lot of noise about chain of command; your people are in the loop. This is a done deal. Understand?"

"Understood, sir."

"In the matter of a Lieutenant-Commander Raymond L. Spinner. You are *not* to go to legal prosecution. Period, end of story. Any questions?"

Dukas looked at Leslie, raised his eyebrows. "This is an order, is what you're saying, Admiral, and I am not to proceed to legal prosecution." He made a horror-movie face at Leslie.

"See that that's what happens."

Dukas dropped the telephone into its cradle. "See?" He wagged a finger. "Spinner gets to Daddy, Daddy gets to his pals on NSC, Daddy's pals get to JAG." He let the phone sit for five seconds and picked it up again and, satisfied that he had a dial tone, called Pilchard. The admiral, waked from deep sleep, listened to him and then said, "I don't care about prosecution right now, Mike. Keep Spinner on ice for twenty-four hours so he can't blab more secrets, and I'm a happy man. You and your guys did well."

"I have an idea," Dukas said.

Pilchard's voice was wary. "I'm up to my ass in ideas."

"I'd like to come in and tell you about it, sir."

"It's your nickel."

"It might mean getting a few people out of bed."

"Dukas, my people don't *go* to bed. This place looks like the Zombie Navy. You want to come in at this hour, do it."

Dukas looked across the bed at Leslie, who was more or less in a pajama top. "I'm on my way," he said.

And so the night turned into a working day.

Day Four

32

USS *Thomas Jefferson*

Soleck yelled, his adolescent triumph simultaneous with the embrace of Alan's harness as the three wire slammed the plane to a halt on the deck. *Home.* Nothing like it in the world; the end to peril and the lure of a rack and a greasy hamburger.

"Three wire and okay!" Soleck shouted.

"Jeez, Soleck, it was a landing. You're not supposed to be surprised." Garcia was laughing.

"Mister Soleck, that was slick." Alan was stripping his harness as he spoke. "Quite an improvement on last cruise."

Soleck smiled ruefully.

Alan grinned back. "Stay with the plane and get gas and weapons. Ms Garcia, will you be kind enough to go down to the intel center and debrief the tape and all the data on the locations?"

"Roger that, sir."

"Master Chief? Want to go down to the ASW module and get the latest and greatest? I'll meet you all in CVIC, okay?"

"Aye, aye, sir."

Alan tossed his empty thermos into his helmet bag, stripped his kneeboard off his leg and pushed it in on top. Under his feet, one of the deck crew popped the hatch in the belly of the plane and let the ladder down. Alan was the first one out.

The deck was empty. He looked around, lost because the island was damaged and there were no marks on the deck. A guy in a flight-deck jersey and a float coat grabbed his shoulder and led him forward, and as he turned he saw a helo turning on the bow. As he watched it, the plane rotated so that her tail showed and he read "USS *Fort Klock*."

Alan realized that Captain Lash was already aboard the *Jefferson*.

His guide went down a ladder that had been cut in the deck and Alan followed, aware of the damage all around him and the repairs that covered it. He saw several bent bulkheads as he went down the ladder well; scorch marks, odd curves where the eye expected a straight line. Like coming home and finding your house had burned; loss, anxiety, anger.

Madje saw him from the passageway, knew he had to be Craik. Craik was thinner than he expected, gaunt. His hair was long for an officer, and his face looked—focused. Set on the next thing. Craik's glance flicked over Madje, read his collar bars, and moved on. Came back and settled on Madje's chicken guts.

"I'm Madje, the flag lieutenant. You need to know that Captain Lash is already aboard—"

"I saw his chopper. Madje? We talked?" Craik was clipped, direct.

"Yessir."

"Let's get this over with. Take me to Captain Lash."

"The admiral wants to see you, sir." Madje reached out to grab Craik's elbow, anxious to convey how important that was to this focused man. He was surprised when Craik turned on him. It was a different look, as if some angry light had gone out of Craik's eyes.

"Of course I want to see Rafe—the admiral. How's he doing?"

Madje smiled. "He's better. In fact, he's mad as hell at Lash, and that's kept him up all day. He tried to go to CIC about an hour ago."

Craik grinned. "That's the best—"

"Commander Craik?"

Craik turned. He and Madje were filling the passageway. The newcomer was a short man wearing a rumpled set of khakis with eagles, and he was standing outside the combat information center. Another O-6 ducked past him; the two captains glared at each other, and the taller man hurried forward without a word.

"Yes, sir?" Craik's voice was gentle.

"What the fuck are you trying to pull, Craik?" The short captain waved a fistful of paper flimsies at him. "You're trying to go over my fucking head? I'll have your ass."

Craik's voice was quiet. "You're Captain Lash, sir?"

"Don't give me that shit, Commander." Lash stepped forward, right into Craik's space, nose to nose.

Craik didn't retreat. "I'm not under your orders, sir. With respect."

"Like fuck!" Lash said, the last word coming out with a shriek. He seemed to see Madje for the first time. "Get lost, Lieutenant."

"Sir!" Madje backed away a step and froze; he was about to take the TAO watch and he needed to get past Lash. Very, very quietly he said, "I, uh, need to get—"

Lash ignored him. "I could arrest you," he said to Craik.

Craik shook his head. Then he looked at his watch. Madje tried to get his hand on the door and failed when Lash pushed forward again.

"What the fuck are you looking at your watch for? You're done, you hear me? You and your fucking plane aren't going anywhere. I feel like I'm in the fucking Russian Navy. This is like a fucking mutiny. I'm not taking your shit, Commander. Now get off this deck."

Craik had backed up this time. He had his back to a steam pipe and a red battle lantern and his face looked as if it was as red and gray as the paint on the bulkhead. A vein on his temple was pulsing. Madje thought that he was scarier than Lash.

"Sir. I don't have time to argue priorities. There's a sub out there with three nuclear warheads mounted in missiles. We have about four hours to find it and sink it. That's our job, sir. Anything else is just ass-covering."

"Listen to me, you pompous bastard—" Lash began.

Watching Lash sweat and swear, it suddenly came to Madje that it was *Lash* who was afraid, not Craik. It was a revelation.

"You listen, sir. I'm getting the sub. It's my duty. It's your duty too; you can ignore it and cover your ass, or you can do it." Craik's voice was still level; he looked at his watch again.

Spittle flew from Lash's lips. "Jesus. You prick. That's the end of your fucking career, so help me—"

Captain Hawkins appeared in the red gloom behind Craik. "Admiral Rafehausen would like to see you, gentlemen."

"Fuck off, Hawkins." Lash was turning back toward CIC. Madje tried not to meet his eye.

"Captain Lash, your immediate presence was required by the admiral. Shall I tell him you refused?"

Hawkins sounded like nothing would please him more, and his over-educated tones and exaggerated patience made every word an insult.

"The admiral is a medical—basket case," Lash spat out, but Madje heard the minute hesitation.

Alan Craik was already walking forward to see his friend.

Rafe looked worse than Alan had expected. In fact, he looked worse than Alan could have imagined. His skin was dead white, his hair was a mass of sweat, and he looked very small in a bed surrounded by support equipment. His head was raised a couple of inches by a pillow. His eyes glittered with life. That was all there was of him, there in the eyes.

"Sir," Alan said.

"Where's Lash?" Rafe whispered.

"He's resisting arrest."

"That—fucker," Rafe sighed. "Wants—me medevaced."

"Yeah. I'd say he was on a power trip."

Rafe's upper body trembled. For a second, Alan thought he was in pain, until he realized Rafe was laughing. Rafe's hand reached out and touched his. "This is my battle," he said clearly.

There was a commotion behind them, and then they all trooped in—Lash, an angry doctor, Hawkins, some junior lieutenant with SWO wings who was probably with Lash. "I want you to pronounce him medically unfit," Lash was saying to the doctor.

"See how you feel when I wake *you* up at one in the morning, Lash." Rafe's voice was thin, but strong.

"I'm not dealing with his interference again." Lash ignored the admiral, spoke only to the doctor.

"Lash, like it or not, I'm in command. TAO, I want Commander Craik's plane armed and out of here before I can say 'Tail Hook.' Got me?" Rafe's voice was still strong.

"Yessir!" Hawkins said.

"And, Hawkins? I want you in as Flag TAO until this is over. Clear?" Still strong.

Lash turned on Alan. "I've had enough of you and your asshole buddy, Craik. I am not taking orders from an admiral doped to the gills and whispering lines you taught him. You are under arrest—"

"Shut up, Lash! I've had it!" Rafe's voice sounded like a pistol shot. There wasn't a noise in the sick bay except the sound of Rafe's heartbeat monitor. "That's better," he said more quietly. "Lash, go back to your ship. I'm ordering you,

395

and every man here, to see to it that my orders are obeyed. Commander Craik is to be afforded every support this goddam battle group has to offer. You know why, Lash? Because it's our duty. That's all." He slumped.

The doctor looked at Lash. "That clear enough for you, sir?"

Lash looked at Rafe for the first time; intimidated and angry. "You could start a war, Admiral. You could start a war and lose the lives of every man in this battle group. For what? You're doing a foolish thing for the wrong reason, Admiral." Lash shook his head. "You're going to start a war with India."

Rafe's eyes were on Alan's now, and they had a bad glitter to them. "We're—already—war," he said. "Carry on!"

"You think he's fit to command?" Lash asked the doctor.

"Yes!" said the doctor, who was also a captain.

"You people are fucking dangerous," Lash said. He rubbed his hands together, as if washing them. And then he left.

When they had gone, Alan found that he was sitting with Rafe again; this time, he was holding Rafe's hand.

"How—was I?" Rafe asked after a while.

"Scary," Alan said.

Rafe choked a little and coughed. "Exc—ellent," he whispered.

Alan found that he was crying. The tears started as a pain in his eyes and suddenly there were tears pouring down his face. "I might be wrong," he blurted out. "What if I'm fucking wrong?"

Rafe squeezed his hand. "Not—my—problem, bud."

Alan thought of Rafe, tall, arrogant Rafe, who had tormented him at his first squadron and taught him how to fly. Who lived to lead his men in the air. Who would spend the rest of his life in a bed like this one, far from the smell of the sea and JP-5 and the bark of the ready room and the kick as the catapult puts you out on the edge. He couldn't stop his tears. He couldn't say anything.

Rafe squeezed his hand again, as if Alan was the one who needed the comfort. "Hey, Spy," he said in a whisper, "go do your fucking job."

Bahrain

Mike Dukas made himself uncomfortable in a borrowed office at Fifth Fleet HQ, not the environment he'd have chosen but all he could get under the circumstances—he'd had his chat with the admiral; he'd got an okay; he'd put things in motion. And here he was, in a borrowed office in the middle of the night, ready to be a sonofabitch.

He had a large coffee, a tape recorder, and a file labeled *Spinner, LCDR R. L.* He tried the desk chair, walked around, placed a straight chair across the desk and sat in it, then got up and pushed the desk a foot to the left and tilted a desk lamp toward it. When he sat again in the straight chair, he thought that the glare was now about as much as he could hope for.

He tried the tape recorder. He sipped coffee. He checked his watch. "Okay, send him in."

Dukas folded his hands over the file and sat there, wishing he looked more like Hollywood's idea of a Mexican drug lord.

Ray Spinner came in. He looked like hell despite his crisp uniform.

"Siddown."

Spinner didn't siddown. He slitted his eyes up as if he, too, wanted to look like Hollywood's idea of a Mexican drug lord. "You're the asshole at the phone booth."

"You're Lieutenant-Commander Raymond Laurence Spinner?"

"What the hell is this? I'm not going to be pushed around, you get me? I'm not some sailor!" But he was trembling.

Dukas flipped on the tape recorder and told it his own name, the date, and the time. "Location is office B314, Fifth Fleet Headquarters. Your name is Raymond Laurence Spinner?"

"Cut the crap. Who the fuck are you and what is this—a rerun of *Law and Order*?"

Dukas turned off the tape recorder. "Commander, your security officer has been told of multiple security violations. I have fourteen other pending issues in this file. We can deal with all of them pretty quickly if you get off your high horse and cooperate."

"You going to read me my rights next?"

"You're not under arrest." Dukas folded his hands again. "We read their rights to people who are under arrest."

"Then what the fuck am I doing here?"

"I believe that Captain Lurgwitz ordered you to be here. Am I right? And you're in the military, so you obey orders."

Spinner sat in the straight chair. "I don't want anything recorded."

"I can understand that, but unfortunately for this interview to be of any use to anybody, and that includes you, we have to record it." He turned the machine on.

"I want a lawyer."

"You're not under arrest, I told you."

"I demand a lawyer."

Dukas addressed the tape recorder. "Lieutenant-Commander Spinner has 'demanded' a lawyer. I have explained that he is not under arrest and that therefore, under the Uniform Code of Military Justice, he neither needs nor will get a lawyer."

"I'm getting out of here."

"I don't advise that."

"I know my rights!"

"I believe that Captain Lurgwitz ordered you not only to appear for this interview but to cooperate with it."

"She can't order me to incriminate myself!"

"In what?"

"The—" Spinner motioned with his hat at the desk. "Whatever you said."

"Right. You can't be ordered to incriminate yourself. If I did allow you to incriminate yourself, I'd be hurting my own case. That's why it's to your advantage to have this on tape." Dukas gave him a little smile.

"All right, cut the bullshit. What's going on?"

Dukas took out his badge wallet and handed it across the desk. "I'm Special Agent Michael Dukas, Special-Agent-in-Charge of the Bahrain office of the Naval Criminal Investigative Service."

Spinner's face showed increased concentration, interest—perhaps recognition. He put the wallet down. "Oka-a-a-y. So?"

"We have a telephone call on tape that you made last night to your father at his office in Washington. No, don't say anything—I don't want you to incriminate yourself. Just hear me out. In that call, you can be heard passing information that was given to you by Captain Lurgwitz. As you now know, that information was false and was told to you to test if, in fact, you'd pass it on."

"That's entrapment!"

"Your home computer's hard drive has an e-mail sent to your father in Washington some weeks ago about a supposed failure on Admiral Pilchard's part. What I guess we'd call privileged information on a sensitive matter."

"Computer was seized illegally—inadmissible!"

"Your laptop had six pieces of classified material on it when it was examined by the Marine guards at the base gate. Plus your home computer had eleven pieces of classified material, including correspondence, a manual on the coding of personnel files, and other—"

"Everybody's got classified material at home, for Christ's sake! Come into the real world, Mike!"

Dukas looked up from the file. "'Special Agent Dukas,'" he said.

"I was trying to relax the atmosphere a little, do you mind?"

"Yes." Dukas looked at something in the file. "Twenty-seven pieces of pornography were also found on your home computer."

"Oh, get a life!"

"Two seem to fall within the definition of child pornography, but we're checking on the ages of the people in the images."

"Oh, great! Is this what you guys do while the world is being overwhelmed by the enemies of democracy? Boy, we can sleep safe in our beds, the NCIS is on the job!"

Dukas folded his hands again. "Last night, you used the telephone of a foreign national—"

"She's *Canadian*!"

"—to call your godmother's house in Washington in order to discuss the passing of classified information with your father. Thus implicating your godmother."

"In what?"

Dukas folded his hands. "Sedition."

It was clear that Spinner didn't remember what sedition was. He turned red, opened his mouth, and then scrambled out of the chair. "I'm outa here. I'm not going to listen to this. You've got nothing—nothing! A mass of, of lies you've put together with Lurgwitz, well, it's well known she hates me because she's a lesbian, that's a fact! And you! Talking to me about pornography, about child pornography, for Christ's sake, you're shacked up with some pretty young stuff yourself, for Christ's sake, you think you're so goddam moral, you knock up your little sweetie and she trots herself down to kill the baby! Is that the moral high ground that you defenders of freedom are coming from? Is that the NCIS uniform code of porking, you can stick it to your girl but nobody else can? I'm outa here!"

If Dukas was surprised by anything that Spinner had said, his face never showed it. His hands, still closed over the folder, made no movement. Instead, he said, "I think you'd better hear what I have to offer."

"What the fuck does 'offer' mean? I didn't ask for anything!"

"You will." Dukas gave him the little smile again. "If you're charged with the things I mentioned, you'll be asking for a lot." He kept his voice low and even. "Sit down."

Spinner slapped his hat against his thigh several times and looked at the doorknob and then sidled toward the chair. "I'm on to any legal tricks," he said. Dukas bobbed his head and Spinner sat down.

Dukas said, "I won't go to legal prosecution. No court-martial."

Spinner's face broke into a huge grin.

"You won't have the ordeal of a military trial with the severe punishments that might lie at the end of it. No hard time, no dishonorable discharge—none of that."

"Hey—" Spinner stood. "All r-i-i-ght." He put out his hand. "Sorry I got a little over-wrought there. I'm sure you can understand, Mike, this has been kind of trying for me. Bygones be bygones?"

Dukas ignored the hand. "However—"

The grin faded. Their eyes locked, and when Dukas bobbed his head again, Spinner sat.

"However, as I'm sure you remember from a course somewhere, Commander, a captain's mast is not a legal proceeding. It's an *administrative* proceeding. People appearing at captain's masts have no right of counsel, and the commanding officer is judge and jury. Of course there's a right of appeal, but then everything becomes public, and the appellate officers can in fact then look into all kinds of stuff.

"On lesser included offenses, you can be brought before a captain's mast on altogether—let's see—eighty-one things.

401

Staff security officer wants to proceed on sixteen of those having to do with security violations; the others can be explained to you if you really want to go that way." He held up a hand. "Not my doing—NCIS would be out of it if there's a captain's mast. Only one thing we'd add, and that would be, because it's on the tape, conduct unbecoming an officer." Dukas smiled. "What you said to me a couple of minutes ago—very unbecoming. And the remark about Captain Lurgwitz—you'd be dead on that one, and the security stuff is open and shut, I think. The others—who knows?" Dukas stared at him. "So you can have the captain's mast." A long pause. "Or you can resign."

"Why would I do that?" Spinner's voice was breathy, whiney.

Dukas sat back, the swivel chair squawking under his weight. "Captain's mast can't do much in the way of punishment—few days in the brig at worst, stuff like forfeiture of pay for a month, loss of liberty. You can take all that. Problem comes with the nonjudicial results. At the very least, I'd say, a letter in your file. In this case—you know what you've done, Commander—the kind of letter that means no more promotions. End of career. You're a smart guy; you've been around; you know what one letter like that can do. And then there are the fitness reports—well, you can imagine the fitness report that'll come after all this."

Spinner stared at him, then looked around the room as if he hadn't seen it before. "That isn't fair," he said.

Dukas mumbled something into the telephone and Captain Lurgwitz, the flag captain, came in. She was forty, smart, political; she had big hips and narrow shoulders and she looked as if she fought a battle with weight, but her face was engaging in its cheerful intelligence. She pulled a chair up to the end of the desk and sat down. Dukas leaned over toward her and said, "I've been explaining to Lieutenant-Commander Spinner that NCIS will not prosecute but that

402

I thought there was the possibility of a captain's mast here."

"It's more than a possibility. Ray, you've really screwed up. I can convene a captain's mast on this stuff in a heart-beat."

"You've had it in for me ever since I reported here!"

"Has Special Agent Dukas explained the outcomes? You know there'll be a letter of severe reprimand, come what may, Ray. Come what may! Plus, I'm now ready to say on your fitrep that you're the worst officer I've ever served with." She sounded almost sad. "You're never going to make full commander, Ray." She put her arm on the back of the chair, turned toward him with her fingers joined just below her right breast. "I heard you make a joke once about some-body who'd been passed over. 'Like a castrated dog with a hard-on,' was I think the way you put it."

Spinner tried to study Dukas's face through the glare from the lamp. He seemed to refuse to look at Captain Lurgwitz. Finally, he said to Dukas, "What's this about resigning?"

Lurgwitz opened the clipboard she'd carried in and detached several pages from it. "You resign from the Navy, effective immediately. I can tell you that the resignation will be accepted—usual separation allowance, airfare to CONUS; you keep points toward your pension. However, the fitrep will be the same." She didn't say that such a fitrep might affect any notions he might have about blessing the Naval Reserve with his abilities. "Sign where the check marks are."

"And if I don't?"

"The mast, and whatever comes out of that. The letter of reprimand. And immediate transfer as assistant fuels officer to the gator freighter that's now in the Indian Ocean. It's normally a jg's billet, but we'll make an exception for you. You'll love it at sea."

Spinner didn't say that he knew nothing about fuel; she of course knew that, meant that his ignorance would be part of the hell of being on board ship. For six months.

"Does my father have to know?" he said, reaching for a pen.

USS *Thomas Jefferson*

In CVIC, they gave him a shiny photograph showing the north side of the bay at Quilon. The Kilo-class sub was clear as day, her two white life rings like target circles and her fat bow obvious. On shore, two heavy derricks showed as long dark shadows stretching like grasping hands over the submarine's hull. One had had a fat white arrow laid over it by an analyst at DNI, and an inset box showed the highest possible resolution, with the derrick arm repeated in grainy black and a white blob like a maggot dangling in the air. The computerized annotation said "Pos Missile."

Yeah. Alan's hands shook as he looked at the picture. He tossed it back on the briefing table in front of Garcia. The closed-circuit television camera was on him, recording him for Donitz in Trin.

"So," he said. "We have no time. If they leave on the ebb, we'll maybe catch them in the estuary. You and Soleck bring us in low." He tried to ignore the camera. "Donuts stays high, over the radar horizon to the south. The only thing that matters is the sub, but the surface ships have AAA and SAMs that can reach out and get us while we chase the sub. The sub will try to get out by going *under* the ships. So we come in low from the west, lay a pattern here—" he pointed at the electronic map—"before they see us. And pop. Okay?"

Off-camera, he placed a dot from a borrowed laser pointer on a spot to the west of Quilon, well off the coast. "We go up and they see us. We're thirty miles south of them, and maybe they shoot, and maybe they call for air, and maybe they do dick-all." He found that he was staring at the blank eye of the camera. He went back to looking at Garcia. "We pop. They take an action, we shoot." He glanced at Simcoe, who was nodding. "My intention is that our harpoon or

Donuts's HARM nails the southern picket ship immediately. If they take no action, we start looking for the sub, laying our second buoy line inshore. If there's enemy air, Donuts makes the call. Worst case, we're conducting an inshore ASW exercise under their guns while we wait for them to shoot."

Simcoe shrugged. "That would suck pretty hard."

"They've been fighting Indian Navy loyalists for three days. The moment we radiate a radar, they'll shoot." He spoke with an assurance he didn't have. Too many guesses.

Garcia raised her hand. "There's what, five, maybe six SOE ships? And we have one Harpoon and the Hornets have a HARM?"

"We'll get support from the battle group," Alan said. His natural tendency to secrecy was overcome by logic. Whom would they tell? "Admiral Rafehausen had a card up his sleeve from the beginning of the exercise. It's still there, ready to be played."

Soleck got it immediately. He grinned and looked at Garcia the way a smart kid looks at the next smartest kid. "The Canuck, Garcia."

She made a V with her fingers and pointed it at her crotch. Universal aviator sign language. *Fuck yourself.*

Alan held up a hand. "The Canadian frigate, HMCS *Picton*. What we have to do, with a little help from our air cover, is take out the southern picket ship; it'll be the only one able to see the *Picton* when she radiates. Everything else will be over the horizon; we'll pass the targets to *Picton*, and she'll take them. Okay?"

Garcia shook her head.

Soleck raised his hand. "The kid in Stevens's plane said the sub got them."

"Yeah, okay," Alan said. "So they have a SAM system on the sub."

"Gotta figure." Soleck shrugged. "Hey, I'm not saying we

405

don't go. I'm just saying we need to be ready to put out chaff and flares."

"Flares. Has to be a MANPAD."

Soleck nodded. "Be prepared, that's my motto."

Garcia smiled at him. "Think of that yourself?"

Alan turned to the CVIC guy running the camera. "That's it. Send it to Trin."

"Yes, sir."

Bahrain

It took a lot to shake Dukas, but he was shaken. Ray Spinner had shouted that Leslie was pregnant—"knocked up," in his words—and Dukas hadn't reacted. Not on the outside. Inside, part of him cringed. Since he had heard it, he had kept it inside, and he had tried to compartmentalize it but had failed. He had tried to make it unimportant. Why should he believe a creep who'd lie about anything and everything? How could Spinner know such a thing, anyway? Why should Spinner know such a thing when he didn't?

But the terrible thing was, he *did* believe Spinner.

"I'm knocking off," he said to Captain Lurgwitz.

"Lucky you," she said.

Lucky me.

33

In the Air, Northern India

Sixty miles east of Delhi, Harry was sitting in the copilot's seat of the Lear jet; Djalik had taken his place in the double seat at the rear.

"You're taking a pretty wide swing around Delhi," Harry said.

"SOP until the emergency's over. Indian Air Force has made it a no-fly zone." Moad gave him a sideways grin. "Wouldn't want to be shot down."

"Nasty, nasty." Harry tried to look out, saw nothing. "How long?"

"We swing around Delhi, and we're about eighty miles out."

Harry had on a headset. "Awful quiet," he said.

"Delhi traffic control is shut down. Mumbai's open. Lahore's open, naturally—Pakistan—and they're actually doing some long-range control over on this side. Truth is, I think they don't want anybody making a mistake and starting a war."

"Maharajah's guy filed us for Patiala. That really where we're going?"

Moad grinned again. "The field is closed, but the maharajah's name opened it for us. A little error in communications—they think this is his plane."

"My, my—I don't think I could pass for the maharajah.

We going to get anything helpful like lights? Burning oil drums? Guys with noses that glow in the dark?"

"They *said* lights. If they *don't* show lights, we're screwed. I'll have to divert—first choice is Amritsar."

"Oh, good, I like places famous for massacres. What if Amritsar's dark?"

"Lahore."

"Shit, then we're in Pakistan!"

"Only if they don't shoot us down when we turn toward the border." Moad shrugged. "It'll be fine. What do you want to do, Harry, live forever?" He checked his GPS and kneepad notes and, eight minutes later, turned to 295 and switched on his headset. Harry listened in. "Lahore Control, this is civilian Lear jet AN 5796 from Chittoor, filed for Patiala. Lahore Control, do you have me on your screen, over?" Moad was craning his neck to look down for the Patiala lights.

The answer came in musically accented English. "5796, this is Lahore Control. Patiala is closed. Over."

"Lahore, Patiala will be illuminated for this aircraft. Over." He put the plane into a descent.

"Wait one, 5796—we are checking that." Crackling silence for half a minute. "Okay, 5796, we have a notice to expect one VIP aircraft for Patiala. You are ahead of schedule. 5796, do *not* turn toward the border. You copy, is it? Pakistan Air Force are very airborne."

"Lahore, I read, do not turn toward border." He put the nose down still farther. "Lahore, I am going through five thousand and I have Patiala in visual. The lights are on." Harry, following Moad's eyes, saw blackness and then found a slender, faraway rectangle.

There was an audible chuckle. "Lucky chap. Okay, 5796, suggesting here you descend to three thousand, turning to 020 eleven miles, then descending to two thousand and turning to 195. On your own then, man—runway is 260–080, suggesting land 080, we have wind here southwest 8, okay?"

"Heard and understood, Lahore. Descending to three thousand and turning to 020. You have me?"

"Oh, we have you okay, man! Don't do nothing crazy!" And then laughter.

Moad gave Harry a look. "Slow night at Lahore Control," he said and put the jet into its turn.

Bahrain

Dukas took the long way home. He drove slowly through the darkness, rubbing his upper lip with his left forefinger, his left elbow on the window ledge. At Manama Mall, he pulled into the empty parking lot and sat there for twenty minutes and thought about a pregnant Leslie. It didn't occur to him that Leslie could be pregnant by somebody else; if she was pregnant, it was his. It didn't occur to him simply to let it go, to let her maybe deal with it herself or, worst case, get so pregnant she'd have to say something about it in two or three or six months. It didn't occur to him to postpone facing it.

What did occur to him was that he had a big problem of his own making, and that you clean up your own messes.

He put the car in gear again and drove home. His face looked angry, although he didn't know it, and in fact he wasn't angry. Not at Leslie, at any rate. At himself, maybe—for not ending things when they had been in Washington, for not sending her back when she had shown up in Bahrain. For not liking to have her around.

USS *Thomas Jefferson*

Alan wasn't angry, although anger lurked there. He couldn't get Rafe out of his mind. White as paper. Almost a corpse.

Alan's thermos was full, and he had a bag of cookies from the dirty shirt; the plane had gas, and they were armed to the turbofans. Alan felt none of the elation that made such moments glow for him in memory. Nothing.

409

He felt the shuttle slide down into tension and then the roar as the turbofans went up to full power, Soleck and Garcia muttering through the ritual in the front seat.

"Everybody ready for a ride?" Soleck intoned.

Alan thought once more of the wraith in sick bay, who would never do this again. He swallowed.

Soleck snapped a salute, and they were gone into the first rays of the sun.

Bahrain

Dukas let himself into the house and was shucking off his jacket even as he closed the door behind him with a foot. Leslie appeared in the vaguely Moorish arch at the room's end; maybe his lights had waked her. She was still wearing the skimpy pajama top.

"You're home." She looked good—rested, relaxed because she had had some sleep—but her face tightened as she got closer and looked at his. "What's the matter?"

Dukas threw his coat on the sofa. He was standing at right angles to her, slowly loosening his tie. When he spoke, he couldn't make the words come out nicely or even neutrally. He *sounded* angry, too. "Why didn't you tell me?"

She didn't say *Tell you what?* or *How did you find out?* or any of the temporizing, stupid things that she might have said. She did give a little gasp, almost a hiccup. He turned to look at her and felt the stab in his chest that he felt whenever he went too deep into her emotions and found again what a *feeling* creature she was. "Why didn't you tell me?" he muttered again. "Am I such a bastard you couldn't even tell me?"

"I thought—I thought you'd think I—" She hugged herself as if she were cold. "Like it was a trap."

Dukas took her by a wrist and led her to the sofa and sank down, pulling her with him. "Oh, Jesus." He didn't mean that to apply to her but to him. He was looking at himself

410

as he supposed she saw him, and then he was wondering how she could think she loved what she saw. "You haven't—done anything, have you?"

"I talked to somebody about it. I'm thinking it over."

"No!" He was surprised at how much emotion jumped out of him. "No, we're not going to do that."

"*We're* not." She chuckled, not very merrily.

"You know what I mean. You can't. I can't—" He had started to say *I can't let you,* but he saw that the words would be stupid. "You can if you—if it's for yourself, not because of what you think I might—" He looked at her. She was twenty-two; he'd be fifty before the baby was in school. His hands came up and cupped her face—an odd gesture for him, not one he'd ever made before. "Let's get married. I mean, yeah—we should get married."

She had a surprising toughness to go with her surprising intelligence and her astonishing emotions. She looked steadily into his eyes, no weakening around the mouth, no boo-hoo. "Can't you say it, Michael?"

"Say—?"

"'Say the magic woid, you get ten dollahs.'"

The magic word was *love.* Dukas was tough, too—tough on himself, tough on her. He couldn't say a word that was untrue. She gave an off-center smile and shook her head, then moved in with her arms around his neck. "At least you're a lousy liar," she said.

"Les—I try, I *will* try. We're good together, aren't we? We get along; you've given me a lot of—fun, what the hell, *happiness*; I don't—very well say—I don't want to give you the wrong idea, no."

She tilted herself a little away so she could look at his eyes again. "You're telling me to take the glass that's half full and not the one that's half empty, right?" She smiled the crooked smile at him again and pulled herself close. She exhaled, and Dukas could hear the raggedness of the breath. Still, she managed to laugh. "Sometimes," she whispered, "somebody could wish you'd lie just a little sometimes."

They held each other, both made numb by the strange intensity of the moment. Only slowly did Dukas come to realize that he'd proposed and been accepted.

Patiala Airfield

The air was heavy and hot and smelled of something bitter, refinery gases or agricultural chemicals. Harry, standing next to the Lear jet, inhaled it and didn't like it and told himself that that was just too bad. In the east, the sky gave no sign yet that morning might be on the way.

"When are you going to tell me where we're going?" Mary Totten said. She had slept for most of the flight and she seemed to be less cranky than she had been.

"Now, if you like."

"I like."

Harry leaned his buttocks back into the hatchway of the jet and folded his arms. The only illumination came from blue taxiway lights and from inside the plane itself, where Bill was still snoring. "Take a seat," Harry said to her.

She shrugged and sat on the second step. "So—?"

"This is Patiala. The main SOE router hub is here someplace. Doesn't matter where; we're not going there. So I figure that the SOE biggies are nearby—according to Bill, the IP is local, no matter what. Someplace within, say, a fifty-mile radius."

"Funny, I had that figured out myself."

"When that cute little jg briefed us on the SOE, she said that the head guy's name is Mohenjo Daro. That rang a bell, but I couldn't say for what. I checked on the web yesterday while we were being entertained by our Indian allies, and I found that Mohenjo-Daro is in fact the name of an ancient city. Across the border in Pakistan, actually. The name is also

412

given to the culture that archaeologists associate with the city—the kind of potsherds and—"

"Come on, move it along!"

Harry smiled. "We're not going anywhere until we find transportation, which isn't going to happen until there's a little life around here."

She told him quickly, a little acidly, of how she had got her rent-a-plane at Trincomalee. "You go on the web for phone numbers, you wake people up!"

"We'll see." In fact, Djalik was on a cell phone in the plane at that moment, calling business contacts of Harry's to get a line on executive—for which, read "armored and pro-tected"—auto rentals. "Okay, I'll skip the fascinating archae-ology bits. Heart of the matter is that Mohenjo-Daro was a damned early site of Hinduism—sort of the Hindu Ur."

Mary didn't respond. Maybe she didn't know Ur.

"So it appears that the head of our cult or terrorist group or whatever the hell they are took a name that has associ-ations with archaic, aka fundamental, Hinduism. So there's an interest in religion and an interest in the past there. Am I boring you?"

"Oh, no, my eyes always cross at this time of night."

"A couple dozen or so Ks from Patiala, there's a site that's never been dug but is believed to be the only other example of the Mohenjo-Daro culture. I picked it off the India Survey map." When she said nothing, he said, a little irritated, "Well, it's a start."

"We're going to an archaeological site?"

"It would be an archeological site if anybody started digging, but you can't. It's privately owned." Harry grinned down at her. "By SOE."

"How come if you're so smart, the Indians didn't do this days ago, being as they're smart people, too?"

"My guess is the SOE has people whose job is to block

exactly that kind of smart—screwing up intelligence, dicking with communications between departments, telling people with good ideas that their ideas stink. SOE is into chaos—they're really good at it."

Later, Djalik came to the hatch and handed out cups of hot chowder from the minuscule galley, and he said, "DelArmCo's got a Humvee they'll let us have with a driver for seven-fifty a day US. They take plastic."

"How quick?"

"They gotta wake up the driver and get him to come in from someplace, plus he's gotta drive here from Delhi."

Harry looked at Mary. She shrugged and muttered something about Harry's having the only idea in town.

"Get on it."

USS *Thomas Jefferson*

Hawkins completed his turnover with Madje. The remnants of the Indian loyalists had ceased attempting to fight and were now too far north to offer any more resistance to the SOE ships, which were standing in with the coast.

"I heard the admiral order us to use the full resources of the battle group," Hawkins said.

Madje pointed at the screen. "I'm going to be selling used cars for the rest of my life," he said.

"Only if we fail," Hawkins said. There was something scary about Hawkins now, too.

It was all scary. Madje had never imagined that he would be in a battle, or that he would have to choose between loyalties to do his job. But he was committed. He wrote out a message for the comm shack to encrypt.

Hawkins took it out into the corridor and walked to sick bay. He walked past the nurse's station and straight to the admiral's side.

"I want to send this," he said.

Rafehausen read it. He smiled, or at least Hawkins read that fractional movement as a smile.

"That's—what—put—him—there—for." Rafe nodded. "You're—my—TAO." He closed his eyes.

Hawkins watched him trying not to notice that one of the alarms on the admiral's instruments had just gone off, hoping the man was only asleep. As a corpsman rushed past him, Hawkins turned and walked back aft to the comm shack.

Captain Fraser of the *Picton* read the message with a mix of alarm and elation. He swung his feet off his rack and slugged back the coffee his steward offered him, pulled a jersey over his head and walked out on the bridge. Dawn was still a few minutes away, but the sky to the east was a pale gray with some pink in it. The sea was almost dead calm.

Fraser grabbed his chart table with both hands and leaned over it; the officer of the deck, who had already read the message, had a grease pencil in his hand.

"We can be on station in an hour, sir," he said, pointing at a location on the chart.

"I want to come up from the south. Make revolutions for thirty knots and come to 000."

"Aye, aye, sir."

"Have the tail cleared away and all the sonars manned when the watch changes. Send the watch to breakfast now, Mister Jeffries. We'll be at battle stations again in an hour."

"Aye, aye, sir."

Fraser met the eye of his executive officer as he came on the bridge and gave him the message. His exec read it over the brim of his coffee mug. He looked up at Fraser. "We don't have to—"

"Belay that," Fraser said. "We'll comply."

The ship began to heel and spray came over the bow.

"Prime Minister might feel differently," his exec said, bracing.

"He's not here. Rafehausen is." He turned to the officer of the deck. "Once we're on station, get me one of those fog banks right in with the coast. See 'em? If you can."

"Aye, aye, sir."

Fraser started to pack his pipe. "I want the helo in the air in thirty minutes, with a full chaff load."

His exec started to take notes.

Radio India

"Confusing reports from both Delhi and Calcutta have been coming in since last night. Multiple suicides, perhaps in the hundreds, appear to have taken place at several locations. No details are available of the method of suicide, but the victims are believed to be members of the Servants of the Earth cult. Police are speculating that the cult are giving up their effort to take over India and are killing themselves in despair. However, an academic expert on the cult has suggested that to the contrary the cult may have completed a master plan and believe its work is finished. Mohan Katragadda, Mumbai."

34

Quilon, India

The submarine *Nehru* didn't have a tugboat to drag it clear of the pier. The sub was short-handed, too, and simply conning the ship to their first launch datum would be difficult and fatiguing. They had missed the first of the ebb dealing with two last-minute desertions, and two men from engineering, fanatics, were dead by their own hands. He wondered what his men would do after they launched their last missile.

Out over the horizon to the north, his little battle group waited, ready to fight the remaining loyalists while he got into deep water and headed west. He leaned his elbows on the curved coaming atop the weather bridge, already feeling the motion of the estuary in his hips. The Kilo-class rolled like a pig, but there wasn't enough water to submerge for another mile. He turned and threw up over the side with the ease of many repetitions. He raised his binoculars again, scanned the air. Nothing.

They really were going to pull it off, the whole absurd plan. He winced as the coaming rose again in the swell and banged his elbows. He tried again to focus on the horizon, lost in the haze.

Two hours, perhaps three, and he'd be over the hundred-fathom line.

And then, chaos. Chaos to the end.

Near Patiala, India

DelArmCo—the Delhi Armored-car Consortium—had provided a Humvee with impact-resistant windows and indoor gun ports and light armor on the bottom and sides. Intended for nervous executives, it was more than Harry thought they needed, but the driver seemed to think it was the greatest thing since instant idlee. A white-turbaned Sikh who loved his job, or at least found his own self-importance in it, he insisted upon showing Harry and Djalik the details of the vehicle's magnificence. The firing ports were treated so reverently by him that Harry thought that they might have to kiss them. "Very nice," Harry said.

"*Very* nice! Magnificently nice!"

"Impressive."

"And safe!"

Harry and Djalik exchanged a look and a smile over that, but Bill seemed relieved; he crawled into the back and deflated into a padded executive seat and stared at nothing with open mouth.

Mary shook her head. "Bill is such an asshole."

"But an essential asshole! Without him, where would we be?" Harry laughed. "We might be back in Bahrain, that's where we might be!" He slapped the roof of the Humvee. "Let's go!"

He had a route already planned on his India Survey map. The driver had objected—No, no, not direct, too long way round—but Harry had insisted. He wanted to avoid towns, although this was the Punjab, and there were villages and small cities everywhere. Nonetheless, the main roads seemed empty, and he questioned his own judgment in seeking back roads until, from an overpass, he saw a military roadblock on the highway they might have taken.

"Roadblock everywhere, everywhere," the driver said. "Army defending border, not being far away."

"Avoid the roadblocks."

"But why, please? DelArmCo very well known—friend to soldiers, police—"

The back roads had more people, but when they saw the Humvee coming, they flinched away, some half-crouching in the ditches, some striding off across the fields. Women in saris pulled children close to them. The driver laughed. "Very afraid, these people." Their fear seemed to please him. "Ignorant people here."

The historic site they wanted was in fact almost fifty kilometers from the airfield. Harry sat in front now with the driver, checking his map and passing it back to Djalik and Mary when, after almost an hour's driving, they seemed to be lost. Bill was mostly asleep.

"Did we pass M'ahra?" Djalik said.

"Yes, yes, M'ahra." The driver pointed back with a whole hand. "Not interesting place." He was used to driving people who wanted to "see India."

Mary was shaking the front of her shirt to cool herself, holding it in thumb and forefinger of each hand and letting the fabric rise and fall like a bellows; tantalizing glimpses of cleavage and brassiere were ignored by Harry and Djalik, but the driver gave a lot of attention to the rearview mirror. "Awfully quiet around here for the home place of a bunch of bad guys," she said.

Harry and Djalik got out and looked around, trying to find landmarks that would agree with the out-of-date map. The entire area was almost semi-suburban, with several factories and scattered office buildings set down in a once rural landscape. They had stopped on the side of a low hill, looking over a shallow valley whose floor rose toward the Himalayan foothills. Close in, there were a couple of small farms and a stream, but the mid-distance was more industrial. Harry put 10x50 Steiners to his eyes and looked. "Cement plant."

"Not on the map. What the hell, the map was made in 1967."

"Looks like kilns. They make bricks around here?"

The driver leaned out. "Yes, making bricks. Very dirty work, dirty people. Not interesting."

Harry handed the binoculars to Djalik, who looked. "It ought to be right there. Right where the cement plant is." The cement plant jutted up from the edge of a scruffy area of green scrub.

Harry shrugged. "Let's have a look." They got back in and he pointed. The driver said again that it wasn't interesting, but Harry said that that was where he wanted to go, and so the Humvee rolled forward, the driver's face, or what they could see of it between his aviator sunglasses and his beard, grim.

The road was cracked macadam, probably broken by cement trucks. They reached the corner of a chain-link fence, within which the two gray-beige towers of the cement plant were contained. No sign of life there, either, but beyond it, next to a muddy stream, two men were shoveling clay into molds; they wore only turbans and dhotis, their feet and arms smeared with clay. They looked up, but, perhaps because of the protection of the fence, did not flinch away as everybody else had. Harry signaled the driver to go on; the road turned to gravel, the chain-link fence continuing on their left, the area within it rubble that gave way to scrub, a kind of dry jungle. The shells of two cinderblock houses that had either never been finished or had been long abandoned were visible through the weeds and vines. Then more jungle, and then the ruin of a one-storey brick building that might once have been a small factory. Faded letters were still legible across the front: *Jo-Lalna Motorized Bicycle Works.*

"Go back now?" the driver said. The road had turned into two tracks with trash trees closing in on the sides.

"Jo-Lalna Motorized Bicycle is an SOE company," Bill said. His voice was lackluster. His forehead was pressed against the armored window. "Wholly owned by the Mumbai Film Entertainment Corporation, LLC."

"I thought you were asleep!" Mary snapped.

"I have total recall."

The driver looked at Harry, his hand on the shift lever to put it into reverse.

"Map."

Djalik handed it forward. Mary pulled herself up and looked at it over Harry's shoulder. His landmark had been a point on the map that, in 1967, had represented a village named Banasar, near which the symbol for "historical point of interest" and the words *Harapan remains* were marked. Now, Harry tried to look back through the window, as if they might have missed a village somehow; then, not seeing one, he got out and looked over the Humvee's roof. He grunted.

"Back up," he said, getting in again.

The driver did so with enthusiasm, which faded when Harry told him to stop opposite the two brickmakers.

"Ask them where Banasar is."

The driver was embarrassed. Worse than embarrassed. "Very low-grade people—"

Harry jumped out. "Banasar?" he called. "Where is Banasar?"

Both men, who had been squatting over the brick-molds, straightened and nodded vigorously.

"Where is Banasar?"

More nodding. Mary stuck her head out. "I think they're telling you that *this* is Banasar."

Harry looked at the stream from which the brick-makers were taking their water. *If that trickle is the "river" on the map, then where the cement plant is now—* He got back in and told the driver to go forward—no, not back, *forward.*

They passed the two unfinished cement-block houses again—had they been part of Banasar once?—and then the motorized-bicycle works, and Harry pointed to go on. The two dirt tracks went straight away through a tunnel of dusty green, the chain-link fence always on the left.

Until, after a couple of hundred yards of bouncing, it turned into a gate.

Harry, Djalik, and Mary got out and looked at recent tire tracks in the dust, and then at an oiled padlock on the gate. Inside the fence were recent marks that showed where the gate had been pulled open, dragging through the dirt in an arc to let vehicles through.

Harry stepped back and looked up and down the fence. It was six feet high, without razor or barbed wire along the top. Not the first line of defense of a major terrorist organization, he thought. On the other hand, there was *The Purloined Letter*.

"I say we go back to Delhi and I'll touch base with the embassy," Mary said. "I've got to knock some heads in DC and I want to know what the hell SOE're doing with those nukes."

"Embarrassing if they're using them to vaporize Delhi."

Mary shrugged.

"The Harapan site is supposed to be private; this is private. Bill says the bicycle place is SOE's; SOE own the archaeological site. I'm going to look inside." He looked down at Mary. "You can wait in the car."

She laughed at him. "What are we expecting to find?"

"A needle in a haystack. The meaning of life. Nirvana. How would I know?"

He rapped on Djalik's window. "Let's go."

Djalik got out and looked at the fence and the gate. "Through or over?"

"Over."

Djalik got out a baseball-bat bag with weapons in it and threw it over the fence. "After you."

Over the Indian Ocean
Four hundred miles south and east of the *Jefferson*, Chris Donitz pulled his probe gently free of Soleck's refueling drogue and dropped into the night, full of gas and ready to play. It was the third time in his career that he'd had to face the animal. He felt more resigned than eager.

He wondered if he was getting old.

A thousand feet below him, Snot wasn't watching his altitude and started a gentle descent.

They were in EMCON, and Donuts couldn't tell him he was slipping. He scanned his instruments and his heads-up display and started north.

Snot caught his plane and started climbing to match Donitz.

One more hour. It was a lonely time, and if he listened too closely, Donitz could hear wild tunes playing in the slipstream outside his canopy. He scanned his instruments again and tried not to think.

Near Patiala
Tire tracks led from the chain-link gate into the scrub jungle. Whatever activity there had been here was recent, the tracks laid over now-bent grass and not worn down to bare dirt. Walking slowly, they came on odd stretches of broken asphalt, as if the trail had once been a paved path or driveway. The scrub pressed in, so dusty that its greens were turning to beige; in several places, saplings had been pushed over by a vehicle and sprung partway back. One actual tree, growing in the middle of the narrow lane, had been hacked down with an axe.

Djalik bent to look at the stump, touched it with his fingertips. "Two-three days at most."

"You good guide, Keemo Sabe. Something you learned in Boy Scouts?"

Djalik unzipped the gym bag and gave Harry a short-barreled

riot gun, then two boxes of buckshot. "Tonto think we need to get out of the middle of the road."

Mary snorted. "Some road. It's so narrow, it doesn't *have* a middle. Bill, get behind me." She didn't offer Bill a weapon—after all, he had his laptop, which he had refused to leave in the car—but she took an H&K prototype machine pistol for herself. "This thing work?"

"Super-high cyclic rate, little-little bullet. Cut a tree down with that thing. Minimal muzzle rise." Djalik was assembling an AK, ramming in a banana clip. "Let's rock." He slung the gym bag's strap over his head and pushed the bag itself around to his back.

They went on, Djalik and Harry in the lead, each on the edge of the narrow road and almost in the scrub, Mary and Bill behind them. They passed, on their right, an overgrown stone shrine, then the remains of a wooden building, maybe a guard's shack or an equipment shed. Then Harry saw more light ahead, a thinning of the scrub and a widening of the road. They spread out, and then they were standing among the trees, looking out into an irregular, open field of several acres, its surface strangely lumpy, with a low mound off to the left. On their right and fifty yards away was a backhoe, pulled back into the trees; opposite it in the field, and stretching away for more than a hundred feet, was what appeared to be a ditch, all but the first couple of feet covered with canvas or tarpaulin.

"The site," Harry said. "The lumps in the grass are probably old foundations or stones." He gestured toward the backhoe. "And they've started to dig."

"With a backhoe?"

"That's the way thieves do it. Not very nuanced." Harry took out the Steiners and glassed the site and the woods around it. "Nobody," he breathed. He trained the binoculars on the backhoe and then on the scrub beyond. "I can see some sort of roof up there." He handed the binoculars to

Djalik. Mary had been reaching for them; when she didn't get them, she said, "Thanks a lot."

"He's a better shot."

"How the fuck would you know?"

Harry and Djalik agreed that they could use the ditch if it wasn't too deep, putting somebody there to cover while somebody else went to have a look at the roof he'd glimpsed—and what was under it. But Harry said that he didn't believe that anybody was there. "Quiet," he said. "Eerie."

"Nice birds," Bill surprised them by saying. Everybody looked startled.

Djalik crept out into the field and used the uneven terrain to make his way toward the ditch while Harry led the rest along the edge of the scrub. Between them and Djalik, the tire tracks were still visible, overlaid in places by the deep imprint of the backhoe's tracks. When they got close, Harry motioned Mary back and went on; he had the shotgun ready as he circled the machine and, finding nothing, waved her and Bill on.

The backhoe had cut a sloping approach to the covered trench so that it could go in and out, the trench surprisingly deep—deep enough, Harry thought, for him to stand in it and still be below ground level.

"Looks like they've been going at this pretty hard. *Very* hard, in fact. That's a lot of digging if they've only been at it two or three days."

"Like they're on a schedule?"

"Like they're in a hurry." From the backhoe's position, he could see the beginning of a grid laid out with string, one line running right along the edge of the trench, others running at right angles. "Somebody sort of knew what he was doing, but that's lousy archaeology—the backhoe."

Then Djalik was waving from the edge of the trench.

"I'll go," Harry said.

"We'll both go."

"Me, too," Bill muttered.

Harry thought that the best cover was the trench itself, and he slid down the incline as fast as he could, glad for the deepening sides to give cover and protection. Bill almost rolled down, then Mary, and they trotted forward in the shadowed, narrow cut, the smell damp and moldy, the dirt underfoot uneven, the light dim. Then they stopped.

"Oh, my God!"

Djalik was looking in under the covering, which was not tarpaulin but shade cloth, the dark mesh that is used to protect plants from tropical sun. "That's why I waved," he said.

Directly in front of Harry was the body of a man, feet toward him. Beyond him was another body; beyond that another. And another. And others, as far as he could see in the trench.

"You're sitting ducks in there if anybody starts shooting from the end," Djalik said. "Perfect enfilade."

Harry was bending over the first body. "Mary, make Bill lie down. You cover the end we came in. Dave, cover the far end."

"Look out for booby traps," Djalik called.

Harry squeezed against the dirt wall to get up by the man's head. The face was contorted, the eyes open, bloodshot. Harry went on to the next one, a woman, then the next. He looked in all at six bodies, thought he could count eleven more pairs of feet sticking up.

"They're cold, but not a mark on them," he said when he got back to Mary. "Jonestown."

"What, suicide?"

"I don't see any sign of dragging, no sign of struggle, no marks. These folks lay down in here and died. Yeah, suicide. Maybe poison."

"Could of been gas," Djalik said from above. "These guys pretty big on gas."

"The point is, they're very dead. Let's get out of here." He shivered. It was like standing in a grave, waiting for the dirt to come down.

When they were gathered again at the backhoe, Djalik kneeling with his weapon ready, Mary said, "With that covering and a fan at the far end, you could move something like Sarin down that trench pretty well."

"With them all lying head to toe like that?"

"If the discipline was good enough."

Harry stared into the dark trench, thinking of that level of dehumanization. "I'd expect to see contortions." He knelt beside Djalik. "I saw at least seventeen in there. You got any sense there were more people than that here?"

"I don't think there was more than two cars came in, maybe three at the most. There's one big tire track, a small one or maybe two small ones. But you know, you put bodies in a trench and you keep a backhoe handy, I expect you to fill in the trench on top of them." He looked toward the place where Harry had seen the roof. "You want to go up there?"

"No. But we have to."

Over the Indian Ocean

His stomach rumbled, and the backs of his arms prickled with tension. Now was the time when Alan would be right, or wrong; when they would find the sub, or not find it. Donuts and Snot were on station, flying combat air patrol circles in the sky to the south; and his S-3 had gone low an hour before, ruffling the wave tops as it drove west towards their first waypoint, where Alan intended to place a line of sonobuoys as a backstop in his sub hunt.

Soleck had them so tight to the sea that spray dotted Alan's window. Outside, the hard morning light filled the sky. His maps and his digital models said that they were safe—over the radar horizon and invisible. At night Alan would have believed it. In the morning sun, with only wavetop haze and some clouds along the coast ahead, he felt that anyone could see them. He felt naked.

"Mister Soleck? Got the pattern laid in. I've marked us for nine buoys; save the rest for the real pattern."

"Roger that. Mind if I do it north to south?"

Alan looked at the Master Chief's pattern. It was a long L, with the buoys spaced too widely apart; merely a safety net in case the sub was not where they expected it. Alan was sure that the sub would try to get under the SOE-controlled surface ships to the north. But he and the Master Chief agreed that it would only cost them some buoys and five minutes to make sure.

North to south meant that the pattern would start closest to the SOE ships. Alan thought he had them located about forty miles to the north. Too close for comfort, but far enough. "Go ahead," he told Soleck.

The plane stood on its port wingtip, five meters off the tops of the swell. Then they were back level.

"No wind at all out here," Soleck commented.

Alan had his hands locked on his keyboard; Soleck's confidence at this low altitude didn't make him feel any better. Next to him, Simcoe's knuckles were white.

The turbofans roared. More spray gathered on Alan's window. The coast was somewhere off to starboard, invisible because of distance and haze and the curve of the earth, but he could see a heavy cloud line and some reflected color. The coast was there, and the sub was in the estuary, or already under the ships.

Or nowhere at all, and he was dead wrong. But that line of thought didn't go anywhere useful. The cockpit was hot; the smell of old electrical gear, dust and human occupation was oppressive. For the first time in years, Alan felt like throwing up.

"Coming up on the mark. Hang on, folks." Soleck's voice

was happy. Alan thought that he sounded like Rafe in the old days.

Near Patiala

It was an old colonial house, one-storeyed, in the bungalow style the British had liked. It might once have been a comfortable place, its long verandah set on a summer night with rattan chairs and tables, plenty of servants who cost almost nothing, whisky and gin in decanters, real ice in a bucket. Now, it was decaying—not yet a ruin but on the way, its roofline swaybacked, its metal roof rust, its verandah's floor rotting through.

"Should be buildings around the back," Harry said. "Servants and that shit. I'll check them out."

"We will." They circled the house, found servants' quarters with small trees growing out the windows, weeds and grass unmarked by anybody's passing, a van and a sedan parked behind the buildings, unlocked and empty.

"Nothing," he said to Mary when they came back. "Whatever there is will be inside the house." He nodded toward the path that many feet had made between the verandah's steps and the trench in recent days.

"This isn't the HQ of a major terrorist organization."

"Kind of counterintuitive." Harry squinted at the sagging house. "If it's empty, we're fucked. I'm out of ideas. You go to the embassy, I go home." He sighed. "If there's something in there—" He shrugged. "Either way, when I go through that door, I'm finished with the Agency." He looked into her eyes. "You'd better believe me."

"I thought you and I might have some fun in Delhi."

He started to say that she had thought she might have some fun with Rao at the palace, but he didn't. She was an attractive woman; she deserved some relaxation when this was over. But not with him. "You believe me?" he said.

She shrugged. "Okay, I believe you. You'll regret it."

"*Je ne regrette rien.*" He signaled to Djalik to cover him from the front of the house. To Mary, he said, "Anybody moves in there, start stitching the place up with that little gun."

"What're you going to do?"

"Knock on the door. Got a better idea?"

He moved into the sunlight from the trees, the riot gun pointed down along his right leg. He felt exposed but oddly good, glad of the heat of the sun on his back and his head. He kept his good eye on the door, trusting his peripheral vision to catch any movement. The door was wood, closed; a screen door stood open, jammed by its own warping against the verandah floor, its ancient metal screen rusted and ripped at the bottom as if a foot had gone through it.

The grass flicked against his boots like little whips. Under it, old flagstones were just visible. The steps were concrete. He went up them lightly, as if he were a guest coming to the house for the first time.

Waiting for the blast of a weapon.

And then he was standing by the door.

And he knocked.

Nobody answered. He tried the door, found it locked. He knocked once more and waited and, when nothing happened, stepped back and kicked with the sole of his right foot just beside the knob. Something crunched, but the door stayed shut, and he had to do it again, harder this time and with some urgency because he heard sounds inside the house.

The doorframe splintered near the knob; the door opened six inches and stopped, two long slivers of soft wood still connecting the bolt to the frame. Harry put his shoulder to it and threw himself down, bringing the riot gun up; the door screeched inward and caught on the floor inside, but it was open enough for him to see the length of a corridor that ran all the way from front to back, doorways on both sides, and close to him on the left an arch of dark, once-polished wood. And within, two bare feet sticking up.

He moved into the corridor, sensing Mary and Djalik moving behind him. He merely glanced into the arched opening and saw the body that belonged to the feet, as dead as the ones in the trench, two other bodies beyond it, a woman stretched on a window seat, another on the floor at an angle. He went on past but saw enough to think *Well dressed*, to register Western clothes and bright colors, to know that shopping bags and luggage were jumbled on the floor, to get that one of the shopping bags was from Harrod's; and then he was past, back against the wall, pushing open a door and thinking *Anything they shoot from inside this room will go right through these walls and me*.

Hearing sounds again, bumping, rattling.

Mary was on the other side of the corridor doing the same thing he was: he opened the door and she looked in; she opened a door and Djalik leapfrogged him and looked in; Bill, clutching his computer to his chest, tottered along behind.

Harry ran past them, gestured at the last closed door and turned into an already open one opposite it, where he thought the sounds were coming from, and found himself in a suite of rooms that led away from him, parallel to the front of the house. The room he stood in was full of potsherds and smelled of the earth; paper littered the floor, written over in small handwriting. Some effort to catalogue what they had dug out in the trench? *These people are nuts*, he thought. But pathetic, too—trying to salvage fragments of their ancient past before the world ended.

A door in the wall directly opposite was closed. He went to it and stood aside and opened it with his left hand, lunging around ready to fire, and through the doorway he could see the next room and, on its far side, a closed door. And, on the floor at the bottom of the door, a woman who was dying.

Harry went forward, checking each room as he came toward her, finding nobody else. The woman was Indian for sure—black-haired, bronze-skinned, a red dot on her forehead. She wore a sari over what looked like a T-shirt. Her heels were thumping on the floor and her face was contorted, and one hand scrabbled at the closed door as if she was trying to get at the doorknob, but she was already slipping away. He smelled excrement, saw her back arch and her legs get rigid, and then she made a sound like a huge groan, and the movements quivered down into tremors, and then nothing.

"Poison, the bitch," Mary said behind him. "There's a room full of computers back there. Bill's ecstatic."

"Yeah, poison. Not like the others, though. Whatever she took, it hurt."

Djalik came in. "That the one was going to backhoe the trench?"

Harry stood. "Check the rest of the house." He put his hand on the doorknob, and it turned. The door swung open. Harry stepped over the dead woman.

35

Over the Indian Ocean

This time it was Alan's wing they stood on to turn. The ocean was right *there*, as close to him as if he were standing on a diving board over it. He forced his abdominal muscles to relax.

Then they were level again, and Simcoe said, "One away." The sonobuoy punched out of the plane with a noise like a baby's plate dropping from a high chair. Alan brought up his sonar screen and watched it until SNBY 1 lit up and began to broadcast.

"One's good," he said.

"Two away," Simcoe said.

In five minutes they had a pattern laid with a bend at the north end to cover a turn, because Alan thought that if the sub made it this far, she'd turn north toward Pakistan. All the buoys were alive and alert, passively watching their section of the ocean and broadcasting their findings.

One buoy transmitted data on the salinity and temperature of the water. It showed that there was no layer; the water was too warm, too shallow. Perhaps down around four hundred meters, out past the one-hundred-fathom line, the sub's might find a layer to hide in.

Alan dismissed that thought. If the sub made it that far, it would have won. Right now, everything depended on the sub having left Quilon on the ebb, headed east-northeast to rendezvous with the mutineer surface ships. That was the only eventuality that Alan could fully cover. His mind kept wandering off down other possibilities, but he forced it back to this; either the sub was here, within thirty miles of him, or all this was for nothing.

"Ready to pop?"

"Anytime, skipper," Soleck said.

Alan reached up over his head and began to arm the systems, warming the Harpoon on the starboard wing, choosing his chaff/flare selection and moving the counter to his chosen pattern—chaff-chaff-flare. The improved-Krivak-class frigates up north had the best ability to shoot him down, he thought, and their missiles, especially their VLS Gauntlets, would home on radar—hence the chaff. The flare cartridge was really inserted as a spacer, so that pairs of chaff cartridges would make big, attractive blobs with a decision distance between them.

Simcoe was putting his thermos into his helmet bag, tidying the cockpit around his seat. Alan did the same and stowed every pen and kneeboard card; if they were in action, the plane would dance around and anything left loose would become a high-velocity missile. Simcoe gave him a nod and switched his own data screen to ESM.

"Get me Donuts," Alan said. He saw Garcia's hand hover over the radio, press a button, give him a wave.

"Cowboy One, this is Chuckwagon, over."

One click, then another. Donuts was staying quiet, just toggling his mike on and off.

"Round up," Alan said. That meant they were going for it; popping to altitude to provoke a reaction. Then he changed to intercom. "Go," he said to Soleck.

At low altitude, every increase in power could be felt across the shoulders as the plane accelerated; the turbofans bit hard on the thick air at sea level and the acceleration was instantaneous. Alan rocked back in his seat and his back muscles burned.

They climbed.

"Radar's warm."

Alan fought the mild g-force and his own fatigue to get the radar cursor to line up on the ship they had most positively identified during the long flight from the *Jefferson*. Before they passed through a thousand feet, he had it. He pushed the radar to on.

He choked a curse. Five bananas immediately displayed, and the farthest away was the Krivak-class he was looking for—it was the northern picket. The other four ships were spread across twenty miles of sea, the closest less than twenty miles north.

"Whoa!" Simcoe gasped.

Nice understatement. Alan got the trackball on the southern Krivak, already in range, for God's sake. He switched to ISAR. The powerful radar beam swept over the SOE ship, looking like a fire-control radar, and the ship obligingly lit up, first a surface-search radar, then, seconds later, an air-search radar. *Somewhere in the night, the bastards had increased speed, and now they were close—too close. In-range close.*

"Got him," Simcoe said.

Alan put his data in the link. They were done hiding; in fact, they wanted a reaction. Alan switched to the radio. "HARM priority two."

Somewhere to the south, Snot cycled his HARM through programmed parameters until he found two, for fire-control radar parameters.

"Launch!" Soleck yelled and the plane slammed to port and they were over, upside down and rushing at the deck, and Alan's arm reached through the pain in his back and toggled the chaff/flare system and they were turning.

"Two contrails!" Soleck added. The plane jinked again.

"Engage," Alan called, his voice a little high. He was holding the chaff toggle down and the sequence was firing, leaving a column of neatly spaced chaff clouds behind them as they fell toward the sea.

Near Patiala

"I am Mohenjo Daro."

A hospital bed stood against the wall opposite the doorway in which Harry stood. An IV stand was on one side and a medical stand and tray on the other; on the tray, a small clay vessel no bigger than a water-glass stood surrounded by flowers—a complete relic from the excavation, turned into a shrine. On the IV stand were a bottle and a drip that ran down to the arm of an emaciated brown man with a shaved skull and a birthmark right above the bridge of his nose. The bed was raised so he could sit up. Except that he had spoken, he might have been dead.

"You are too late," he said.

"Harry O'Neill."

"Not whom I expected." Daro smiled, or tried to; it was clear that he hardly had the strength to do even that. "I don't know whom I expected. Shiva, perhaps." He tried to smile again.

"You're under arrest," Mary said. "I have the power to take you from here to an appropriate authority, and I'm going to do just that."

Daro had something in his left hand, Harry saw; he thought it might be some sort of trigger, although he thought that would have been wrong for this man. The fingers moved and he saw that what was in the thin hand was only a plastic control that led to the IV. *Morphine*, he thought. *The man's dying of cancer.*

"Do as you must," Daro said. His voice was fading a little. "It makes no difference. I am an agent of chaos. You are agents of chaos. What we do now is a detail."

Mary was going to say something else, and Harry put his hand on her shoulder to stop her. He said, "Your people stole

436

three nuclear devices from the government facility at Ambur."

"Yes." He tried to smile.

"Where are they?"

Daro moved his head a fraction of an inch and tried to raise it, as if he wanted to look beyond the bottom of the bed. "Is Vashni dead?"

"There's a dead woman in the doorway. Suicide—poison, I guess."

"Vashni—" He rolled his head and looked at the IV. "Did she bury the others?"

"I think we came too soon."

"Well— Burial is a detail. But I had promised them that they would lie in the earth of our home." He looked at Harry with astonishingly innocent eyes. "We were all born here, you know. When it was a city."

"Three thousand years ago."

"That is why I came here to die. To return." He tried to smile and succeeded this time, a look of radiance, of certainty. "'When it is done,' I told them, 'we will lie in the earth of our beginnings.'" He looked at Mary. "You may arrest me, if you like."

Harry bent forward. "Where are the nuclear devices?"

"Oh, didn't you find that out? You did so well even to come this far. You are an African, I think. Yes. The newest people, but with great insight. Never mind. It will all be over soon." A spasm moved across the ravaged face; his hand moved on the control, allowing more morphine to flow.

"What will you get from destroying the American fleet?"

The face was blank, then clouded as the morphine took hold; then Daro seemed to regain strength. "I am the one who is supposed to talk in mysteries, young man, not you." He did something like laughing. "That is a guru joke." He gasped; the hand moved on the control again. "What American fleet?"

437

"The American battle group that's heading for Sri Lanka. Where your submarine is going."

"Oh—" His other hand moved as if he wanted to gesture with it. "I know nothing of battle groups or America. Why would I care? I am bringing an end to the world, young man. Chaos! Chaos, chaos, chaos—first chaos, then destruction, then creation. The world—your world—will end." He smiled the smile of a rather naughty child. "And good riddance." He seemed vastly amused. "Oh—what a world—what people—!" His left hand moved over the control and held it. Harry, realizing what was happening, merely swayed forward on the balls of his feet. The radiant smile appeared again as the morphine flowed—and flowed, and flowed. Mohenjo Daro was killing himself.

"Goddamit—!" Mary flung herself at the bed.

"Let him be."

"He's mine!" She was wrestling with the hand and the emaciated arm. The IV stand toppled and the needle tore out. She was panting, holding the arm, Daro's body half out of the bed.

"You're wrestling with a corpse. He's dead."

Mary heaved the body back on the bed and put fingers at Daro's throat. "The shit, he is!"

Harry was already kneeling over the woman in the doorway. He put a hand inside the neck of the T-shirt, pulling on a thin gold chain, trying to ignore the contorted face. When he found the gold USB key, he tore it loose and walked back through the house.

"Where's Bill?" he said to Djalik, who jerked his head. Harry followed the direction and found a room that might once have been an office. Now, its two wooden desks were covered with computer equipment; cables writhed everywhere across the bare floor. On a chair by the only window, Bill was staring at the screen of his laptop.

Harry thrust the USB key at him. "Decrypt it."

Bill stared at him as if they were strangers. "I'd have to use up my battery."

"Yeah, Bill. Use up your battery."

Bill began to type, and Harry went out and got Djalik and they went looking for a generator, which they found in one of the outbuildings—a brand-new Honda with five twenty-liter gas cans beside it. The cable was neatly coiled on the gas cans. "They were done with it," Harry said.

"These folks were done with everything, Harry."

They carried the generator to the window and ran the cable in and started it up, and by then Bill had opened the files in Vashni's USB key. Mary was looking over Bill's shoulder. She looked up when Harry came in. "How'd you know?" she said.

"He valued her."

Mary pointed at the screen.

Vashni had been organized. Her files were in folders; the folders had a master list and a descriptive index. Harry leaned over Bill's head and scrolled down until he came to a folder titled "Final Chaos".

"Open it."

The file had five parts. One was the plan for the final move to "the birthplace"—the place where they were now. It even included the rental information on the backhoe. One file was about mass suicide and the means that were preferred. One was about disinformation through two SOE-owned public relations company. One was about money.

And one was about the missiles.

The submarine would sail from a small port city called Quilon under the protection of rogue elements of the Indian Navy. Once in open water, it would go deep and proceed to a datum of the captain's choosing, and there it would launch the missiles at three targets: Karachi, Bahrain, and Mecca.

"Bahrain!" Mary cried. "Jesus!"

"*Mecca.*" Harry's mouth had turned to cotton. The holiest

place in Islam. He had been there. He had been inside the Kaaba. Tears sprang to his eyes.

And then he was in motion, yanking out his cell phone, punching in numbers with shaking fingers, and hearing the sound that meant the phone could not find a signal.

"I have to go to the plane. The satphone."

"Call WMD."

"I'm calling Fifth Fleet; they can get the targets to Craik."

"Fuck Craik—it'll take that sub days to get where it can hit all three targets. WMD can organize a real response. The Air Force out of Germany—the Saudis have a navy—"

"Mary, once that sub goes deep, they won't find it. It's Craik or—" He shrugged.

"Call WMD!"

Harry looked at her. He was about to say *Call them your-self,* but he saw that she meant to stay where she was. She was sitting on an intelligence coup—all those computers. "I'll send the car back for you." He turned and started out, shouting for Djalik. He glanced back from the doorway. "Unless you want to come now."

"Unh-unh, baby, these computers could be huge. I don't dare miss them."

"Your call."

He was through the middle room and almost to the corridor when she shouted, "I'll give you a rain check."

But he was gone then, not caring what she'd give him. He grabbed Djalik and started running for the car, explaining as they went.

The Indian Ocean

Captain Fraser on the *Picton* heard the "Engage." He turned to his helmsman. "Execute," he said. His orders were already issued and explained.

HMCS *Picton* leaped forward, her gas turbines instantly transferring power to her screws. The pale gray bow slashed

440

through the low swell and raised a bow wave, and in seconds she was moving at well over twenty knots out of the coastal haze and into the brilliance of the morning sun.

"New contact," his air-warfare station said. "Four bandits range six zero angels 24, noses hot."

"Radiate," Fraser said. The SPS-49 shot out through the morning air, hot for the first time in two days, as *Picton* announced her presence across the EM spectrum. "Watch our friends."

"Aye, aye, sir," his AW said.

He turned to his fire-control officer. "As you bear."

He put his unlit pipe in his mouth and bit down on the stem.

Snot heard "Engage," but it took a moment to register because he had just watched four new contacts blossom on his heads-up display; all detected passively and fed into the link, and they were sixty miles away and closing and a fist closed on his gut. But not hard enough to keep him from doing his job.

He put the seeker head of the HARM squarely on its target and fired. He'd never shot a HARM, and the flash and the change in weight through the plane surprised him; he actually started a sharp left bank before he caught it. The missile climbed away at first and then turned north and he lost it, already getting his nose back on the four bandits.

"Going hot," Donuts said.

His voice made Snot feel better at once. He turned his radar on, too.

The HARM was a fast missile and it burned through the cool air for several seconds in a shallow climb; the warhead was already comfortable with the location and parameters of the target. After thirty seconds it was much lower, tearing through the haze just above water level.

* * *

"Missile two's in the water," Garcia said. Her voice was tense, the tension of a girl on an amusement ride. "That was fucking beautiful, Soleck."

Alan didn't have to see Soleck to know the quality of the idiot grin on his face.

"We're too low," Alan said. *Too low to use our Harpoon; too low to keep the rest of the SOE ships in contact.*

Soleck started a slow climb, shallow and headed south, keeping his power in reserve for the next flight of missiles.

Donuts said, "Fox two." Then, "Fox three."

Snot saw that one of the enemy planes had jinked or declined the engagement or whatever the fuck and turned away long before the merge. The other three came on.

Donuts had Sparrows, and he shot them both from the middle of the envelope while Snot stayed below and behind him with his nose hot, waiting for someone to blink. He wanted to get one this time; he needed a little bit of tail aspect to make his Sidewinders count. All-aspect was a great phrase, but against a good plane, you wanted a nice quarter shot.

Then it all happened at once.

One of the MiGs blew up less than a mile away and one of the others turned south, and Snot went to afterburner on his butt and then realized the other guy now had a look up his tail pipe and Donuts yelled something—

The HARM popped up to a few hundred feet in its terminal phase and detonated within a few meters of its target emitter, a fire-control radar on a stubby mast just aft of the bridge of the Krivak-class and almost on top of the missile racks. The explosion was small as missiles go, but the shrapnel and the precision of detonation meant that the two remaining SAMs detonated in sympathy, and the bridge was annihilated. Every antenna aft of the bridge was scythed down.

Several seconds later, the fireball ignited the fuel for the SS-NX-27 Gadfly on the starboard side and opened a seam.

"Scratch one Krivak," Simcoe said. "She's off the air across the board."

Alan's fingers were flying as he placed each of the other enemy emitters in the link—the second Krivak, far to the north; an improved Godavari just over the horizon; and two unknown hulls that showed as LW-08 radars; his data card said they were Nilgiri-class light frigates. He didn't think any of them could see the *Picton*, although it was all much closer than he had expected. *A knife fight with missiles*, he thought.

In Alan's ear, Donuts said, "Stupid fuck!" and then, "Eject!"

Donuts watched Snot's plane break in half, the rear half a fireball. He thought he might have seen something separate from the front before he had his own hands full again.

He made a shallow S-turn and put an IR missile into the guy who had popped Snot and then swiveled his head because somewhere there was another plane that had broken off the engagement early, and sure enough, he was high. Snot's original victim was low and in a turn.

I've lost my wingman and I'm in a sandwich.

Donuts turned and dove, backed off on the power to let the low guy stay in front of him until he liked the tone, and then he gave him a missile and rolled left, his vertical stabilizers parallel to the ground. The high guy overshot him, and Donuts pushed his throttle to the metal and put the nose up, burning a hundred pounds of fuel a second to get altitude and safety. Behind him, his missile detonated and the coiled wire inside the warhead took a third of the target's wing.

The pilot didn't eject.

Donuts grayed out starting to turn. He was out of missiles;

situational awareness said he'd probably missed one of his targets, and he didn't have time to look.

"Leakers," he croaked.

"Leakers," Alan heard Donuts say. Alan guessed that Donuts's wingman had gone down. "We could have company," he said to Soleck.

"Holy fuck," Simcoe muttered.

Just to the north, the SOE ships had every radar on, and launch warnings played around the edge of the screens. Missiles, their own warheads broadcasting their radars, jumped into existence from the enemy ships and began to move at supersonic speeds across the digital sea.

"Oh," Alan said. He'd never seen a sea battle, hadn't imagined its intensity. Even the computer couldn't cope with the signal density.

"Incoming," Simcoe warned.

Soleck started to dive.

As the cockpit pulled across the horizon, Garcia caught a glimpse of the whole battle spread out in shades of blue and white to the horizon. Uncountable threads of clear white showed, contrails and launch exhaust, some laser-straight and some in mathematical curves, a warp and weft of missiles against the high blue sky and the flat blue sea. Almost at her feet, the first *Krivak* burned, the smoke black and thick. Three contrails leaped at her like fingers trying to drag her plane into the sea.

On Alan's screen, six new signals appeared at the southern limit of the digital ocean and moved an inch a second, spreading like an opening hand as they advanced.

Simcoe said, "Holy fuck."

Alan found that he couldn't breathe.

Soleck rolled the cold top of the plane toward the missiles, hiding his engines under the wings; Alan fired his chaff again, aware that the new threats might be IR missiles. He thumbed his mix to chaff-chaff-flare-flare, keeping his attention on the surface-to-surface missiles that had appeared from the south. They had all been tagged by the computer, which indicated Harp 1c. Six times.

"Where're those from?" Simcoe shouted.

"Canada."

A fist punched at their plane. Something rang against the base of Alan's seat and his head was slammed back. He saw red and breathed copper. The cockpit seemed to pulse; something sounded like breaking glass.

"Everybody still back there?" Soleck asked from far away. The plane rolled again.

Alan saw blood on his keyboard.

Simcoe said, "Commander's hit."

Alan said, "Bullshit." Then he could see where the ricochet had sliced his arm. On the screen in front of him, the six Harpoons vanished into their targets. Drops of blood had spattered across the shards of his screen. "It's nothing. Chief, you got a dressing?"

"On the way." Simcoe put a hand in his helmet bag. "Hey, look at that!"

Both of the Nilgiris and the northern Krivak had vanished on ESM.

Air whistled through a hole in the fuselage where the SAM had hit them.

Alan ground his back teeth together. In fact, the arm hurt quite a bit now.

Garcia said something and Alan missed it. He blinked and felt worse, his mouth full of copper and salt, and he threw up into his helmet bag.

A strange high beeping seemed to fill the after cockpit. Alan didn't take it in at first; he threw up again.

Soleck's voice said, "How bad's he hurt?"

Simcoe was out of his harness, a lock-blade knife in his hand, cutting the sleeve of Alan's flight suit back to the elbow and putting a heavy compress over the wound. It was a long slice with a lot of blood. Alan's vision tunneled.

"How bad's he hurt?" Soleck said again.

Alan could hear him perfectly. Everything started to make sense again except the high beeping noise. He said, "I'll be okay. Chief's putting a—thing—on my arm."

"Hold on, skipper."

Simcoe cut the tape with his big knife. Alan had never carried first aid gear in his helmet bag and he wondered why. "Master Chief? What's that noise?" he asked. The plane shuddered and turned suddenly, and Simcoe was lying across him for a moment. Then he struggled back to a crouch. Alan tried to wave an arm. "Chief?"

Simcoe ignored him. He wasn't plugged in; couldn't hear a thing over the rush of air.

"Stop fussing! Get strapped in before Soleck does another trick!" Alan wanted to shout; it came out as a croak.

Simcoe folded his knife against his thigh and threw himself back into his seat, hands already pulling at his harness clips. The tone of the air whistling into the airplane's wound changed and got into a harmonic with the beeping alarm. Simcoe pushed his helmet cord back into the socket.

Alan looked at his computer screen and found that a fragment had shattered it. He couldn't do anything.

Simcoe said, "Uh oh."

"Tell me."

"Our sub just made contact with buoy four."

Soleck was turning so that Alan's window looked north and west over the burning wrecks of four ships.

The sub wasn't under the ships. It was already twenty miles behind them.

"*Fuck,*" Alan said. Under his breath he said, "*I'm not done yet.*"

446

36

Patiala Airport

Harry ran for the Lear jet, his brain screaming *Mecca, Mecca, they're going to nuke Mecca*. He had told Djalik, whose face was grim behind his sunglasses. Now, Moad tried to tell him something about problems with the local airport and fuel, and Harry blew past him, growling, "Later!" and threw himself into the aircraft. Moad was left to hear about it from Djalik.

Harry tried the satphone, found that the auxiliary power was off, headed for the cockpit. By then, Moad knew about Mecca and was right behind him, shouting, "What can I do, what can I do—?"

"Get me some power!"

"Get out of my way—" Moad pushed his boss aside. Harry yielded; the plane was Moad's specialty.

Moad gave him a look, flipped switches. "Get on the fucking phone, Harry!"

Djalik hung back in the hatch, out of it.

Harry threw himself back into one of the club seats with the satphone in his hand and began to punch in numbers from his laptop—Fifth Fleet Headquarters. He counted nine rings, then ended it and tried it again. Six rings this time, and then a distant voice said, "Fifth Fleet HQ, Petty Officer Nicco speaking, sir."

Allahu Akbar. "I have to speak to Admiral Pilchard. Now. This is a vital matter of national security."

447

He was aware how foolish it sounded. The voice, however, remained the same, said simply that it would get the duty officer.

But the duty officer thought it was foolish—didn't say so but began to give Harry the runaround: who was this? what was the nature of the information? who was speaking? what was his rank and unit, sir? and would he speak with the flag lieutenant's assistant, instead?

Harry shouted an obscenity and ended the call.

He began to punch in Valdez's number.

Over the Indian Ocean

Alan looked at the wrecked computer screen and tried to think his way through it. The sub had run somewhere, had used its surface ships as a decoy. *Ruthless.* If he had ever doubted that SOE would use their nukes, his doubts were dispelled. "Soleck?"

"Skipper?"

"Get us over our buoys."

The sub's last location on the buoy line was ten minutes old, putting it at least a mile beyond the line.

And then what?

Then the hundred-fathom line and so much depth that the Kilo-class could go anywhere.

And they'd never find it.

Patiala Airport

Harry was on the verge of cursing—not taking the name of Allah, no, but calling curses down on cell phones and distance and time—but he held himself together. Valdez hadn't been home. Mavis was home. But Mavis would get the same runaround at Fifth Fleet that Harry had. He told her, anyway, and shouted into the handset to tell Valdez and pass the message to Pilchard or what the hell was his name, Alan's assistant, like a city in the Dakotas—what was it? "Pierre—

it's Pierre, or—Lapierre, that's it—try to get him—Mavis, this is *important*!"

Now he was trying to get Dukas. He realized that his hands were shaking and his blood pressure must be up somewhere above two hundred. He heard himself groan. Like an old man in pain.

"Dukas." A voice that had been waked from sleep.

"Oh, Mike, thank God!"

"Who's this? Harry? Hey, man—"

Harry went right through him. And the hell with going secure. "Get to Fifth Fleet and get to Al Craik! He's after a submarine that has three nukes and he has to be told that the targets are Karachi, Bahrain, and Mecca! Did you get it? Mike? Karachi, Bahrain, a—"

Dukas didn't say any of the stupid things people like to say. All he growled was, "Is this solid?"

"A-1! Urgent, Mike—I mean, *urgent*!"

"I'm on it."

And he hung up.

Bahrain

Captain Lurgwitz fielded Dukas's call. "This is the real deal?"

"He says A-1, and he's the best. Urgent, he says."

"I'll say!" She put him on hold, pulled up comms, and said, "Get me the TAO on the *Jefferson*. Now!"

It took less than a minute to pass the names of the three cities to Captain Hawkins.

USS *Thomas Jefferson*

"Chuckwagon, do you read, over? Chuckwagon, this is Wagonmaster, do you read, over?"

"Go ahead, Chuckwagon." Soleck frowned at Garcia. The *Jefferson* was supposed to be in EMCON.

"Message for your passenger. Tell him the targets are Karachi—"

Over the Indian Ocean

Karachi, Bahrain, Mecca!

Alan tried to blot out what *Bahrain* meant—his two children, Mike Dukas, friends, the naval base—and to focus on the hope and the problem that the message had brought. Out there somewhere was a datum, selected by Mohenjo Daro or the sub's captain, from which the three cruise missiles would be fired. Around the datum would be a circle—all the possible points from which a sub with those missiles could hit those three targets. *Mecca, Karachi, Bahrain*—

Alan didn't have a chart of the western Indian Ocean, and the computer didn't, either. He guessed that there must be a launch point somewhere southwest of Karachi that would let the sub fire missiles at all three of its targets simultaneously. Maybe not. Mecca was a hell of a long way to the west.

West, anyway. Straight toward the hundred-fathom line.

His mind raced, looking for a solution, grabbed an idea.

He called the *Picton* and told Fraser what he knew.

"I'll sprint and drift for a while. See if the tail gets a zone." Fraser sounded worn.

Simcoe shook his head, then shrugged. When Alan was off the radio, he said, "Won't get no zone out here. The water's warm straight to the bottom."

Alan didn't want to hear more bad news. "Whatever. Look, we need all the help we can get."

Simcoe said, "That sub's still running on a snorkel. They need to, to save power, right? Not a nuclear sub. He needs to run his diesel for as long as he can."

Alan nodded dully. "Yeah."

"So he'll make noise. Look at these lines, Commander. He's making boo-coo noise." Simcoe was pointing at his screen.

Alan unstrapped his shoulders, tested his back. His left arm was hot and swollen, but there wasn't any more blood coming out of the bandage, which, by contrast, felt cold and sticky. He was light-headed. He leaned out across the aisle between them and looked at the minutes-old graphs on Simcoe's screen. The sub was, indeed, making a lot of noise.

Alan reached over Simcoe and pointed at the track. "Show me his course while he was in our sonobuoy field."

Simcoe played with his keyboard. "There."

A straight line traveling WNW—perhaps 290 true. Alan leaned back in his own seat. He was breathing hard. "He doesn't have any reason to turn. He's heading straight for his launch point."

Alan tried to lean forward in his harness and the pain in his left arm stopped him cold. He swore, wriggled, found a position from which he could reach his good arm across his body into his helmet bag and extract a fistful of charts there. He pulled open an ancient TPC of the northern Arabian Sea and spread it across the ruins of his keyboard.

"How far's a Tomahawk go?" Alan said, mostly to himself. Time was playing tricks with him. He was fully aware, and then a little out of it, and then back. "Eight hundred miles?"

"Depends on fuel and payload. Those nukes have to mass a lot more than a ship strike package." Simcoe had undone the top of his harness and leaned over the chart.

"Okay. Wild-assed-guess worst case, twelve hundred miles." Alan tried measuring with his fingers; he was too unsteady. He ripped a piece of paper off his kneeboard and used it to measure distance: *Mecca, Bahrain, Karachi.*

"If he's going to shoot them all at once, he'll launch here." *Here* was a pencil mark on the chart, deep, deep ocean five hundred nautical miles due west of Socotra Island. Alan did a calculation in his head and then dismissed it as absurd, did it again. "He's at least *ninety hours* sailing time away."

"Deep water, minimal ASW assets. We'll never find him." Simcoe was back at his station, looking at the grams. "That's where he's going, though. Lines up like that with his course."

451

"He can shoot Karachi anytime. He can shoot Bahrain in a matter of hours." Alan took a deep breath and found that hurt, too. "We have to get him right now."

Simcoe smiled. "That's what I think. We know where he has to go, we can guess his course; Mister Soleck can take us here—" Simcoe indicated a point just a few miles to the west—"and we drop a new pattern—small, tight—and see if he comes into it."

"That's two miles short of the hundred-fathom line." Alan tried to sit up straight. "No, never mind. Go for it."

Simcoe started telling Soleck where to fly.

To the east, Donuts had watched Snot's chute hit the water and had seen a Canadian Sea King hovering over it. He'd finished his long evasion turn and climbed back to find the sky empty. He turned south for the tanker, all too aware that he was leaving Craik alone in the sky.

The fuel on a second SSM caught fire and burned white-hot on the southern Krivak. The open seam cracked; the ship broke in two and sank in seconds. Most of the crew were already dead; many by their own hands.

Both of the Nilgiri-class frigates were afire, their remaining ammunition adding to the conflagration started by the *Picton*'s Harpoons. Very few crewmen were attempting any damage control. Again, most of them were dead.

The *Picton* pulled in her tail and began a long dash for the last datum on the sub. She could make thirty knots—six times the speed of the Kilo submerged. She would be their last hope, and a slim one. Once the sub made it over the shelf and into the deep water, only luck would get her.

They flew due west, almost over the sub's projected course, until Alan's best guess and Simcoe's experience said they were ahead of her. They laid five buoys in a straight line

452

across a mile of sea, a very tight pattern that gave them a sensory net almost three miles across. By the time the last buoy was in the water, the sub was almost due to arrive.

Alan sat with his head all the way back in the seat, trying to follow it all from radio calls and what he could see of Simcoe's screen. He thought about the sub and about Stevens: the sub had a SAM. Maybe a rack of them, maybe just a guy who ran to the flying bridge and shot a MANPAD.

"Soleck?"

"Skipper!"

"Soleck, if that sub comes up, you put your rockets on him. Got me? Pri-one."

"I hear you, skipper."

"Master Chief? Tell me your thoughts about prosecution."

Simcoe didn't take his eyes off his screen. The sub was now officially late. "If I get a fix, I'd put an active buoy down. We only have one torp and we have to be sure, right?"

"Right."

"Okay. Active buoy. On the first ping, Mister Soleck starts us on lineup and we drop the torp."

"Roger that," Alan said. He was not thinking his best, but he knew he had wanted to say something—Ah! "Torp may have gotten fragged."

Simcoe sat back, his head snapping around. "Jesus fuck," he said. "I forgot."

"Yeah." Alan nodded blearily. "But we go with it. Go active. Stevens must've gone active, right?"

Simcoe probably had no idea what Craik was talking about. He was suddenly busy on his screen.

He'd just got a passive sonar hit from buoy 14.

"North end of the pattern. He's changed course slightly, going about 300 true." Simcoe's voice went up an octave. He had his fingers on the toggle to drop an active buoy.

They only had four buoys left.

The plane waggled back and forth and suddenly the wings came level and Simcoe grunted and pulled his toggle.

"Away," he said and they were turning hard, like a shit-hot break over the carrier, the turbofans screaming along with Alan's back and arm. His heart was pounding. It was all on them now, and he was out of it—his screen busted, his station unimportant. All down to Simcoe. Simcoe looked like a batter waiting for a pitch. His mouth was open.

Back into a second turn. Water just out Alan's window. Alan was puzzled to find that there was a crack in it. They were below a hundred feet. Air rushing through the hole in the fuselage.

"Going active," Simcoe said.

Alan pushed himself against the turn and the g-force and the pain to look over at Simcoe's screen.

Garcia said, "Bingo!" and Simcoe grunted.

"Mister Soleck? Torp run. Get me a broadside shot, sir."

"Roger, Simcoe. 120 true." Again, the hard turn. Water out the cracked window again. Alan watched Simcoe's screen as another pulse went out from the active buoy; Simcoe's head came up like a pointer's. "He's going for the surface. Fast."

Soleck pulled the nose up, nearly stalling; pulled power off the plane and pushed the nose over and down until he was just barely airworthy and moving at less than sixty knots. All that in a few seconds, because he was ready to pull that very maneuver, because Skipper Craik had said the sub would surface.

Less than a mile in front of him, the bow shot into the air and crashed back, throwing spray into the oily swell. The tower was already clear. Soleck figured ten seconds until they had a man on the bridge. In ten seconds, his plane crossed three hundred meters, and the bridge of the sub seemed to fill the windscreen. By then, two men were shouldering launchers. *That's how they got Stevens.*

454

Soleck fired his entire rocket pod, the firing a continuous push that tried to turn his plane to starboard with every launch. The S-3 had no sights, no computer, no nothing to guide his rockets. Just pilot skill. Soleck walked the rockets across the water by eye, from the first impact until he saw hits. Then he banked away to port, his right hand flying from the firing toggle to the throttle and pushing it all the way forward.

Garcia was on the radio, telling the Canadians and the *Jefferson* that they had the sub on the surface.

Simcoe waited until the turn was done. "Torpedo," he said sharply, the one word suggesting that he could have got it in the water faster on the last pass if Soleck had let him.

"I got him!" Soleck shouted.

"Maybe twice." Garcia had the roller-coaster-ride voice again.

They were turning hard again. "Three-inch rocket might not hit anything important," Simcoe insisted.

"Cleared their fucking bridge, though," Soleck exulted. "I think I see smoke."

The surfaced sub flashed by under Alan's window.

The plane was turning again, getting the lineup for the torpedo. The torp needed some run time to arm the warhead and get a clean look at the target. Their wings were level. The active sonar put out another pulse.

"I see him." Garcia finally sounded tense. And then, "Movement on the bridge."

They were flat and level and a few feet off the water. There was a loud clunk and the plane was suddenly lighter. "Torpedo away," Simcoe said.

"Launch!" Garcia warned.

Alan had toggled the launcher to flare-chaff-flare; his arm moved of its own volition and the spike of pain came a moment later. He pulled the toggle down and held it, listened to the reassuring sound of the cartridges' firing. The aircraft was more than two miles away from the sub, and Soleck was turning into the sun.

"Torpedo running!" Simcoe shouted. Alan could hear him on his headphones and also over the sounds in the cockpit. He was that loud. Alan breathed out, kept his hand on the launch toggle.

Thud, thud, thud.

"Missile one in the water."

The tail lifted, as if they had encountered turbulence. "Missile two found a flare," Garcia said, her voice flat. "Sub's still on the surface," she added.

"Get us out, Soleck," Alan said. He hadn't contributed much, but he'd thought it through. Had to be ready for the next step. "Soleck, I want twelve miles between me and that sub."

The plane leaped forward. "On the way."

"He's still on the surface."

Simcoe was looking at his watch. He had the Kilo on the surface just a few hundred yards from two passive buoys from the pattern and his active buoy was a few dozen yards astern of the target. He could track his own torpedo as well as the target. He said, "Torpedo's going deep." His voice was breaking as he said it.

Alan already knew the torpedo had failed.

Alan nodded. "Sinking?"

"Maybe." The word sounded like a cry. "Why are they staying on the surface?"

It came to Alan then—they were on the surface because they could shoot one of their payload, maybe more. Never Mecca; not from here, but Pakistan might be in range. And perhaps—

Alan hit his press-to-talk switch. "Wagonmaster? This is Chuckwagon, over. Do you have us in the link?"

"Roger, Chuckwagon."

"Wagonmaster, give me a far-on circle from this datum

and tell me if a TLAM-C can hit Karachi? Or Bahrain? My screen is fried, over."

"Roger, Chuckwagon. Wait one."

Static silence; time to think about two children and many friends and thousands, perhaps millions, of civilians.

"Torp's still running. It went right under their stern." Simcoe was sobbing with frustration. "Goddam it. Under. Under."

Soleck made a turn; they drove on, four miles a minute. A minute passed.

"Chuckwagon, this is Wagonmaster. Karachi for sure. Bahrain's right on the edge of range."

"Roger, copy all. Torpedo went Tango Uniform. Chuckwagon out."

"They're going to shoot a missile," Alan said to the cockpit. He had another trick to try, and then he'd have to face the final options. Like asking Soleck to fly the plane into the conning tower. He looked at his watch. "Soleck?"

"Thirty more seconds, skipper, and you'll have your twelve miles."

Alan had the Harpoon hot; it had been hot since the opening of the first engagement. He didn't have a screen. He spent ten seconds thinking it through.

"Garcia."

"Sir?"

"See your screen? On your armrest?"

"Yessir."

"Put the cursor on the sub."

"Done."

"Bring up the Harpoon targeting menu. Got it?"

"Roger."

"Put the Harpoon on the Kilo."

"Got it."

Alan looked at his watch. "Range?"

"Thirteen nautical miles."

457

Simcoe said slowly, "His bow's coming up."

To fire a missile. "That'll get more of his superstructure clear of the water. Garcia? Know how to put in a waypoint?"

"Roger that, skipper."

"Bring the missile into the target from 120. Full broadside, biggest return."

"Done."

Alan looked at the red Lucite cover on his missile. The light was green. He wished there was time to crawl up front and check her work. There wasn't. "Turn us into the target." He reached up and lifted the Lucite cover against its spring. The plane turned under him, his extended arm heavier in the acceleration, as if the missile switch weighed ten pounds. He kept it there, his back and arm unnoticed.

"Opening his torpedo tubes," Simcoe commented.

"Bow on," Soleck called.

"Missile away," Alan said. He pulled down on the missile release switch and let go the toggle. Nothing happened. Time stretched.

Whoosh. Loss of weight, a kick in the starboard wing, an audible roar and a heavy vibration. Then gone.

"Missile in the air." Alan hunched forward, shoulders set as if he were flying the missile. He had time to thumb the releases on his shoulder harness and lean across to Simcoe's computer. None of that safety crap mattered now.

"Follow it in?" Soleck asked.

"Yeah."

On the screen, Alan watched the missile turn away from the submarine and fly east; plenty of room, longer range, more chance for the warhead to arm. Well out to the east, it turned; perhaps the computer exaggerated it, but it seemed to skid uncertainly, and Alan found that his adrenal gland did have something left. His breath stopped.

The missile began to curve back west. The curve straightened, and the missile ran faster.

Ahead of them, there was a flash so bright that it jumped through the cockpit to the back.

"Hit," Garcia shouted.

Allahu Akbar.

Coda

Mike Dukas and Leslie Kultzke were married in the relative cool of the morning in the Navy chapel, Bahrain. The Episcopal chaplain married them—the closest to a Greek Orthodox clergyman that they could get.

For Harry O'Neill, the ceremony was a clash of feelings. He had been raised as an Anglican; now, as a Muslim, his presence at the familiar service brought back memories, some old, some more recent—old worship, recent fights with his father. That he wore a Muslim cap with his beautiful suit merely externalized that conflict—a life split into a before and after. Yet he smiled, ignored a few startled looks at his headgear, kissed the bride and shook the rather rattled Dukas's hand.

Now, standing under a broad tent in the Craiks' garden, he sipped papaya juice. A sense of separation from the event remained, but he smiled; the separation would always be there now, he knew, more so since he had broken with the Agency and they had responded by canceling two big-money contracts with his company. Still, he smiled; others smiled. It was a wedding.

"So," he said to Henry Valdez. The red-haired Mavis was a dozen feet away. Harry looked toward her and said, "Your turn next, Valdez?"

"No way, man. I'm too young to die." He might have

elaborated on that, but Mavis swung to his side. "Right, Mave?" he said.

"Right, whatever you said." She was drinking champagne, perhaps not used to it this early in the day; her eyes looked dazzled and her pale skin was flushed. "Harry, when do I get on the magic list at Fifth Fleet with all you *guys*?"

"Hey, Mave—"

Harry waved Valdez to silence. "You don't, Mavis. Nobody does. We're bad people at Fifth Fleet now."

"I thought you walked on water over there! If that isn't an offensive ecumenical mixture of religions—is it? Anyway—" she sipped champagne—"I was pissed off when I wasn't allowed into the sacrosanct precincts of the American Navy along with my Latin lover, here."

"That's history, Mavis. The special relationship has been canceled." He sipped his juice, looked over the top of the glass at her. "Want to leave my employ for a good Christian?"

"Oh, darlin', damned few of the Christians pay as well as you do, and anyway, you got Rickie." She was holding Valdez's hand, now leaned against him and giggled. Then she looked back at Harry. "Weddings make me sad, so I drink too much. Don't worry, Harry, I won't make a scandal." She stared around her in the tent. "It is awfully early in the day to be drunk, though, isn't it."

Harry whispered "Take her home" to Valdez and ambled off. What Valdez and Mavis did was their business, unless they did it in public, when it became his business.

A Bahraini jazz trio—guitar, keyboard, sax—was playing oldies with the odd bit of soft rock thrown in. The music, volume kept deliberately low, floated in the warm air like a scent. Harry saw people he knew, smiled, waved, said a word or two and moved on. He wanted to find Dukas and Al Craik and to settle at their sides for a little, and then he would go. Spotting Dukas and Leslie—like Valdez and Mavis, holding hands—on the far side of the tent, he made his way toward them, moving around groups, squeezing between people. A *lot* of people, he reflected; half the Navy seemed to be there, although the group at the actual wedding had been quite small. He saw one of Alan's pilots, a gangly kid named Soleck with a pretty woman in a uniform with wings. He saw an NCIS agent he knew named Rattner, with him somebody newer named Greenbaum and a pretty woman he had been told was a Canadian nurse whom Greenbaum had met during an investigation. He smiled at both men, unable, unwilling to get close enough to talk, saw the pretty woman lean in tight to Greenbaum to whisper in his ear, her eyes on Harry. Asking who he was. *Oh, yeah, the black Muslim. Isn't he supposed to be really, really rich?* Both Greenbaum and Rattner leaned toward her to tell her about him, but not, he thought, to tell her that he had lost his ticket to the ball, wasn't one of them anymore.

"Happiness to the bride," he said, and he kissed Leslie for the second time that morning. She looked a little over-whelmed, a little nervous, but almost pretty. *Women never so radiant as when they are brides and when they're pregnant, and she's both.* He knew that, too. "Congratulations to the groom," he said, shaking Dukas's hand. Dukas rolled his eyes and made a face. "You know what this shindig cost?" he growled.

"He doesn't really mean that," Leslie said. "He's pretending to be a cynic."

"I don't have to pretend; I am a cynic. Gloom, doom, and no hope."

"You married me—that seems pretty hopeful." She had an arm around Dukas's waist and she looked, Harry thought, possessive and sure of him. "You didn't bring your wife?" Leslie said after a quick look around the tent.

"Yasmin is very shy. She doesn't speak English and she feels out of place among—" He hesitated too long before saying "people she doesn't know," and the words overlapped with Dukas's saying "Christians."

"Oh, you should have brought her anyway! Rose and I made a women's room in the house—we could have visited in there and she never would have had to come out here." She meant it, he saw. He told her that she would have to come visit Yasmin at their home; Yasmin would love to meet her.

"Oh—" Leslie glanced at Dukas. "We won't be here so much, I'm afraid."

Dukas grunted. "We're doing the honeymoon bit in Italy. Househunting. I'm going to be the SAC at Naples."

He waved a hand. "Spinner got a job in DoD, you know that? Nice to have connections. You screw the Navy, leak classified information, you get a better job in the Pentagon. Really swell." He was more than angry. Leslie said something; he stirred, shoulders and upper arms, part shrug, part shiver. He seemed to have calmed, and then he said in a bitter voice, "You hear about Pilchard?"

Harry had heard about Pilchard—the admiral was already back in the states, they said, pulled out of his command of Fifth Fleet and called home for "reassignment." Then the Craiks found them, Rose beautiful and beginning to look a little pregnant, Alan drawn a little fine, his smile just a shade thin. "I heard you mention Admiral Pilchard," he said when they had finished greeting each other, and Rose was done telling Harry how gorgeous he looked. "You know what happened?"

"He got bounced."

"Yeah, right out of the Navy. Retirement—for letting me fire on a sub that was carrying WMDs."

Rose gave Harry a look. "Honey, it's a wedding—lighten up!"

Dukas grunted. "Like me."

The two women started to tell their men how happy they should be—look at the day, listen to the band, watch the pretty girls—and Rose said, "Be like Harry! *He's* happy. *He* knows how to behave at a wedding."

"Absolutely. I'm so happy at weddings I'm thinking of having another myself." He smiled at all of them. "I'm allowed four wives, you know."

Then they all laughed, not entirely merrily, and the talk turned to other people, lighter matters. Harry told them about flying Mary Totten and the lugubrious Bill back to the maharajah's palace and the gathering of CIA people there in the past weeks. "Sort of like flies on a pile of shit— they've got thirty people there at last count. The hotel is full."

Alan said that Fifth Fleet had had to lay on an every-other-day flight, but how did Harry know so much?

"I have sources, m'man." He grinned. "The maharajah and I rather hit it off, don't you know."

"And Mary's in charge? A dream come true. Now all she'll need is a guy who'll stay in one place for a few hours."

"Actually, I think she found one." His smile was slow, secret. "You'd have to ask Dave Djalik."

Alan looked stunned. "Djalik?" He looked at Rose, then back at Harry. "*Djalik?*"

"Don't ask, don't tell. But the maharajah is a fount of information."

Other people came up and began to talk to the bride and groom. Harry muttered his congratulations again and then made his goodbyes to them and said that of course they'd be seeing each other again—somewhere, sometime—and then he and Alan were moving toward the garden gate. Neither of them said anything, and when they were at the gate, waiting for Harry's driver to bring up his car and its escort, they stood looking out at the street, the celebration behind them muted and almost distant. Finally, Harry said, without looking at Alan, "How bad is it?"

"I don't know yet. You?"

Harry drew himself up. "The Agency threatened me, but I know things they don't want spread around. I think they had some idea they'd out me—convince other Muslims that I was a wholly owned CIA subsidiary. Get me killed. Or worse. Now, they won't—a Mexican standoff." He watched his car pull in close to the gate and a bodyguard get out and look up and down the street. "But it's different now."

"Yes, it's different now."

The bodyguard nodded, and Harry put his hand on the gate. "But not between us."

Alan put a hand on his shoulder and squeezed, and then Harry opened the gate and went out.

Peace Maker

Gordon Kent

Alan Craik is back from sea duty and rapidly tiring of life behind a Pentagon desk when he learns that his best friend, a CIA agent, has been kidnapped in Central Africa, just as Rwanda is about to be engulfed in violence. Before long, Alan flies out to join the US fleet of the African coast, ready to launch a bold rescue mission. But as events spiral wildly out of control he and his wounded friend find themselves stranded in the middle of the continent with war raging all around.

ISBN 0-00-651295-X

Top Hook
Gordon Kent

In *Top Hook*, US Navy Intelligence Officer Alan Craik finds himself in the middle of a major espionage crisis when his wife Rose, also a naval officer and now about to fulfil her long-cherished ambition of becoming an astronaut, is suddenly accused of spying. With Rose's career and reputation at stake, Alan will have to risk everything to uncover the real spy, one of the highest-ranking and most powerful officials in the CIA – and he must do so before the spy's machinations result in a major naval action between the USA and a new and robust enemy.

'Here's a thriller that really flies. Gordon Kent knows his subject at first hand and the expertise shows on the page: high stakes, pounding tension and the best dogfights put on paper. A lot of thrillers these days, you come away feeling like you've been in a simulator. Gordon Kent straps you into the real thing. Enjoy the ride!'   IAN RANKIN

ISBN 0-00-651296-8

The Double Eagle

James Twining

In Paris a priest is murdered, the killers dumping his mutilated body into the Seine. Only he has taken a secret with him to his death. A secret that reveals itself during his autopsy and reawakens memories of Depression-era politics and a seventy-year-old heist.

Jennifer Browne, a young and ambitious FBI agent is assigned to the case. This is her last chance to kick start a career that has stalled after one fatal error of judgement three years before.

Her investigation uncovers a daring robbery from Fort Knox and Tom Kirk, the world's greatest art thief is the prime suspect.

Tom, caught between his desire to finally get out of the game and his partner's insistence that he complete one last job for the criminal mastermind Cassius, faces a thrilling race against time to clear his name. A race that takes him from London to Paris, Amsterdam to Istanbul in a search for the real thieves and the legendary Double Eagle.

0-00-719015-8